3Score Publishing

But I'll Remember This

Pam Nixon grew up in Lincolnshire.

She has a degree in English from St Hilda's College, Oxford and an MA in Modern English literature from the University of Reading.

During her career she taught English in various establishments, some stranger than others.

She and her husband lived for some time in Cyprus and travelled extensively in the Middle East. They now live in the servants' quarters of a Victorian house in North Oxford.

They have four children and six grandchildren, one in Rouen, two in Sydney and three in Reading.

Pam Nixon has had poetry published. This is her first novel. An earlier version was shortlisted in a national competition for unpublished writers.

Praise for But I'll Remember This

'Elegantly ironic style' Maggie Hartford Oxford Times

'I started to read your book a chapter at a time but after meeting Mike and Alithea I couldn't put it down. The plot intrigued me, the situations touched my emotions, and the style of writing whipped me along. …..There seems to be very little written about the rarefied life of the 1950s upper middle class schooldays, family attitudes and the break in of atheist and socalist ideals and certainly little expressed in such a racy, amusing way.'

'I sat down intending to read a chapter or two and finished the whole book four hours later. Now I feel bereft.'

'I have found it difficult to lay down the book for long this week, and finished it last evening. I am full of admiration. I smiled through most of the reading. You might have been talking about me often in describing Phyllida, and my mother. An evocative story. THANK YOU for such pleasure. I could go on….. '

'I finished your novel last Thursday. Once I picked it up I had to go on reading; it was utterly compelling.'

'I did so much enjoy your novel. Thank you and many congratulations. Reminiscent of early Jane Gardam I thought. Have you started your next one yet? Don't delay, your fans are eager.'

'We both loved your book. D. said "you had brought all the loose ends together at the end very elegantly". ….the school bits, really funny and reminiscent, very enjoyable.'

'What Alan Bennet did in 'The History Boys' you have done for women of our generation. Once started I couldn't stop reading. I found it most therapeutic and only wish you had written it 20 years earlier.'

BUT I'LL REMEMBER THIS

Pam Nixon

*Best wishes
Pam Nixon*

3Score Publishing
STONESFIELD, OXFORD

Copyright © 2014 by Pam Nixon.

All rights reserved. No part of this publication may be reproduced, distributed or transmitted in any form or by any means, including photocopying, recording, or other electronic or mechanical methods, without the prior written permission of the publisher, except in the case of brief quotations embodied in critical reviews and certain other noncommercial uses permitted by copyright law. For permission requests, write to the publisher, addressed "Attention: Permissions Coordinator," at the address below.

First published July 2014
Reprinted August 2014
Reprinted October 2014
Reprinted January 2015

3Score Publishing
Sothams Farmhouse, Pond Hill
Stonesfield, Oxford
England OX29 8PZ

www.3scorepublishing.co.uk

info@3scorepublishing.co.uk

Publisher's Note: This is a work of fiction. Names, characters, places, and incidents are a product of the author's imagination. Locations and public names are sometimes used for atmospheric purposes. Any resemblance to actual people, living or dead, or to businesses, companies, events, institutions, or locations is completely coincidental.

Book Layout ©2013 BookDesignTemplates.com

Ordering Information:
Quantity sales. Special discounts are available on quantity purchases by associations such as book groups and others. For details, contact the publishers at the address above.

But I'll Remember This   Pam Nixon - 1st ed.
ISBN 978-0-9928950-0-6

*To Ron for his unfailing support
And to Judith who will remember at least some of this*

*The author would like to acknowledge the help of the following:
Jan Mark in whose creative writing class I was first encouraged to continue with this novel,
Lisanne Radice and Jane Gardam for encouragement and helpful criticism,
and, most of all, Elizabeth North who was a wonderful, inspiring mentor and friend.*

Thanks also to my writing friends Janet Cunliffe-Jones, Leela Dutt, Ruth Heald, Mary Stableford and Elizabeth Wade for their support and comments.

I'd like to thank my family for all their enthusiastic interest including my sister Judith for permission to use her painting on the cover, my daughter Sarah Good for her professional editing input and my granddaughter Ruby Haran for help with Megan's conversation.

I'm grateful to 3Score for their support particularly to Peter Clifton for his initiative in starting the group and to Gillian Clarke for sensitive and careful proof reading.

Most of all thanks to my husband for all the shopping, cooking, technical support and for appreciating the humour.

CONTENTS

PART 1

    December 1997   11

PART 2

    Autumn Term 1955   25

PART 3

    Christmas 1955   159

PART 4

    Spring Term 1956   207

PART 5

    Easter 1956   235

PART 6

    Summer Term 1956   255

PART 7

    Summer 1956   297

PART 8

    Interim   309

PART 9

    The Past Unearthed 1997 - 2000   329

PART 1

December 1997

CHAPTER ONE

I'd been rather looking forward to the funeral. Fiona had implied there might be a mere handful of mourners and I'd pictured a little group of us huddled round the coffin in the Angel Choir, candles giving off faint warmth, a suggestion of incense in the chill of the musty air - something exquisitely austere after the excesses of Christmas. Now I'm here, the reality, the long nave of the great cathedral filled with prosperous-looking people, is rather disappointing - that woman a few rows in front for example – what a hat!

And where the hell is Fiona? I hope she hasn't let me down. Thanks to her powers of persuasion I've left my husband sulking, the house in a mess and somehow had found myself agreeing to ring Ursula, a woman I usually try to avoid. I'd rather hoped Ursula would say, 'How bourgeois' as she would have done back in the 70s - but not any longer. She'd agreed with Fiona that we all ought to go to our old headmistress's funeral.

'She was a great lady,' Ursula had pronounced, sounding uncannily like her aunt, wife of the former Dean. I suspected she hoped she might meet someone important.

It always amazes me the way people reconstruct their past. While Fiona was on the phone persuading me to come to the funeral and reminiscing about how much she'd admired Miss Cutler, I'd been recalling their various battles - a skirmish over the half inch frill of petticoat showing below Fiona's regulation navy skirt, all out war over

Fiona's refusal to accept a place at a teacher training college – 'We don't really feel you are university material Fiona.' Still, I supposed, although Miss Cutler had probably won the skirmish, Fiona had certainly won the war, so perhaps, after all these years, she could afford to be magnanimous.

I hadn't even imagined Miss Cutler could still be alive until Fiona had told me that she was dead; yet here I am, standing in the cathedral while the congregation all around me are bellowing out, *City of God*, that we used to sing at every school commemoration service in this very building.

My neighbour pushes a hymn sheet in my direction; I don't need it. It must be forty years since I last sang this hymn but the words are hard-wired into my brain:

City of God how broad and far
Outspread thy walls sublime!

Although I no longer subscribe to the words the tune is irresistible, so I perjure myself by joining in:

Unharmed upon the eternal rock
The eternal city stands.

The organ groans into silence and there is much scraping of chairs as we all settle back. What's happened to the pews? And I still can't see Fiona.

Sitting there in the cathedral my mind drifts back to my first day as a boarder at the High School. Homesick and terrified, I'd been standing on the edge of a chattering mob of day girls. Ursula had been the first to notice me. She'd asked what I was called and visibly sneered at my response.

CHRISTMAS 1997

'Phyllida! What a peculiar name!'

'My cousins call me...' But she'd already turned her back. For a moment it had seemed likely that the others would take their cue from her. Then Fiona had saved me. Although only eleven, she'd already begun to cultivate what Alithea once derisively referred to as her 'social manner'. She turned towards me.

'What do your cousins call you? ...Yes, Dilly's easier. We'll call you Dilly.'

Later, at break, as we stood together, slurping our milk through straws, she told me that Ursula was a stuck up goody-goody who thought she was somebody because her uncle was Dean at the cathedral. And so a pact was formed. From then on Fiona and I positively basked in Ursula's disapproval. We found it hilarious.

Unfortunately, however, my mother disapproved of Fiona. It was about the one thing that she and Steve had ever agreed about. My mother thought Fiona was dangerously 'sophisticated'; Steve thinks she's 'very worldly' which I suppose comes down to the same thing in the end.

Somehow Steve knows by instinct when it's Fiona on the phone. On Christmas evening we'd had a houseful. I'd been helping put grandchildren to bed until I'd been called away by an insistent ringing. It was Fiona and almost as soon as I'd answered, there was Steve in the doorway, a doom-laden presence. Sounds of childish shrieks came from upstairs, screams of inane laughter from the television in the next room. I couldn't hear a word Fiona was saying. I gestured to him to close the door.

'There don't seem to be any dry bath towels,' he announced.

'Is that a philosophical statement or an oblique way of asking me to do something about it, because – look! – I'm on the phone.' He left, closing the door as loudly as possible without actually slamming it but I knew that wouldn't be the end of the matter. And of course it wasn't. He'd argued about the foolishness of driving up to the funeral on my own, in winter. He'd complained about the expense to me and the inconvenience to him, but all the time I knew the real objection was that it had been Fiona's idea.

Still, despite Steve, here I am in the cathedral; I give up looking for Fiona and try to concentrate on what's happening next.

So when this corruptible shall have put on incorruption, and this mortal shall have put on immortality... The lesson from *I Corinthians*, read by the mayor, is coming to an end. I've begun to realise that this is a civic funeral. Our old headmistress had a long retirement - time enough to become a local personage - over ninety when she died - although in the last few years she, as Fiona put it, 'hadn't been quite herself.' Which, I suppose, is true, to some extent, of all of us. Fiona, for example - once, even in a crowd like this, I'd have been able to identify her by her red, no auburn, she'd always insisted on 'auburn' - her auburn curls – but no longer. So would I recognise any other characters from my past? Alithea, if, by any unlikely chance, she were here, and Mike? Surely I would recognise Mike. But then what about me? Would I really want to meet Mike again after all these years?

Thoughts of Mike send my mind off in another direction, back to another very different funeral, to Rosa's father's funeral, to a summer afternoon forty years ago. According to the school timetable I should have been playing rounders with the rest of the sixth form; instead, I'd carried on cycling past the playing fields to the cemetery. I remember the group of Yorkshire miners bearing the coffin; I remember the singing of the *Red Flag* and I remember, most of all I remember, being moved to tears by that tall, dark young man with a resonant Welsh voice proclaiming *Do not go gentle into that good night* over an open grave. Mike! I think, Mike! and I remember what it was like to be eighteen again.

And so, returning to the present, I finally admit to myself why I'm here. During the last few days, in order to justify driving two hundred miles in the depths of winter to a place I haven't visited in years, to attend the funeral of a woman I'd almost forgotten about, I've invented several reasons for making this trip.

It would be a diversion from the inevitable after-Christmas flatness; I was doing it out of loyalty to Fiona; I felt a certain nostalgic curiosity to revisit the place where I'd spent my schooldays. But now I recognise my real motive for making this absurd journey: a little bit of me has never given up hoping for news of Mike. Yet I know it's most unlikely that Alithea will be here. Even though Fiona and I had never revealed Alithea's most scandalous secret, Miss Cutler must have regretted ever employing such an exotic character to teach English. They'd hardly have parted on friendly terms.

Back in the present a bent figure is hobbling towards the lectern. Surely that can't be Dr Mount? I remember bobbing a graceless curtsey to him one Speech Day as he presented me with the Frederick Mount Essay Prize. My view is impeded by the woman in the amazing hat, but I consult my order of service. Yes, it's him, bent and frail but definitely Dr Mount about to give the address. Somehow I feel that if this character from the past can suddenly reappear, so can others and

I'm filled with an irrational hope.

One last hymn and the blessing is pronounced:

The Grace of our Lord Jesus Christ, and the love of God, and the fellowship of the Holy Spirit be with us all now and for evermore. A loud but ragged 'Amen' echoes back from the fan vaulting. We rise and the coffin is borne out to a Bach fugue.

The person in the hat turns round – Fiona. I might have guessed.

Outside the West Door we shiver, uncertain what to do next. The hearse moves off, followed by a small party of close friends, perhaps family. I scan the crowd still half hoping I might see and recognise Alithea, but instead spot Ursula being gracious to the officiating clergyman.

'Oh there's Ursula,' says Fiona. 'Looking rather more conventional than you'd led me to expect.'

'Well, she and Clive are very in with the new regime you know. Clive's advice is much sought after.'

Some time back in the sixties Ursula had changed her name to Su to mark her dramatic conversion to the extreme left. Since then she has been through several transformations: the dungarees to indicate her enthusiasm for the Chinese Cultural Revolution, the ethnic look, during which phase she'd resembled a Peruvian peasant in distressed circumstances, even, on one occasion, full African robes in order to show solidarity with some oppressed persons or other. I'd rather hoped, sooner or later, to see her in a burqa. Disappointingly, as her politics have become more mainstream her enthusiasm for ethnic minorities seems to have cooled. In any case, under all her disguises, I've always retained my image of the Ursula of our schooldays, the Dean's niece, primness personified, with her Persil-white shirt,

CHRISTMAS 1997

impeccably knotted tie, perfectly plaited hair and socks that always stayed up. Why, unlike the rest of us, did she never lose her garters? And what about that blue rosette that she'd worn on her prefect's blazer during the 1955 General Election? Something, I imagine, she has long preferred to forget.

Now here she is in her latest transformation, suitably dressed in black, even a hat, the kind that looks like a lampshade.

'She's reverting to type,' I explain.

Fiona looks me up and down critically.

'Well you always look much the same, Dilly.' Regret or affection, I wonder? Fiona herself never could resist the temptation to be smart. Even now, though she is supposed to be part of the tweeds and green wellie set, she's not so much dressed as expensively upholstered. Everything about me, on the other hand, is flapping loose; my lovely purple scarf is floating in the wind, my hair is coming down, even my earrings are swaying. I'd forgotten about that east wind. 'Nothing between us and the Urals,' locals used to say, as if it were a cause for pride. My long black coat that, in London, makes me feel like a character in a Russian novel, is proving rather inadequate. It would, I'm now all too aware, be no use at all in Moscow. While searching for my gloves, scrunched up somewhere in my pocket, I realise with dread that Ursula has seen us.

'Put your gloves on,' says Fiona. 'You must be freezing. Oh hello Ursula!'

Ursula/Su approaches, smiling. We all pretend to be delighted to see each other.

Greetings over, Ursula, attempting humour I think, enquires,

'And how is your enormous family?'

Just at this moment I'm grateful for Anna, the only one of my five children to have a conventional career. Anna, I tell Ursula, is doing a job swap in Sydney.

'Sydney!' says Ursula. 'I thought she had some sort of job in publishing. Are there any publishers in Australia?'

'Only ones like HarperCollins and McGraw-Hill.' She gives a tight smile but continues, undeterred,

'But why Sydney? It's funny, but I can't say I've ever wanted to go to Australia.'

'I expect Australia will manage to survive.'

Fiona gives a snort, which she hastily turns into a cough. Ursula gives another tight smile.

'And Jonathan? Still working on the land? He and Rupert used to be such friends,' she adds, untruthfully.

'He has his own organic farm now,' I say, slightly exaggerating the size of my son's smallholding.

'Oh yes, your people were farmers weren't they?'

'My uncle, but Jonathan's philosophy is very different. He's a passionate environmentalist.'

Ursula titters. I give her a hard stare.

'Sorry Dilly, but farming and philosophy – it sounds so incongruous – but anyway how marvellous to have such a useful son. I'm afraid as a family we're just boringly academic. I must tell you about Rupert.'

Which, of course, is what this was all leading up to.

Fiona stands by looking on with an air of detachment and I realise that this middle class bitching about children's educational achievements and careers is now a matter of indifference to her. She lives in a world of social connections in which, no doubt, other snobberies play their part. Fortunately we're interrupted.

CHRISTMAS 1997

'Ursula! Phyllida!' – and, in a cooler tone, 'Fiona!'

Another figure from the past - Miss Carr, once the formidable Head of English - incredible! She must be eighty at least but she looks much the same, except smaller.

'Phyllida! I hoped you would be here. Was that your poem in that recent collection? What was it called? - The publisher with the sanguinary name? On the whole I found it most pleasing although there was a line in the second stanza...'

Ursula, I am delighted to see, looks annoyed.

People begin to disperse. Fiona and I walk across the Close to her hotel. I'm regretting that I didn't ask Miss Carr if she ever heard from Alithea when Fiona says,

'So you still write poetry?' I admit to this vice. There's a moment's silence. I suspect Fiona, like many other people, fears I might expect her to read it.

'But you've always been so amusing, Dilly. Couldn't you write a best-seller?' Fortunately we reach the hotel at this moment so I'm saved from replying.

I flop into a squashy chair in the lounge. Fiona lowers herself into another and orders tea; we start to thaw out.

'Do you have to go back to London tonight?'

I mutter something about finding somewhere to stay.

'You could stay here.'

Why, I wonder, do the wealthy have so little imagination? But I'm underestimating my friend.

'There are two beds in my room. They won't notice; anyway they've charged me for two.'

I call Steve, and then, as we laugh together over his reaction, we're thirteen years old again, plotting against authority, passing notes in class, pulling faces at smug Ursula behind her back.

Over dinner we're soon on to the subject of Ursula, which causes more hilarity until Fiona says,

'I was surprised to hear that son of hers went to his father's old school. I thought they were supposed to be so left-wing?'

'Don't get me started on that.'

'Still he's done very well.' She pauses. 'None of yours went to Oxbridge did they?'

'No. They thought big northern cities were the cool places to be.' I hope I don't sound defensive.

'And they all went to comprehensive schools. I suppose having so many children you couldn't afford to send them anywhere else.'

'Steve wouldn't have heard of it.'

'Well I was appalled when I heard the High School had gone comprehensive. We had such a wonderful education. Better than my children, for all the money we spent on them.' She starts to recall old members of staff: 'inspirational', 'always demanded such high standards', 'so many extraordinary women.' 'The English teaching was marvellous, Miss Carr...'

'And Mrs Davis.'

'Mrs Davis?'

'Surely you remember Mrs Davis?'

Alithea had once caused Fiona such outrage I can't believe she's forgotten her. She frowns, thinking.

'You must remember! Masses of dark hair, silver jewellery, wine glass rings on our essays, Ursula telling us about her uncle – you remember Ursula's uncle, the Dean – so shocked by the sight of her – Mrs Davis – walking through the Close on a Sunday in jeans and a sloppy-joe, or was it a duffle coat? He said she looked as if she'd come straight from the Left Bank. They were holding hands; she and her... Mr Davis... Mike.'

I realise I've stopped in mid speech. Fiona looks at me; I pull myself together, 'He, the Dean, said it set a bad example to the choirboys – holding hands that is.' Fiona still seems vague.

'Oh I think I remember. She wasn't there long was she? Just our final year.'

During the night Fiona snores and I lie awake for a long time remembering that final year at school, all its strange events and those violent emotions that, from time to time, still continue to haunt my life.

PART 2

Autumn Term 1955

CHAPTER TWO

Tuesday was always shepherd's pie, so it must have been a Tuesday when it all began because I remember the shepherd's pie in its enamel dish was still steaming on the orangey-varnished dresser when the headmistress came in.

'Shepherd's pie, how delicious!' she said as, followed by her dog, she squeezed between the table and the bulging dresser. The juniors down at the dark end of the table pushed their chairs in as far as they would go and she just made it. A smell of damp dog mingled with the smell of shepherd's pie. The dog raised his nose to sniff the food but lowered it promptly. Evidently even a mongrel collie had that much discernment.

Tuesday evening then, in September, early in my eighth autumn term, still light outside at seven o'clock, gleams of watery sunlight, the sycamores in The Close just beginning to turn and the rooks calling, soaring and wheeling round the cathedral towers. Enter the headmistress – Why?

As she bent over to confer with our housemistress, the dog sniffed at her broad tweed-clad bottom. Some of the juniors got a fit of nervous giggles and Becky Simon – it had to be her – knocked over her glass of water. Matron looked furious.

'Go straight down to the kitchen Becky and ask for a cloth.'

I poked shepherd's pie around my plate. Hunger struggled with revulsion. I could cope with the watery potato but the stench of the pinkish meat was too much. Could the Head really believe it was delicious? Perhaps, some time back in her Edwardian childhood, she had actually eaten delicious shepherd's pie. Had she no sense of smell?

Probably it was just something she felt she ought to say. Complaining about food showed weak moral fibre. It was ten years since the grown-ups had been able to say 'Don't you know there's a war on?' but you felt they still missed the opportunity.

This was the worst meal of the week, apart of course from Saturday lunchtime's mouse stew, called that ever since, a few years back, Caroline had found an actual mouse's head in her helping. Being a well-brought up child of the vicarage she'd merely put it to the side of her plate but the rumour had soon spread round the table. There'd been a lot of horrified sniggers but we'd been told not to fuss; Matron had somehow managed to imply it was Caroline's fault. Miss Manzonni, our housemistress had said nothing, just tightened her lips, but the gleam in the dark eyes in her plain, intelligent face made me suspect she might have been oddly amused.

Now Becky returned with a greasy cloth and slopped it around ineffectually. Her shoulders shook from time to time with ill-suppressed laughter. I felt sorry for her. Once you're in that state every thing seems funny and I could see she was heading for big trouble.

The servers piled the dirty plates and the remains of the shepherd's pie into the dumb waiter. With a creaking of ropes the dishes disappeared down to the basement kitchen. The pudding was hauled up. Matron served out jelly and custard. The headmistress and her dog left the dining room.

'No pudding for me, thank you Matron. Rebecca, you had better come and see me later.' Miss Manzonni rolled up her napkin and followed the Head. The blandness of the jelly and custard was a relief after shepherd's pie.

'For what you have received,' said Matron threateningly, 'may the Lord make you truly thankful.'

AUTUMN TERM 1955

Brenda and I, the two most senior boarders, were left in charge of the clearers. I was nominally Head of the Boarding House but Brenda, though a year below me, had her own ideas of how things should be done. She began to order the two fourth years around as soon as Matron had gone. There was no point in competing, so I moved over to the bay window to see if anything interesting was happening.

Looking out of the window was one of our favourite occupations. The juniors down at the bottom end of the table couldn't see much but by the time we were seniors, sitting at the top end near the window, we had a clear view of all the south side of the Cathedral Close.

The cathedral dominated our view and echoed through our lives. The great clock struck every quarter except when the assizes were in progress. The judge had ruled it should be silenced on the nights he spent in his official lodgings but it never kept us boarders awake; the familiar sound mingled with our dreams. Similarly bell-ringing practice on Thursday evenings was just a background to our struggles with irregular French verbs or quadratic equations. The full performance wove into the pattern of our Sundays, and every Saturday we wandered back from the local shops hardly registering snatches of anthems and plainsong as the choirboys rehearsed for the following day. So it was hardly surprising that our main source of entertainment was the clergy.

Unfortunately they weren't that interesting, being mainly, at least in our opinion, terribly old. There was one young one, dark and good-looking, a little like Gregory Peck. However, disappointingly, it was rumoured that he had taken a vow of celibacy.

'He's very High,' said Caroline who, having survived the mouse, was now in the Lower Sixth. Although her father had a country parish she seemed well up on cathedral gossip.

Sometimes, but rarely, we might see some of the Grammar School boarders. Andrew Strong was the favourite, fair and broad shouldered. Caroline's contemporary, Jane, had once been kissed by him, under the Roman arch near the sweet shop. The fact that they had both been twelve at the time and he had only done it at the instigation of one of her friends didn't really detract from the glamour. The story had passed into Boarding House legend and added to Jane's reputation of being rather wild, even though she was so brainy.

About a year ago some new characters had appeared on the scene. A group of actors from the local repertory company had taken lodgings a little further up the Close. Every evening they passed the Boarding House on the way to the theatre. The men weren't dazzlingly attractive but there was an air of bohemian raffishness about the group as a whole that we found fascinating. I thought they were much more interesting than either the clergy or the Grammar School boys. One Sunday in the dusk of an early spring evening, I'd passed the window of their lodgings. There were no curtains and the lovely proportions of the eighteenth century room were half-revealed, shadowed by firelight and lamplight. The room was sparsely and casually furnished; the group were sprawling on chairs or cushions, learning lines, reading the papers, making toast. There was a sense of purposeful leisure, companionship and physical comfort that appealed to me immediately. A line from one of our A level set texts came into my mind, *There is a world elsewhere.*

It was in the hope then, of seeing these wondrous creatures that I stood by the window, slightly bored, irritated by Brenda's bossiness and depressed by thoughts of the coming term. But there were no actors in sight. They must have set off for the theatre while the Head's visit had been claiming all our attention. A little white-haired figure waddled out of the south porch and set off across the Green. It was the Suffragan Bishop who, because he took his title from the local port, was known to us as the Fish Bish. Now he was heading home after Evensong, his purple and scarlet robes making a dramatic and enjoyable splash of colour in the gloom.

'Red and purple!' said Brenda who had seen off the last of the clearers and now joined me at the window. 'Anyone knows they don't go.'

'You'd better tell the Archbishop of Canterbury.' She gazed at me with her rather protruding pale eyes, trying to decide if this was a joke.

'Oh there's Algy after all,' I said. 'He's late.'

The leading man had been Algy to us ever since we'd seen him in *The Importance of Being Earnest* the previous year. A slightly built young man was crossing the road but it wasn't the actor. He came straight up to the Boarding House and clanged the bell. Miss Cutler's bicycle was still leaning against the basement railings. Her dog started barking; Miss Manzonni's Old English Sheepdog joined in. The door was opened; we heard general greetings and instructions to the dogs to be quiet. Brenda and I gazed at each other amazed; who on earth could he be? There was nothing more to see; so, reluctantly, we clattered up the back stairs to the attic.

The attic was the Sixth Form study. The year before we'd been allowed to redecorate it but already the yellow distemper was shedding flakes over the broken-down sofa and the lino. A few last rays of sunlight slanted through the small window. It wasn't considered cold enough yet for us to be allowed to light the oil stove so Jane and Caroline, hunched over the ink-stained table doing their prep, were wearing their blazers for extra warmth against the autumn evening chill.

Although it made the attic more cramped I was glad that these two, who had just come into the Lower Sixth, had joined us. I'd had a year of Brenda's undiluted pomposity and pretentiousness. She irritated me intensely and this was made worse because I knew I should feel sorry for her. She had no father - I naively assumed he must be dead - and sometimes she wasn't able to go home for half term. Jane and Caroline came from more normal families. Caroline, a vicar's daughter, was rather a prig but I liked Jane who was clever and funny.

Now she raised her head expectantly, her high-coloured face with its sharp nose alert, ready for news.

'A man, a young man, has come to see Mazzy.' I said.

Caroline looked up and gazed at us with her dark eyes. Her soft face wore its typical expression of troubled innocence. All thoughts of prep ceased as we speculated on what he could possibly have come for.

'I thought at first it was Algy,' I said. 'But it wasn't, though I have the feeling I've seen him somewhere before.'

Jane was all for finding out at once.

'One of us could go down, knock on the door and ask for something.'

But what? We tried to come up with something plausible.

'Anyway she'd just tell us to go away and come back later when she wasn't busy,' said Caroline.

'We could go down to the dorm and look out of the window so we could see him as he leaves.'

'We don't know how long he'll be there. It's getting dark and Matron's putting the juniors to bed just across the corridor.' The more ingenious Jane's suggestions, the more reasonable were Caroline's objections.

'It's only a man,' said Brenda. 'Really!' She rolled her eyes at me trying to suggest a world-weary sophistication, although her long sallow face and sneering expression just made me think of a sour camel. Only a man! Anyone would have thought she regularly met the species for cocktails, danced till dawn every weekend and indulged in intimate candlelit dinners instead of, in reality, just having an unrequited crush on one of the Grammar School day boys.

Eventually Jane persuaded Caroline, who was always seen as good and sensible and knew how to use her innocent brown eyes, to go downstairs just as the young man was leaving and ask if she could borrow the big French dictionary. We spent some time, lurking at the top of the attic stairs, listening for sounds of departure and then Caroline set off. I tried to appear as indifferent as Brenda but this break in routine had cheered me up enormously and I hoped there might be some further developments.

'Well?' we all asked, as she returned.

'He's a young man.'

Brenda yawned. 'Tell us news not history, dear.'

'Let me finish, Brenda. Not bad looking, but a bit pale and skinny. I feel I've seen him somewhere before.' She thought for a minute, 'I know! He was at Early Evensong on Sunday. Do you remember? He crossed himself and genuflected in the Creed at *"born of the Virgin Mary"*. I thought maybe he was a new ordinand - very High anyway.'

Caroline sounded disapproving. Her father was inclined to evangelism. I remembered that he had brought a busload from his parish to hear a Billy Graham rally being relayed to the cathedral the year before. Quite a few of his parishioners had declared for Jesus and they had driven off into the night singing *Showers of Blessings*. Ursula, being the Dean's niece, had told us that, privately, her uncle thought it all very vulgar and, of course, very American.

There was a clattering of feet on the stairs. The attic door burst open and Becky Simon precipitated herself into the room.

'How dare you come in without knocking!'

I felt that should have been my line but Jane was always quicker off the mark. Brenda looked put out but made up for it by declaring the juniors had no manners nowadays. Then Caroline told Becky,

'Go out and, this time, knock and wait to be told to come in.'

As usual there was nothing left for me to say.

Becky went out, knocked, waited, then came in with exaggerated politeness. I did actually find her quite amusing, although, as everyone else disapproved of her, I never admitted it.

'Mazzy wants to see Dilly in her room now.'

'Please,' said Caroline.

'I don't think she said "please".'

I wanted to laugh. Caroline looked confused.

'Get out!' said Jane.

Why did my housemistress want to see me? I started to wonder what I had done wrong.

'Crumbs!' said Jane. 'It must be something to do with that man. I know! He saw you at Evensong on Sunday and it was love at first sight because you looked so irresistible in your school beret and he came to ask Mazzy if your affections were already engaged. You'll have to tell her about Christopher.' She laughed, exposing large, strong white teeth.

'Shut up about Chris. You know we're finished.' I slammed out.

'If he's as High as Caroline says, you'd better not let him know you're a Methodist though,' she shouted after me.

I skidded round the corner at the bottom of the attic stairs, nearly crashing into one of the juniors as she wandered past in her dressing gown. Baths were running and there was a smell of soap and toothpaste.

'Be careful, Dilly!' warned Matron but I was already halfway down the next flight, anxious to find out why I had been sent for.

The housemistress's room, as always, smelt of dog. Rags, lying before the empty grate, thumped his tail as I came in. Her cat sat, dribbling, on the worn arm of a chair. There were books on every surface and a pile of exercise books on the floor, though a little table had been cleared to make space for a decanter and three sherry glasses, now empty. This was unusual.

'Sit ye down! Sit ye down.' I obviously wasn't in trouble then. I moved a pile of essays from a chair and sat down next to the drooling cat. But the next minute the jovial tone changed. Mazzy's face became grave.

'Dilly dear, I have some rather sad news.' Panic struck. (The young man must have been a policeman – one of my family had been in a fatal accident!)

'I know you will be sorry to hear that Miss Rush is very ill. In fact she is in hospital.'

I tried desperately to look suitably grief-stricken but felt a huge upwelling of relief, almost, I'm afraid, of joy. My first thought was that it didn't matter that I hadn't yet memorised the fair copy of my last Latin prose, the second, that I might get out of extra Latin for weeks to come. The third, and more sobering, was that I actually needed the extra lessons. And this, at last, helped me to look suitably regretful.

Miss Rush in hospital! I thought. It was difficult to imagine the retired Latin teacher lying there helpless, meekly obeying doctors' orders - impossible in fact. I pictured her angry little face peering out over a stiff, white hospital sheet and felt sorry for the nurses.

'Her cat will miss her. And so will Miss Christie, of course.' I added hastily. Miss Rush shared a house with a retired maths teacher and an over-indulged cat that would only eat cornflakes if they were from the top of the packet. I realised, too late, that I hadn't said I was sorry. But Miss Manzonni had moved on.

With some incredulity I heard that the pale young man was to be my new Latin tutor.

'He was at Oxford with Mrs Davis and is staying with her and her - her husband'.

It was quite remarkable how much disapproval she managed to put into that last word. Young married women were a recent phenomenon at the High School and one that the older members of staff didn't much care for. Mazzy went on to say my new tutor was very brilliant and was hoping for a university appointment but in the meantime was working on a translation of Aristophanes. I began to feel rather terrified. I dreaded to think what a brilliant young man, who was obviously a Greek scholar as well, might make of my Latin proses. All the same, it would certainly provide some variation in the general monotony and the others would be most interested. This thought had occurred to Miss Manzonni as well.

'One last thing, Phyllida. I know you're a sensible girl but some of the others...I don't want any silliness over this arrangement.'

'Of course.'

But how was I to stop 'silliness?' The juniors would be bound to show off every time he came to give a lesson. I could just imagine Becky Simon. And it wasn't just the juniors. Jane's scream of laughter when I told them the news in the attic must have been heard through the whole house - so much for no silliness.

CHAPTER THREE

'The boarders are obviously sex-starved.'

Audrey Dawkins, a day girl, happening to overhear me telling Fiona about the previous evening's excitement, laughed scornfully as she spoke. Perhaps she had a point. That morning, eager to tell Fiona about my new Latin tutor, I'd nearly fallen head over heels down the Harstans, a steep flight of ancient steps that led from the Cathedral Close down to the main school. But I'd soon realised, from her lack of reaction, that outside the Boarding House, the story seemed less sensational.

Audrey's sneer, however, made Fiona rally round immediately. Audrey was the year below us and couldn't be allowed to get away with making contemptuous remarks to her superiors. Besides Fiona and I had recently seen her in town one lunchtime kissing an American airman - the city was surrounded by airbases. Audrey had not been wearing her school beret.

'We should really report her for that,' said Fiona. 'But at least without her beret no one will realise she's a High School girl.'

Now here was Audrey again, big-busted and brassily blonde, lounging around near the back row of the form room, which we, the Third Year Sixth, had made into our own little enclave. It was bad enough having to share a form room with the Second Year Sixth without having the likes of Audrey shamelessly eavesdropping and flinging out words like 'sex-starved.'

'Audrey!' Ursula squeaked. Fiona looked at Audrey coldly.

'At least that's better than making yourself cheap with Americans.'

Audrey went rather pink and flounced off.

'Not even an officer,' Fiona added.

There were four of us in the third year sixth; the other three, Fiona, Ursula, who, inevitably, was Head Girl, and Rosa, her Deputy, were day girls. Ursula, Rosa and I, were doing Oxbridge entrance; Fiona had stayed on because she'd caught chickenpox halfway through her A level exams. This was hard on her but a relief to me. Ursula and I were still more or less enemies and Rosa had always been an enigma.

Fiona was already by far the most sophisticated of us. While I perched on a desk swinging my feet, she was reclining languidly, her chair tipped dangerously against the radiator, apparently admiring her legs, clad in the thinnest lisle stockings she could get away with. Her shoes were slip-ons with fringed leather tassels. She tended to be plump but her ankles were slim and she made the most of them.

Neither Latin tutors nor Grammar School boys were of the slightest interest to Fiona. She'd recently been taken out to dinner, at one of the best hotels in the city, by a man of twenty-five and had made him buy her out-of-season strawberries for dessert.

'I could see the waitress thought I was a horrible little gold-digger,' she said with some satisfaction. 'She just slammed the plate down in front of me.' The school authorities may not have known the details of Fiona's social life but they sensed enough to regard her with suspicion. They had only recently, and with some reluctance, made her a prefect. But their suspicion was unjustified. Her behaviour with men was confident, dignified and rather proper. They didn't get much in return for out-of-season strawberries apart from the benefit of her company and conversation.

I ought to have known Fiona wasn't likely to be impressed by a pale, skinny Latin tutor, even if he was translating Aristophanes.

'He won't earn much from that,' she said. 'What will he charge for your lessons?'

'Five bob an hour I suppose, same as Miss Rush. I used to give it to her in an envelope at the beginning of every lesson. My father said it was probably so she didn't have to declare it for tax.' Ursula looked shocked.

'That's against the law.'

'Well you can't really blame her,' said Fiona. 'Teachers' pensions are measly. I wonder if this Mr Marlow has private means?'

Rosa said nothing. I wondered what she was thinking. Small, pale, serious and phenomenally clever, she often gave the impression that she found our conversations trivial. Her background was rather mysterious. None of us had ever been to her house. She lived in one of the little redbrick terraces downhill from the Cathedral. In the city, 'Downhill' indicated more than a mere geographical location; all the best people lived 'Uphill'. She had a noticeable local accent and while she didn't exactly drop her aitches she pronounced them very carefully. Some people had been surprised when she had been made Deputy Head Girl. But, although Miss Cutler was something of a snob, Fiona and I were, for different reasons, considered unsuitable and Rosa had a certain air of quiet authority that, despite the dodgy aitches, made her respected by the juniors.

'Is that make-up you're wearing Fiona?' said Ursula, changing the subject. Her round pink face shone with Pears soap and disapproval.

'Just a touch - I got so freckled this summer.'

'And mascara,' said Ursula, relentless.

Fortunately Miss Carr, our form mistress, came in at that moment and we all leapt to our feet with a polite chorus of 'Good morning

Miss Carr.' The register was called and we filed out of our semi-basement classroom up to the assembly hall.

'Ursula's even worse now she's Head Girl,' Fiona muttered. 'What's my make-up got to do with her?'

'Nothing,' I agreed, although I did feel at times that Fiona rather overdid it, especially with the mascara.

The prefects sat in chairs along the side of the high-windowed hall, which had something of the air of a Victorian chapel. Miss Cutler stood ready at the lectern behind a large open Bible. The choir were grouped to her left. Behind her a portrait of the first headmistress gazed sternly down, as though disapproving of the immodest amount of leg displayed by girls in the mid-twentieth century. The lower forms sat cross-legged on the floor. Ursula, who was a cantor in the choir, opened the proceedings.

'O Lord, open thou our lips,' she sang in her clear, pure voice.

And, as we did every morning, we chanted back

'And our mouth shall show forth thy praise.'

Mr Marlow arrived the next evening soon after tea had been cleared from the dining room and we sat side by side at the top end of the table. He began by enquiring about my lessons with Miss Rush. I explained that I always brought in a piece of prose that I'd been set to translate into Latin. (Usually very inadequately, but I thought I'd leave him to find that out for himself.) Miss Rush then went through it, corrected it, told me to make a fair copy and learn it by heart to recite to her the following week. If I wasn't word-perfect her rage could be terrifying and I'd been so alarmed by Miss Manzonni's account of Mr Marlow's brilliance that I'd made a big effort to learn my most recent fair copy. I offered to recite it.

AUTUMN TERM 1955

'And why should you wish to do that?'

He gazed at me enquiringly. His eyes, I noticed, were grey and he had quite nice eyelashes. His accent indicated that he had been at what my mother always reverently referred to as 'a good school.' He continued to gaze, expectant. I realised I needed to explain further.

'Miss Rush believed I would eventually get the rhythms of the sentences into my head. She wanted me to write Latin prose like Cicero.' Even as I said this I recognised the total absurdity of such an ambition and was unable to repress a half smile.

'And do you aspire to write Latin like Cicero?' He smiled too, so I felt a bit more relaxed.

'Well no, but I need to improve my A level grade because I'm trying for a State Scholarship in the summer.'

'For A level you need to write something grammatically correct. There are not many extra marks for style but in any case our main concern at the moment is the Oxbridge entrance paper, not the State Scholarship. We will concentrate on translation into English.'

The door burst open and Becky Simon charged into the room.

'Oh sorry!' she said, unconvincingly. 'I thought I had piano practice in here.'

'Use the piano in the San.'

'I think Mary's in there.'

'Well sort it out with Matron.'

'Yes, Dilly. Sorry Dilly.' She backed out staring at Mr Marlow; I knew she'd be back. Mr Marlow produced a book.

'I thought we might try some Catullus to start with. Do you like Catullus?' I admitted to total ignorance of Catullus. Mr Marlow was already making me feel inadequate. He started to read a poem aloud which made me feel slightly uneasy. While he was reading, I assessed his attractions - rather wispy mousy hair and bony wrists, but there was something quite endearing about the latter. I was trying to work myself up to falling in love with him. I felt it would alleviate the boredom of another year at school.

'*Atque in perpetuum, frater, ave atque vale.*' he concluded and looked at me expectantly but, before he could ask my opinion, there was another crash at the door and Mary Nicholls fell through shrieking,

'Becky, you beast!'

'Really!' said Mr Marlow. 'This is impossible.'

At prayers before supper Miss Manzonni had much to say on 'Silliness', unspecified, as well as discourtesy to guests and the reputation of the Boarding House. Mary and Becky were sent off to bed early.

I took Catullus up to the attic.

'Hugh Marlow,' Jane read from the title page. 'I'm going to draw a big heart with an arrow through it and write "Dilly loves Hugh" underneath.'

'Don't be silly,' I said, as calmly as possible. You never quite knew how far Jane would go.

'Mag - del – en College Oxford,' read Brenda over Jane's shoulder.

'It's pronounced Maudlin,' said Caroline, whose father was an Oxford graduate.

'Well who's supposed to know that?' said Brenda, offended. She raised her nose in the air and did her sour camel impression. Jane, who had been studying the book further and whose Latin was much better than mine, gave one of her shrieks.

'I say listen to this! *Da mi basia mille*'

Brenda, who was doing A level sciences, looked blank. Caroline and I tried to look as if we knew what *'basia'* meant.

'Kisses,' said Jane, 'Kisses! Give me a thousand kisses!' I grabbed the book back. 'His girlfriend is called Lesbia,' she added. 'Do you think she is?'

'Is what?' asked Caroline.

'A lesbian, like Mazzy and Robbie?' Jane had gone too far again. We all accepted there was a great friendship between Miss Manzonni and Miss Robson. The latter, previously head of history, was now headmistress of a girls' grammar school down South. She'd always worn tweeds and an aertex shirt with a tie and her hair was close-cropped but lots of teachers wore odd clothes and, although Jane claimed she'd heard the two of them call each other 'darling', no one, up to now, had ever actually uttered the word 'lesbian'. I'd only just learnt what it meant.

'I shouldn't think so,' I said, after an awkward pause. 'After all, he is expecting her to kiss him.' I felt I had dealt with Jane in a mature manner. Nevertheless I thought that as long as Mr Marlow continued to come to the Boarding House there would be many further outbreaks of 'Silliness'.

The same thoughts had obviously occurred to Miss Manzonni. A few days later she sent for me again and talked a great deal about the necessity of leaving the dining-room free for piano practice. However, she continued, Mrs Davis had kindly offered a solution. She had suggested that Mr Marlow could teach me at their digs.

'After all,' she added, almost as if reassuring herself 'Mrs Davis will be there as well.' From what I already knew of Mrs Davis I didn't quite see her in the role of chaperone but anyway I could hardly hope Mr Marlow would make advances to an immature schoolgirl. Especially one who'd already confessed to an ignorance of Catullus.

I thought about this new arrangement. On the one hand any deviation from ordinary school life, any change of scene was to be welcomed. On the other hand, I told myself, I'd rather this had been anywhere other than the Davis's lodgings.

CHAPTER FOUR

The main reason for my reluctance to go to the Davis's lodgings wasn't because of any particular dislike for Mrs Davis herself. I'd had my reasons for feeling antagonistic when I'd first heard she was coming to teach at our school but I was now beginning to find her rather interesting.

Her arrival had caused quite a stir. For a start she was young and married, a rare enough combination in our school, but, even more remarkably, she was very striking, dark, good-looking, with extraordinary clothes and a tendency to wear dangling, silver earrings.

'Honestly! She looks like a gypsy,' said Ursula.

'Oh, more like an art student,' I said. Even if I hadn't already been attracted by Mrs Davis's bohemian appearance Ursula's disapproval would have made me want to defend her.

It was true that, along with the rest of the Sixth Form, I found this strange woman rather challenging. Besides teaching English she had, as the newest member of staff, been landed with General Studies. This had always been regarded as a relaxation period, forty minutes of chat during which, if you sat at the back, you could catch up with a bit of homework, doodle, or possibly even read a magazine under the desk. Even Ursula had been known to prepare a few lines of the *Aeneid* when under pressure. Now, with Mrs Davis, everyone had to participate. She made no effort to disguise her opinion that she found us all very ignorant and very provincial. She herself was a Londoner

'Hampstead I expect,' said Ursula. 'My father says they're all atheists and Socialists there'. For, unlike most of the staff, Mrs Davis had already made her political sympathies very clear.

This had an interesting effect on Rosa; in the past she had always held back in discussions, but now, with Mrs Davis's encouragement, she had gained a new confidence. She began to speak with quiet passion in defence of Trade Unions, the Welfare State and comprehensive education, things that most of our parents regarded with disapproval. Her arguments defeated us and Mrs Davis backed her up, unfairly some felt.

In the previous week's lesson Rosa had suddenly shocked us all by declaring, 'I'm working class.' We were embarrassed. This idea had not yet become fashionable and we knew, although it was never said openly, that one of the High School's aims, perhaps its main aim, was, whatever our backgrounds, to turn us into nice middle class girls. To have reached the Sixth Form, to be Deputy Head Girl, to be trying for university, for Oxbridge indeed, and still to say you were working class shocked us and her defence of comprehensive schools was felt to be, as Fiona put it, 'rather ungrateful.'

When Ursula, no doubt quoting her parents, suggested that the Welfare State was encouraging fecklessness amongst the working class, Rosa's already pale face went alarmingly white.

'I suppose,' she said, in a tightly furious voice, 'you think my dad is feckless, scraping by on a disability pension after ruining his lungs down a mine, while my mum has to go out cleaning to make ends meet.'

There was an appalled silence. Ursula turned even pinker than usual.

'I didn't mean your father, Rosa,' she said. 'I was thinking of people in council houses who buy televisions on hire purchase.'

'You weren't thinking at all Ursula,' said Mrs Davis. 'Whatever has people buying televisions on hire purchase got to do with anything? That was a ridiculous non sequitur.' Ursula's smug, pink face turned bright red; she looked as if she might cry. For once I felt sorry for her.

'So your father was a miner was he?' said Mrs Davis turning to Rosa. 'Where from? My husband comes from a mining background too - from South Wales.'

'How peculiar,' said Fiona later. 'Mrs Davis obviously doesn't come from that kind of background herself. Why would she marry a coalminer's son? She must have met more suitable men at Cambridge.'

'I think she went to Oxford,' I said.

'Well you know what I mean,' said Fiona.

'Anyway,' I said, 'people do sometimes marry someone from a different class. My mother thinks my father comes from a lower class than she does. I've told you before how she looks down on my aunt and uncle.'

'I thought that was just because they were English,' said Fiona.

Both Fiona's parents were Scottish and were always complaining about the barbarous country they were compelled to live in. My mother was also Scottish and made similar complaints. It was another bond between Fiona and me.

'It's a class thing too,' I said, and left it at that. My mother rather looked down on Fiona's parents as well. They came from Glasgow; she was Edinburgh.

Nevertheless the lesson had reminded me of why I had been ready to dislike Mrs Davis when I'd first heard she was to be our new English teacher. It wasn't that her political views had caused me any concern. In fact it had been delightful to see Ursula so thoroughly crushed and this alone had made me think there might be something to be said for them. What had upset me had been her reference to her husband.

I'd never actually seen Mr Davis. Well, at least only from a distance. Jane had once called me to the dormitory window to admire a man she'd seen walking through the Close. By the time I joined her he'd almost disappeared.

'You should have come sooner, even better looking than the divine Mr Weaver. I think I'd almost give him ten. Quel smasher!'

Jane had recently devised a scheme for giving marks out of ten to all the males in our limited acquaintance. The highest score so far was the aforementioned Mr Weaver but because of his rumoured vow of celibacy, she'd only awarded him a nine.

'Who do you think he can be?' She continued to describe the stranger in glowing terms.

'You make him sound like a hero in a women's magazine story.' This was meant to be derogatory but Jane took it as a further reason to award the stranger ten. I tried to make my point more forcefully.

'Or one of those men they use to model cable-knit sweaters in knitting pattern books. The type that's always photographed staring into the distance while the wind ruffles his hair.'

'Well obviously you prefer weedy types like Christopher.'

'Very funny!' Then I had a sudden intuition. 'You know what! I think he might be that new English teacher's husband, the legendary Mr Davis. Chris was always on about him when we were going out together. I got sick of hearing his name.' I brooded over this for a moment. 'Actually I blame him for our break-up.'

Jane wasn't interested in my thwarted love life.

'You mean he's married? Damn! Only nine then.'

AUTUMN TERM 1955

My ex-boyfriend's obsession with his A level history teacher and what I'd then thought of as this man's stupid ideas had been a source of irritation all the time I'd been going out with Christopher. Not only did I blame Mr Davis for the break-up of our relationship, but I also felt he'd been at least partly responsible for the slow progress of our romance.

I remembered, for example, a frustrating afternoon the previous March. I'd been seeing Christopher illicitly ever since we'd met at the joint Sixth Form party for the two Grammar Schools back in January but we hadn't progressed much beyond holding hands as we'd huddled together against the cold on winter Saturday afternoons.

But spring was coming. Now, somewhere above us, among the black ash buds, in the overgrown graveyard that we'd selected for our trysts, a thrush was singing energetically and the chestnut leaves were already showing signs of stickily unwrapping themselves. It was the first Saturday it had been warm enough to stop walking about. We sat down on a flat tombstone.

Fiona had nicknamed Christopher the Grecian Urn, and it was true his ears did stick out a bit but, as I gave a sideways glance at him, I thought, he really wasn't bad looking. After all he was tall, apparently free from boils and acne and, above all, male. I had been wondering when, if ever, he would get round to kissing me. Sitting there in the spring sunshine my heart had begun to beat faster. He seemed about to put his arm round me but then, thinking better of it, began,

'You know our history master.' (Not again! - I thought) 'You remember I told you he was a Socialist, well the other day he told us he was an atheist as well.'

'Is he a Communist?'

'No, he says he's a Socialist and an atheist but not a Communist.'

'So what's the difference?' I said. 'He might as well be a Communist and have done with it.'

Christopher, although he was doing Scholarship level History, wasn't altogether clear about this. I edged a bit closer but he didn't respond and instead started to tell me what Mr Davis had to say about the Soviet Union.

Christopher, after university, was planning to be ordained. I wondered whether, being rather High Church, he might think it was irreverent to kiss a girl on sanctified ground. Perhaps I should suggest the Arboretum next Saturday?

Irritated as I was by Christopher's obsession with Mr Davis I was, nevertheless, interested enough to ask Ursula about him. Her father taught Classics at the same school. Ursula pursed her lips looking even more prim than usual. Then she shook her head slowly before pronouncing,

'My father says he's little better than a Communist. He's been giving the boys all sorts of ideas.'

'Well I suppose that's what he's there for,' said Rosa, who could be unexpectedly witty at times.

'Not those sort of ideas,' said Ursula.

I wanted to hear more but Ursula never had much time for idle gossip. She jumped up, putting an end to any further discussion of the suitability or otherwise of Mr Davis's ideas.

'Dilly, I've called a meeting about the House rounders matches - attendance at the practice yesterday was very poor. You'd better come too and back me up.' Ursula was then a House Captain and I was her reluctant and ineffectual deputy. I lingered a little as she bustled off.

AUTUMN TERM 1955

'Rabbit's having yet another busy day,' I said to Fiona. Rather to my surprise Rosa laughed. I'd never associated her with anything so childish or, I suppose, although I'm ashamed to admit this, anything as middle class as *Winnie the Pooh*.

The final blow to our rather inadequate romance was struck near the end of the summer term. Christopher told me that Mr Davis had invited his History group to a post-exam party.

'And he's asked us to bring our girlfriends, so do you want to come?'

I was fairly sure it was no good even asking if I could. The idea of a boarder going out with a boy on a Saturday evening was unimaginable. I wasn't even supposed to have a boyfriend. If Mazzy ever wondered why I needed permission to go down to the public library every Saturday afternoon she'd probably just explained to herself that I was a keen reader.

Christopher tried to persuade me to ask permission to come to the party. He suggested I could say that his history teacher's wife would be there. However he rather spoilt any illusion of respectability this might have given to the occasion by saying that his friend Dave Whatley had already met her.

'He says she's really..,' he paused to find a suitable word, 'glamorous.' I knew he really meant sexy.

While I was discussing the problem with Fiona, Ursula overheard us.

'You'll do well to stay out of it Dilly. I heard my father say he can't see that man lasting long at the Grammar School. Fancy asking his pupils round for a party! Do you know, at the end of last term he actually took some of them to the pub! My father says teachers should never socialise with their pupils. It's bad for discipline.' She sat back; lips pressed together, her prim little face glowing.

I couldn't imagine anyone wanting to socialise with Ursula's father, who looked as grim as his brother-in-law the Dean, but all this convinced me further that it would be no use asking if I could go to the party. Soon afterwards Christopher's cousin, who was in my form and who had obligingly carried notes between us, told me that he'd invited his previous girlfriend to go with him instead. I'd lost my first ever boyfriend, all because Mr Davis had decided to give a party.

I'd already begun to dislike the legendary Mr Davis. After this I felt I detested him. Now it looked as if I might have to meet him. I resolved to be very cold and dignified if I did.

CHAPTER FIVE

By the next General Studies we'd moved on. It was quite possible that after her attack on Ursula Mrs Davis had been told to lay off politics. Ursula may have talked; her uncle was, of course, in close contact with the Bishop and the Bishop was Chairman of the Governors. Anyway, whatever the reason, we were now struggling to discuss art.

On the Tuesday morning of my first visit to the Davises, Mrs Davis gave back our latest essays. She'd given us a challenging title, *What is Art for?* By 'Art' I think we all assumed she meant paintings.

Most people agreed that pictures were for hanging on walls to make the house look nice and therefore should be pretty and portray something recognisable unlike modern art as practised by people like Picasso. Somehow I had begun to despise this view and I wanted to impress Mrs Davis with my greater sophistication although I had no clear ideas about how to do so.

Led by Fiona, as usual, I'd begun to develop an interest in paintings. It had come about in rather an odd way. Fiona had noticed that Audrey Dawkins and her friends were sticking pictures of the local football team inside their desk lids. It was just one more example of the indignities we had to suffer in sharing a formroom with the year below.

'So common!' said Fiona. She decided we must start a counter movement by buying postcard reproductions of famous paintings. These could be tastefully arranged inside our desk lids in a kind of miniature art gallery that would raise the tone of the formroom even if we couldn't entirely turn back the march of the barbarians. She had discovered an art shop, a tiny place, on a cobbled street that plunged downhill from the Cathedral Close, where we could buy these cards and we took to visiting it in our lunch hours. Fiona's tastes were already formed; she chose several Constables, some English watercolourists and, I think, an early Turner. I was more eclectic, although that wasn't the word I would have used at the time. There was El Greco's *Grand Inquisitor* in his pink robes and his spectacles, because we'd been shown it in one of our European History lessons. There was Franz Marc's *Blue Horses*. Was this because I still liked horses, or because of the energy of the composition? (I'd like to think the latter). And there was Seurat's *La Grande Jatte* and so on. Fiona said there was no linking theme. She pointed at the Seurat,

'Why not just have French Impressionists?'

Sometimes I wondered where Fiona's knowledge of art came from. I liked her parents; they were friendly and cheerful but they seemed ordinary enough. They both had noticeable Glasgow accents and the family, Fiona, her parents and an older brother, when he was home from university, lived in a small thirties semi on a road lined with similar houses. There were no signs of high art around the place, just silver-framed wedding photos and two almost identical photos of Fiona and her brother as babies lying naked on their stomachs on a fur rug. The one original painting was a watercolour of Loch Lomond that had been painted by an aunt. Even then I knew it was very bad.

Anyway, regardless of Fiona, I was finding my way around, trying to discover what I liked and why. Truth to life was not the only criterion I decided and I tried to express this, no doubt clumsily, in my essay. I finished in a burst of inspiration with a quotation from one of our O level set texts:

> *...Art was given for that*
> *God uses us to help each other so,*
> *Lending our minds out.*

Now Mrs Davis flung our essays back at us contemptuously. I nervously read the comment on mine, 'C+, your use of the Browning quotation was apposite; otherwise you have said very little, very wordily indeed.' Ursula was leaning towards me trying to see my mark. I put my hand over it.

'And as for yours Ursula,' said Mrs Davis, 'The banality of your argument was breathtaking. Not what one might hope for from an Oxbridge candidate.'

I removed my hand.

The only girl who had managed to construct a coherent argument, apparently, was Rosa. She had defended the Socialist Realists now painting in the USSR.

'But Rosa do you think the only purpose of art is to educate? Some people might say this was propaganda.'

'But,' said Rosa, 'A painting like *The Tractor Driver's Supper* is something working people can relate to.' Audrey Dawkins started an ostentatious yawn but stifled it quickly when Mrs Davis looked at her. The rest of us were silent. We didn't really know what they were talking about.

In the end Mrs Davis said she disagreed with Rosa but she would 'defend to the death anyone's right to hold different opinions.' She added that she and her husband often argued about Socialist Realism. I was impressed. My parents argued about boring things such as how often we had to visit my father's brother or whether or not my mother's housekeeping allowance was adequate. I couldn't ever imagine them debating the merits of 'Socialist Realism' whatever that might be.

At the end of the lesson Mrs Davis called me aside and reminded me that I was to have my first Latin lesson with Mr Marlow after school that afternoon.

'Come to the staffroom and we can walk up together,' she said. Still smarting from having been told I had said, 'Very little, very wordily indeed,' I decided I would say nothing at all on our way to her lodgings on the other side of the cathedral.

Mrs Davis raised the subject of my essay as soon as we were out of the school gate and had started to walk up the Harstans to the Close.

'You were the only one apart from Rosa who showed you had given some genuine thought to the subject but you must get your ideas clearer before you start to write.' I muttered that the trouble was I didn't think I had any clear ideas. Mrs Davis continued to hold forth on art and I said things like, 'I see' or 'I'd never thought of that' until we turned into a quiet little cul-de-sac of shabby Georgian houses, a strange rather secret place; even now still unknown to tourists. Mrs Davis creaked open a small iron gate and we walked up a brick path slippery with moss. Michaelmas daisies straggled about in a quantity of wet grass. It was a mild afternoon but there was a distinct drop in temperature as we entered the stone-flagged hall, which smelt of damp and paraffin. A flickering Aladdin stove attempted to give out faint warmth. A door opened and a thin stooped figure huddled in shawls appeared.

'Oh it's you dear, and a High School girl! Young life about the place, how nice!' I waited for Mrs Davis to introduce me but she merely nodded, so I smiled as nicely as I could, having been brought up to be polite to the old. The elderly lady shuffled back in.

'Who was that?'

'Oh, our landlady Mrs Herbert, the widow of some Canon or other, always popping out to make sure she doesn't miss anything.'

'Perhaps she's lonely.'

'God! You sound like Mike. He can't help being charming to everybody. She adores him'. I presumed she was referring to her husband. It wasn't what I had expected of someone that Christopher had told me was both a Socialist and an atheist. I was also registering the blasphemy and the casual use of Mr Davis's Christian name.

We crossed the hall passing a shallow stepped staircase with a delicately curved banister and pushed open a door covered with the tattered remnants of green baize. We were now in a corridor leading to a narrow staircase.

'Mind that lino,' said Mrs Davis. 'Those holes are lethal in this half-light.' We went down the steps into a semi-basement kitchen.

I stopped in the doorway, amazed. I'd never seen a room like it. Compared with the rest of the house it was warm and seemed to be used as an all-purpose living-dining-work room. There were several bookcases constructed of planks resting on bricks, a happy improvisation that delighted me. There was a large square table laden with books, marking, dirty plates and mugs, a jar of marmalade, a lump of cheese, a full ashtray and a brown pottery jug with a strainer of coffee dregs balanced on it. This, I thought, accounted for the less than pristine state in which our essays were often returned to us. A crumpled newspaper, the *Manchester Guardian*, lay on a scruffy sofa that was partly covered by a striped rug. One wall had been distempered orange and there were some posters for exhibitions of contemporary art.

Mrs Davis looked at the littered table and at the kitchen range, clogged with cinders and leaking ash. She frowned and went to the door.

'Hugh!' she shouted. There was a thump from above and then footsteps. Hugh Marlow came into the kitchen looking rumpled and sleepy. He glanced at the table.

'Oh shit! I didn't mean to sleep so long. I didn't mean to sleep at all, but I got so cold writing I just crawled under the blankets to get warm. Allie darling,' he went over to her and flung an arm round her shoulder, 'Mea culpa. Don't be too cross! I'll clear up now.' Mrs Davis removed his arm.

'Dilly is here. Extra Latin – had you forgotten?' Hugh looked slightly discomposed. Made aware of my presence, I thought he was on the verge of saying 'shit' again, a word that, up to that moment, I had only seen written on walls. My horizons were expanding almost too rapidly. He used really bad swear words, I thought, and yet he also spoke Latin. Of course, I thought, swearing sounded sophisticated rather than rough if you had a public school accent.

He swears in an educated manner, I explained to myself.

At that point there was a clattering in the corridor. Someone was dragging a bike through the green baize door. I realised with dread that the Socialist-atheist was back.

'Hello! Who's this? Hugh's pupil? Well! Some people have all the luck. I never get lovely girls to teach.' This flattering comment made in a slight Welsh lilt was accompanied by a dazzling smile and I couldn't help noticing that he had intensely blue eyes. I immediately forgot all my resentment and my contemptuous remark about knitting patterns. I struggled to remember Mrs Davis's warning, 'He can't help being charming to everyone,' I repeated to myself but it was no good. I blushed; I couldn't stop smiling; I felt slightly giddy. He tugged off his bicycle clips and dumped them on the table.

'See you've neglected the household chores again, Hugh. Hello, darling!' (this last presumably addressed to his wife). There was already so much to report back to my companions in the attic we probably wouldn't get any prep done at all that evening.

Rather to my relief the Davises took themselves off, presumably to a cold bedroom, while I had my lesson. I wondered if they too would crawl under the blankets for warmth and was rather shocked by myself. It was the kind of speculation Jane would make.

Hugh Marlow was a good teacher. He didn't paralyse my brain by glaring at me over the top of his glasses like Miss Rush but led me on stage by stage.

'Make an intelligent guess,' he kept saying and somehow, with this encouragement, over the following weeks my guesses became more intelligent. I began to see for the first time ever that this might be literature, like Milton and Shakespeare, rather than just some tortuous puzzle. Even during this first lesson I became absorbed and was quite surprised when Mrs Davis reappeared pointing out we'd been working for an hour.

'Would you like some tea Dilly?' she asked. I knew that Matron would have left out bread and jam for me in the kitchen but I was reluctant to leave this extraordinary household especially when Mike Davis almost immediately followed his wife into the kitchen.

Mrs Davis made toast spread quite generously with butter. I remarked appreciatively on this.

'But butter's off ration now.'

'So much the worse for us boarders. When it was rationed Matron had to give us each four ounces a week. Now it's unrationed she's cut it back to two again. She says she can't afford to give us more.'

'Really! It sounds like *Jane Eyre*.' Encouraged by this I expounded disloyally on the inadequacies of Boarding House food. The story of the mouse stew was greeted with a mixture of horror and laughter. I felt I was being a social success.

'Tell me,' said Mrs Davis. 'Why a Boarding House?' I'd never given this much thought but said some people lived on farms, which would mean a long bus journey to the nearest grammar school.

'And what about you?'

'Our local grammar school is co-ed. My father wanted me to go to a girls' school.' (That, at least, was what he'd told the local education authority when he'd asked for me to board at the High School. My mother had said the local grammar school was rough but I thought this might offend Mr Davis's socialist principles.)

'Quite right,' said Mr Davis, 'Pretty girls like you should be kept locked up.'

'You're not amusing, Mike,' said Mrs Davis.

'Dilly's amused. Aren't you Dilly?'

Actually I was beaming with pleasure. If I'd been a cat I'd have been writhing around purring. Remember, I said to myself, he can't help being charming to everyone. But it was no good.

'Give her some more toast, Allie,' he went on, 'She looks as if she needs feeding up.' This was less flattering. Ursula, in a French lesson, had once described me as 'maigre'. I knew I was no Brigitte Bardot but I'd felt that was unnecessarily spiteful.

'Boarding schools aren't meant to be hotels,' said Hugh. 'The food was pretty grim at Winchester - and it was cold, but it's meant to be character building.'

AUTUMN TERM 1955

'Well that accounts for a lot,' said Mike Davis. The look he gave Hugh at that moment was very far from charming. There was a moment's silence.

'Supper!' said Mrs Davis, springing up. She started chopping onions vigorously. She poured some oil into a pan. The onions sizzled and smelt delicious. It was obviously time to go.

'You cook with oil?' I said, gathering my books together and stuffing them in my satchel.

'Yes, I'd prefer to use olive oil but you can only get that at the chemist's in this backwater, and even there, if you say you want enough for cooking, they think you're mad.'

I'd already heard of people cooking with olive oil. There had recently been an angry letter in the *Yorkshire Post* from a Scarborough hotelier complaining about the growing fashion for foreign holidays and foreign food. He'd referred contemptuously to olive oil and asked what was wrong with good old British lard. Olive oil, for me, was still inextricably connected with the dusty little bottle of bright yellow stuff lurking on the bathroom shelf at home. We used it for earache; the idea of cooking with it had made me shudder. Now I was prepared to reconsider.

Mrs Davis stirred in some mince, of distinctly better quality than the meat in the Boarding House shepherd's pie and started opening a tin of tomatoes. Tinned tomatoes on soggy toast were regularly served up at breakfast in the Boarding House but now it seemed they had other uses. Then she reached up to a shelf to bring down a packet of long spaghetti. I longed to stay and see how she cooked it but I didn't want to outstay my welcome.

'Goodbye Dilly. Come again soon,' said Mike Davis. He frowned. 'Dilly, Dilly? Is that short for Dilys by any chance?' Much as I should have liked by this time to claim a Welsh connection I had to admit to Phyllida.

'Phyllida,' he said, 'now I've heard of that name somewhere before.' I desperately hoped he wouldn't remember where. Not for the first time I wished that my mother had spent her pregnancy knitting bootees and matinee jackets like any normal woman instead of lying on the sofa browsing through *The Golden Book of Modern English Poetry (1870-1920)*.

'You're rather late dear.' Mazzy met me in the hall before I could knock on her door to say I was back.

'Yes I was discussing my General Studies essay with Mrs Davis. She gave us rather a difficult title, *What is Art for?*'. Mazzy raised her eyebrows. She looked amused. (I suspect now that she found Mrs Davis rather pretentious.)

'Dear me! That certainly is a big question. Well don't take advantage of her kindness will you?' I promised I wouldn't. 'Matron has left some tea for you in the kitchen.' I thought of saying I'd already had some tea and then thought better of it. I remembered it was shepherd's pie night again. It might be as well to fill up on bread and marge and anonymous jam while I had the chance.

I hadn't really lied, I told myself, just moved events around a little. Mr Davis had called me a pretty girl. Could he possibly think that even though half-starved I was quite attractive? He'd looked at me as if he thought so. I knew my mother thought I was very plain. She was always lamenting over my straight hair and telling me not to read too much because glasses, as she put it, 'would be the last straw.' Of course I must remember, 'He charms everyone' but he didn't *have* to say I was pretty did he?

There was a violent red sunset; the window in the basement kitchen was almost on a level with the rough lawn and the grass was a luminous green; the Michaelmas daisies in the weedy flowerbed blazed in a purple fire. It all seemed part of the strangeness of the evening.

In the attic, after supper, Jane asked if I'd done the poem about kissing. I said, rather shortly,
'No, we read one about a pet sparrow.'
'A pet sparrow!' said Caroline, 'Not in a cage I hope.'
'No, she tied its leg to her wrist with a bit of silk.'
'Now that is cruel!' Her big brown eyes started to brim with tears.
'It died.'
'I'm not surprised.'
'That Lesbia again!' said Jane and whooped with laughter.
Really they were all so silly and childish. I couldn't be bothered to tell them anything.

CHAPTER SIX

The following Saturday I went home for the weekend. Sunday was Harvest Festival and it was a family tradition that we always went to Uncle Frank's for the occasion. I was looking forward to telling my cousin Frances about the Davises. Frances was about my age, the youngest of Uncle Frank's three daughters. When we were younger I'd been very close to her but she'd left school after O levels and was now at home on the farm helping in the house and looking after the poultry. She was expected to stay there until she got married. Ellen, her eldest sister, had married a farmer the previous year and was already pregnant. Only Amber, the middle one, had managed to break away.

Since she had left school I was beginning to find Frances and I had less to say to each other. Now there would be something to talk about, although I couldn't quite imagine how she would react to my account of the Davis household.

Fiona's reaction had been disappointing. My attempts to describe the amazing kitchen fell flat.

'Ugh! It sounds rather squalid.' I told her about Mrs Davis's cooking. 'Oh! spaghetti bolognese! I had it in an Italian restaurant in London last Easter when Auntie Elsie took us to see *Salad Days*'.

I ought to have guessed; of course Fiona would already know about spaghetti bolognese. She always got there before me. I'd only ever eaten tinned spaghetti on toast, which my mother liked because it was easy. Now I hoped that Frances would be impressed by, or at least interested in, my extraordinary experience and my fascinating new acquaintances.

On Sunday morning I spent some time trying to put my hair up like Mrs Davis's but without success. My hair was straight and fairish not dark and wavy. It kept slipping out of the clips. Also I couldn't really see properly. We lived in a characterless modern house on the outskirts of the town. It had been described by the builders as a 'chalet-bungalow', which meant there was one upstairs bedroom crammed under the eaves. I'd insisted on having this as my room because it seemed the only interesting space in the house, but even on this sunny September day, it was full of dark corners and the dressing-table mirror was in one of them. I gave up and came downstairs with my hair flowing loose over my shoulders. My father said I looked 'arty' by which I think he meant 'immoral' and my mother said it didn't look smart. I re-tied it in my usual ponytail, which didn't suit my father either.

'That's one of the ugliest styles ever invented. You look as if you're always just about to wash your neck.'

'If you had it cut dear you could have a nice perm,' said my mother. I didn't even bother to reply.

'I used to like your plaits,' said my father.

This temporarily united my mother and me. We both told him not to be silly.

'That nylon blouse has seen better days,' my mother said, thereby immediately losing my transient goodwill. 'What about that nice Fair Isle jumper Aunty Nettie gave you? It would go perfectly with your tartan skirt.'

'Too hot,' I said, flinging myself sullenly into the back of the car.

The farm was in the next county beyond a wide estuary. Nowadays the estuary is crossed by a toll bridge; back then there was only a ferry. The estuary tides were unreliable and it wasn't unknown for the boat to stick on the mud banks, stranding passengers for hours. The ferry port itself was a melancholy collection of dark brick houses set among flat fields intersected by turgid watercourses which lurked behind high banks, known locally as dykes. To board the ferry, we had to drive slowly down a long pier stretched out over the mudflats. My mother never liked going to Uncle Frank's anyway and all these things contributed to her gloom.

Even though we didn't run aground this time it still looked as if we might be late for the service. Once over the other side the landscape improved. It began to fold into gentle chalky hills and the villages were of a warmer brick. On the straighter stretches of road my father began to drive faster than usual; the speedometer reached forty and my mother kept gasping,

'Tom, slow down!' which made him even more irritable.

'Oh look Dilly, lovely horses!' she exclaimed at one point obviously trying to restore me to good humour. I was furious. How old did she think I was? Twelve? Suppose Mrs Davis had heard her. The mere thought made me nearly die with shame.

We arrived in the village near the farm just in time. Uncle Frank's new car, pale blue with a gleaming chrome radiator like a shark's mouth, was parked on the verge and Uncle Frank himself, constrained in his Sunday suit, his neck a burnt red against his white collar, was glancing anxiously at his watch. Our little black Morris stuttered to a standstill. We hurried into our pew just as the Minister was mounting the pulpit steps.

Sometimes in future Septembers, as I contemplated tins of beans and packets of soup piled up in some dusty school hall, I would think nostalgically about the little plain brick chapel with its clear glass windows open to the surrounding fields and gardens; those very fields and gardens where the apples and plums, the cabbages, carrots and marrows, now piled so generously in front of the communion table, had recently been growing. The hedges were being destroyed but there were still great vases of beech leaves tinged with gold providing a background for lavish bunches of dahlias and chrysanthemums. The combine harvester might now throw out square blocks of compressed straw in its wake but someone had managed to find two traditional sheaves of corn to adorn the pulpit.

There was no organ and the hymns were accompanied by a piano played by whoever could be coerced into volunteering. That Sunday it was Frances. All my cousins had learnt the piano. Now Ellen was too heavily pregnant and Amber had given up some time ago after a spectacular row with her music teacher, so Frances was plodding more or less accurately through *We plough the fields and scatter*. She was helped along by a little white-haired man, who played the violin, like some character out of a Hardy novel.

During the sermon my mother's face expressed a kind of resigned contempt. It was not the kind of sermon she had been accustomed to in the Church of Scotland - she always made it clear that she didn't see herself as belonging to the non-conformists - 'chapel people', as they were called locally, a term which infuriated her.

'In Scotland,' she said 'Chapel is where the Papists go.'

'*Come ye thankful people come.*' The service was nearing its end. During this final hymn I contemplated Amber a few rows in front of me. Her long red hair lay loose over her shoulders. 'She manages to get away with it,' I thought.

AUTUMN TERM 1955

All be safely gathered in
Free from sorrow free from sin,

the congregation sang enthusiastically. Somehow in Amber's case I doubted it.

'A grand sermon Reverend Taylor,' said Uncle Frank.'Champion! Wasn't it, Margaret?' rather unwisely turning to my mother.

'A very nice homely little address, very appropriate,' she said in her most Edinburgh voice.

She stood among the other women like some elegant long-legged bird, a curlew or an oystercatcher perhaps, in a hen-coop. The other women wore fitted coats that bulged out over their substantial bottoms and bosoms. They had solid felt hats in navy or the colour that, in those unenlightened days, was known as 'nigger brown'. My mother's hat was bright pink and looked to me horribly like a man's trilby, worn rather dashingly on the side of her head.

'Smashing hat, Aunty!' said Amber suddenly appearing beside us. I realised with a kind of surprised gratitude that Amber rather admired my mother.

In the farmhouse kitchen the range was roaring away and there was a smell of roast meat. Aunty Joyce bustled about, stout, hot, red-faced, shouting instructions to her daughters.

'Sit down, dear, do,' said my mother to Ellen, 'You shouldn't be on your feet all the time in your condition.' She flung a meaningful glance at Ellen's husband who, oblivious to all else, was discussing wheat prices with my father and Uncle Frank.

'Don't say that Margaret,' said Aunty Joyce. 'Ellen's the only one that knows what she's doing. Our Frances is like Dilly, in a dream half the time, and as for Amber...'

Being rather sensitive to the influence of names I sometimes wondered if Aunty Joyce regretted the uncharacteristic fit of fancy that had caused her to name her middle daughter Amber. She often explained that she'd been convinced it would be a boy this time and hadn't thought of any girls' names. Then, seeing the reddish glint in the baby's hair, the name Amber had, as she put it, 'just popped into my head.' It was most unlike her and she probably regretted it now, but would it really have made any difference if Amber had been called something sensible like Mary or Ann?

Now here was Amber slithering up to my mother to have more conversation on the subject of hats while Ellen was helping dish up the Yorkshire pudding and Frances, getting more and more flustered, was dropping forks.

'You seem to get a lot of time off,' said my mother. 'I thought nurses often had to work at weekends.'

'Oh I couldn't miss Harvest Festival,' said Amber smoothly.

She was, I thought, a most unlikely nurse.

'I expect they thought a hospital matron would be able to keep an eye on her,' my mother had said when we heard Amber had managed to get away from home. I suspected Amber had been so difficult that her parents hadn't been entirely reluctant to let her go.

We ate in the big kitchen; a white starched cloth was draped over the dark green, chenille table-cover. The Yorkshire pudding came first, huge, puffed up slices of crisp golden batter covered with onion gravy served straight from the oven by the side of the range. The following courses always seemed an anti-climax.

'Very little beef for me, Frank,' said my mother as usual. She took one potato and shuddered away offers of cabbage and more gravy.

'Come along Margaret. You don't eat enough to keep a fly alive,' said Uncle Frank. 'You all look as if you could do with feeding up.'

'Take some more potatoes Tom,' said Aunty Joyce to my father.

'Not too many, dear,' said my mother 'You don't want to be up all night with indigestion again.'

'I'd like another potato,' I said quickly. My mother looked at me reproachfully but couldn't find any reason to object.

'That's right, Dilly,' said Uncle Frank. 'I like to see young ones with a good appetite. How are your studies going?'

'OK,' I said. 'I've got a new Latin tutor.' It gave me exquisite pleasure to mention this connection with the Davises.

'Latin!' said Aunty Joyce. 'That won't help you look after a husband. Will it?'

'If she has any sense she'll have a career like her aunts,' said my mother.

(She was always telling me that her unmarried older sisters, one a teacher and one a doctor, had a much better life than hers. 'They have their own money for one thing,' she frequently said. 'They don't have to beg for every penny.')

'Well perhaps so,' said Uncle Frank, 'After all she's clever.'

'Does that mean it's clever not to get married?' asked Amber.

'Amber you do twist things so,' said Aunty Joyce. 'Your father just meant....'

'No good at figures though,' interrupted my father, perhaps thinking a little modesty about his daughter's achievements was called for.

'Well girls aren't,' said Uncle Frank.

'I am,' said Amber. 'I like Maths; it was my best subject.'

'Oh well, you!' said Uncle Frank. There was an awkward pause.

The subject of education was a controversial one in my father's family. My mother had often told me how my father's teachers had wanted him to go to university but that his parents wouldn't hear of it. He'd done his accountancy exams at night school; something she resented far more than my father seemed to. Education in her Scottish family had been regarded as almost sacred. She herself had been considered too delicate to go to university but both her sisters had degrees.

Uncle Frank realised it was time to change the subject.

'You'll never believe what happened this morning,' he began. 'A fellow turned up with a truckload of beasts.'

'Never!' said my father.

'That's right, on a Sunday an' all. What do you think to that?'

'What did you say?'

'Well I was forced to take them of course. But I asked him if he knew what day it was? "Sunday," he says; so I asked him if he remembered the fourth commandment?'

I noticed Amber's green eyes were fixed on me. She gave a slow wink. Frances had told me that her sister sometimes went to the pictures on Sunday when she was away from home but that Uncle Frank must never find out. I was rather flattered that Amber saw me as a potential Sabbath breaker. As a child I'd been rather afraid of her. She used to tease Frances and me when we were younger. I wondered if the Davises went to the cinema on a Sunday.

'I don't suppose he did,' said my father, referring to the fourth commandment. 'They don't seem to teach them anything nowadays.' This got all the older generation started on the general decline in manners and morals. There was no discipline in schools, no young person could spell and what was all this nonsense about teenagers? No one had heard of them in their day. It had a unifying effect and lasted through the apple-pie and custard and cups of tea. Then Ellen went off with her husband to visit her in-laws while Frances and I were sent into the scullery to help Aunty Joyce with the washing-up.

'Where's Amber?' said Aunty Joyce.

'I think she went for a walk.'

'Not in those shoes she didn't.' I said no more. I had definitely seen her hovering near the coats in the passage but I thought it might be best to keep quiet about it.

The washing-up seemed endless. Aunty Joyce kept on producing more and more snow-white, beautifully ironed tea towels from the drawer and we wiped and stacked a mountain of crockery. The used tea towels joined the now gravy splattered tablecloth in a pile destined for boiling in the copper on Monday morning. Eventually we got away, leaving her scouring saucepans before she turned her attention to getting tea. I wondered how all this endless toil could be reconciled with Uncle Frank's views on Sabbath observance but perhaps housekeeping didn't count as work. After all you didn't get paid for it.

We were told to go and seek eggs. Frances and I wandered through the stack-yard gathering a few eggs from under a rusty harrow, a few from a bale of straw while the hens shrieked at us from the rafters but we both had other things on our minds.

'Let's leave them here, walk over to the woods and pick them up on our way back,' I suggested and we set out onto a chalky cart track through rolling stubble fields. Below the hills the flatlands were smoky-blue in the distance and you could just see the watery glint of the estuary. A few golden beech leaves blew towards us from the woods where we used to play as children.

'*Season of mists and mellow fruitfulness*' I murmured to myself. Mrs

Davis had indicated she didn't think much of Keats.

I was wondering how best to introduce the subject of the Davises when Frances asked,

'Do you ever see that boyfriend of yours?'

'I see him around from time to time. We're quite friendly.'

'Do you miss him?' she went on. I thought about this.

'I don't actually miss *him*. I did miss having a boyfriend but now...' I was about to say that now I had something more interesting to think about but before I could get any further Frances said,

'I don't think I shall ever have a boyfriend.'

After this, even in my Davis-obsessed state, it seemed unsympathetic to go on. Frances started to tell me how Aunty Joyce was beginning to despair of her.

'She keeps saying, "Our Ellen had been courting for a year when she was your age."'

'Where did Ellen meet Brian?'

'At the Young Farmers' but she's not like me. At school she was always in the thick of things.'

I couldn't think what to say. I knew Frances had been unhappy at boarding school. Shy by nature, this had made her even more insecure. She couldn't banter and exchange friendly insults with boys but what would happen to her if she didn't manage to get married?

'I'd like to get away,' she said.

'But what would you do?'

'I wondered about asking if I could go to training college. I sometimes teach in the Sunday School and I like that.' I contemplated the idea of Frances as a teacher. I thought she could just about cope with infants.

We started to wander back discussing this possibility. We were just going to pick up the eggs from the stack-yard when a movement by one of the ricks stopped us. It was Amber and she was not alone.

She was leaning back against the straw-stack clutched in the arms of a stockily built man. He had rather greasy-looking black hair cut in the style known as a DA, which, as Jane had told me, stood for Duck's Arse. He appeared to be biting Amber's neck and I thought for a moment she was being attacked until I saw the expression on her face.

'Sensual' I thought. Last year I had carelessly described Keats' poetry as 'sensual'. Miss Carr had been scornfully amused,

'Sensuous was the epithet you were seeking, Phyllida. Sensual has quite another meaning.' I got it now: Keats was sensuous: Amber was sensual.

'It's Barry Wilson,' whispered Frances.

'Who?'

'His family keep the White Swan.' This made it even worse. Both our families regarded pubs as the abode of the devil. I noticed that one of Barry's hands seemed to have wriggled up under Amber's tight sweater. Neither Frances nor I dared move. Amber made no objection to the hand under her sweater but when he took it out and started to slide it down the contours of her pencil skirt clad bottom she gave it a sharp slap. Even Amber it seemed had her limits. We decided she could look after herself. Frances signalled to me and we crept round the house, coming in at the front door.

'Whatever are you doing coming in that way?' said Aunty Joyce. 'I hope you've wiped your feet properly. What have you done with the eggs? You're dozy enough on your own Frances but with Dilly you're both in a right dream. Where's Amber? Upstairs, I suppose, reading those silly magazines of hers. Your mother's having a lie-down in the room, Dilly. She says she's not feeling too well. You girls had better help me get tea.'

The rest of us were already sitting round the dining-room table when Amber slid in, a bit flushed.

'What's that silly scarf doing round your neck, Amber?' said Uncle Frank. 'You girls and your fashions! I don't know! Whatever next.' Frances and I were careful not to look at each other. I did however look at Amber once or twice in the course of the meal. An odd thought struck me. Amber was happy with her body. In fact she was more than happy. She was revelling in its power.

Years later, on a hot night in Rome, glancing in the mirror, I'm surprised for a moment to see a fleeting resemblance to my cousin Amber.

Back at school that night I dreamed about Amber and Barry. At least I dreamed of two figures clinging together, but then, mysteriously, as is the way in dreams, I seemed to be in Amber's place. In real life I would have been revolted by greasy Barry but in my dream he seemed not unlike Mike Davis. I woke up sweating. The cathedral bells were ringing for St Michael and All Angels and I was filled with guilt.

CHAPTER SEVEN

For the next few weeks I was constantly expecting news of Amber. I thought she and Barry might announce their engagement and then there would be the most appalling row. Finally a letter arrived from Frances, several sheets of pink notepaper covered with her round handwriting describing the matinee jacket and bonnet she was knitting for Ellen's baby, the doings of her Sunday School pupils and a brief reference to the Young Farmers' Club Social but no mention of Amber or Barry.

Perhaps, I thought, they might have entered into a secret engagement like Jane Fairfax and Frank Churchill or perhaps they might suddenly elope like Lydia Bennett and Wickham. Uncle Frank would have to track them down to their sordid hideout and insist on their marrying. Having had very little experience of life most of my ideas were based on the classics of English literature. Before long I was to experience what is known in educational jargon as 'a steep learning curve' but at the time I was still hopelessly naïve. What never occurred to me then, was that Barry Wilson had simply provided Amber with a little excitement to liven up an otherwise boring Sunday afternoon.

When I went to the Davises for my first lesson after the Harvest Festival Sunday I tried very hard to put all thoughts of my dream out of my head, being determined not to blush when Mike Davis appeared; however I was soon blushing for another reason.

'I've been reading some poetry lately,' he began. I knew with horrible certainty what was coming next.

> '*The Ladies of St James's*
> *Go swinging to the play:*'

I cursed my mother; I cursed Austin Dobson, the almost forgotten Victorian author of the poem and I cursed Mike Davis's phenomenal memory. I had a despairing feeling that he would be able to rattle off all seven verses. I had to admit he had a wonderful voice. He sounded like Richard Burton in *Under Milk Wood*. All the same, by the time he reached,

> '*But Phyllida, my Phyllida!*
> *Her colour comes and goes;*
> *It trembles to a lily, -*
> *It wavers to a rose.*'

my colour had wavered to beetroot.

'Mike, stop it! That's enough. Can't you see you're embarrassing Dilly?' I looked gratefully at Mrs Davis.

'I hate my name,' I said, as soon as I had recovered enough to speak. 'I wish I had an ordinary name like Mary or Anne or even Gillian.'

'Still that might be quite boring.' said Mrs Davis, 'At least it shows you have interesting parents. That's what I always feel about being called Alithea.' I looked blank.

'My mother was writing her thesis on Restoration Comedy while she was pregnant.' This was no help. Restoration Comedy had never been on the English syllabus. All I knew was it had a reputation for being rather improper.

I could, of course, have said, 'My mother was lying on a sofa reading Victorian poetry,' but it didn't have quite the same ring to it. Once more I was made aware of the gulf between Alithea's background and mine. Still it was encouraging to think that Alithea might find my mother interesting. Perhaps she was, if being unlike anyone else's mother was interesting. I always had to invent excuses for her lack of skill in domestic matters. Before my first term she'd sewn on my school nametapes with such large, uneven stitches that the other girls assumed I'd done them myself. They'd all laughed at me but it was better than having them laugh at, or, more likely, be shocked by, my mother's sewing. I wondered whether I would ever find any group where I felt I fitted in.

I also wondered how I would have felt if Mike (as I had secretly started to think of him) had been allowed to continue to the end of the poem,

But Phyllida, my Phyllida is all the world to me.

Of course I knew that wasn't true, but on the other hand... In the meantime I had to remember to tell the others that I'd discovered Mrs Davis's Christian name, which had been the subject of much speculation. It was wonderfully strange, as one might have expected.

Tuesday and Thursdays when I had extra Latin in the Davises' kitchen had replaced Saturday afternoons as the high point of my week. I stayed later and later; Mazzy said nothing. Perhaps she hoped they might contribute something to my wider education, which indeed they did.

We were now well into autumn. During those dark evenings in the cavernous kitchen I felt my mind was almost physically expanding. They talked about politics, or films and plays that I had never heard of and, especially in Alithea's case, the frustrations of provincial life. Those glamorous figures the local actors were apparently condemned to perform silly farces or drawing-room comedies while in London there had been this amazing new play called *Waiting for Godot*.

Alithea Davis started to bring the *Observer* into the Upper Sixth classroom. Miss Carr was already in the habit of bringing the *Sunday Times* and I noted that their theatre critics, Hobson and Tynan, didn't always agree. It was all very confusing. I had no confidence at all in my own opinions. In any case I was unlikely to see any of the plays they discussed and, from what I'd heard Alithea say about it, I couldn't imagine the audience at our local theatre would be ready for *Waiting for Godot* for quite some time.

If Mike had anything to do with it, sooner or later the conversation turned to politics. I began to be vaguely aware that Hugh and Alithea shared a more sophisticated approach to the Arts. On the other hand, politically, Alithea broadly agreed with Mike and Mike liked to taunt Hugh with their differences. Mike's political views startled me. I listened in a kind of fascinated horror while he attacked the Royal Family. Listening to him I also began to feel rather guilty, remembering that when I was ten I'd helped Frances collect pictures for her Royal Wedding scrapbook. Of course, I told myself, I'd been very young at the time. Mike also spoke critically of Churchill whom my parents regarded almost as a demi-god.

What made him most angry however was the number of American airbases around the city. As he ranted about this I thought of Audrey who could talk of nothing but her American boyfriend, the one Fiona and I had seen her kissing earlier in the term. The Americans had always seemed rather glamorous figures to me, with their smooth, well-pressed uniforms, such a contrast to the thick, coarse cloth worn by the RAF, and they always seemed open and friendly but Mike said they were a menace. Their very presence endangered us.

Hugh said the Americans were here to defend our freedom.

'Freedom!' said Mike. 'What about all those anti-Communist witch hunts back in the dear old US of A?'

Occasionally Alithea tried to draw me into their arguments but I knew so little. We didn't have television at home. In the Boarding House we didn't even have a wireless. We were allowed the *Children's Newspaper* and the *Daily Telegraph*, the latter being Miss Cutler's choice. It was also the paper my parents read at home. I looked at it from time to time and saw nothing there to contradict the views I had been brought up with. My mother's sisters in Edinburgh were both Liberals and sometimes argued with my father but their disagreements never got very far because my mother would start crying or say she had a headache or both. 'Arguments make me nervy', she always said.

During the election earlier in the year, Jane had put up a 'Vote Conservative' poster in the dormitory window. Mazzy had made her take it down, which had made Jane suspect she was a secret Labour voter. I'd defended her at the time.

'I think she might be a Liberal though,' I conceded. 'My aunts are.' This sounded a bit more respectable. Certainly, although she was always careful to sound impartial, I knew Mazzy's views were somewhat to the left of Matron's, which wouldn't have been difficult.

More and more often the Davises and Hugh seemed to forget I was there; so, besides national and international politics, I learned a good deal about the politics of the staffrooms in both schools, which, if I am honest, I found rather more fascinating. It was no doubt very unprofessional of the Davises but they were young and careless; they saw themselves as just passing through. They had no loyalties to either school, no long-term prospects to attach them to the city or the neighbourhood. The place provided a living for the time being but their sights were set on London. This was something I didn't really take in at the time. Staff did move of course, especially the younger ones, but we were used to a lot of stability. One or two of the older teachers seemed built into the very fabric of the school. They'd even taught some girls' mothers.

Occasionally the Davises tried to draw me out on the subject of the High School staff. Once Alithea started to ask me about Mazzy. She wondered what 'such an intelligent, interesting woman... quite cosmopolitan in some ways... what was she doing in this backwater?' I'd never thought, until that point, why any of the staff were there – they just were. Now I started to think about my housemistress and piece together the various fragments she had let drop about her life. We knew her father had been Italian. 'He was a Liberal,' she said but had added that Italian Liberals were not the same as British Liberals. 'He kept a dagger by him. He had enemies.' This was very odd but then, after all, he had been a foreigner.

After one holiday, Mazzy told us, she had been to Israel. Foreign holidays were still quite unusual among the people I knew. My parents disapproved of them. The practice came under the heading of 'flashing your money about'. Unfortunately one of my Edinburgh aunts visited France fairly regularly. This was usually tolerated as a regrettable necessity because she taught French as well as Latin, although sometimes, suspecting my aunt of enjoying these trips, my mother would say it all sounded rather silly to her. I supposed, as she taught some Scripture, Mazzy could be excused for going to Israel but it did seem somewhat extreme. I knew she had been to London University and had friends in London, so, for the first time, I wondered why indeed she was here.

'I suppose,' I said, feeling rather awkward, 'she might have come because of Miss Robson.'

'Oh, a lesbian passion,' said Alithea, 'that explains it!' I couldn't bring myself to look at Mike or Hugh for several minutes. Alithea was worse than Jane. 'After all, I suppose I'm here because of you,' she said to Mike, sounding resentful.

'And why is Hugh here?' asked Mike. Hugh didn't answer.

'Don't start please, Mike,' said Alithea. There was a tense silence.

Another thing that puzzled Mike and Alithea about this conservative, provincial city, so alien to both their backgrounds, was the importance of the Church of England. Hugh could perhaps have enlightened them but he usually remained silent on this subject, merely looking superior.

Alithea complained one day about a girl in the Lower Sixth who had spent the whole of her English lesson in tears.

'She'd had a big row with her boyfriend at the weekend,' I said, having heard Jane and Caroline discussing the sad affair at some length when we were meant to be getting on with prep in the attic.

'Oh why was that?' said Mike, who always seemed to take what I sometimes felt was a rather unmanly interest in affairs of the heart.

'Really Mike! Who cares?' said Alithea, 'I just hope she'll have got over it before next lesson and stops snivelling.'

'I gather they argued a lot about religion,' I said. 'Peter, her boyfriend, is rather spikey - High Church.' I explained seeing they looked bewildered. 'He said,' I added bravely, 'that the Virgin Mary was always a virgin, but she said Jesus had brethren. He said this meant cousins.'

'He was perfectly correct,' said Hugh. The other two were gazing at me, for once united in amazement.

'And then,' said Alithea, 'did they argue over how many angels could dance on a pinhead? Dear God!' she added, inappropriately, 'This place is obsessed by religion.'

'It's living in the shadow of this bloody great cathedral,' said Mike. 'They should pull it down and build workers' flats on the site.' He saw my face and started to laugh. 'I didn't mean it Dilly. I'm an historian. I don't want the evidence destroyed but they could make it into a museum as they do with churches in the Soviet Union.'

I stayed silent not knowing what to say. I loved going to Early Evensong. I loved the music; I loved the *King James Bible* and the *Book of Common Prayer*. The rhythms of the language still echo through my mind. It's a part of my education I'll always be grateful for.

In fact I didn't have time to say anything. Hugh was so enraged by this iconoclasm that he stopped looking superior and in no time at all he and Mike were involved in a ferocious argument.

After that Mike often returned to the subject of religion. He seemed bewildered by the popularity of the Student Christian Movement. Even my explanation that it was one of the few places where the two grammar schools could mix seemed inadequate to him.

'Well,' I said, 'I suppose it's also the only place where we can talk about things and have arguments.'

'Such as?'

'Well the colour bar in South Africa and last term we had a debate on gambling.' I remembered that last occasion rather bitterly. I'd been chosen to propose the motion *Gambling is un-Christian* and had, I knew, made a good speech. Christopher's friend Dave had opposed me. His speech had been flippant and rather incoherent but all the boys had voted against me because I was a girl and all the girls had voted for him because he was a boy. He had admitted as much to me afterwards, which was nice of him but not entirely consoling. Now I recounted this episode to the Davises. Alithea was indignant and said girls really ought to learn to support each other. While I considered this novel idea Mike burst out,

'That's another thing. Dave Whatley - the brightest of my history set and he's set on being a bloody vicar, him and his great pal Thompson.' (Thompson was Christopher's surname.) He stopped and looked at me.

'Dilly's blushing!' he said. 'Come on Dilly, which is the one? Whatley or Thompson?'

'Neither,' I said but Mike continued to tease me about them both every time their names were mentioned: I didn't really mind.

Afterwards I thought about Alithea saying girls should support each other and remembered that Fiona had voted for me. I told Alithea this the next time we were walking back to her lodgings.

'It was really nice of her because she can't usually be bothered to come to SCM.'

'And Ursula?' asked Alithea.

'Oh, she voted for Dave Whatley.'

These evenings at the Davises were particularly important to me because school seemed dreary. A lot of the syllabus was a repeat of the previous year's and the life seemed to have gone out of it. Some of our contemporaries were already at university and their letters made us all the more aware of the narrowness of our lives.

Alithea made things more interesting but someone so totally urban wasn't the best person to teach Wordsworth. She told us she preferred the Metaphysicals. When I said I knew nothing about them she lent me her Nonesuch edition of Donne. At first I was disconcerted - 'sucked', 'snorted,' - was this the language of poetry? But some of the love poems seemed to have been written for someone in my emotional state and I soon became obsessed. Even reading *On his Mistress going to Bed* I refused to be shocked. How feeble Jane's torrid historical romances seemed in comparison! However, I thought, I must keep the book out of her hands. I couldn't bear to have it desecrated by her ribald shrieks. I also realised that on no account must my parents set eyes on it. My father thought English literature was a suitable subject for girls to study, as it didn't sound too intellectually demanding. The highest praise my mother could give to any work of literature was that it was 'delightful'. Somehow I couldn't imagine her being delighted by the poetry of John Donne.

History lessons also seemed duller; our previous teacher Miss Elliston, with her flowery summer dresses and upswept glasses had interspersed dictating notes with entertaining little anecdotes about the private lives of historical characters. This year she'd been replaced by the plain, earnest Miss Seymour, who was more interested in economic history than gossip about dead celebrities. A level History no longer provided any light entertainment and in the Scholarship lessons she made us feel completely inadequate.

One day she asked us which newspaper our parents took. Fiona said hers took the *Express*. Miss Seymour said nothing but the scornful expression on her blotchy face made me glad my parents took the *Telegraph*, which I knew was regarded as a more respectable paper; however she obviously wasn't impressed by that either.

'We get the *Daily Herald* when we can afford it,' said Rosa. Fiona looked at me. We both knew it was a Labour paper but, as we'd been listening to Rosa's political views in General Studies for several weeks, I couldn't think why she found this surprising or significant. I was beginning to find Fiona rather irritating at times. I knew she was baffled by my enthusiasm for Alithea Davis, possibly rather hurt by it too. Up till then we'd always agreed about which teachers we liked and which we didn't, with Fiona taking the lead in these judgements.

'I would recommend the *Manchester Guardian*,' said Miss Seymour. 'I could save mine for you, Rosa.'

'It's all right,' said Rosa. 'I can read it in the library in town.' Fiona looked at me again and raised her eyebrows. One lunch hour we'd seen Rosa in the library Reading Room absorbed in the *Daily Worker*.

'Do you think Rosa's a Communist?' Fiona asked me after the lesson.

'Honestly Fiona you're worse than the bloody Americans,' I said, leaving Fiona gaping at me, as well she might. Apart from anything else I don't think she had ever heard me swear before.

CHAPTER EIGHT

'Where is everybody?' enquired Miss Seymour one wet Tuesday in October. 'Fiona?'

'Training college interview,' I said. 'Under protest,' I added. Fiona had no intention of going to training college but the headmistress had insisted. Miss Seymour almost smiled and continued to call the register. There were, it seemed, a number of training college interviews that day and we were also moving into the season of winter coughs and colds. The A level History class was reduced to two, me and a very pretty blonde girl called Hazel Atkins, one of Audrey Dawkin's gang.

'Well,' Miss Seymour said, 'I was intending to start a new topic today but there is absolutely no point without the others. I think you had best go to the library and learn your notes on the over-expansion of the Spanish Empire for next week's test.' She gathered up her books and left.

'Gone to make herself a cup of tea,' said Hazel.

'I'm sick of being sent to the library,' I said. 'It happens to Fiona and me all the time. No one can be bothered with us in the Third Year Sixth. Let's stay here. We could test each other.'

'Or,' said Hazel, 'we could go to the physics lab. It's usually empty. No one would find us there.'

The physics lab was not much more than an ill-equipped cupboard only slightly larger than the prefects' room. We perched ourselves on a couple of stools and I started to ask Hazel questions about Spanish expansion in the New World. Hazel was rather vague on the subject.

'In last year's paper,' I said, hoping to motivate her, 'we got *Account for the rise of the Spanish Empire in the 16th century,* so this summer, it's quite likely we'll get something about the decline of Spain in the 17th century.' Hazel yawned and admired her nails. They were beautifully manicured and painted a subtle shade of pale pink, slightly more noticeable than clear varnish but not striking enough to attract the attention of the authorities. I was reminded of a song I'd heard from a popular musical,

The girl that I marry will have to be
As soft and as pink as a nursery.

I looked at Hazel sitting on the other side of the lab bench. She seemed out of place in these drab surroundings.

Her nails will be polished
And in her hair
She'll wear a gardenia...

I wasn't sure I'd ever seen a gardenia but I knew if I tried to put one in my hair it would certainly fall out. In the meantime I scrunched up my hands to hide the state of my nails.

'Have you got any training college interviews coming up?' I asked, as we didn't seem to be getting anywhere with Spanish imperialist ambitions.

'No, I'm not applying,' she said.

'How've you got out of that? Cutler made Fiona apply.'

'I told Cutler I didn't like children.' I tried to imagine Miss Cutler's reaction to this unfeminine sentiment.

'I'm thinking of becoming a beauty consultant,' she added. I hadn't known such a career existed but I was sure it wasn't one considered suitable for a High School girl. No wonder she hadn't been made a prefect. However I'd been miserably aware since the morning that I had a spot coming up on my chin and I had a Latin lesson that evening.

'Is there anything I can do about this spot?' Hazel immediately became animated.

'Whatever you do, don't try to squeeze it,' she began. She may not have known much European history but she could have done a PhD on spots, blackheads and the treatment thereof.

It was unfortunate that Miss Carr happened to be passing along the corridor and heard what she rightly suspected to be idle chatter coming from a usually unoccupied lab. She was not pleased. Hazel, I think, was generally considered to be a lost soul but, as Miss Carr pointed out, I was a prefect and an Oxbridge candidate. I ought to be trusted to pursue independent study unsupervised.

'I thought no one would mind Hazel and I being...' I began. An expression of agony crossed her face.

'What did you just say Dilly?'

'Hazel and me' I said hastily but that wasn't right either. If I couldn't recognise a gerund requiring a possessive pronoun I shouldn't apparently be even thinking of university. So, prompted, I began again, 'Hazel's and my being...' I thought it sounded as if I was translating from some obscure archaic language but Miss Carr was satisfied at last and at least it distracted her from my more serious offence.

That afternoon as Alithea and I trudged uphill through the drizzle she seemed rather distant. Eventually she said,

'What possessed you to waste a free period in the physics lab gossiping with an empty-headed girl like Hazel Atkins?'

How they did go on about us in the staff-room! I thought resentfully. Hadn't they got anything better to talk about? Aloud, I said,

'I'm getting tired of being sent to the library to revise things we did last year, when no one can think what else to do with us.' Although she pointed out I could have done some background reading, Alithea wasn't totally unsympathetic, which made me feel able to speak much more frankly than I would have been able to with any of her colleagues. I started to try to explain why life seemed rather drab, apart, as I told her, from the time spent at their place. At this she gave a rather knowing smile that made me feel slightly uneasy. It's likely she knew more about my growing feelings for Mike than I allowed myself to be aware of. If so, had she already realised how she could make use of them?

After my lesson, Alithea told Mike and Hugh how dissatisfied I was with life. All they could think of to recommend was wider reading. Hugh suggested Greek Tragedy.

'In translation of course,' he added.

'Or *Das Kapital*' said Mike grinning, 'In translation of course.' This was so clearly said to annoy Hugh that I didn't take it seriously but Alithea said it might be an idea to learn something about Marx.

'You should talk to Rosa more,' she said. 'I've told you about her, haven't I?' she said to the men. 'A very interesting girl.' I felt a surge of jealous rage. Had Rosa been there I would have killed her with a glance, 'Named after Rosa Luxemburg, can you believe! Her father is an invalid - progressive fibrosis. He reads a lot. Of course he's dying,' she added casually. I was shocked and mentally resurrected Rosa with apologies. 'She's the only one with any ideas,' she continued. 'The others all just parrot their parents' bourgeois views.' Rosa's life hung in the balance again. Also, even in my Davis obsessed state, it occurred to me that there was something illogical about this. Wasn't Rosa just repeating her father's Marxist views?'

This obviously occurred to Hugh as well. He smirked and said,

'Oh, clearly an original thinker!'

'Oh Hugh!' Alithea spread her hands in what I thought was a rather continental gesture and laughed. 'Well we should ask her round. You'd see what I mean then.' No! No! No! I thought.

'The thing is,' said Mike, 'is she as pretty as Dilly?' I expect the joy I felt was obvious. Alithea looked at him for a moment and then gave me an oddly assessing glance. I thought perhaps she was wondering why Mike thought I was pretty.

'No,' she said. 'No, she's rather a plain girl,' (live Rosa, live!). She paused for a moment. 'Dilly,' she said, 'I keep meaning to ask you. What on earth do the boarders do all weekend?' I wondered why she had changed the subject so suddenly but after seven years at the Boarding House this was at last, unlike dialectical materialism, a field in which I felt I was an expert.

'Well,' I began, 'on Saturday morning we have shoe cleaning.' I thought for a bit and realised there wasn't much else to say. As juniors we'd been subjected to a relentless programme that included Guides, a compulsory walk with Matron and hymn practice with the local Vicar, but, as seniors, no one knew quite how to occupy us. 'I suppose we can do as we like during the day, as long as we finish our homework and are there for meals. If we go out we have to say where we're going. We can't go out after tea unless there's something organised.'

'Such as?' asked Mike. I was about to mention some trips to the despised local theatre but Alithea interrupted him.

'So you're hanging about at a loose end all weekend?'

'Well, not all weekend, not on Sunday. There's the morning and evening services and in the afternoon we have to write home and then do our mending while Miss Manzonni reads to us.'

'What does she read?' asked Mike sounding interested. I was about to list some of the classics Mazzy had read to us but Alithea cut me short again. At the time I thought perhaps she didn't like Mike taking so much interest in my life; Later, much later, I realised she'd had her own agenda.

'So you're free most of Saturday. There can't be much for you to do in this place. My God! I was so lucky to grow up in London!' I noticed Hugh didn't protest about Alithea's blasphemy.

In the sixth form we were already beginning to get a picture of Alithea's teenage years. She sometimes dropped remarks about how she used to queue at the Old Vic for returns to see Gielgud or Olivier in Shakespearean productions. At other times she would recount interesting conversations she'd had while sitting around in South Kensington coffee bars, discussing life, art and music with students from the Royal College of Music or the Royal College of Art. It made me feel very inadequate.

The best I could offer was to say I sometimes met Fiona for coffee in Boots' cafe on a Saturday morning or went to her house for tea on a Saturday afternoon. Alithea seemed to have stopped listening.

'Who's Fiona?' asked Mike.

'A friend of Dilly's. Stop interrupting, Mike,' said Alithea.

'Well that's all really,' I said.

Hugh appeared totally indifferent to all this. Perhaps, I thought, the sixth formers at Winchester, when they weren't busy torturing the younger boys as in *Tom Brown's Schooldays*, might spend Saturday evenings listening to talks by cabinet ministers or famous writers or scientists to prepare them for their splendid future careers. What, I wondered, would he make of our Saturday evenings? In winter we jostled for a place near the common room fire; in summer we played games in the garden. But anyway he wasn't interested.

Mike, on the other hand, had seemed fascinated by every detail. I suddenly remembered, that only last term, I might have been seen racing across the lawn, pursued by Jane or Caroline, flinging myself against the wall screaming, 'One, two, three block!' as I reached 'home'. If Alithea hadn't kept snubbing him what might I have carelessly revealed? Had I really behaved so childishly such a short time ago?

Fortunately Alithea reacted sympathetically as I'd been hoping.

'You know Dilly, if you really are at a loose end on a Saturday afternoon you're very welcome to come round here,' she said casually. 'We can talk about what you've been reading.'

'Yes, and then Allie can explain why your opinions are rubbish' said Mike. 'But do come Dilly. Now we all know exactly what we're going to say to each other before we've said it. It's just like a scene from *Huis Clos* – "Hell is other people". What a genius! Nothing Jean-Paul doesn't know about the human condition.'

I had absolutely no idea what he was talking about.

'Well from a Christian perspective, your Sundays...' Hugh began.

'You see what I mean!' said Mike.

Alithea attempted to deflect another outbreak of hostilities by asking what I was reading at the moment.

I thought quickly. The tall bookshelves in the common room mainly contained books that other people had thrown out. I'd long since worked my way through Dornford Yates, Ian Hay, Warwick Deeping and Jeffery Farnol and had begun to recognise their inadequacies. In the Lower Sixth, when work hadn't been so pressing, I'd read a lot of classics from the school library but, just then, in my bored frame of mind, I was indulging myself by re-reading a novel by Georgette Heyer. I knew it would be unwise to admit this to Alithea, so I said I'd just read *The Loved One*. 'Just' was stretching the facts. I'd read it some months before. I'd bought it with a book token my aunts had given me and it had left a strong if not entirely agreeable impression.

'Well don't bother with *Brideshead Revisited*,' said Mike. 'It'll give you all the wrong ideas about Oxford.' But Alithea said Waugh was a brilliant satirist and suggested I looked in the library in town for his other works.

I went quiet. Since the departure of Christopher I hadn't really had the heart to go to the public library, especially as the girlfriend, who had preceded and then superseded me, was now working there. That summer I'd been demoralised by the sight of her looking cool and pretty in a dress of fashionable waffle piqué, with her hair in a smooth pageboy.

'Why don't we lend you some books now?' said Alithea.

'Miss Manzonni,' I began, encountering my housemistress in the hall on my return, 'Who said "Hell is other people"?'

Mazzy pressed her lips together rather disapprovingly but I could see from her eyes that she was suppressing some amusement.

'This is Mrs Davis again I suppose?' I didn't contradict her; it was near enough the truth.

'I don't think you will find it useful to read Sartre just at the moment Dilly.'

Jean-Paul Sartre, I thought. I'd heard of him somewhere although I couldn't remember where.

'It looks as if Mrs Davis has been lending you some books?' I had been prepared for this and pulled out a novel by Arthur Koestler that seemed the most respectable of my haul.

'Oh yes,' she said, 'he seems rather fashionable at the moment.

Well, wider reading is important just in case you get an Oxbridge interview, but don't neglect your schoolwork will you?'

'Dilly, you naughty girl!' said Jane when I unpacked my satchel in the attic later that evening. 'D H Lawrence, isn't he banned? I thought you could only buy his novels in France.'

'I think that's just *Lady Chatterley's Lover*,' I said.

'*Sons and Lovers*' said Brenda, 'Whatever's that about then?'

'It's about a coalminer's son who becomes educated,' I said. 'Mrs Davis says it's largely autobiographical.'

'Correct me if I am under a misapprehension Dilly but didn't I hear Mrs Davis say in General Studies that her husband's father was a miner?' said Brenda.

'That dreamboat? Really?' said Jane.

'Goodness! Does Mr Davis have a very common accent, Dilly?' said Caroline.

'Well,' I said, 'he's Welsh so I'm not sure, really.' I felt my face becoming flushed again.

'Oh Dilly's in love with Mr Davis!' said Jane. 'I thought Mr Marlow was your favourite.' I panicked for a moment and then said,

'Don't be silly. Mr Davis is married and Mr Marlow is a drip.'

'Of course,' said Jane 'you're still pining for that twerp Christopher. I forgot.'

I encouraged her to be witty along these lines for the next few minutes, until Caroline pointed out we had work to do and I told myself, hard as this would be, I mustn't talk about the Davises so much.

I decided not to take up my invitation until I'd read at least some of the books I'd been given. I wanted to be prepared for intelligent discussion when I felt brave enough to go. That Saturday evening, having managed to get a chair next to the common room fire, I started to read the slimmest of the Davis's offerings, *Lucky Jim*, and was shocked. It was true that I could see the novel was, as Mike Davis had claimed, very funny, and I felt some sympathy for Jim Dixon, but his drunkenness and lying appalled me. I tried to think what I could say, when they asked what I'd thought of it, that wouldn't make me sound priggish.

In the meantime I kept studying myself in the mirror. Did Mike really think I was pretty? My mother had always assumed I was so plain no one would ever marry me and thought it fortunate I seemed to be turning out quite clever because I could be a teacher like her unmarried sister Nan. She'd been quite surprised when I'd first admitted to her that I had a boyfriend. At first she'd been impressed but then she'd started to enquire about his social background, something about which I'd tried to be deliberately vague.

Now I assessed myself as dispassionately as possible. My hair was straight but so was Amber's and though it wasn't such a striking colour as hers it was thick and glossy. My eyes were big but greenish, to my mother's regret. ('I had always hoped for a blue-eyed daughter') and my lashes though long, were, as Fiona had pointed out, rather fair (I still hadn't had the nerve to follow her advice about mascara). My mother said my mouth was too big but, despite the occasional spot, I had a good complexion and altogether I decided I wasn't as plain as my mother thought. In a few years' time, my looks were to become extremely fashionable but of course I wasn't to know that then.

All the same, I thought perhaps my appearance was worth a bit of attention after all. Remembering how I'd admired Hazel's exquisite pink nails when we were in the physics lab, I got to work on mine with an emery board; even though I didn't have any nail varnish they looked surprisingly better.

CHAPTER NINE

'So you didn't come to see us on Saturday?' Alithea accosted me on the Monday morning while I was on corridor duty at break.

'No,' I answered rather distractedly. 'Single file and don't run,'- this latter remark being addressed to a rabble of Upper Thirds who had just been let loose from their Maths lesson and were rushing towards the milk crates. 'No talking Becky! – No, sorry, I thought about it,' I added, 'but...'

'Well,' she said, 'I can see you're busy at the moment, but don't forget - any time - perhaps this weekend?'

After that, although she didn't mention it again, I felt I had as good as promised to go round there the following Saturday afternoon.

'I'm just going to change some books,' I said to Mazzy. She looked up from a pile of marking.

'All right, dear.'

I hadn't actually said I was going to the library I told myself. It was up to her if she chose to think so. I was taking back *Lucky Jim* and would probably be offered another book. And anyway I wasn't doing anything wrong. But I knew that if I said I'd been invited to the Davises it would be thought odd. We never met teachers socially. We imagined them living out their mysterious half-lives in dismal digs. That is if we ever bothered to think about them at all.

With this in mind I didn't walk straight across the Close but edged round it as if I were going through the mediaeval arch by the SPCK bookshop, towards the steep street that led downhill to the main part of the town. Instead of going through the arch, however, I turned right, walking softly past the Regency terrace where Miss Cutler lived courtesy of the Dean and Chapter, until I reached the north side of the cathedral. My heart was thumping and I felt slightly shaky. I had been invited, I kept reminding myself.

Through the bow window at the front of the house I could see the flicker of firelight. Mrs Herbert seemed to be asleep in her chair. I tried the front door and it was open, so I quietly let myself in, crossed the hall, went down the back stairs and pushed open the green baize door. But, at that point I nearly turned back because I could hear the unmistakable drone of a sports commentary on the wireless. I was disappointed. I associated the sound of sports commentaries with the boredom of Saturday afternoons at home - my father listening to football, rugby or cricket while my mother paced the house complaining about the tedium of her life and demanding that he picked up the crumpled newspaper at his feet. I'd hoped the Davises were about to reveal a more exciting way of spending Saturday afternoons. However, having come this far, I felt the public library would be an anti-climax and continuing down the dark corridor, I tapped on the kitchen door.

'Hallo? Come in!' It was Mike's voice and he didn't sound entirely welcoming. I sidled round the door.

'Dilly!' Mike had been sprawled, tie-less in one of the tatty armchairs but, on seeing me, he leapt to his feet, in spite of his revolutionary tendencies he'd obviously been well brought up, and switched off the wireless. There was no sign of either Alithea or Hugh. I felt overwhelmed by shyness.

'Mrs Davis said...' I began.

'Yes, yes! I know, but perhaps she forgot to say this Saturday she and dear old Hugh were going to Nottingham where some pretentious little film club is putting on some arty black and white French film, with subtitles, though those two won't need them of course,' he said. '*Les Enfants du Paradis,*' he added in an exaggerated French accent that was presumably meant to be an imitation of Hugh, or possibly, Alithea.

He looked at me thoughtfully for a moment and then suddenly smiled.

'Well better you than Joan Seymour at any rate,' he said. I could make no sense of this at all.

'I'd better go.' I said.

'No, no, Dilly. Sit down. I'd offer you a cup of tea but I doubt I can find a clean cup.'

I looked around. In the light of a grey late autumn afternoon the bohemian charm of the place was less obvious. The sink was full of dirty dishes and on the table there were greasy newspapers that had recently held fish and chips. A cigarette had been stubbed out on a greasy plate and there were several overflowing ashtrays among some empty beer bottles. In daylight the orange wall looked rather grimy and one of the posters was torn at the edges. The fish and chip papers surprised me most; according to my mother eating fish and chips out of newspaper was very working class. I cleared some books off a chair and sat down. Mike flopped back and lit a cigarette. He offered me the packet but I shook my head. I'd have liked to accept but I was an inexperienced smoker and didn't want to look silly.

'No, sorry,' he said. 'I suppose you shouldn't.' His glance flicked towards the wireless for a moment but then he leant forward and, taking another puff, stared at me intensely. I looked around for a clean space where I could deposit *Lucky Jim*.

'What did you think of it?' said Mike.

'It was very funny,' I said, 'but...'

'Alithea hates it,' he said, not waiting to hear my reservations. 'She thinks it's anti-intellectual. I can't get her to see it's just anti-pretentiousness. But then she's somewhat deluded by pretentiousness at the moment.' There was nothing I could say to this so I waited expecting some further insights into *Lucky Jim*.

'And what do you think of your Latin teacher?' I was discomposed. He gave another intense, blue-eyed stare. This, combined with the impression that he hadn't shaved that morning, made him seem a tragically romantic figure.

'You mean Mr Marlow?'

'Yes, Mr Marlow, dear old Hugh.'

'He's a good teacher,' I began cautiously. I wasn't used to teachers asking me their opinions of each other. We all knew there were some members of staff who didn't get on too well but to us they always presented a united front. However even I was beginning to realise what lay behind these questions, so I added, 'But I suppose he is a bit pretentious.' I could see this was well received and wondered how much further I could go. 'He's quite weedy, isn't he?' I ventured. I wanted to add. 'I don't believe anyone could really prefer him to you, Mr Davis,' but hadn't quite got the nerve; however I expect my face expressed what I was feeling.

Mike smiled; he gazed at me with what seemed tenderness,

'You're a sweet girl, Dilly. You know what; you're a really sweet, lovely girl.' I felt I might possibly die of happiness. Filled with a spirit of exquisite self-sacrifice I said,

'If you want to listen to the football I could do the washing-up.'

I knew from reading *Woman's Own* that this was the way men liked to be treated and women were supposed to get satisfaction from caring for their man, although I couldn't actually say I had seen any evidence of this in real life. Aunty Joyce toiled incessantly for her family but complained about exhaustion and lack of adequate help from her daughters. My mother did much less and complained even more; however at that moment I would have done anything for Mike.

At home, press-ganged into helping, I would sullenly swill cups under the tap or dry up with a soggy tea towel in gloomy silence. Now I washed and rinsed assiduously, not just drying the crockery but almost polishing it. As I worked I was aware that Mike was looking at me from time to time, which made me self-conscious. Once I caught his eye and he smiled, which caused me to drop a cup, chipping it against the sink.

'Don't worry love. Allie gets so mad about doing the washing up she's always breaking stuff. There's hardly an unchipped piece of crockery in the whole bloody place.' I was so moved by being called 'love', however casually, I nearly dropped another cup. When I'd finished I wiped down the rather slimy wooden draining board, disposed of the fish and chip papers, even rinsed out the tea towel and hung it up to dry. I felt like one of the merry young women who smiled out of the magazine advertisements, rendered ecstatic by the advent of a new washing-up liquid; all I lacked was a frilly apron. Even Aunty Joyce might have approved although she would probably have boiled the tea towel, which was in no way up to her standards.

In the background the wireless rumbled on. Whichever teams were playing Mike was not impressed; occasionally he swore and then looked at me apologetically. I then gave him a saintly and understanding smile.

'Shall I make some tea?' I asked.

'You're an angel,' he said which I took to mean – yes. He was still sprawling casually in his chair. The top button of his open-necked shirt was missing and I noticed the dark curly hairs on his chest.

The inside of the teapot was heavily stained and I scoured it out rather self-righteously, before warming it conscientiously and measuring out the tea. Mike switched off the wireless. 'Do you follow any team, Dilly?' he asked.

'No. Not at all.' I thought of telling him about Audrey and her friends and their pictures of the local football team. Then I wondered if he would think Fiona and I with our little art galleries inside our desk lids were, like Hugh, also being pretentious, but, before I could say more, he continued,

'Quite right, rugby's the game, or 'rugger' as our posh friend calls it.' He was obviously still brooding on Hugh. To distract him I brought over the tea, clearing the ashtrays and beer bottles off the table as I did so. I handed him his cup feeling as if I were performing a sacred rite – and yet - I thought - he could have got up and helped himself. The word 'lazy' floated into my mind but I suppressed it.

I sat down and sipped my tea cautiously, afraid if I gulped it down my stomach might rumble which would be shameful. There was a silence. There were a lot of things I wanted to ask but I didn't know how to start.

'Thanks Dilly, a lovely cup of tea,' said Mike. 'You'll make some lucky bastard a smashing wife one of these days.' I didn't know where to look. 'The place looks a lot better.' It did, but anyway it was getting dusk and the room was recovering its romantic shadowy charm. Mike leaned over and switched on a lamp made from an old wine bottle. I noticed again how unshaven he looked. The dark stubble on his chin seemed to have grown thicker during the course of the afternoon. I wondered what it would be like to be kissed by a man with a beard. 'It takes a woman's touch,' he continued, 'though that sort of talk makes Allie furious. She says I could learn to help if I tried but I wasn't brought up like that. My mother never let me do a hand's turn. "You get on with your studies," she always said. She used to bring cocoa and biscuits up to my room at nine o'clock every night. "Brain food" she called it. Allie doesn't see things like that. She says we're both working and I should do my share.' Although I desperately wanted to sympathise with Mike I thought Alithea was making a fair point but I said nothing and he went on, 'Of course she's not really used to doing housework herself. They have a housekeeper at their place, a German Jewish refugee who's been with them since the thirties - quite part of the family.'

'Does Mr Marlow do any of the housework?'

'Hugh, that bloody public school boy! What do you think? He was at Winchester you know with Allie's brothers. Call themselves Socialists – ha!' This was presumably a comment on Alithea's family. Hugh certainly showed no Socialist leanings. In fact I'd heard Mike describe him as somewhat to the right of Louis XIV; however it did do something towards explaining how one of the ill-assorted trio had ended up in this strange household. But then what about Alithea and Mike? I tried to reconcile the background I'd just had sketched out for me with Alithea's previous references to her home life. On the one hand there was the miner's terraced cottage where a humble little Welsh woman waited hand and foot on her brilliant son, toiling up to his chilly attic bedroom with a mug of steaming cocoa. On the other there was the spacious London house where the inhabitants held intellectual dinner parties in between dashing out to attend plays, concerts, art exhibitions and political meetings; their every need met by this loyal and doubtless grateful, refugee.

'How did you meet Mrs Davis?' I asked.

Mike laughed, 'At the University Labour Club. We were both in a production of *Mother Courage* – Brecht you know.' (I didn't) 'You're thinking we're an odd pair, aren't you Dilly?'

'Well, not really,' I said politely but, remembering my mother's account of the social embarrassments she'd had to suffer on her marriage to my father, I couldn't help adding, 'but at your wedding? Did your families...' I stopped, feeling perhaps I'd gone too far.

Mike looked at me rather oddly, then he grinned.

'Could you see Allie in white with a veil promising to L*ove, Honour and Obey?*' The mere thought of this made me, much to my mortification, splutter into my tea. Mike handed me a rather grimy handkerchief.

'I'm glad you find it funny. It is rather risible. All you need to get married Dilly, is quarter of an hour at the registry office and two witnesses.'

Of course - I thought - that was how Socialist-atheists would get married.

I realised it was getting late and thought perhaps I should go. Suddenly Mike leaned forward. He gave me another intense look.

'Tell me Dilly, have you got a boyfriend?'

'Not at the moment,' I said, trying to make it sound as if this was a brief temporary interlude. He continued to gaze at me obviously expecting more.

'I used to go out with Christopher Thompson.'

'No! Not really. You can do better than that. When did you finish with him? He didn't bring you to our party - I'd have remembered. He was with some rather dim girl - fairly pretty but she didn't have a word to say for herself.'

If I had the slightest trace of resentment left about that unfortunate party this was enough to dissipate it completely. But I felt I ought to tell him what had really happened and was pleased by his indignant reaction when I did.

'If only we'd known,' he said, 'I'd have written to that dragon of a house-mistress myself and said you had to come.'

'She's not really a dragon,' I said. 'It's just being a boarder – well, you know.'

'But I don't,' he said. 'You can't expect girls of eighteen to live like nuns in this day and age.' I suddenly felt a surge of fury. He was right. It was ridiculous. Why did we put up with it?

'But anyway,' he said, 'if you had been allowed to come you might still be wasting your time with Thompson.' I might have said that even a weedy boyfriend was better than none but I had a flashback to Christopher at a Church outing he'd invited me to the previous Easter – skinny, in grey flannels and a blazer, his open-necked shirt partly revealing a hairless chest. I wondered how often he needed to shave. Probably not every day. I looked at Mike and once again, I expect my face showed too much of what I was feeling. There was a silence and then he suddenly jumped up.

'You'd better be going Dilly.' He sounded quite stern and grown up. Then he softened again. 'It's getting late; I don't want you getting into trouble with the dragon.'

I picked up the cups and took them over to the clean sink. I rinsed them under the tap and, as the tea towel was still wet, placed them on the irredeemably slimy, splintery, draining board.

'Thanks Dilly,' said Mike, 'you're a darling. Allie would have been in a foul mood if she'd come back and found the place the way it was.'

Even though it was delightful to be called a darling and he was giving me one of his most irresistible smiles, it was perhaps the feeling that I was being dismissed that made me say,

'Well I expect you could eventually have managed to stagger to the bin with the fish and chip papers.'

He looked rather startled for a moment, but then smiled again,

'I suppose I might have done - eventually.' I smiled back, but just as I was going out of the door I thought of the question that had been bothering me.

'Mr Davis,' I said, 'have you got a sister?'

'No, why do you ask? I'm a spoilt only child I'm afraid.'

'It's just - well I'm an only child too but my father's always telling me I've got to help my mother in the house. If you had been a girl or if you had a sister, a clever sister, would your mother have told a girl to get on with her studies and brought her up cups of cocoa?'

This time Mike's amazement lasted for more than a moment.

'Well, Dilly,' he began slowly. 'Well, probably not but then it's different for girls.'

'Why?'

'Well they need to learn to do housework - unless you're called Alithea Miller that is.'

'But why don't boys need to?'

'Has Allie been giving you girls all that Simone de Beauvoir stuff?'

'No. Is she the one who's married to Jean-Paul Sartre?' I was rather proud of my recently acquired knowledge.

'Not married exactly - but anyway never mind Sartre and his bloody mistress. The fact is Dilly, it's more important to educate boys because usually men earn the money.'

'You sound like my uncle Frank.' I must have looked disappointed because Mike started to be charming again.

'Of course I don't mean clever girls shouldn't be educated. Intelligent men want intelligent wives but it's lovely to find a clever girl like you who isn't above doing the washing-up. I'm afraid we men expect rather a lot.'

I noticed that his smile was slightly crooked. I melted.

'That's all right Mr Davis. I'm glad I was able to help.'

'I tell you what. When you're round here why don't you just call me Mike.'

'I'll try,' I said, overwhelmed. He came to the door with me and held my hand for a moment, looking down at me with that intense blue-eyed gaze. I thought for a moment he was going to kiss me.

'Come and see us again soon,' he said.

On the way back I wondered why he had called his wife by her maiden name. Did it suggest something unsatisfactory about the state of their marriage? And if it did, what was that to me? Just as I reached the Boarding House I remembered I hadn't given him back his handkerchief.

'You're very late Phyllida.' Mazzy sounded cold; the use of my full name was never a good sign.

'Oh I just dropped in at the Davises to give back one of the books they lent me.'

'I really don't think you should be bothering Mrs Davis on a Saturday afternoon. She deserves some time with her husband.'

'She told me I could.'

'I must have a word with her.'

If, on Monday morning, Mazzy had a word with Mrs. Davis she would say she'd been in Nottingham today. Perhaps I should tell

Mazzy this immediately but then it would all come out that I'd been chatting to Mr Davis on his own for some time, even if I pretended I had been to the library first. Of course there was nothing wrong with talking to Mr Davis was there? I said nothing.

That evening I sat by the common room fire attempting to read *Sons and Lovers* but I found it hard to concentrate. My face was hot from the fire but, as usual, there was a draught from the ill-fitting sash windows making my back cold. I twisted in my chair listening to the Vicar banging the piano in the dining room and the shrill sound of the juniors' voices as they practised the next day's hymns. Occasionally the Vicar raised his voice in anger. The juniors were fond of teasing him. They liked to request particularly morbid hymns pretending that they were their favourites. There was one that began something like, '*In the old green churchyard there are many tiny graves*' that was guaranteed to put him in a rage. Soon they would all come bursting in and wind up the ancient gramophone or get involved in a noisy card game.

In the meantime Jane sat on the other side of the fireplace snorting over a lurid historical novel.

'Oh I say! Listen to this!' She started to read out loud, dramatically,

"*'Ha!' Eleanora exclaimed. She turned towards him, her winsome face alight with passion. "Good childbearing hips I have. Is that what you are thinking my liege?"*"

Brenda stared at Jane with her pale protruding eyes. She was obviously wondering if Jane really admired this writing. Eventually she smiled to be on the safe side and continued knitting the fawn jumper that had been occupying most of her spare moments all term. Caroline looked up from the tray cloth she was embroidering as a Christmas present for her mother.

'Really Jane! Where do you find these books?' She looked at the lurid cover and added, 'What must they think when you get them out of the library?'

I continued to read *Sons and Lovers* but I was less interested in the state of the Morrells's marriage than in the possible breakdown of the Davis's. I didn't think I actually knew anybody who was divorced. If Alithea left Mike and ran off with Hugh...But why would she want to? I remembered that I had once thought of trying to fall in love with Hugh; such a ridiculous idea seemed to belong to another life, almost to another person. But just suppose she and Hugh didn't return from Nottingham. Suppose they fled to London to live in sin, would I be able to find some way of going round to see Mike? - Do his washing up? – Even learn to cook spaghetti bolognese or other dishes from Elizabeth David's *Italian Food*, that I'd noticed among the other junk on their kitchen table, until he realised that he couldn't live without me, that it was me he'd really loved all along. It was a plot I was familiar with through the novels of Georgette Heyer though mine lacked the Regency embellishments. At this point the fantasy grew hazy. I remembered that in theory my mother approved of divorce, because the Catholics didn't allow it. Still I didn't think she'd be very happy about her only daughter marrying a divorced man especially not a Socialist-atheist and as for my father... Had I got good childbearing hips? I wondered. Probably not, I had my mother's slim build and she said having me had nearly killed her. She had been more or less an invalid ever since.

The juniors charged in.

'Quis?' shouted Mary Nicholls, holding up a pen.

'Ego' shouted several people at once.

'I egoed it first,' yelled Becky Simon. A scuffle broke out and

Matron came in to complain that we seniors weren't controlling the noise.

Sometimes life at the Boarding House was intolerable.

CHAPTER TEN

'I gather we have you to thank for that unusually tidy kitchen we found on our return yesterday,' said Hugh.

I'd been both disappointed and relieved when I saw him sitting on the other side of the choir stalls as usual. He and Alithea had evidently decided against elopement. Normally after Evensong he greeted me with a brief nod but that Sunday he was loitering in the south porch almost as if he'd been waiting for me.

'Although,' he added, 'Alithea felt dear Mike had got off rather lightly.'

And how much washing-up did Hugh do? I wondered - not much, according to Mike.

'Did you enjoy the film?'

'Yes, indeed! It's a splendid example of the genre, very long though. I'm afraid we got back rather late, much to Michael's displeasure.' Michael? – I couldn't think who on earth he was talking about for a moment - 'He seemed to appreciate your company but, by the time your history teacher turned up in the evening, I'm afraid he wasn't as welcoming as he might have been.'

Miss Seymour had been there in the evening! 'Better you than Joan Seymour.' Had Alithea asked her to call in as well? Hugh's tone and his sly smile seemed to imply more than his words. I couldn't believe he was being so tactless. I sensed Brenda, Jane and Caroline hovering in the background and imagined Brenda's pale eyes protruding even more than usual. I wished them all in hell. I started to think how I would answer their inevitable questions as soon as he had gone.

'Well, see you on Tuesday,' he said and walked off briskly.

'Six, definitely no more than six,' said Jane as he disappeared round the West End of the cathedral.

'Really, Jane!' said Caroline. 'I don't think it's very nice to talk about men like that.'

'Why not? They judge the way we look.'

'That's different.'

'Why?'

'Well you know, men...'

Caroline gave up. I knew she believed men were our superiors, stronger, more intelligent. Perhaps she thought this gave them the right to make these judgements. After all they were expected to do the choosing. My mother had much to say on the subject of girls who 'chased after men.'

'Is she as pretty as Dilly?' I remembered and felt guilty. Mike had no right to judge Rosa by her looks. But I wasn't able to feel too indignant about it.

'Anyway,' said Jane, dismissing Caroline's protests. 'What exactly have you been up to Dilly dear.' She flashed her strong white teeth at me but it seemed a threat rather than a smile. I was expecting the question and by now had ready an expurgated version of events, emphasising that I had gone on the wrong Saturday owing to a misunderstanding and leaving out the tête-à-tête over tea.

'You were there for a conspicuous length of time. There must have been a formidable quantity of washing up,' said Brenda.

'The place was in a right mess,'

'Mummy says intellectual women are hopeless housekeepers,' said Caroline. 'That's why she wants me to do a secretarial course instead of going to university.'

On Monday evening I expected Mazzy to summon me and ask why I hadn't mentioned that Mrs Davis had been in Nottingham on Saturday afternoon. Alithea, passing me in the corridor, had murmured, 'Thanks' and given me a conspiratorial smile. Surely she must have held forth in the staff room about the French film? But when Mazzy called me back at the end of evening prayers it was only to ask whether Becky Simon had been behaving any better lately and it began to look as if Alithea had said nothing.

There was one repercussion, however. In our scholarship lesson Miss Seymour handed back my essay saying,

'This might have been better, Dilly, if you had spent more time on research instead of playing the little housewife.' She then flushed an unpleasing shade of puce. I was astounded. The essay had been handed in the previous week, well before I had done the Davises' washing-up. Her remark was not only unjust but also downright silly. I had a feeling that she didn't like me at all. I suddenly had a strange thought. Could she actually be jealous?

'What on earth was all that about?' asked Fiona later. It was lunchtime and we were toiling up the Harstans. School dinners were served in what had once been a mediaeval tithe barn situated half way between school and the Boarding House. The day was windy and my words blew away.

'Can't hear,' she said, puffing.

'Tell you later.'

We managed to head adjacent tables. I leaned towards her and, as quietly as possible, once again gave an account of my Saturday afternoon and what I knew of Miss Seymour's part in the events.

Fiona frowned.

'It all sounds very odd to me. What was Mrs Davis doing going to the cinema with Another Man?'

'He's not exactly Another Man,' I said. 'He's an old school-friend of her brothers. I expect she looks on him as just another brother.' I thought about the embrace that Hugh had given Alithea at the beginning of my first lesson. Was this a brotherly embrace? I had no experience of brothers. I thought of Fiona's older brother on whom I had once had a mild crush. He was now a medical student in Glasgow so we didn't see him very often. I had no recollection of his ever hugging her and I didn't feel inclined to ask her if he ever did.

Fiona was distracted by the arrival of the puddings.

'Dead man's leg, I hope,' said one of the juniors at her table. 'I'm starving.'

'I hope not,' said Fiona, 'or that'll take all my calorie allowance for today. She was trying a new method of slimming. She fiddled with her little cardboard calorie counter, 'And don't use that disgusting name,' she added.

'Chinese diarrhoea,' said the server dumping down a tin dish. Fiona was furious, unreasonably I thought. These were the time-honoured titles given to jam roly-poly and chocolate semolina. We might have become more squeamish but you couldn't expect the juniors to show similar sensibilities. Still at least it took her mind off the Davises.

On the way back to school however she started again. Eventually, I said,

'Anyway, I don't believe Mrs Davis could prefer Mr Marlow to her husband. He's not nearly as good-looking.'

'Looks aren't everything,' said Fiona. 'Mr Marlow seems more Mrs Davis's social equal.'

'What on earth does that matter?' I said. 'You sound like my mother. Mr Davis isn't just good-looking. He's clever and he's funny and kind - though perhaps a bit lazy,' I added hastily in case I was sounding too infatuated. Fiona was not entirely deceived.

'Be very careful Dilly. You don't want to fall for a married man. I think I'd stay away from the Davises if I were you.' She might as well have told the moth to stay away from the candle flame.

Jane, fortunately, seemed less interested in the time I had spent with Mike than in mocking Hugh's intellectual pretentiousness.

'Do you think this is a splendid example of the genre, Dilly?' she enquired, waving her pseudo-historical novel in front of me. 'It's a good thing you're having extra Latin with Mr Marlow. You can learn to talk like him. I expect they all go on like that at Oxford so at least you're getting in some practice now.'

'I don't suppose I'll get into Oxford,' I said. 'I'm only being entered as an also-ran. Ursula and Rosa are the favourites.'

'A metaphor!' said Jane, 'and a splendid example of the genre too.' She hooted with laughter.

'Oh shut up! You think you're so funny, don't you!'

The next week was half term and once we were back at school the Oxbridge entrance exams hurtled toward us with terrifying rapidity. The Davises and Hugh reminisced about their entrance papers and their interviews. Mike and Alithea seemed to assume I would get in but down at school Ursula was, as I had said to Jane, clearly the favourite. We were both intending to read English. Rosa was going to read History. Miss Seymour thought a lot of her but I sensed the general attitude in the staff-room was more ambivalent. Rosa was clever; everyone agreed about that, but was she really Oxbridge material?

'They really are a set of reactionary snobs.' Either Alithea had forgotten I was there or she didn't care and thought it was all right to speak freely about her colleagues in my presence. 'Joan says she is one of the brightest girls she's ever come across and yet they keep going on about "not really Oxbridge material". What they really mean is she's working class.'

'So am I,' Mike pointed out, 'and they took me. Mind you,' he added, 'there were times when I wished they hadn't.' He assumed the upper-class drawl that he sometimes used when imitating Hugh; he was a good mimic,

'"You know what, dear boy; they keep sending me these grammar school types who don't know any Greek." That's what I overheard one of my tutors saying.'

'Well of course knowing Greek is quite important,' said Hugh. This was unwise. Mike turned on him and I thought, now I know what they mean when they say, 'his eyes were blazing'.

'What's so fucking important about Greek?'

Over the last few months I'd got used to 'bloody' and 'bugger' but this really shook me as did Mike's rage. I'd never heard anybody say 'fucking' before. I had no idea what it meant but somehow I knew it was extreme language. I also knew the row wasn't really about Greek and I looked at Alithea to see what she was going to do. I was taken aback to see she seemed to be suppressing a smile.

Mike continued to rant incoherently about the insignificance to the world of yet another translation of bloody Aristophanes and the true nobility of people like Rosa's father who had managed to educate themselves while ruining their lungs hacking out coal underground to warm the effete members of the upper class.

'I hardly imagine your family ever goes short of coal – one of the perks of the trade isn't it?' said Hugh when he could get a word in. He was leaning back in his chair looking superior. I had a strong desire to hit him and then to go and give Mike a hug. Naturally I did neither of these things but just stood there feeling awkward. I'd been on my way out and my satchel was getting heavy so I shifted it to the other shoulder. This slight movement made the others remember I was there.

'I think Dilly is waiting to say goodbye,' Alithea reminded them. Mike turned to me.

'Dilly I'm sorry, inexcusable language but... don't Dilly, whatever you do, don't...' He seemed unable to get out whatever advice he wanted to give me. It looked for a moment as if there were tears in his eyes. I could hardly bear it but Alithea gestured to me, 'Scoot,' and I scooted.

Alithea hadn't yet, as far as I knew, invited Rosa round but obviously from what Mike had said to Hugh, he must have started to visit Rosa's father regularly. Nor had I yet taken Alithea's advice and talked to Rosa about politics. I didn't know how to begin such a conversation and I thought she would despise my ignorance. Also I didn't want to upset Fiona any more than I had already. I could see she didn't like my friendship with the Davises and I still felt some loyalty to her. Anyway she was my best ally against Ursula. Unctuous Ursula would be even worse when she got into Oxford or Cambridge. Perhaps she would even get a scholarship and then she would be unbearable.

However, one day Fiona was off with a cold. Rosa and I were both on prefect duty in the dinner hour supervising the juniors as they straggled out of the tithe barn, full of stew and steamed pudding. We were delayed on the way down by Becky Simon, who was hanging around under a stone archway halfway down the Harstans.

'What do you think you're doing?' said Rosa.

'Just feeding the poor gargoyle.' We looked at the small stone gargoyle on the side of the arch. Becky had crammed its gaping mouth with leaves from a creeper growing over the wall. I wanted to laugh but Rosa just looked annoyed.

'Go straight back to school,' she said. Such was her authority that Becky did so, immediately.

'I don't envy you dealing with that one every day,' she added, as Becky scurried off. From Rosa this was almost an invitation to friendship and made me feel I could ask,

'Are you going down to the public library?'

'No,' said Rosa, never one to waste words.

'I thought you might be going to look at the *Manchester Guardian*.' I decided not to mention the *Daily Worker*.

'Oh Mr Davis brings it down when he comes to see Dad. He's really kind like that.' As social exchanges went, this was a record for Rosa and a faint flush coloured her usually pale face.

'He charms everybody,' I remembered. It confirmed my idea that Mike's appreciation of my washing-up might have been the cause of Miss Seymour's strange outburst. Was every female in the place infatuated with him? Was this why Alithea was flirting with Hugh - if that was what it was - in order to get her own back? But that didn't make sense. I really hoped Mike liked me but it was Alithea who had insisted I should go round that Saturday afternoon. Had she forgotten she was going to the cinema with Hugh or had she asked me round to keep Mike from complaining too much? She seemed to be throwing us together. The thought excited me but then I remembered, 'better you than Joan Seymour.' Was she using Miss Seymour as well? Of course Joan Seymour was grown up and she and Mike both taught history and they were both left wing but, from what Hugh had hinted, he obviously liked me better. A wild idea came to me. Was Alithea perhaps planning to run off with Hugh and trying to make it as painless as possible for Mike? 'You're a sweet girl Dilly', 'you'll make some lucky bastard a smashing wife one day'. I felt dizzy with hope. And yet I knew it wasn't really that simple. Something odd was going on and I couldn't understand what. I wished I could talk to Fiona about it but I had a feeling I might not like her interpretation.

Meanwhile, there, on the Harstans, I persisted with Rosa.

'I've started to read the *Manchester Guardian* too.' I gave a rather nervous little laugh. 'It gives a very different picture of the world from the *Telegraph*.'

'Well of course.'

'I really don't know much about politics. Most people I know are Conservatives; in fact my father says this government isn't Conservative enough for him. But my aunts, my mother's sisters, are Liberals. There are still quite a lot of them in Scotland, apparently.' I was aware that I was babbling but Rosa's silence was rather demoralising.

'Liberals!' said Rosa in tones of contempt. However she walked back down the steps with me. 'I sometimes read the *Telegraph* as well,' she said. 'It's useful to know how the enemy thinks.' She smiled at me quite amiably but I was lost for a reply. Even my father at his most outraged didn't refer to the Labour opposition as the enemy.

CHAPTER ELEVEN

When the dreaded exams finally arrived they passed in a blur. My wrists ached; my fingers got covered in ink; my handwriting sprawled.

'Well, Dilly, it's fortunate you're not entering a handwriting competition.' Miss Seymour, who happened to be invigilating that afternoon, glanced at my script as she was gathering in our exam papers. 'And just look at your hands.' I looked and unwisely ran them through my hair.

'Oh Dilly, now you've got ink on your forehead!' Ursula sniggered and exchanged pitying glances with Miss Seymour. Rosa was staring out of the window, pale, cold and aloof as the wintry sky outside. I wished she would turn towards me, smile or something. I had the feeling she didn't much like Ursula, who was always very patronising towards her, but on the other hand she was Joan Seymour's special protégé so it was understandable she didn't want to take sides.

After they were over I tried to forget about the exams and concentrate on applying to other universities, but I kept getting reminders. At my next lesson Hugh wanted to go over the Latin papers with me. I'd found them both almost impossible and didn't want to reveal my problems to him but he was actually quite sympathetic. A few days later I was hanging up my coat in the sixth form cloakroom when I heard Alithea's voice coming from the top of the stairwell.

'Dilly found the Cambridge Latin paper very difficult. Even Hugh said it was nasty.'

'Well, I understand Dilly's Latin is very weak.' It was, of course,

Joan Seymour speaking, 'Ursula's Latin is much sounder...' I moved away. I didn't want to hear any more but it left me depressed for the rest of the day. I dragged myself up the Harstans, thinking gloomily of the pile of homework in my satchel, only to be astounded by a message on the noticeboard by the back door. There in Mazzy's dramatic italic script: 'Dilly, Interview!' I rushed round to her room and found there was a telegram from Oxford.

'I expect someone dropped out at the last minute,' she said, curbing my excitement. I thought this very likely and when at school the next morning I found Ursula had heard nothing I began to think they must have mixed us up. A further telegram from Cambridge, however, convinced me that they couldn't both have made a mistake. Rosa had also been asked to go for interviews but Ursula had heard nothing.

In spite of Mazzy's attempts to stop me getting above myself I set off on my journey to the unknown South in a cheerful mood. I didn't really expect to get into either university and my thoughts were both unworthy, whatever happened now I'd done better than Ursula, and frivolous, I was getting out of Games. It was a bitterly cold day. I looked out of the train window; watched tree branches bending in a brisk east wind and thought with satisfaction that netball would be even more hellish than usual.

Returning from my adventure I was bursting to relate my experiences and Fiona was bursting to hear them but we both had enough manners, if not enough compassion, to keep quiet in front of Ursula. I could see that Fiona was also curious about Rosa who had returned even more pale and silent, seeming reluctant to answer the most basic questions about her interviews. Fiona asked me to tea that Saturday and once we were in the privacy of her chilly bedroom we could talk freely at last but I hardly knew where to begin. Fiona fairly inevitably wanted to know about my clothes.

'You did get a hat didn't you?'

Fiona had been adamant about the necessity of wearing a hat for interviews. This had caused an argument at home. My father had asked why my school beret wouldn't do. This was silly of him because it had started my mother on a well-worn theme; if only they had been able to afford to send me to a proper boarding school I would have had a nice Sunday uniform like my cousins. As it was she'd persuaded me to buy something rather like the felt pudding basins they'd been forced to wear. I told Fiona this and added that I'd managed to leave it on the train.

'Oh, Dilly, you are hopeless!' What I didn't tell her was that I'd been distracted by an American airman's attempt to pick me up on the journey back from Oxford. He definitely wasn't an officer so I knew she wouldn't approve but I'd rather enjoyed the episode and it had put my hat right out of my mind.

'Anyway,' I said, 'my tweed suit was OK, a bit boring but better than the awful school uniforms the posh girls were wearing.'

'You mean the girls from public schools?'

'Yes they all looked hideous.'

'Still, schools like that do give you a certain something.'

'Yes, spots and greasy hair by the look of it.'

'Dilly!'

'Still,' I said, feeling I'd been unnecessarily unkind, 'I expect the poor things couldn't help it. My cousins were only allowed to wash their hair once a fortnight when they were at boarding school.'

'How disgusting!' Fiona said no more on the advantages of a public school education; instead she asked me what Rosa had worn. I immediately felt guilty.

Rosa had gone to Oxford first and when I arrived there after my cross-country journey from Cambridge I bumped into her on the steps of the college we were both applying to. After my exclamations of pleasure at seeing a familiar face I asked her if she'd finished her interviews.

'I'm supposed to be going to see the Principal. But I don't think I'll bother.' I looked at her in amazement and thought for a moment that the ever-impassive Rosa was actually going to cry.

'But why ever not?'

'They don't want people like me here. I don't fit in. All these stuck-up girls...'

'Oh I know,' I said. 'Cambridge was full of them.'

'Well I won't go there then neither – either,' she corrected herself.

My attempt at empathy had gone badly wrong. Trying to put things right, I said,

'But you mustn't let them intimidate you. Some of them are really spotty and they're wearing the most hideous uniforms.' As soon as I'd spoken I realised I'd been stupid. Rosa was wearing an ill-fitting jacket and skirt in a cheap material and a hat that was far too old for her. I suspected it was really her mother's. She'd actually have looked a lot better in her school uniform. I quickly tried another line of argument.

'Come on Rosa, Mr Davis came from a...Mr Davis is a miner's son and he came here'

Her pale face flushed pink. 'Mr Davis will understand.'

I didn't much care for this. I felt I had first rights to Mike's understanding but then I remembered, 'Is she as pretty as Dilly?' and Alithea's response, 'No, she's quite a plain girl,' so feeling magnanimous, I managed to persuade Rosa to go and have an interview with the Principal after all.

'And did she go on to Cambridge?' Fiona asked me at the end of this story.

'I don't know. I didn't see her again until we were both back at school and she won't talk about it.'

At that point, Fiona's mother called out that tea was ready and that we must be frozen up there. Did we want to have it by the living room fire? While we were helping her carry things through, She asked me about my actual interviews. I said everyone had been very nice to me and that I'd had an interesting discussion about Evelyn Waugh with one of the tutors at Cambridge.

'Why have you been reading Evelyn Waugh?' asked Fiona.

'Mrs Davis suggested I should.'

'Oh, her!' said Fiona. 'I suppose all the tutors were very dowdy,' she added.

I said, 'No, not all of them.' One of the tutors at Oxford had been particularly smart. I told Fiona that she'd been wearing the same shade of nail varnish that Mrs Davis used.'

'Bright scarlet from what Fiona tells me of Mrs Davis,' said her mother with a laugh.

'No,' said Fiona, 'it's Pale Cream by Peggy Sage.' I made a mental note.

To get us off the subject of Alithea I said that the Principal of the Oxford college had suggested that, if they offered me a place, I should consider leaving at Easter and spending a few months in France.

'You can't do that!' Fiona almost shrieked, 'and leave me with Ursula and Rosa!'

I tried to reassure her. 'Firstly they probably won't have me and secondly I've got to try for a State Scholarship in the summer.'

There were other reasons for not going to France that I didn't go into. To begin with I knew I'd never be allowed to do such a thing. When I was about fifteen, some of my year had gone on a French exchange, but my mother had vetoed the idea immediately it was mentioned.

'They're all RCs you know. If we had a French girl here she'd want to go to the Roman Catholic church. Just think; the priest might even call and then what would we do? Then she'd expect elaborate meals. Your Aunt Nettie is always going on about French cooking. She seems to like that kind of food but your father couldn't stand all that grease and garlic, not with his digestion and we certainly wouldn't be offering wine. If you went back there they might expect you to drink and even go to Mass. Anyway,' she had added, 'French girls are very sophisticated.' I wasn't sure how she imagined this sophistication would manifest itself in our small town; perhaps she thought the hypothetical girl would attempt to seduce my father. Still, in spite of my mother and in spite of Fiona, I might have fought to go to France this time, even though the thought of how a cultured French family might react to my appalling accent was rather terrifying. However overriding everything else was the fact that I couldn't bear to be separated from the Davises.

CHAPTER TWELVE

A few days later the unimaginable happened. I was offered a place at Cambridge. Of course I was happy. How could I not be? When I arrived for my next Latin lesson, Alithea had already told Hugh and Mike. Over tea Mike teased me, saying that women were even more outnumbered by men at Cambridge than they were at Oxford.

'Don't go wild Dilly, will you? Don't forget me completely, nor our friend Hugh here, of course.' Hugh gave a rather chilly smile.

I wondered whether in fact I would have any opportunity to go wild at Cambridge. My college seemed a long way from any of the men's colleges, stuck out among the potato fields. The food had been fairly dreadful as well, nearly as bad as at the Boarding House.

Soon after, the conversation turned to Rosa. Rosa had not gone for her interview at Cambridge and was in disgrace at school. Even the Davises were not as understanding as she had hoped.

'What will she do if she doesn't get into Oxford?' Alithea asked Mike.

Why should he know? I thought jealously.

'Oh, I advised her to try for London.'

When? I wondered and realised Mike must now be a regular visitor at Rosa's.

'The LSE I suppose,' said Hugh, looking knowing.

'No, University College.'

'Oh, the Godless Institution on Gower Street,' said Hugh. 'Your idea no doubt.'

'Why is it called that?' I asked.

'Well,' said Hugh, 'in the past only Anglicans could go to Oxford or Cambridge, so University College London was founded to take non-conformists, atheists, even Jews.'

'What do you mean – even Jews?' said Alithea. I remembered she'd once mentioned that her father was Jewish. 'Though not of course practising,' she had explained.

'Just Hugh's anti-Semitism showing,' said Mike grinning.

'I am not anti-Semitic.'

'Yeah, yeah, we know. Many of your best friends are Jews.'

'All right you two,' said Alithea as if they were squabbling children.

I thought it was time to go.

'You off Dilly?' said Mike. 'I'll come out with you. I've run out of fags. And I don't suppose Hugh will part with his superior brand.'

'You can have one if you like,' said Hugh.

'No thanks. I prefer my working man's Woodbines.'

I found myself walking along the dark street with Mike.

'Neo-fascist bastard,' he said. I assumed he was speaking about Hugh. 'What does she see in him?' I felt inclined to tell him he'd scored nine on Jane's chart and Hugh had only managed six but I thought it might need rather a lot of explaining. We'd just stopped at the corner under a street lamp where our ways diverged. I looked up at his half-shadowed face and said passionately,

'I really can't think.'

He leant towards me and gently put a finger under my chin. I stood very still and suddenly his face was very close. He said softly,

'That's for getting into Cambridge and for being such a sweet kid.' And he kissed me lightly on the lips before speeding off towards the newsagents.

I stood on the corner trembling so much I had to lean up against the nearest garden wall for at least a minute. It was misty; there was a smell of damp leaves and the cathedral clock was striking six. I stayed against the wall, re-living the exquisite moment while looking at a spider's web between the lamppost and the wall. The web shone silver in the lamplight; little drops of water on it glittered and I thought it was the most beautiful thing I had ever seen. I wanted to tell everyone but I knew I could tell no one. Fiona would have been horrified and I could imagine Jane's shrieks only too well.

I was getting cold; I could hear voices and footsteps; people were approaching through the mist. I realised I must move on before Mike returned. It would be terribly awkward if he found me still standing there.

By the time I'd reached the Boarding House, prep was under way in the common room and Brenda had once again usurped my place at the head of the long table, something she had been inclined to do lately. While I indulged in buttered toast and intellectual conversation at the Davises, she'd started to take advantage of my absence to assume my responsibilities. I was beginning to get annoyed by it and I stood by her chair until she shifted her books.

'Sorry,' she mouthed. 'Thought you weren't coming.' I gave her a world-weary glance. After all, these things must be important to her in her limited existence.

That night I lay awake in the dormitory listening to the steady breathing of the others and the creaking of the iron bedsteads as they turned in their sleep. I relived the scene and remembered Mike's words,

'Sweet kid.' This wasn't entirely flattering. Would he have called me a 'kid' if I hadn't been wearing my school uniform? I imagined suddenly appearing before Mike looking sophisticated, having at last succeeded in putting my hair up – or perhaps in defiance of my father – flowing loose - no I'd look older with it up - up would definitely be better. But what would I be wearing? Nothing I had in my existing wardrobe, that was for sure. I let these details remain hazy while I played out a little scene in my mind...

'Dilly!' he would exclaim, 'but...but you're beautiful. You've heard I suppose. Alithea has finally run off with that bastard Hugh. I was in the depths of despair. But now you are here everything seems changed. I always thought of you as a mere child but I see I was mistaken. Of course you must go to university first but I will wait for you.'

Even in my infatuated state I realised this sounded both improbable and silly. The sober sound of the cathedral clock booming out eleven reminded me I'd be tired in the morning if I didn't get to sleep. Love, I thought, was very exhausting.

The next morning, before school, the Boarding House phone rang and Mazzy said my mother wanted to speak to me.

'There's a telegram from Oxford,' said my mother, sounding rather gloomy. From her tone I assumed it was a rejection.

'Oh, so they don't want me?'

'No dear, they're offering you a place but the Minister told us the Cambridge offer is more prestigious.'

'What does he know about it?'

'There's no need to be rude, Dilly. I've told you about the new Minister. He's a very nice young man. Quite an intellectual. We're getting a very different kind of sermon now - although of course it's quite beyond most of the congregation.'

'I couldn't care less what his sermons are like. He has no right to come interfering.'

'Couldn't care less! You know I hate that expression. What ever is the matter with you, Dilly? I hope you're not getting above yourself.'

'Sorry,' I said. 'But you might have been a bit more pleased about Oxford.'

'Well, your father thinks you should listen to the Minister.'

At school I went straight to the staffroom and asked for Miss Carr.

'I've been offered a place at Oxford,' I said. 'But my father says the Cambridge offer is more prestigious.' Miss Carr looked at me kindly over her half-moon glasses.

'Well, my dear,' she said, 'who is going to this university? You, or your father?'

'You mean it's my choice?'

'It's your life Dilly.'

My mother was not impressed when I repeated this conversation to her and pointed out that as my father would have to make some contribution to top up my grant he should have some say in the matter. But it really was my choice and there was nothing much they could do about it.

Once again I was the centre of attention in morning prayers. Soon after that Rosa heard she hadn't got a place.

'Mike says,' said Alithea to Hugh, a few days later, 'Rosa wasn't just put off by those Roedean types. She had a horrible interview with one of the history tutors. Apparently this woman asked Rosa about her background and said - can you believe this! - that before the war she used to teach the daughters of bishops but ever since the 1944

Education Act she's had to teach girls who don't even know what a bishop is.'

'Well, I see her problem,' said Hugh. 'You do need some cultural background to get the most out of Oxford.'

'Oh Hugh. You are a snob!' said Alithea.

'Anyway, Rosa knows what a bishop is,' I said. 'She could hardly not, coming from our school.'

'That's not the point,' said Hugh. 'You must learn not to generalise from the particular, Dilly.'

I'd been listening anxiously for the clattering of Mike's bike. I was sorry he hadn't come in time to hear Alithea call Hugh a snob. I wondered whether he regretted kissing me and I wanted to hear what he would say about my Oxford offer. Now I couldn't repress my anxiety any longer.

'Mr Davis is late.'

'Oh,' said Alithea, 'he won't be in for ages. He's helping with rehearsals for the end of term concert.' She gave a little smile. Had he confessed to her about the kiss? Or did he feel guilty and was deliberately keeping out of my way?

'I didn't really expect you today, Dilly,' said Hugh, 'Now you've got your place at Oxford there's no great urgency to carry on at the moment. We'll have to think what to do about improving your A level grade later. Do you really need this State Scholarship?'

'Miss Cutler wants me to try for it,' I said. I wasn't really sure whether it was a financial necessity or not. My father liked to be mysterious about his income. I felt distracted, still hoping Mike might appear but not being able to think of any excuse to stay.

'Oh, I expect she'd still like a cup of tea,' said Alithea. 'Would you like one Hugh?'

'No thank you!' Hugh snapped and he left the kitchen, slamming the door behind him. Alithea raised her eyebrows, shrugged her shoulders and put the kettle on. Sometimes with the three of them I felt I was watching a play in a language I didn't quite understand. I drank my tea as slowly as possible but Mike still didn't appear.

CHAPTER THIRTEEN

It was nearly Christmas. We'd started singing Advent hymns at school assembly and in the cathedral. End of term exams were over and there was a general air of relaxation.

I tried not to talk about Oxford in front of Ursula and Rosa but Ursula still tried to put me down whenever the opportunity arose. Much of our spare time that term had been spent knitting squares to make into blankets for an East End settlement supported by our school. Alithea made her contempt for this patronising charity fairly clear but Miss Carr insisted that we all contributed, even hopeless knitters like me. Now the squares were being sewn together and Ursula was organising the project. She took a good deal of pleasure in pointing out that most of my squares just weren't - in fact some of them were almost triangular.

'I can't think how you do it Dilly,' she said, feigning tolerant amusement. 'Surely there's nothing easier than knitting a simple square!' Fortunately, once the blanket was completed, Ursula, always one for worthwhile activities, decided to put on a Mummers' play with some of the juniors. It was to be performed at the end of term assembly. This took up her dinner hours leaving Fiona and me the chance to slope off into town where Fiona pronounced judgement on the clothes displayed in shop windows and I admired the confidence of her opinions. Rosa remained as uncommunicative as ever.

In the Boarding House the juniors were busy making Christmas cards and also rather sticky, uneven calendars intended as presents. It made for a cheerful atmosphere but also created a great deal of mess. Jane, Caroline, Brenda and I were already on our way out to carol-singing with the Student Christian Movement when Matron stomped into the common room.

'Just look at this! And I suppose I'm not going to get any help from you sixth formers this evening, now you're off carol-singing.'

The two long tables were covered with magazines, scraps of paper and glue, so we hastily started to help clear up in case carol-singing was vetoed at the last minute. We didn't want to miss out on this exciting occasion that provided an opportunity to wander about in the dark with the grammar school boys and might lead to some surreptitious hand-holding if nothing else.

The group assembled near the South door of the Cathedral. Our music teacher and Dr Penney from the Grammar School were bustling around handing out roneoed sheets of carols. It would have been appropriate if there had been snow, or at least a crisp frost, and lanterns. Instead we had to make do with a damp chill and electric torches but it was still quite thrilling.

Once outside the Boarding House the others went off with their friends but Fiona scorned school societies and Rosa never took part in SCM meetings; I supposed she, too, was a Socialist-atheist ; so Ursula and I were inevitably thrown together. Almost immediately we were joined by Christopher and his friend Dave.

I liked Dave Whatley. I'd met him several times when I was going out with Christopher and I knew his father kept a corner shop. Once, at the end of the previous Easter term, when my parents had just collected me from the Boarding House my mother decided she needed something to supplement our supper. My father stopped the car opposite the nearest shop, and I was sent in to buy a tin of peas. I'd just been paying for this when Dave himself had appeared from out the back. He'd introduced me to his father and I'd chatted to them both for a bit. When I came back with the peas my father wanted to know what had kept me. My explanation had not been well received.

'I suppose Christopher comes from a similar background.' said my mother and when I admitted this was more or less true the rest of the journey passed in silence.

'Bet we begin with the grovel carol,' I heard Dave say to Christopher.

'*All poor men and humble*' announced Dr Penney.

'Told you so,' said Dave. I was slightly shocked. This was a Davis-type remark, not what you would expect from someone who, Mike claimed, intended to become a vicar.

'By the way, congratulations!' said Christopher generously. It turned out that he'd just been rejected by a group of Oxford colleges. He was intending to try again next term. Ursula was also going to try for another college. They started to talk about this, while Dave told me he'd just heard he'd got into Keble.

'So I'll see you in Oxford in two years' time,' he said. That at least, I thought, was one advantage in being a girl; I didn't have to do National Service.

By this time we had reached the Sub-Deanery where the carols were to start. Last summer term we had been there for a garden party and I had thought then that if could choose any house in the world it would be the Sub-Deanery It was a long low house; the front was Georgian but some of it was much older. You went into the hall and then ascended by a double staircase to a gallery. A drawing room opened off the gallery and from there long windows opened onto a tangled garden that grew on top of the Roman wall. At the time of the garden party it had been full of floppy roses and spikes of lavender. Now, in winter, we went no further than the panelled hallway. The Sub-Dean, white-haired and rosy faced, rather like Chaucer's Franklin, came out beaming. We launched into the grovel carol,

All poor men and humble,
All rich men who stumble,
Come haste ye nor seem ye afraid.

Moving on round the Close we sang to Miss Cutler, who opened the door and tried to listen through Biff's barking.

'Someone should strangle that beast,' said Dave.

The next stop was the Deanery, a rather grim Victorian building. I wondered whether, if you were appointed Dean, you could ask to be demoted so you could live in the Sub-Deanery instead. Ursula's uncle, the Dean, smiling austerely, asked us all in and we stood around rather uneasily in the chilly Gothic hallway.

As we finished *Past three o'clock and a cold frosty morning*, the Dean's wife appeared. She approached our little group,

'Well Ursula,' she said, 'this is disappointing news. What are you going to do now?'

Ursula muttered something about trying for St Anne's.

'And if you don't get in there, what then?' Ursula said she had already applied to Durham.

'Durham!' said her aunt. 'You won't even hear decent English spoken up there.' Beastly woman! I thought. For once I wanted to defend Ursula.

'Actually,' I said, 'Miss Carr says the English course at Durham is really good.' Her aunt turned to stare at me.

'Are you the girl that got into Oxford?' she asked and, without giving me a chance to reply, added, 'Well, I hear they take all sorts nowadays.' Even Ursula looked ashamed by this rudeness. Dave gave a kind of soft whistle. What would she think if she'd known about him, the son of a man who kept a corner shop, getting a place at Keble? There ought to have been something we could say but I couldn't think what; also I wondered why I should be described as 'all sorts'. She knew nothing about me.

The cow! I thought to myself, the rotten cow! I remembered Caroline once rebuking Jane,

'Mummy says calling someone a cow is obscene.' Well good! The fucking cow, I added to myself with satisfaction. The Davises had extended my vocabulary in more ways than one.

From the Deanery we made our way towards the Bishop's Palace, the climax of the evening, but on the way we passed the end of the lane where the Davises lived.

'We should go and sing a carol to Trotsky.' said Dave.

'Good idea,' said Christopher, 'we might convert him.'

'In fact,' said Dave, 'I think it's our Christian duty and if we can't save him we might have some effect on his lovely wife.'

'You're just hoping she'll be wearing that tight red sweater,' said Christopher. Ursula actually giggled and I suddenly noticed that she and Christopher were holding hands. It must be all off again between him and his semi-permanent girl friend. Well I didn't care but I did wonder how Christopher would be received at the Deanery.

'Come on Dilly,' said Dave. 'Let's go.' They turned down the little lane.

'You boys!' called our music teacher, 'Dilly! Ursula! Where are you going? This way please. The Bishop is expecting us.' I had a sudden inspiration.

'Oh Miss Hurst,' I said, 'I think they've heard of a very lonely old lady living down there, Mrs Herbert. She's a canon's widow,' I added, knowing that Miss Hurst had a great respect for the clergy, especially the higher ranks.

'Well I don't know...' began Miss Hurst.

'Come on, Sir,' called Dave to Dr Penney. 'We're going to convert Mr Davis.' This might well have wrecked my diplomacy but Dr Penney, who wasn't much older than Mike, seemed amused.

'Not much hope of that I'm afraid, Whatley.' Mike's atheism seemed to be something of a joke in the Grammar School. Not for the first time I noticed that the boys seemed to have a more relaxed relationship with their staff than we did with ours.

'Now where is Dr Penney going?' said Miss Hurst, as the whole crowd started to follow Dave and Christopher. 'I can't believe he's given way to those silly boys. This is your fault Dilly.' This seemed rather unfair but I didn't care. We were outside the Davises and that was all that mattered.

'A very short one, please, Dr Penney. The Bishop will be waiting.' Dr Penney ignored her. He'd probably overheard her comments on his weak discipline.

'This Endris Night,' he suggested - he preferred the more obscure carols.

At the third *By by lullay*, Mrs Herbert appeared beaming in the open doorway and before Miss Hurst could do anything about it everyone was in the hall and Mike, Alithea and Hugh had appeared from the basement to see what was going on. Alithea was wearing slacks and the famous red sweater, her hair was loose and she looked rather flushed.

AUTUMN TERM 1955

'Mrs Herbert has asked if we could sing *O Little Town of Bethlehem*,' said Dave who seemed to have struck up a rapport with the canon's widow while at the same time managing to have a good ogle at Alithea.

'The Bishop...' squeaked Miss Hurst but was ignored. Alithea caught sight of me and signalled to me to come over.

'Dilly,' she said quietly. 'I'm afraid we're all a bit tiddly. Hugh's just heard one of his translations is going to be broadcast on the Third Programme soon and he bought several bottles of Algerian red to celebrate. In fact Mike's more than a bit tiddly. Can you do anything to get this lot out of here?'

If she had just left things as they were we would all have departed without any trouble. *O Little town of Bethlehem* was coming to an end and Miss Hurst was already moving the group bishopwards although Dave and Christopher and therefore, of course, Ursula and I were hanging on until the last minute. Then, because Alithea had called me over, as the crowd thinned out Mike caught sight of me.

'Dilly! terrific news about Oxford - well done!' and he enveloped me in a bear hug, wreathing me in fumes of what I supposed to be Algerian red as he did so. For a moment I felt the roughness of Mike's tweed jacket against my face and heard the thump of his heart.

'Mike!' Alithea hissed at him. He loosened his grip and I released myself with a mixture of ecstasy and confusion. He glowered at Alithea.

'You've got your friend over there. Why can't I give Dilly a hug?' He was definitely drunk. Hugh had slid away into the darkness of the basement stairwell.

'You're embarrassing Dilly.'

'Am I?' He caught hold of my hand and gazed at me rather blearily.

'Am I embarrassing you Dilly?'

'It's all right,' I said, as, reluctantly I slid my hand out of his grasp. 'It's all right - but I've got to go.' Only Dave, Christopher and Ursula were still in the hall; they were all staring at me. I hoped they were the only ones who had seen this little drama. If Jane had any idea of what had happened it would be all over the school, with embellishments.

'I think he's been drinking,' I said quietly, trying to sound lightly amused but probably just sounding defensive. 'That's what Mrs Davis was trying to tell me.' I added, attempting to fill the silence.

'Come on you stragglers!' someone shouted from outside. 'Miss Hurst is in a bit of a bate. She says the Bishop isn't used to being kept waiting.' Presumably Miss Hurst was now out of earshot.

'Goodbye, goodbye, such a lovely treat!' called Mrs Herbert, happily unaware of her lodgers' inebriated condition. We stepped out into the night. Under the cover of darkness Dave at last managed to say something,

'So are you telling us Mrs Davis was warning you our revered history master was likely to kiss you because he was drunk?'

'No, of course not. She just said he'd had a bit to drink' (I thought that sounded better than saying 'drunk' to Mike's pupils) 'and we should go - anyway he didn't kiss me.'

'Looked like it to us. Didn't it Chris?' Much to my relief they were beginning to treat it as a joke.

'He was just congratulating me on getting into Oxford.'

'Well I've just got into Oxford. He didn't kiss me. Come to that neither did Mrs Davis. I'd have liked that. Shall we go back and see if Mrs Davis'll kiss me if I tell her I've got into Keble.'

'Oh shut up! I've told you he didn't kiss me.' I was beginning to quite enjoy this. I'd never really been teased by a boy before. I decided

Dave was rather amusing. Jane thought he had too many freckles to rate more than a seven but I thought I would tell her he was definitely worth eight, at least.

By this time we'd reached the Bishop's Palace. We scrunched up the drive and caught up with the others at the door. The Bishop, all affability, led us into a vast drawing room. Christmas cards filled every available surface. I was impressed. Ours at home only just overflowed the mantelpiece.

'Oh, Bishop,' said Miss Hurst, 'I do hope we haven't kept you waiting.'

'Crumbs,' I said to my little group. 'She's practically genuflecting.' The boys looked startled for a moment. Girls weren't expected to make jokes, but then they laughed. Ursula looked disapproving. Her momentary lapse into normality seemed over. Now we were in a lighted room she was no longer holding hands with Christopher. She went over to talk to the Bishop whom, of course, she knew. Mince pies were handed round on silver trays and there were glasses of some kind of non-alcoholic punch smelling strongly of cloves, which made me think of toothache.

I felt exhilarated. Whether Mike had kissed me or not, and to be honest I wasn't quite sure, it was the second time he had embraced me. I could still feel the roughness of his jacket against my cheek and hear the powerful thump, thump of his heart. For years, the smell of cheap red wine would evoke that rapturous moment.

Where it would all lead I couldn't imagine but at that moment I believed anything was possible. I felt confident a wonderful future was before me in one way or another and in the meantime I was enjoying joking around in a friendly way with Dave and Christopher.

'Well Dilly,' said Jane when we were all back in the boarding house. 'I saw you with Christopher. So that's on again is it?'

'Not at all. Actually I think something's starting up between him and Ursula.' Thank heavens, I thought, that was all she'd seen. 'Anyway Dave Whatley is much more amusing.' I thought it was quite a good idea to give her someone else to tease me about.

'Oh,' said Caroline, 'I thought he was going out with some girl in 5B.'

'I'm not actually bothered - it *is* possible just to be friends with boys you know.'

'And anyway you prefer mature men don't you?' said Jane. I panicked.

'Such as?' This was stupid but fortunately, once Jane had an idea she didn't let go.

'Your beloved Latin tutor, of course.' Relieved, I let her run on merrily about Hugh until lights out.

Before registration the next morning Fiona asked how the carol-singing had gone. As Ursula was off organising something, I felt free to tell her about the appalling behaviour of the Dean's wife including her rudeness to me.

'"All sorts" - what could she have meant by that?'

'Well,' said Fiona, 'Perhaps it was your accent.'

'My *accent*?' I said, 'But I've had elocution lessons!'

Ursula bustled in at that moment so we dropped the subject. I started worrying she might say something about Mike's hug but she was full of Becky Simon's latest misdemeanour for which she seemed to hold me responsible.

After our English lesson Alithea asked me to stay behind for a moment.

'I'm very sorry about yesterday evening Dilly.' She looked rather pale and tense. 'As you may imagine, Mike is rather the worse for wear this morning but he asked me to say he didn't mean to embarrass you in front of your friends.' I didn't know whether I liked the sound of this or not but I murmured something reassuring and then said,

'Mr Marlow must be very pleased that his translation is going to be broadcast.' I thought this was a clever and tactful way of changing the subject.

'Yes,' she said, 'he is.' She paused, 'It might be better to keep quiet about yesterday's incident. If someone took it the wrong way... Well, we'd be sorry if you weren't allowed to come round any more.'

I wondered, uneasily, what she thought was the right way to take Mike's embrace; however the mere idea of being banned from my paradise so appalled me I promised I would say nothing to anybody.

CHAPTER FOURTEEN

'Two more days and we shall be
Out of this academee,'

sang Becky Simon. She threw a cushion at Mary Nicholls but it missed and landed at Matron's feet just as she came in the door.

'Over-excited,' said Matron, 'you know the cure for that Becky, don't you – early bed. Go up and start getting washed – now. And pick up that cushion.' She sighed and said to me, 'They get worse every year.'

'Well not long now, Matron,' I said, trying to sound sympathetically mature. 'Where are you going for Christmas?'

'My sister and I are going to stay with my married niece in Pontefract.'

'Oh well, that'll be nice.'

'I don't know about that, Dilly. Her children are very badly behaved; she doesn't seem to know how to say "No" and I expect I shall get roped in for doing the vegetables as usual. Anyway Pontefract isn't exactly the centre of the universe, you know.'

As I knew nothing of Pontefract except the eponymous liquorice cakes I could only say 'I suppose not'. Matron's gloomy attitude to Christmas seemed to be rather similar to my mother's. She was fond of saying it was 'no rest for a housewife,' although our Christmas dinner only involved a rather small chicken and a bought Christmas pudding, very black and inclined to stick to the roof of your mouth. Mazzy seemed rather more cheerful about the approaching festivities. She was going to spend the holiday with Miss Robson and was looking forward to 'walks on the Downs and a good go at the *Times* crossword.'

My own feelings as the holiday approached were increasingly bleak. I almost wished I was Becky's age and could still be excited about hanging up my stocking. Latin lessons were over for the term, so I hadn't seen Mike since the carol-singing. I wanted to know if he still remembered the hug he had given me; I couldn't bear the thought of not seeing him for almost three weeks.

On the last morning of term I gave Alithea a Christmas card. I didn't quite have the courage to address it to Mike as well but I'd chosen something non-religious and artistic, a Bruegel skating scene.

'Oh thank you, Dilly - goodness I nearly forgot - I put aside some books for you. I thought you might like to do some general reading over the holidays. Is there any chance you could drop round and pick them up before you go home?'

'I'm sure that will be possible,' I said in a self-controlled way but inwardly I felt like shouting for joy. I bounced through the rest of the day and even managed to be suitably enthusiastic about Ursula's production of the Mummers' play although Fiona and I privately agreed it had been tedious beyond words.

'Mutterers' play more like,' said Fiona. 'Why couldn't she at least have got them to speak up?'

'I've just got to go and pick up some books from Mrs Davis.' I stood in the hall poised for a quick getaway.

'Is this essential, Phyllida?' Mazzy's voice was cold with disapproval. 'Why could Mrs Davis not have given you the books at school today?'

'She forgot to bring them.'

'Did she indeed!' She clicked her tongue. Mazzy seemed to be becoming less and less amused by Alithea's influence on me and more and more hostile. I wondered if Miss Hurst had realised more than I'd thought about the Davises' state at the carol-singing. I was sure she hadn't seen Mike's embrace but had Ursula perhaps dropped hints?

'When are you expecting your parents?'

'Oh they won't be here for at least half an hour and my luggage is all ready.' I indicated my trunk and satchel.

'Well I don't know where you're going to put any more books, let alone have time to read them. Remember you have mocks early next term. If you made an arrangement with Mrs Davis I suppose you must keep to it. But this kind of thing can't go on you know, Dilly.'

What kind of thing? I wondered, but I was too anxious to get away to give it any more thought.

Alithea had the books all piled up ready for me on a corner of the kitchen table. There was some Leavis ('They don't like him at Oxford but he is important.'), I think there was *Brighton Rock* and there was definitely Sartre's *Nausea* ('I don't think you will find it useful to read Sartre just at the moment Dilly' - Well Miss Manzonni, we'll see about that!) and Simone de Beauvoir's *The Second Sex*.

All the time she'd been talking I'd been listening anxiously, hoping Mike wouldn't be delayed at school again. As I heard the, by now, familiar sound of him dragging his bike into the corridor; my heart started thumping. Would he say anything about the other evening? Would he feel uneasy? I needn't have worried. He flung open the door and, on seeing me, said 'Dilly!' in tones of surprise and delight. He was wearing his tweed jacket with the leather-patched elbows; I remembered the feel of it against my face and involuntarily touched my cheek. He came over to the table and picked up *The Second Sex*.

'For God's sake, you're not going to fill Dilly's head with that rubbish are you? She's a sweet, gentle, feminine girl. Don't corrupt her with the ideas of that Frog virago.' I remembered Hazel, *as soft and as pink as a nursery*. 'Sweet, gentle and feminine'. Did I really want to be like that?

'Take no notice,' said Alithea. 'He's just trying to be provocative.'

Hugh, who had been staring out of the basement kitchen window at a dank, ivy-covered wall ever since I'd arrived, turned round as if he'd only just become aware I was there.

'I expect you're looking forward to the holidays,' he said politely. He flicked open his gold cigarette case and offered it to me, 'As term is over,' he said. I felt very flattered but I didn't dare take a cigarette. My parents might notice the smell of tobacco smoke but, I thought, I really must try to master smoking before I go to Oxford.

'I haven't smoked since I was in the third form,' I said, making it sound as if it was something I'd tried long ago and decided to give up.

'Really?'

'Yes, at the end of the Boarding House garden.' I paused, remembering the smell of the giant angelica we used to lurk under on summer evenings. I had a sudden nostalgia for those distant days when I was a dirty-kneed little tomboy; nobody would have described me as sweet and feminine then.

Hugh seemed to have already lost interest but Mike wanted to know how we'd got hold of the cigarettes.

'We used to say they were for our big brother.'

'I don't imagine they believed that for a moment.' Mike sounded surprisingly disapproving.

'I don't suppose it did them much harm,' said Alithea. She was leaning against the sink, which was, as usual, full of dirty dishes, smoking one of Hugh's cigarettes in her long cigarette holder. I noticed she was wearing the nail varnish I particularly admired which Fiona had identified as Peggy Sage's Pale Cream. I thought I might ask for some for Christmas but who could be persuaded to give it to me? I desperately needed to have some spending money, not just for nail varnish but for clothes and bus fares, so I could meet Fiona in the holidays, in other words, independence.

Hugh paced up and down smoking; he seemed gloomy. Feeling sorry for him, I asked when his play was going to be broadcast.

'Well it's not exactly my play,' he said with a little snigger that made me dislike him again. 'It's a translation of *The Clouds* by Aristophanes'

Mike had flung himself into a chair and was smoking one of his own cigarettes from a crumpled packet.

'Christ!' he suddenly shouted. He'd dropped some burning ash on his already rather holey grey flannels.

'Oh Mike, not again!' said Alithea, sounding quite wifely for once. 'You'll definitely have to get some new ones now.'

'Do you have to blaspheme?' said Hugh. 'Some of us mind quite a lot you know.'

'You,' said Mike, 'are a whited sepulchre; that's what you are. All this church going and then you translate that filthy play. I hope you won't listen to it, Dilly.' I wasn't sure whether he was joking or not.

'And you,' said Hugh, 'despite all your atheistic talk, are just a Welsh puritan at heart.'

'Boys! Boys!' said Alithea. She took another drag on her cigarette and blew a series of smoke rings. 'What will you be doing in the holidays Dilly? Apart of course from all your reading. Will you be going to lots of parties?' I felt amazed that she could have so little idea of what my home life was like.

'Hardly,' I said. 'There aren't too many parties in a little town like ours.'

'Where is it exactly that you live?'

I told her.

'Oh yes, I know,' said Hugh surprisingly. 'My mother was at school with the Vicar's wife. It's apparently rather a dead end hole.' He turned to Alithea. 'You know those ugly little towns in the Pas de Calais? Well imagine one of those with no boulangerie, no patisserie, no charcuterie.'

'My God!' said Mike, ignoring Hugh's strictures on blasphemy. 'No boulangerie, no patisserie, no charcuterie!' - pronouncing all the French words in exaggerated imitation of Hugh's accent - 'How on earth do they manage? Actually,' he went on, 'I believe there's a very interesting Saxon church. I keep meaning to go over on the bus and have a look at it.'

'We could all go,' said Alithea. 'We'll be back here soon after New Year. If Hugh can borrow one of his father's cars he could call on his mother's friend while you...we look at the church and we could call on you too Dilly. You are on the phone, aren't you?' I gave them my home telephone number with a mixture of delight and terror. I longed for them to come, but the thought of them all crowding into our regrettably bourgeois bungalow and being entertained by my parents, made me curl up inside. However I thought it would probably come to nothing.

'Well,' said Mike, suddenly springing up out of his chair, 'Opening time - I'm off.'

'You're going to the pub?' said Alithea in a tone that from anyone less sophisticated might have sounded like disapproval.

'That's right. I'm taking my sixth-form history group out for an end of term drink.'

'I see, and I assume no one else is invited.'

'You assume correctly. This is an all-male outing. Anyway, as a Welsh puritan, I don't approve of women going to pubs.'

'That's not amusing.'

'It's not meant to be, but no doubt Dave Whatley will be disappointed, judging by the way he was leering at you the other evening. Bye Dilly, see you in the New Year.' He sauntered out grinning to himself. I didn't know whether he meant in the holidays or next term but anyway I was disappointed. If he'd waited a minute we could have gone together. I didn't actually expect he would kiss me again but there was always a chance. I rather hoped he might be waiting for me outside but by the time I'd gathered up my books and left the house he'd disappeared. Then, as I came round the West front of the cathedral, I saw my parent's car was already outside the boarding house. Clutching the books, I started to run.

My mother was sitting in the tatty armchair in Mazzy's study, drinking a cup of tea. She'd apparently had what she always described as 'one of my dizzy spells.' Matron came and removed the tray looking rather tight-lipped. She didn't approve of my mother. I don't think she believed in her illnesses and made it plain she felt sorry for my father. Fortunately for me the little drama had distracted attention from my lateness.

My father and I loaded my luggage into the car.

'*Nausea*,' he said, catching sight of the Sartre. 'Whatever next! I hope,' he went on, 'you're not going to spend all your holidays with your head in a book. Try to be some company for your mother and stop her complaining to me all the time. And another thing, it's time you learned to cook, then we wouldn't have to have all this tinned stuff.'

'Well, I know how to make spaghetti bolognese.'

'I wasn't talking about foreign food. Ask your Aunty Joyce for her recipe for steak and kidney pie, but not in your mother's hearing.'

Once in the car my mother recovered rapidly. She was looking forward to having me home. She chatted on happily about plans for a shopping expedition and having some people round one evening now that I was there to help her. She was also full of the new Methodist Minister and his wife. I was still feeling rather resentful about this man's unwanted advice over my choice of university. But I began to feel more warmly towards his wife when my mother, after saying the couple had 'absolutely no money' and two young children, added that, in spite of this, the wife hadn't 'let herself go'.

'She does her hair up very nicely in a little sort of bun; it looks very smart. You must ask her how she does it, Dilly.' I thought that at least this might make my mother stop nagging me about a perm.

'Perhaps they'd like a baby-sitter some evening,' I suggested, temporarily roused from the lethargy that always overcame me when my mother started talking about local affairs. My mother agreed that they probably would.

'Good! Then I could actually earn some money.'

'Oh no! You couldn't possibly expect to be paid. I told you, they're terribly hard up.'

'What do you want money for anyway?' asked my father. 'I should hope I can afford to keep my own daughter.'

'Other girls earn money,' I said. 'If I wasn't a boarder I could have worked on the Christmas post. For a start I'd like to buy some nail varnish.'

'Nail varnish!' exclaimed my father, as I knew he would. I

remembered what Mike had said about the same old arguments. *Hell is other people* I thought. The grey fog of boredom seeped back through my brain, filling my whole being with inertia.

'Oh!' said my mother, 'I nearly forgot. Guess what? You're invited to the Vicarage on New Year's Eve. Apparently the young people are having a party.' The grey fog retreated slightly. The Vicar's daughter went to a real boarding school and I only knew her by sight. I couldn't think why I was suddenly being asked to her party.

'Of course it's because you got into Oxford,' said my mother. 'Someone told the Vicar's wife and she rang up. She says she's dying to meet you.'

I thought this was all most peculiar. Was I some kind of freak to be exhibited? But still, it was a party. I remembered that the Vicar's wife was a friend of Hugh's mother and thought for one wild moment that perhaps he and Alithea and Mike might be invited. Then I realised this was unlikely; they would be classed as grown-ups not 'young people', as my mother referred to teenagers.

'However,' said my mother, with a sidelong look at my father. 'I don't think you'll be able to go, dear. It says 'black tie' and that means an evening dress.'

'Black tie!' my father exploded, 'Evening dress! How old are these children?'

'Well, I'll need an evening dress next year,' I pointed out.

We drew up outside the front door. Once inside, the comfort of squashy armchairs and a cheerful fire made me forget for the time being how dull home could be.

'Don't worry,' said my mother, while my father was putting the car away in the garage. 'I'll get round him.' Which she did.

No sooner had this decision been made however than my mother began to have regrets.

'The Stewarts will be very disappointed not to see you at Hogmanay,' she said. Mrs Stewart was a friend of my mother's because, so I assumed, she was a fellow Scot. I could think of no other possible reason for continuing the acquaintance. The Stewarts, as usual, had been invited to see in the New Year at our house. Traditionally this would take the form of drinking coffee, eating mince pies and listening to Jimmy Shand and his Band on the wireless until Big Ben struck twelve. At this point my aunts usually rang up to wish us a Happy New Year which always made my mother cry. Remembering this ritual made the impending party seem an exciting alternative although I couldn't imagine what it would be like and, as the time drew nearer, had increasing moments of panic at the thought of it.

PART 3

Christmas 1955

CHAPTER FIFTEEN

At the service on Christmas morning, the new Minister, rather surprisingly, treated his bewildered congregation to an excerpt from Milton's *Ode on the Morning of Christ's Nativity*. This made me feel more kindly towards him, despite his unwanted advice about universities. My father was less impressed.

'Folk had no idea what he was on about,' he complained. My mother and I exchanged superior smiles.

'Apparently,' said my mother, 'he and his wife have smartened up the Manse like billy-o, even though they haven't much money. They've got rid of all that dark wallpaper and painted one wall lime green – rather fun!'

'Well don't start wanting lime green walls in our house,' said my father.

On Boxing Day we traditionally went to Uncle Frank's to help eat up their enormous turkey, the pork pies and the spiced beef. My mother dreaded this carnivorous feast but my father insisted and after the deathly hush of Christmas afternoon at home I was longing for life and people. Even if Uncle Frank and Aunty Joyce could be tiresome it would be nice to talk to Frances and it would be interesting to see Ellen's baby. I told myself that if I got married I would have a big family and Christmas would be a lively affair. I thought four children would be about right. Of course I couldn't have known then that my fourth child would turn out to be twins.

We exchanged Christmas presents as soon as we arrived at the farm. Aunty Joyce was not an inspired present giver. A box of pale blue notepaper ornamented with forget-me-nots had been last year's offering. The year before had been worse, padded coat hangers with knitted covers she'd bought at the Chapel Sale of Work. This year, as she handed me a floppy parcel wrapped in holly-patterned paper, I braced myself for another handmade horror and had my fixed smile ready. I was all the more amazed therefore when I discovered the jade green sweater I'd just unwrapped was made of Orlon. It had fashionable bat-winged sleeves and could never have been made by any local knitter.

'Is it all right?' she asked. 'Amber got it for me. It seems she has a friend who has a shop. It's supposed to wash well.'

'It's super!' I said beaming. Amber herself gave me a pair of sheer nylons.

'Those won't last five minutes,' said Aunty Joyce.

'She's not allowed them at school you know,' said my mother but I thanked Amber with genuine enthusiasm.

'Home again, Amber!' said my mother. 'You were lucky not to be on duty at Christmas.'

'I've got to leave tomorrow though,' Amber said. 'New Year's a busy time for us.' She looked amused as if her words had a meaning we hadn't altogether understood. My mother looked at me and raised her eyebrows.

Conversation at the dinner table was mainly about Ellen's new baby. Always one to do the right thing, Ellen had produced a son six weeks earlier. Francis Wesley or Young Frank, as he was always to be called, was of course, a perfect baby and Ellen, apart from on the one or two occasions when she had inexplicably ignored Aunty Joyce's advice, was a perfect mother. Ellen and Brian had spent Christmas Day at the farm and were coming round for tea later after visiting Brian's parents.

'I hear she had rather a difficult time,' my mother murmured to Aunty Joyce. They dropped their voices and muttered sinister things about the horrors of childbirth. Uncle Frank and my father talked loudly about the economy while Frances and I strained to eavesdrop on our mothers. After all it was as well to know what you might be letting yourself in for in the future.

The reproductive system of the rabbit, part of the O level Biology syllabus and the only sex education we'd had so far, wasn't entirely adequate. There were too many details missing. We'd found it all fairly incredible anyway. Frances had at first insisted there must be another way for humans that we hadn't been told about. I'd finally persuaded her to face the truth but still... our parents. We couldn't bear to imagine it!

Now I thought about Ellen. Surely, I thought, like the heroine of Jane's novel, she had 'good child-bearing hips'. She was a well-built girl. 'Hefty' was my mother's rather unkind description but it seemed this hadn't saved her from fearful agonies to judge by the older women's expressions.

'Well, Dilly,' said Uncle Frank thinking it was high time to change the subject. 'Three more years of study, eh!'

'You'll be quite an old maid by the time you've finished,' said Aunty Joyce.

'At twenty-two!' said my mother. 'Hardly!'

'You're not an old maid until you're twenty-five,' said Amber. 'So don't give up hope yet, our Frances!' Frances reddened and looked miserable.

'Oh thirty surely!' said my mother - she herself had been married at twenty-nine.

'I tell you, Amber,' said Uncle Frank, 'you'll never get a husband if you can't learn to be a bit less forward. Too much to say for yourself, you have.' I wondered if this was true. Amber didn't seem to have any problem attracting men. I remembered Barry Wilson in the stackyard; what had happened to him?

'Three more years of study!' repeated Amber, 'How can you bear it?'

'Well,' said my mother, 'you'll have your nursing exams.' Amber gave her a curious sliding glance with her green eyes and said nothing. My mother looked at her sharply but no one else seemed to notice anything.

'Dilly's been invited to the Vicarage, to a Hogmanay party,' said my mother, perhaps wanting to show that I wasn't inevitably headed for learned spinsterhood.

'New Year at the Vicarage!' said Uncle Frank. 'Going up in the world are we?'

'It seems to be since she got into Oxford,' said my mother, with what was meant to be a deprecating laugh. 'People are funny. I was invited to a charity coffee morning at Redbourne Manor the other week for the first time ever.' I felt deeply ashamed of my mother and it got worse.

'Of course,' she said, 'I didn't really care for the new people who have bought it. Rather a Jewy looking couple I thought.' I felt I must speak or I would hate myself, and also my mother, forever.

'My English teacher is partly Jewish,' I said, 'and she's terribly clever and interesting.'

'Oh well, they're clever all right, the Jews' said Uncle Frank. 'Of course it was terrible what Hitler did but...' His unspoken words seemed to hover in the air above the remains of the reheated

Christmas pudding.

'Is Miss Carr Jewish?' said my mother. 'You've never mentioned it before.'

'No, Mrs Davis, the new one.'

'Davis,' said Uncle Frank, 'Davis? That's not a Jewish name.'

'Her husband's Welsh,' I said. It was just bliss to mention him.

'The Welsh are a rum lot and all,' said Uncle Frank. Aunty Joyce looked nervous. She probably feared that Uncle Frank might thoughtlessly start on the Scots, though he was just as likely to expound on the peculiarities of Lancastrians or even the inhabitants of the West Riding.

'Nice singing voices though,' he conceded, 'musical, the Welsh. Still, Jews are often musical too.'

'Yes indeed,' said my mother. I hoped I'd made her feel guilty, but perhaps it was the mention of Hitler that made her want to compensate for her previous remark, 'Look at Mendelssohn.' We all contemplated Mendelssohn for a moment or two in silence and then Aunty Joyce, probably fearing my mother was going to turn all intellectual on them, said,

'How about a nice cup of tea? Put the kettle on Amber. Goodness! Look at the time! We'll have Ellen and Brian round with that blessed baby before we've got the pots washed.'

Ellen and her husband duly arrived and everyone indulged in an orgy of baby worship. Young Frank was charmingly plump and rosy and just beginning to smile. Perhaps it was worth the indescribable agonies of childbirth if this was the end result. Even Amber seemed quite taken with him.

'*Twenty tiny fingers,*' she started singing, '*Twenty tiny toes,*'

'What's this rubbish now?' said Uncle Frank.

'*The Stargazers*,' said Amber. Uncle Frank shook his head. 'Radio Luxemburg' she explained, winking at me. I wasn't sure this growing complicity was justified but I was quite flattered.

'Would you like to hold him, Dilly?' asked Ellen.

'Don't give him to Dilly. She'd be sure to drop him,' said my father but Ellen handed the baby over.

'Support his head, dear,' said my mother hovering anxiously. I was enchanted by him and for a few moments I almost envied Ellen but then she handed me my Christmas present, an embroidered dressing-table set.

'For your bottom drawer,' she said with a sly smile. It seemed to embody the whole dreariness of conventional married life. The Davises had shown me that marriage didn't have to involve embroidered dressing-table mats. I was sure Alithea had never had a bottom drawer.

'That girl is up to something.' My father and I had no need to ask which girl my mother meant. We were driving slowly home in the dark of Boxing Day evening.

'What sort of friend owns what sort of shop? That's a lovely jersey Dilly but she can't have bought that on a student nurse's pay.'

'It was from Aunty Joyce and Uncle Frank.'

'I daresay but Joyce would never have paid what it really cost. Amber must have got it cheaply. What did she do to get it I wonder.'

'Now that's enough!' said my father. 'She may be a bit wild but she's been properly brought up.'

'Still,' said my mother, 'you must admit, the girl is over-sexed.' This was going too far. My father exploded so violently that even my mother was silenced. For the rest of the journey I sat in the back of the car wondering if I was also over-sexed. I spent a lot of time when I should have been revising, fantasising about Mike and some of my fantasies would have horrified my mother.

CHAPTER SIXTEEN

'You can't walk in that get-up,' said my father on New Year's Eve. 'I'll drive you down to the Vicarage.' I was wearing my new evening dress, sea-green net over taffeta. The silver sandals I was going to change into at the Vicarage were in my school shoebag. I swung it nervously while I waited for my father to get the car out and nearly knocked over a vase of bronze chrysanthemums that had been bought that morning in honour of the Stewarts' impending visit.

At the door of the sitting room I looked back. A coal fire was blazing brightly and the trolley was set out with the best china. Home had never seemed so attractive, so comfortably safe and familiar. Then, just as I reached the hall, the front door bell ding-donged.

'Yoo hoo!' cried Mrs Stewart. 'It's only little old me and my better half.'

'I say!' Mr Stewart pretended to be overcome by my appearance. 'So who's this stranger? This elegant young lady.'

'Goodness me!' said Mrs Stewart. 'It seems no time at all since you were so high!'

Perhaps I was glad to be going out after all.

At the Vicarage my father was so outraged by the sight of some boys, whom he judged to be no older than seventeen, wearing dinner jackets and drinking sherry, that he nearly took me straight home again.

'Remember, no alcohol, promise.' I promised. 'Have a nice time then. I'll be here sharp on midnight.'

'It may go on a bit longer.'

'Never! It's Sunday tomorrow, remember. Even...' He stopped himself probably realising that it wouldn't be very tactful to start on the regrettable laxity of the Established Church towards keeping the Sabbath Day holy, on the very doorstep of the Vicarage.

He left me standing in the hall, which was nearly as vast as the Deanery's but warmer. I remembered that the Vicar's wife, who was said to have 'money of her own,' had had central heating installed, which most people agreed was 'quite unnecessary' and even 'unhealthy'.

'Sherry?' said the Vicar's wife, coming forward to greet me. I stammered a refusal. I wondered how close a friend she was to Hugh's mother and whether I should say I knew Hugh but there was something so intimidating about her tightly waved iron-grey hair and upright bearing that I couldn't find the courage.

'Monica!' she called to her daughter, 'This is Philippa. Get her some orange squash can you?' I decided to leave this uncorrected. Philippa made me sound a bit more normal. 'Perhaps you two know each other? Philippa is local. I expect you've seen her about.' Monica denied all knowledge of me, which I was sure, was a lie. I had certainly seen her about when she was home on holiday from boarding school. She usually wore a silk headscarf tied under her chin like royalty. When I was younger I'd longed to get to know her because at that time she'd had a pony.

'Anyway' the Vicar's wife continued, 'she's frightfully brainy and has just got into Cambridge.'

'Oxford,' I said.

'Well I knew it was one or the other. Now introduce her to some nice boys.' Up to this point Monica had been looking at me with indifference. Now, I could see this was changing to fear and loathing.

'Oh,' I said, 'I'm not really at all brainy. Everyone was surprised when I got in...' But it was too late. Monica stalked off. I supposed I was meant to follow and trailed after her into a huge drawing-room. The bay window was filled by a sixfoot Christmas tree covered in multi-coloured lights and there was a log-fire roaring away superfluously in the baronial style fireplace. Groups of girls stood around, decked out in net or taffeta and pink lipstick; they were giggling together and giving surreptitious glances towards groups of boys who ignored them.

'This is Philippa,' said Monica, taking me straight over to one of these groups who had been boasting about their fathers' cars. 'She lives locally. She's frightfully brainy and has just got into Oxford or Cambridge; I can't remember which. I expect she'll tell you all about it.' So threatened, they all uneasily made their excuses and removed themselves as far away from me as possible. I spent what seemed like hours wandering round from group to group, standing on the edge pretending to be terribly interested in what people were saying and smiling when they all laughed, although most of the time the jokes were incomprehensible to an outsider. For the sake of something to do and because I just couldn't face any more orange squash, I accepted some fruit punch but it didn't taste like the Bishop's and I rather suspected that it might have been alcoholic.

Eventually I took refuge in the lavatory. It was quite nice in there. It was an old-fashioned one with a willow-patterned bowl and a broad wooden seat. There were some old copies of Punch on a shelf and I entertained myself looking at cartoons until I heard someone shout it was supper time.

Mince pies and sausage rolls interspersed with sprigs of holly were spread out on a large polished table. There were also turkey sandwiches and bits of cheese and tinned pineapple skewered on cocktail sticks stuck in a half grapefruit. Various people exclaimed at this novel arrangement.

'Oh it was Monica's idea,' said her mother. 'Very fancy!'

I was in the middle of eating a bridge roll with cheese spread when the Vicar's wife summoned me into the kitchen to come and meet a friend of hers. Standing by the Aga was a tweedy-looking woman. I wondered for a moment whether she was Hugh's mother but then the Vicar's wife said,

'My friend is thinking about sending her daughter to your school as a boarder. Now tell me, Philippa. What kind of girls are the other boarders?'

I thought about this for a moment. I knew there were girls whose boarding fees were paid by their local authorities. Although never explicitly stated, we gathered it was because they had problems at home. I had the sense not to mention this.

'Quite a few are farmers' daughters,' I began. I could see this didn't impress the Vicar's wife but her friend seemed eager to be persuaded.

'The fees at St Ethelreda's keep going up and up.' she complained. 'And after all, Philippa here is going to Cambridge.'

'Oxford,' I said but was ignored. I had begun to realise why I had been invited to this party.

'There's Caroline,' I said to encourage her. 'Her father's a vicar.' They immediately tried to work out who exactly Caroline's father was. He was eventually identified.

'Very low,' murmured the Vicar's wife. 'My dear,' she continued to her friend, more loudly. 'Believe me, a good school is the important thing. All sorts of people go to Oxford and Cambridge nowadays. (Here we go again, I thought). Listen I'll tell you something. A very

CHRISTMAS 1955

dear friend of mine has a son who has recently graduated, a very brilliant young man. He was terribly in love with a girl he met there. He knew her brothers at Winchester.' (I stayed as quiet as possible). 'Anyway this girl fell for some very working-class boy, rather good-looking I understand but with absolutely nothing else to recommend him. I think she may even have married him. Poor Hugh is completely distraught and won't settle to anything. He's still mooning round after her. His mother is so worried.'

'But where did she meet this boy?'

'At Oxford, that's what I'm telling you. A miner's son I believe, on some sort of scholarship.'

'But how on earth did she get to know him?'

'Oh well. She comes from a very odd family. Left wing intellectuals, father Jewish, you know the type. Apparently they were both mixed up in university politics.'

'Well it sounds to me as if your friend's son had a lucky escape.'

They suddenly remembered me.

'Goodness me, Philippa. I forgot you were here. Do go, dear. I didn't mean to keep you away from the fun.' I left obediently in search of fun.

As nobody seemed willing to include me in whatever fun was going I returned to the lavatory. I glanced through the cartoons again while thinking over what I had just heard.

It seemed odd to hear Mike described as a boy. 'Working-class boy' sounded like the Teddy boys who hung around the street corners with drainpipe trousers and greasy quiffs. 'Nothing much else to recommend him.' How dare she! And then Hugh, 'Terribly in love.' I didn't think Hugh was capable of such violent emotions. But, 'Still waters run deep,' as Matron was fond of saying about quiet girls whom she suspected of various kinds of deviant behaviour.

'Someone's been in the bog for ages,' said a boy's voice. He banged on the door. I slid out blushing while they stared at me.

The fruit cup, or whatever it was, started to take effect on the party. It grew louder; dancing began. A boy with horn-rimmed glasses was in charge of the gramophone and people started shouting out requests. He put on something very loud and raucous.

We're gonna rock, we're gonna rock around the clock tonight. There was some screaming and the Vicar put his head round the door but went away again immediately. People started jiving. I had never actually seen anyone do this before so it was quite interesting but the record suddenly stopped. A broad-shouldered fair boy, rather less pimply than most and with a faint resemblance to Jane's favourite, Andrew Strong, had lifted the arm of the record player.

'Monica and I want something smoochy.' There was some protest but what he said obviously went. Monica and he were indeed smooching and so were a number of others. A rather flabby boy suddenly asked me to dance. I had seen one or two other girls refuse him. He grasped me with clammy hands and steered me onto the floor. I hadn't a clue what I was meant to be doing and I don't think he had much idea either. We stumbled around to the music for a bit.

On the record-player someone that my father would have described as 'one of those blasted American crooners' sang *Hey you with the stars in your eyes.* Obviously feeling he needed to make conversation, the flabby boy said,

'Have you taken your O levels yet?' I was furious. How could he think I was that young? Me, who was suffering hopeless passion for an unhappily married Socialist-atheist and was reading, or anyway just about to read, Sartre, as soon as I could find the time.

'Good heavens, yes,' I said. 'I'm going to university soon.' After that he abandoned me at the first opportunity.

The dreadful evening was coming to an end. Somebody switched on the wireless. I felt quite homesick when I heard the sound of Jimmy Shand and his Band. Big Ben started to strike.

'It's 1956 everyone,' screamed Monica. There was some cheering and we got in a big circle for *Auld Lang Syne*. I found myself next to the clammy-handed boy. We escaped from each other as soon as possible and I went in search of my coat.

Soon afterwards I found my father standing in the hall looking disapproving. I felt a rush of affection for him.

'Well come on then,' he said. 'Have you said your goodbyes?' The Vicar's wife was standing just behind us.

'Thank you very much for inviting me.'

'Well, I hope you didn't feel too out of things, dear.' So she'd noticed.

'It was very interesting.'

'Interesting!' said my father when we got outside. 'What's that supposed to mean?'

'It was the best I could do.'

'You didn't enjoy it then?'

'They were all snooty boarding school types.'

'Well don't say that to your mother. You don't want to go upsetting her.' I promised I wouldn't.

CHAPTER SEVENTEEN

'From what you said yesterday I got the impression you didn't enjoy the party very much.'

It was Monday morning and we were sitting over breakfast. My father had already left for the office and, with him at last out of the way, my mother was hoping for a more detailed account of the party than she'd been able to get from me so far. During the previous day I'd given some thought to how much I should reveal. If I said too much about my sense of social inadequacy this would only make my mother depressed and nervous. This was never a good idea and certainly not at New Year when she would be missing her sisters in Edinburgh. They would be visiting neighbours, eating black bun and drinking hot ginger wine even, perhaps, when pressed, taking 'a wee dram, just for the once'.

I decided to make the experience sound trivial and amusing. I gave a little laugh. 'Well, there was quite a bit of smooching.' This was a serious mistake; I ought to have known my mother better.

'Smooching?'

'You know - necking, kissing'. My mother gasped.

'But what did the Vicar say?'

'Oh he wasn't there most of the time. He just put his head around the door when the music got a bit loud.'

'And his wife?'

'She was in the kitchen talking to a friend. They called me in to ask about the High School. The friend is wondering about sending her daughter to our school as a boarder. I think that was why I was invited.' I hoped this would distract her. Normally my mother would have been pleased and interested by this but she was too outraged by the idea of immorality at the Vicarage to take it in.

'Well I think that was most irresponsible of them. And Daddy tells me they were serving alcohol.'

'Just sherry when people arrived, though there might have been a bit in the fruit cup.'

'I hope you didn't take any?'

'I had orange squash,' I said, almost truthfully.

'And that,' said my mother, 'is the Church of England for you. You'd have been better off staying at home. The Stewarts may not be very exciting but they're decent people, very kind and that's what counts, isn't it?'

I supposed it did count for something but I hoped I would never have to resign myself to such low expectations of friendship. I was also a bit worried. My mother had a way of making me say more than I intended. I never wanted to go to another party at the Vicarage but I didn't want her spreading it around that I'd been shocked. It would be unfortunate to be thought prudish as well as brainy.

'Don't say too much about it, will you?'

'I'm not going to waste time complaining to them if that's what you mean. I hear the daughter can wind her father round her little finger. If you ask me she's quite out of control.' (I knew she would talk.) 'Now what can we do today to cheer ourselves up?' I guessed she would be proposing a bus trip into the nearest large town and a cup of coffee at the Tudor Café, but at that moment the phone rang.

'It's somebody for you, Dilly. Anthea or something.' My mother seemed puzzled but not hostile. 'She sounds awfully nice,' Sounding 'awfully nice' almost certainly meant what was called 'well-spoken'. My heart started thumping. I rushed into the hall and grabbed the phone. As I'd guessed, it was Alithea.

'Hello Dilly! Did you have a nice Christmas?' The polite preliminaries over, Alithea started to explain. 'We're in your area. We've just dropped Hugh off at the Vicarage to see his mother's friend while Mike and I look at this Saxon church but we've promised to rescue him in half an hour.' At this point the pips went. 'Oh damn!' There was a clanking of pennies into the box. 'Half an hour – but then we're going on to see this artist friend of his, Hugh's that is, and we wondered if you'd like to come with us?'

The dreadful party faded away like a bad dream. My mother was disappointed but bore up bravely.

'I don't suppose they'd think of asking me along as well?' she said half-hopefully but pretending it was a joke. I muttered something evasive. 'Oh well, I know young people like to be on their own sometimes.' I felt sorry for her and this made me feel guilty and resentful. Why couldn't she make some kind of life for herself instead of depending on me or settling for boring people like the Stewarts?

I was in my bedroom admiring myself in my Orlon sweater and experimenting with some lipstick when the doorbell ding-donged. What, I thought, would Alithea think of people who had a chiming doorbell? I suddenly looked round my room. It was unlikely they'd come up, but suppose they did? I seized a picture of Harry Llewellyn on Foxhunter winning a gold medal at the 1952 Olympics and put it face down in a drawer. That pale blue paint and flowered wallpaper would have to go as soon as I could persuade my parents to redecorate but there was nothing I could do at the moment. Why had I still got all my Beatrix Potter collection in the bookcase and *Just William*? Why those glass animals on the windowsill? My whole past life was here.

My room must be changed to reflect the new me. But now it was more urgent to go down and make sure my mother wasn't saying anything too embarrassing. I defiantly left my hair loose and stormed downstairs.

'Here she is,' cried my mother, 'all harum–scarum, last minute as usual!' They were all standing around in the kitchen. I couldn't believe they were actually there in these prosaic surroundings. Mike was standing by the sink looking out over a garden transformed by the bright frosty morning from its usual wintry dreariness. Hugh leant nonchalantly against the red Formica topped table while Alithea was energetically refusing coffee.

'Really,' said my mother, 'It won't take a minute. The kettle's boiling.' She hovered over the tin of Maxwell House, teaspoon at the ready.

'No, we must go. Our friends are expecting us for lunch. Hugh got rather held up at the Vicarage.'

'Oh the Vicarage!' said my mother. I was terrified she would start on the party.

'Perhaps when we bring Dilly back,' said Alithea.

'Oh yes,' said my mother, 'and then we can all be more comfortable in the drawing room.' I wished she wouldn't call it that. It was true my grandparents' Edinburgh house, now lived in by my aunts, had a drawing room - but in a bungalow?

Mike turned round,

'Dilly!' he exclaimed, 'you look smashing. She looks even prettier out of school uniform, doesn't she?' he said, turning to the others. Alithea smiled; Hugh looked impassive. He obviously didn't want to be associated with such extravagant flattery. Mike addressed my mother, 'You must be so proud, having such a pretty, intelligent daughter.' My mother looked around in a confused way as if she expected to find another, more attractive, daughter lurking in some corner of the kitchen, before she realised he meant me. Normally she'd have regarded such effusiveness with suspicion. 'Laying it on a bit thick' she'd have called it. It was a tribute to Mike's charm that he could get away with that sort of thing. I didn't for a moment compare it to Mr Stewart's 'Elegant young lady.' Now my mother looked at me again. Had she perhaps underestimated my looks?

'Your hair's a bit of a mess dear.' She looked at Alithea. 'I suppose you have a natural wave like me. I'm always telling Dilly she should have a perm.' No one was listening to her. We were all heading for the door.

In the drive was a most amazing car, low slung and gleaming; the kind of car you might see on the cover of a book about the Bright Young Things in the twenties. But I did wonder how there would be enough room for all four of us.

'Hugh's teaching me to drive,' said Alithea. 'Do you mind sitting in the back with Mike, Dilly? I'm afraid it will be a bit of a squash.'

'No, of course not,' I managed to say, almost faint with happiness.

My mother waved us off. She seemed a lonely figure standing there in the doorway and I felt a pang of guilt, which I suppressed.

'What a nice house,' said Mike as we drove out of the gate. I assumed he was just being charming again but he continued, 'so light and I suppose it's what they call "labour-saving." My mother would love it.' He sounded as if he meant it. I was disappointed in him. Also, he was wearing a thick sweater and I was reminded of my earlier comment to Jane about male models in books of knitting patterns. His reference to his mother made me wonder if she'd knitted it, perhaps as a Christmas present. I wondered where he and Alithea had spent the holiday; I knew they'd been away and found it difficult to imagine Alithea in a miner's terraced house. I pictured Mike's white-haired old mother wrapping up the sweater with tears in her eyes knowing that she wasn't going to see her only son at Christmas... On the other hand if Alithea's father was Jewish did they actually celebrate Christian festivals in her family? And then as Mike and Alithea were atheists... At this point even my imagination failed me.

(As I'd already worked out, Mike could only be about six or seven years older than me, I don't know why I imagined his mother as frail and ancient. The woman was probably barely fifty.)

I was roused from these speculations by a sudden juddering. Alithea's driving was rather erratic and we suddenly seemed to be proceeding by a series of leaps and jolts. Mike put his arm round me to steady me and I immediately forgave him his taste in domestic architecture and any slight resemblance he might have to a male model.

'Let the clutch out slowly, Allie,' said Hugh.

'Can you drive?' I asked. I'd stopped calling Mike 'Mr Davis' since the Saturday afternoon we had spent together but I couldn't quite bring myself to say 'Mike' especially not in his wife's hearing. His arm was still resting lightly on my shoulder and I didn't want to break the spell and have him take it away but I wondered why he wasn't teaching Alithea to drive himself.

'Yes, I learnt in the army, in Germany during National Service, but Hugh here is a bit touchy about who's allowed to drive his Alvis.'

'It's not my Alvis. It's my father's. He collects vintage cars.' This last remark was presumably for my information. 'It's not an army lorry Mike and he's rather particular about who drives it.'

'Which, I suppose, is why Allie is being allowed to destroy the gears.'

'Well my father knows Alithea.' Remembering the information I'd gathered the previous evening, I felt this was rather a nasty remark. Cautiously I leaned a little towards Mike and he tightened his hold on me. Alithea obviously felt it was time to change the conversation. She half turned round and the car slid towards the frosty verge.

'For God's sake keep your eyes on the road,' said Mike. 'Do you want to kill us all?' Even Hugh was too shaken to protest about the blasphemy. He suggested they should change places and that Alithea could learn the art of driving by observation.

Once this change had been made Alithea turned round again and I expected Mike to remove his arm but he stared at her rather defiantly; she didn't appear to notice anything.

'These people we're going to have lunch with, Dilly, are very interesting. Well at least Ben is. He's a very talented artist and has spent some time in America where apparently he's picked up a lot of extraordinary new ideas about painting. Danny, his friend - well Danny's very interesting too in his way. Ben met him in a pub in the East End. He hasn't had much formal education but he's very keen on learning about painting and devoted to Ben so he does all the domestic things - he's a very good cook; so Ben can just concentrate on his art.'

'They sound like characters in a novel,' I said. I hoped this didn't sound silly but I'd certainly never come across this sort of thing in real life, and I found it amazing to think such people might be living locally. 'How do you know them?' I added more sensibly.

'Oh, Ben was at school with Hugh and my brothers. At least he was until he was expelled.'

'Well, encouraged to leave early,' said Hugh. 'You do tend to exaggerate, Alithea.' I looked sideways at Mike. He looked gloomy - almost bad-tempered.

'Why are they here?' I'd always thought artists lived in London or perhaps somewhere picturesque in the South of England. My mother often complained that our district was a cultural desert.

'Oh they found this place to rent very cheaply. In fact doesn't your mother's friend, the one you saw this morning, doesn't she know the people who own it?'

'Probably,' said Hugh. 'I expect Ben's mother was panicking about him again. She wanted to get him out of London. I don't think she realised he'd take Danny with him.'

'Well anyway,' said Alithea. 'It allows Ben the absolute peace he needs for his work.'

At this point Mike made a noise that sounded like something I'd seen written in Victorian novels, 'Pshaw!' Once again I felt there were things going on that I didn't quite understand. I also began to feel rather nervous about meeting these strange people. I wished I could just be driven around all day with Mike's arm around my shoulders, admiring the sunlight on the whitened fields and the trees and hedges all furry with thick frost.

We began to climb from the flatlands up a low chalky escarpment. After a few miles driving along the ridge, Hugh turned sharply in under a pretend ruined gateway. It had a gothic arch and both sides had been left artistically jagged. There was a little room built into one side of it pretending to be a gatehouse but the pointed window was grimy and cracked. The drive led across an expanse of rough grass towards the castellated façade of the house.

'Gothic revival,' I said, pleased to be able to identify the architecture.

'Bellingthorpe Castle' said Hugh.

'Although,' said Mike quietly, 'it's no more a castle than that fairy in there is Leonardo da Vinci.' Alithea looked at him frowning but I think she'd only half-heard him. I had heard but only half understood.

'I hope,' said Alithea, 'you're not going to be difficult, Mike.'

'Dilly and I reserve the right to be as difficult as we like. Don't we Dilly?' I felt torn. Of course I wanted to make common cause with Mike. On the other hand I was about to meet some real bohemians at last and I didn't want to be thought dull and bourgeois. I smiled at Alithea, trying to look as if I thought they were both joking and I was joining in. The car scrunched to a stop on the weedy gravel at the front of the house. No one came out to greet us but when Hugh pushed the great studded front door it swung open easily and we walked across the black and white tiled hallway towards the stairs. Unidentifiable things were standing around, covered in dustsheets. Every sound echoed in the silence.

'Hallo,' called Hugh. Somewhere on the landing, a door opened.

'Come on up,' someone called back. We headed up the stairs towards the open door and I found myself in the most wonderful room I had ever seen.

CHAPTER EIGHTEEN

My first impression was of sunlight, music and sunlight. Something joyful was being played on the record player. Later I found it was a Mozart horn concerto, but at that moment it just seemed part of the sunshine. Then, as my eyes adjusted to the brilliance, I saw the white room, the arched windows with their fine tracery of panes, the view of the frosty park outside, the flames from the wood fire roaring up the chimney and the multiplicity of strange and brightly-coloured objects filling the room. Coming, as I did, from a world of brown furniture I was particularly entranced by some scarlet painted kitchen chairs.

A short young man with longish dark hair was standing at an easel. Rather pretentiously, he was wearing a blue artist's smock. Of course I didn't think it pretentious at the time; it was what I expected an artist to look like. At least we were spared the beret. He made no effort to welcome us and in fact seemed to resent the interruption caused by our arrival. Then he flung down his brush and said

'Hopeless!' The easel was covered with a series of squiggles; I assumed he was trying out paint and couldn't get the colour he wanted. 'After being so inspired by Pollock in the States,' he said, 'I'm trying to develop in an entirely new direction but I can't seem to get there.' As I'd never heard of Jackson Pollock this meant nothing to me but I did at least now realise that the squiggles on the canvas were intended to be a painting. He went over to the gramophone and, rather to my regret, stopped the music.

'Hey!' said Mike. 'Don't treat Mozart like that.' But no one took any notice.

*

Some years later, visiting MOMA on a trip to New York, I stop in front of one of Pollock's paintings and recall Ben's struggles. As far as I can remember the squiggles he'd been producing hadn't looked remotely like a genuine Jackson Pollock. Later still however, I find that he had, towards the end of his life, managed to produce some quite convincing Pollock pastiches. Perhaps, by that time, he'd given up hope of ever becoming an original painter.

*

Alithea obviously felt she should try to take Ben seriously.

'Oh,' she said, 'I don't know. From the photographs I've seen of Pollock's work I should say you've managed to grasp the elements of his technique. The danger lies, of course, in being too derivative.' Ben completely ignored her and turned towards Hugh.

'What do you think?'

'What, exactly,' asked Hugh, 'are you trying to achieve?' Ben went off into a long speech full of tonal values, impasto, semi-abstraction and other technical terms. Mike, who was standing behind him, raised his eyebrows at me and grinned. He was clearly indicating, 'What a charlatan!' and I couldn't help smiling back; on the other hand I didn't want to be like people who said Van Gogh couldn't even draw a chair with straight legs. I remembered Alithea telling us that people who said, 'I don't know anything about art, but I know what I like,' were beneath contempt. Until you did know something about art, she had said, you had no right to express any opinion, so I said nothing.

Alithea had wandered off while Ben was absorbed in talking to Hugh and was looking at the paintings hanging all round the walls. I followed her. It was an oddly varied collection. Some reminded me of the posters of Cubist paintings that I seen in the art room at school; there was an angular portrait that looked a bit like a Picasso and then there was a perfectly recognisable but very untidy kitchen table displaying mundane things like a packet of cornflakes portrayed in a style that I described to myself as 'scratchy'.

'His Bratby phase,' Alithea murmured to me. 'I suppose he has a certain skill in pastiche. He'll never find his own talent until he stops being so easily influenced. So far the only thing one can say about his painting is it's eclectic.'

I'd never heard this word before but I thought I could guess what it meant so managed to look intelligent. I remembered Fiona's critical comments on my desk-lid art gallery and wished I'd known the word then.

('I don't have a linking theme Fiona because my tastes are probably more eclectic than yours.' That would have shut her up.)

Alithea had obviously been rather put out. She wasn't used to being ignored and I had the feeling that her previous description of Ben as 'very interesting' and 'a talented artist' was being revised.

'You know,' said Ben, looking at Hugh meaningfully, 'your opinion matters more to me than anyone's.'

'Yes, well,' said Hugh, 'I don't think you should take too much notice of my opinion. Alithea knows a great deal more about painting than I do.' But Ben didn't seem very interested in Alithea or her opinions. Mike, I noticed, was no longer smiling. In fact I thought I had never seen him look so grim.

A door to the side of the fireplace was flung open. A cheerful voice called out, 'Luncheon is served everyone,' and a young man appeared staggering under the weight of a huge tray.

'Quiche Lorraine,' he announced.

'Hallo, Danny,' said Alithea.

'Hallo, darling,' said Danny and then, catching sight of me, 'well what have we here? A golden-haired princess!' I had never encountered the camp manner before and the absurd compliment made me giggle foolishly. I liked Danny immediately; his friendliness was a relief after the intense and gloomy Ben. Mike however didn't appear amused. I had the wild hope that he might be jealous, although this didn't seem very likely. Danny was a strangely elfin-looking creature. In later years when the children watched *Star Trek* I used to look at Mr Spock and be reminded of Danny.

On first inspection I thought quiche Lorraine was something like Aunty Joyce's egg and bacon pie but after a few mouthfuls I realised that good as Aunty Joyce's egg and bacon pie might be, this was something of a different order.

'This one,' said Ben, leaning towards me with a bottle in his hand, 'is a Chinon Blanc but you may prefer the Alsace.' These were the first words he had addressed to me and they did nothing to make me less terrified of him.

'Um, I don't drink,' I muttered.

'Not at all?' He sounded incredulous.

'This Chinon is quite superb,' said Hugh. 'Where on earth did you find it? There can't be a decent wine merchant within miles. Try some, Dilly. You can't not drink when you go up to Oxford.'

'Oh my godfather sent me several cases at Christmas,' said Ben.

'She doesn't have to drink if she doesn't want to,' said Mike. 'Do you have any beer by any chance? I don't have Hugh's sophisticated tastes. It must be because no godfather ever sent me cases of wine for Christmas.'

'All right, all right! Mike,' said Alithea, 'you've made your point.

Just try a little of the Alsace, Dilly. I think you'd like it.' I agreed to try a little and sipped it cautiously. I was disappointed at first; I think I'd expected something rather like lemonade but mysteriously nicer; however after a few sips I got used to it and agreed to try some more.

'Oxford!' said Danny. 'Well not just a pretty face then.' This cliché seemed exquisitely witty and set me off giggling again. It may have been his camp tone or the effect of the wine. Mike obviously thought the latter and censoriously removed my glass.

'I'm not a child,' I said to him.

'Legally,' he said, 'you are.' This was humiliatingly true and I sulked. The others were talking about art.

'Seeing the Rothkos when I was in the States,' said Ben, 'was the most sublime experience of my life.' Mike raised his eyebrows at me. I smiled reluctantly. I was still annoyed with him and anyway, although I didn't know what a Rothko was, I was prepared to allow a painting to be a sublime experience. 'Of course,' Ben continued, 'Paris is finished. New York is where things are happening.' I was appalled. I hadn't even got to Paris yet and it was finished. I was too late.

'I'd love to see the Rothkos,' said Alithea. 'Do you think we'll ever get a chance to see them over here?'

'It's hard to imagine,' said Ben. The wine seemed to have mellowed him and he was talking to Alithea quite amicably now. 'We're so behind the Americans.'

'Well thank God!' said Mike, 'Yes we're behind the Americans if that means we haven't yet set up a committee for un-British activities, if we don't yet hold witch hunts and suspect our intellectuals of being Communist sympathisers. Even though we may be a little paranoid about a peace-loving nation like the Soviet Union, we're still behind the Americans in some respects, I'm glad to say. We won't be bothering about the Tate acquiring a few over-priced canvases when, thanks to their war-mongering, the H bomb wipes out London.' As he became more impassioned Mike's accent became stronger and Hugh leant back regarding him with a mocking smile before coolly interjecting,

'A peace-loving nation like the Soviet Union? Even you can't be that deluded.' A tremendous row broke out. They sat elbows on the table, smoking furiously and stubbing out their cigarettes on their plates. Little piles of ash formed among the cheese rind and apple cores, remnants of the second course. Rather to my relief no one offered me a cigarette, in fact they seemed to have forgotten about me and I didn't feel capable of joining the debate even if I'd been able to get a word in edgeways.

Danny, who wasn't saying much, caught my eye. He signalled to me to pick up the remains of the quiche and started gathering up some of the debris. I followed him through the door by the fireplace into what had evidently been a corridor and was now a makeshift kitchen. It was a relief to have something to do, a relief to be alone with kindly, cheerful Danny.

'Better make some coffee I think,' he said in quite a normal, sensible voice. I noticed he had a slight cockney accent. 'Oh dearie me!' he reverted to camp. 'Love's roundabout, dearie, Love's roundabout!' I looked at him enquiringly. 'You don't think that's really all about politics do you? I adore Ben, Ben loves Hugh, Hugh loves that Alithea.'

'And who does Alithea love?' I asked. I rather hoped he would say 'Hugh.' He shook his head.

'Don't ask me dearie. Women are a mystery to me - herself, probably, or perhaps she's still attracted to that gorgeous Mike. She wouldn't get so mad with him if she didn't feel anything. I'd go for him myself but he'd be horrified wouldn't he? Now I've shocked you. Sorry. You're very young, aren't you?'

I felt extremely awkward. I knew enough to know that what he was talking about was against the law.

'And you love Mike, don't you? And he loves Alithea.' He looked at me kindly. 'Cheer up dearie. You'll get over it.'

'But I don't want to get over it. Anyway I'm sure he does love me a little bit at least.'

'Oh yes,' he said, 'he probably does love you a little bit. Why wouldn't he when you look at him so adoringly.'

'I don't,' I said in horror.

'Oh but you do. Don't be ashamed of it. There's nothing wrong in loving people.' He looked so sad that, in attempt to console him, I rushed in, gabbling,

'I'm sure Ben must l-l-like you a lot Danny.' – I couldn't quite bring myself to say 'love'- 'You're so nice and friendly and that was a delicious meal and Ben said you decorated that room yourself and - those scarlet painted chairs – they're beautiful!' I paused for breath and Danny patted my arm.

'Thanks,' he said, 'you're a sweetheart.' At that moment Alithea came in.

'Things seem a lot happier in here,' she said, sounding surprised. 'Is there any chance of some coffee, Danny? We need a distraction to stop Mike and Hugh punching each other's heads in.'

'Ooh dear, that would never do, would it? Give us a moment, madam, and my assistant and I will have it ready in no time. Grind some beans for me ducky,' he said to me. 'I'll go in there and finish clearing if you think it's safe enough. Do I need a mop for the blood on the floor?'

By the time we had the coffee ready some sort of peace seemed to have been restored. There was a new record on the gramophone. It was the kind of thing my father referred to as 'that American jazz'. He tended to call any popular music without lyrics 'jazz' - the other kind being 'those dashed awful crooners' - but in this case he would have been right.

'You actually heard Miles Davis in New York?' said Mike. The music seemed to have made him more friendly towards Ben. Whatever he felt about his painting he seemed to share Ben's taste for jazz. I was amazed to hear them discussing it seriously. Alithea and Danny in the meantime started to talk about food.

'It's no good complaining you can't get olive oil here, darling. You can't get good Normandy butter in the south of Italy. Look for the local stuff. They all keep pigs round here - local pork pies, smashing lard! I have my sources.' Hugh was left with no choice but to talk to me. He started to tell me about the standard required for the examinations I would have to take at the end of my second term at Oxford.

'Two books of the *Aeneid*,' he warned me. 'You've improved a lot but you must learn to work faster. You'll be expected to prepare big chunks for translation each week. Why are you re-taking Latin by the way?' I explained again about the State Scholarship.

'Why didn't you all try last year? Surely that Rosa girl would have got one if she's as bright as they say she is?'

'We never take it in the second year. I think it's a way of making sure we stay on for the whole of the Third Year Sixth.'

'That's absurd! You should take the advice they gave you at Oxford; leave at Easter and go to France. Unless you really need this State Scholarship for the money,' he added quite kindly. He smiled at me and

I thought he wasn't bad really although I couldn't think how I had ever imagined falling in love with him.

The sun had gone and it was dark outside. The big beautiful windows let in a lot of cold air and people kept throwing logs on the fire, huddling closer.

'Nearly opening time.' said Ben. 'Fancy a pint?' he said to Mike.

'You bet!'

I wondered when we would be leaving. We had high tea at home at five thirty and my mother had talked about coffee that evening. She would be expecting us back by seven at the latest. Danny said he would stay behind.

'The locals are beginning to give us looks when Ben and I go together. I'll make some sandwiches for when you get back.' This made me even more anxious about the time. I wondered if I should offer to stay with him. I'd never been in a pub, but I thought I'd quite like to see if they really were the dens of iniquity my family believed them to be. I also hoped I could have a quiet word with Mike about not staying there long. I'd noticed he had a slightly protective attitude towards me and would probably be more understanding than the others about what my parents were like. Once in the car I found myself in the back with Mike again, but the terrifying Ben was on the other side of me and I felt too inhibited by this to say anything during the short journey.

'No ladies in the public bar please,' said the landlord as we entered. I sensed he thought Alithea and I shouldn't be there at all. The public bar was lively with locals gathered round a darts board and there was a glowing coal fire. The saloon bar felt dank; the air smelled stale as if it hadn't been used for a long time. Hugh brushed the dark green moquette seat of a hard armchair before sitting down cautiously and stayed huddled in his the coat. There were no signs of exciting debauchery.

'This is a good brew. Is it local?' said Mike.

'Same again?' asked Ben. I began to despair. Mike by now was in a much better mood. In fact I noticed he seemed quite jolly and any sense of responsibility towards me seemed to have disappeared. Fortunately Alithea seemed to share Hugh's distaste for his surroundings and vetoed Mike's second pint.

Back at the castle Danny had prepared a pile of sandwiches and was drawing Alithea's attention to the quality of the local ham. Ben opened some more wine and put on some more Miles Davis. I had no watch and didn't even dare ask the time.

They seemed to be settling in for a long evening and Ben was just offering to open another bottle when Alithea said,

'Oh God! I'd forgotten. We've got to drop Dilly off. We'd better go.'

I felt as if I was a nuisance but at least we were leaving.

CHAPTER NINETEEN

'You can't learn to drive in the dark.' said Mike, as Alithea was about to get into the front passenger seat. Alithea, rather resentfully I thought, climbed into the back beside him. I felt slightly resentful too. Worried as I was about the time, I'd still been looking forward to sitting next to Mike on the way home and hoped he'd put his arm round me again. Of course if Mike didn't want to be with me... As we drove off I could hear them arguing quietly and furiously but I couldn't hear what they were saying. It was freezing hard and Hugh skidded once or twice. He drove more and more slowly and then said,

'I don't know where the hell we are. All these roads look the same. I think we're lost.'

'What time is it?' I asked.

'Quarter past nine.'

'Oh no! My parents will be frantic.'

'Well,' said Alithea. 'As soon as we pass a telephone box you can give them a ring.' This casual reaction made me realise she had no idea what my parents were like.

Hugh obviously felt some distracting conversation might lighten the atmosphere.

'What did you think of Ben's work, Allie?'

'He doesn't seem to have found his own style yet,' said Alithea.

'He needs to get his spiritual life in better order before he can find his true nature,' said Hugh. 'For a start, he must break this unhealthy relationship with Danny.'

'Jealous are you?' said Mike in a somewhat unpleasant tone, as even

I had to admit. Hugh jammed on the brakes causing the car to slide sideways across the road.

'That,' he said, 'is a most offensive remark.' Oh no! I thought - don't let them start fighting. There isn't time. Just then we saw a telephone box.

Public telephone boxes made me nervous. I was always terrified I'd press button B instead of button A and cut myself off just as I'd got through. This time I panicked even more when I realised I hadn't the right change. Fortunately I had enough sense to reverse the charge. My father accepted the call and almost shouted,

'Where are you?' I looked at the name in the phone box.

'We're near Hibbleston.'

'Hibbleston! What on earth are you doing there? Your mother's been beside herself. I've only just managed to stop her calling the police.'

'We got lost,' I said.

Alithea was in the front when I returned to the car. She had a torch and was looking at a map, so I got in the back beside Mike.

'The trouble is,' she said, 'I've got no idea where we are.' I told her the name in the telephone box and so she managed to find it on the map. We set off again.

'At least someone has some sense,' said Mike. 'Clever girl Dilly!' He put his arm round me again. At first I was too worried about the recriminations awaiting me at home to really appreciate it. Gradually, however, I relaxed and allowed myself to lean against him.

'Oh Dilly,' he murmured. 'Why can't I just be happy with a nice simple girl like you?' This was hardly flattering and perhaps I might have protested that I had hidden depths if only he cared to find out, but he followed this up by kissing me on the lips and this time it was not done lightly. I was dazed with happiness and sat there with my head on his shoulder for the rest of the journey, which now seemed all too short. I wondered how, over the next few months, I could subtly reveal to him the complications of my personality and make him realise that he could indeed be happy with me.

When we eventually reached my house it was nearly ten o'clock. It was far too late to ask them in for coffee. I could see my parents' bedroom light was on.

'I'll be in trouble,' I said.

'Shall I come in with you?' asked Mike.

'Don't be stupid,' said Alithea. 'I'll come in with you Dilly if you like.' I accepted her offer gratefully.

'Goodnight Dilly, my darling,' said Mike.

'You shouldn't take him too seriously, you know,' said Alithea as I was ringing the doorbell. I thought she might be jealous and I wondered if she'd been aware of the kiss; if so, did she mind?

My father came to the door looking grim. But Alithea turned on the charm and my father began to soften visibly as she dramatised the horrors of the journey.

'And then I must admit we were later setting off than we intended. We just couldn't get the men out of the pub. Could we Dilly?' Oh no! I thought - now I really am in trouble.

My father said very little after she'd gone except,

'You'd better go and say goodnight to your mother. She's gone to bed but she couldn't sleep until she knew you were back.'

As I passed the kitchen door I saw the tea trolley set with all the best china. I knew it must have been there since the early evening when my mother would have been happily anticipating a sociable evening with some interesting new people. Even then I realised there was something horribly poignant about it. In later years the image of that tea trolley came back to haunt me whenever I regretted the sadness of my mother's life.

As instructed I went to say goodnight. My mother had obviously been crying but she was so relieved to see me that, at first, she wasn't at all angry. But then, as I bent down to kiss her, she drew back suddenly.

'Have you been drinking?' She pushed me away and wouldn't speak to me again.

Back in my own room, I first thought with dread of the recriminations there would be in the morning. Had it all been worth it? Although there had been some bad moments, I believed it had. I felt I had lived a lifetime in a day. 'Mike,' I murmured to myself and in spite of my worries couldn't help smiling. And then, worn out by my experiences, I fell asleep almost immediately.

The next morning it felt as if somebody had died. Until my father left for work, my mother addressed all her conversation to him in a low solemn tone. Afterwards her only remarks to me were of the 'Could you pass the marmalade, Phyllida' variety. 'Phyllida!' This meant things were really bad. As we did the washing up together she kept her face averted and stared out into the garden. The frost had gone and a general grey sogginess pervaded everything. It was a question of who would crack first and I knew it would be me. Eventually I said,

'I'm sorry you were so worried last night but...' Before I could get any further all my mother's feelings came out in a rush. The ostensible reason for my being in disgrace was that I had been drinking.

'You know how strongly I feel about it. There's a weakness in the family you know. My Uncle James...' Great Uncle James was always referred to when the subject of alcohol came up. He had taken to drink as a young man, got into debt and been packed off to Canada. The shadow of Uncle James lay over us all and just one sip of the stuff was seen as the first step on the road to perdition.

'I only had a little white wine. It seemed rude to keep refusing.'

'They had no right to press it on you and Daddy says you went to a pub.' In vain did I try to say that it had been very dull, I had only drunk ginger beer and that I believed English country pubs were more respectable than Scottish city drinking dens. According to my mother, nice people, especially nice women, didn't go to pubs.

Of course really she was reacting after a terrible evening worrying about my whereabouts, imagining a crashed car on a dark and frosty road. But this wasn't something I really appreciated until my own children were teenagers. At the time it just seemed that once again she was trying to restrict my freedom and prevent me growing up.

However instead of admitting how worried she'd been, my mother chose to concentrate all her anger on the fact that I'd been drinking. Eventually she extracted a promise from me not to touch alcohol again until I was twenty-one and so we made a kind of peace; but this wasn't the end of the matter. When they'd arrived the previous morning my mother had been charmed by Mike and impressed by Hugh and Alithea. Now, however, she felt some resentment towards them for not taking up her invitation to come back for coffee. Looking hurt she put the best cups away and over the next few days asked me a great many questions about where exactly we had been, who had entertained us for lunch and how we had spent the day.

I said far too much. The trouble was my head was full of it all and I wanted to talk. Also I felt some guilt about Mike and while I certainly wasn't going to say anything about the kiss in the back of the car I think she guessed that something dubious had been going on.

'You say those two young men live together in that castle. Are they both artists?' As I described Danny's role in the household and praised his cooking she began to look more and more severe.

'It seems a funny sort of arrangement. I hope they don't get into any sort of trouble.' I looked at her, all wide-eyed naivety.

'Why should they?'- although by now I knew perfectly well what she meant.

'Well you know, two young men... This Danny seems an odd sort of character. Cockney you say? Not quite the same social class as his friend then?'

I tried to introduce a distraction,

'Well, I suppose Mr Davis isn't the same social class as Mrs Davis or Mr Marlow.'

'Yes, but he's educated isn't he? I thought he seemed a very nice young man, very nice manners. He was very charming.'

'Yes,' I said, 'he is.' She looked at me sharply. 'Very charming to everyone,' I added hastily. 'His wife finds it rather irritating.'

'I don't know why she should. There's nothing wrong with having nice manners. I thought she seemed rather hard, a bit sophisticated, Jewish you said?'

'Her father is.'

'I see. And Mr Marlow - I hadn't realised he was quite so young. When Miss Manzonni said he would give you extra Latin lessons I had imagined someone rather older.'

'You knew he'd just graduated.'

'I suppose I didn't take it in at the time. You won't go falling for him will you?' she added, in what was meant to be a jokey tone.

'For heaven's sake! If any male so much as says "hello" to me you think I'm going to elope with him. He's a very good teacher.' This was a mistake. It was designed to make sure she didn't suspect my feelings for Mike but it was enough to convince my mother that I was cherishing an unrequited - or perhaps worse - a requited passion for Hugh.

My mother was always terrified by any hint of sex and rather foolishly I added to her terrors by insisting I wanted to listen to Hugh's translation of *The Clouds* when it was broadcast on the Third Programme one evening later that week. I should have known better. Not only had Mike warned me against Hugh's 'filthy play' but I'd also heard Hugh telling Alithea how, unlike the Victorian versions, his modern translation would restore the bawdy humour of the original. I can only suppose I so wanted to be able to join in a discussion of the play when we met again after the holidays that I didn't think about the effect this bawdy humour might have on my parents.

That evening just as my mother wheeled in the tea trolley, I fiddled with the dial on the radiogram until I found the right spot.

'What's this then?' said my father looking up from the *Daily Telegraph*.

'Dilly's Latin tutor has a play that's being broadcast this evening - on the Third Programme,' said my mother.

'The Third Programme, eh!' said my father, smiling. 'I suppose we're in for a lot of this high-brow stuff now you're off to Oxford.' He took his tea and returned to the *Telegraph*. In cultivated accents the actors' voices boomed out their lines. Hugh's translation had certainly restored the power of the original Greek. My mother looked anxiously at my father. He appeared to be still absorbed in the newspaper but he rustled it from time to time and gave several little coughs. My mother shook her head at me.

'I think we've had enough of that now dear. Turn it off.' I was quite relieved really. It was awful listening to that kind of thing with my parents.

Next morning at breakfast the atmosphere had turned chilly again.

'That was rather a strange play of that young man's.'

'It was just a translation.'

'But why translate smut when there must be so many nicer things to choose from. I'm sorry Dilly, I'm afraid I'm old-fashioned and anything seems to go nowadays but smut is smut even if was written in Ancient Greek. What sort of things do you read with him in your Latin lessons?'

'Poetry,' I said.

'Poetry by whom?'

'Catullus.' My mother didn't know anything about Catullus but she made a phone call to my aunts that evening.

'Aunty Nan says Catullus wrote love poetry,' she said the next day. 'She seemed rather amused that you were reading it. Not a usual choice she said.'

'It's not all love poetry,' I said. 'There's one about his brother's death. *Atque in perpetuum, frater, ave atque vale.*' I hoped she would be impressed that I could quote Latin but she made no comment. Instead my father was instructed to speak to me. The next evening, while my mother invented some task in the kitchen, he cleared his throat and, looking extremely awkward, began,

'That young man.'

'Which young man?' I decided to be deliberately obtuse.

'That Latin teacher - your mother seems to have the idea you're getting involved with him.'

'What! How can she be so stupid?'

'Don't let me hear you call your mother stupid. I don't know what my father would have said if he'd heard me say such a thing. There's no respect nowadays - ever since the war. Anyway,' he said, 'I'm glad to hear there's nothing in it.' He hated this sort of conversation and was glad to be able to bring it to a swift end. However I felt inclined to challenge him.

'I don't know why you're both so against me having boy friends. I'll be nineteen soon. Most girls of my age have been out with lots of boys by then.'

'That's modern times for you.'

'No it isn't. Aunty Joyce is always on about how she was married at nineteen.'

'I don't think you should ever get married.'

'Why do you say that?'

'Well you don't like housework and you're always reading.' I nearly retorted this was also true of my mother but realised it would be tactless. Then I thought of Alithea, a chaotic household, wide literary knowledge and two men fighting over her, but this menage would hardly be my father's ideal model for married life. 'Study hard,' he continued, 'and then you can spend the rest of your life in an Oxford college. You're not cut out for real life.'

'If we'd lived in the Middle Ages,' I said, 'you'd have put me in a convent.'

'Now then, you know what I think of Roman Catholics.'

'If we'd lived in the Middle Ages we'd all have been Catholics.'

'You know what,' he said. 'Since you got into Oxford you've got too fond of arguing. You're getting above yourself.'

The day before term began my mother sent me on an errand to the shops. As I left I heard her pick up the phone. To my surprise when I came back she was only just putting the phone down. She greeted me with a kind of forced jollity that seemed odd but, at the time, I didn't think much about it. I couldn't wait to get back to school, to see the Davises and talk about the day at the castle.

PART 4

Spring Term 1956

CHAPTER TWENTY

'Good news, Dilly dear.' Miss Manzonni called me over as the others were filing out of her room after prayers on the first evening back. 'Miss Rush is much better and you can start extra Latin with her again on Tuesday.'

'But Mr Marlow?' Her face became stiffly disapproving.

'Mr Marlow has gone back to London. I believe he is hoping to go to America shortly to do some research.' I couldn't speak. 'And Dilly, you are not to go running over to Mrs Davis's all the time, now there is no need. Married people deserve some privacy. They don't want some schoolgirl hanging around all the time. You're not at university yet, you know and while you're here you must keep to the Boarding House rules. Matron needs help with the juniors and Brenda shouldn't have to be doing your job all the time. There was some excuse for neglecting things while you were doing Oxbridge entrance but now you must buckle down and get back to routine.' She started to talk about God and the sin of pride and the necessity to do one's duty in the path of life that had been allotted to one. At one time this would have had me in tears of repentance but I'd been infected by Socialist-atheism and while I felt full of miserable foreboding I also felt resentful.

I probably looked as resentful as I felt because eventually she seemed to realise she wasn't getting anywhere and tried another approach. I was to pay special attention to Rebecca Simon. With all her faults she was a clever girl and looked up to me. Mazzy felt I had already influenced her for the good and wanted me to make sure she continued on the right track.

'I want you to make this your special task for the term,' she said. 'I'm relying on you and I'm sure we will all see a great improvement in her by Easter.' She smiled encouragingly, 'And now I mustn't keep you any longer from your unpacking.'

I was desperate to speak to Alithea but when I approached her, after our English lesson the next morning, she wouldn't look at me.

'I'm sorry, Dilly,' she said, apparently preoccupied in gathering together her books. 'I haven't time to hear what you have to say just now.'

I felt slightly sick. She was furious with me. She must have seen Mike kiss me in the car. But - I argued with myself - she hadn't seemed cross when she'd come with me to the door of my house.

'You shouldn't take him too seriously.' It had sounded like a friendly warning. I ran through the scene at the front door. She'd been so charming to my father. It had been silly of her to mention the pub but she couldn't have known how my parents would react. She hadn't been trying to get me into trouble, I was sure.

Walking back from school with Fiona that afternoon, I had another idea - Mike had told her he was in love with me! This was terrifying but exciting at the same time. It was a raw January day but I decided to hang around for a while. Perhaps Mike might try to meet me. I'd seen Alithea walking some way ahead of me, chatting to Miss Seymour. Once they were safely round the other side of the cathedral he might miraculously appear.

'Come on, Dilly.' said Fiona. 'This isn't the weather to be hanging around and I'll miss my bus if you keep dawdling.'

'You go ahead,' I said. 'My shoelace is coming undone. I'll see you

SPRING TERM 1956

tomorrow.' I sheltered in a gateway but then thought he might not see me so I stood in the wind. I was aware that, probably, my lips were blue, my nose was red and my hair was straggling out from beneath my school beret, but if he really loved me I supposed he wouldn't mind. Everyone had gone ahead by now. 'Please let him come!' I said, almost audibly.

'Hello Dilly,' said a voice behind me. It was Becky Simon.

'Why are you so late?' I snapped at her.

'Ursula put me in prefects' detention.' She didn't seem at all concerned. Reforming her would be a hard job.

'Why are you standing in the cold talking to yourself?' she asked. She really was a tiresome child.

Over the next few weeks I ran over the same things again and again. Sometimes I was convinced Alithea was angry with me. Sometimes I believed Mike must have confessed to her that he loved me - but then why did he give no sign?

I played games with myself. – If I can get to the top of the Harstans before the cathedral clock finishes striking, Mike will be waiting for me. Sometimes I tried prayer – apologising to God for my recent neglect of Him. I wondered if I should promise to try to convert Mike from his atheism if only God would arrange a meeting.

Alithea's coldness towards me continued and other people began to notice. If, in English lessons, any other girl offered an answer or opinion, Alithea would pointedly ignore my waving hand. After one such lesson, Fiona said,

'Mrs Davis doesn't seem as friendly towards you this term.'

'Well I'm not going there for Latin any more, so I don't see her that much.'

Fiona looked rather doubtful but then she said,

'Well yes, and of course now you've got into Oxford I suppose she has to concentrate on Ursula.'

Alithea had certainly begun to be much nicer to Ursula, which had added to my unhappiness, but Fiona's explanation made me feel slightly better. Perhaps that was the reason Alithea seemed to have no time for me. Then, one break when I was on prefect duty, I saw her at the end of the corridor. She saw me at the same moment, turned briskly and walked off back to the staff room. There was no doubt about it; she was avoiding me.

It turned even colder. The temperature in the Boarding House was intolerable. When we had to go up to the dormitory after breakfast to make our beds we put our dressing gowns on over our school uniforms and wrapped scarves round our heads. Becky Simon even wore her eiderdown. In the attic in the evenings we worked in our coats and tried to write wearing gloves. The oil-stove gave out a foul smell but very little heat. It was a relief to get down to school.

'This form-room's freezing,' complained Audrey Dawkins. Brenda and I assured her she didn't know the meaning of the word.

'Anyway,' said one of her friends. 'Audrey's got her love to keep her warm.' I'd forgotten all about the American airman but apparently the romance was progressing rapidly. Audrey had removed the footballers' pictures from inside her desk lid.

'She's stuck up the Stars and Stripes and a picture of Hank or Chuck or whatever he's called,' said Fiona. He was actually called Bobby and, from a glimpse of the photo, he seemed to be nice-looking in an open-faced, white-toothed-smile kind of way, although his hair was rather short. I envied her.

While Brenda and I were complaining about conditions in the Boarding House Rosa suddenly spoke.

'If the temperature drops below fifty-eight degrees in school,' she said, 'we've the right to pack up and go home. That's the law for any place of work. My Dad told me. Surely it's the same for the Boarding House. You ought to object.' I was unhappy and resentful enough to feel reckless so I decided to speak out that evening after prayers.

As soon as I had spoken, Mazzy's whole face sagged with sorrow. She gazed at me with sad, dark eyes. I was apparently being self-indulgent and thoughtless. I should have realised how tight the Boarding House finances were. If the heating bills went up then many girls wouldn't be able to afford to come here. Afterwards I felt she had missed the point. The local education authority should be made to give more money. She ought to be campaigning on our behalf but of course she wouldn't. She had a soul above physical discomfort and she concluded by telling me that if I really had my mind on my work I wouldn't be aware of the cold.

In fact the cold made it difficult for any of us to concentrate on work but I couldn't concentrate anyway. We were meant to be revising for our mock A levels but I was tired of what seemed endless exams and I couldn't stop wondering what was going on at the Davises. Why had Hugh gone back to London? Had he had a fight with Mike? Had Mike won back Alithea? Were they blissfully in love and didn't need me any more? But Alithea didn't look blissful. She seemed pale, tired and bad-tempered. Then I had another idea. Perhaps they'd all discussed me after that day at the castle and Ben had said I was dull and immature - not worth bothering with. But then would Mike have taken any notice of Ben's opinions? All these ideas went round and round in my mind, over and over again.

Alithea did more than just ignore me. In General Studies she treated my contributions to any discussion with contempt. It was more than simply not being friendly. After one such lesson Fiona asked,

'Why is Mrs Davis being so beastly to you?' At first I didn't know what to say. I'd already given Fiona an expurgated account of my day at the castle. Now more explanation seemed necessary. I tried my best.

'That day I told you about... Mr Davis paid me quite a lot of attention... maybe she was annoyed. But I think maybe he did it because he was annoyed because she was making up to Mr Marlow and he didn't like his friends.'

'Who didn't like whose friends?' asked Fiona. But she was sympathetic. When I tried to explain further, she said none of them sounded very nice and I was well out of it. She asked me round to tea that Saturday. When I arrived her mother looked at me, concerned,

'You look tired, Dilly. Have you been over-working?'

'No,' I said truthfully. Her kindness made me want to cry. She gave us tea on our own in the living room by a generous fire.

One evening it seemed slightly warmer.

'Perhaps Mazzy's been praying for better weather,' said Jane, who knew about my protest, and she whooped with laughter.

'That's blasphemous, Jane,' said Caroline. I cautiously opened the attic window.

'I can smell snow,' I said.

The next morning we woke to a world of pure white beauty. Snow lay thick and soft on the branches of the sycamores; snow so deep that the gravestones in the Close were only just visible as low humps. The juniors rushed out into the garden to start a snowball fight but were called in by Matron saying they would all get soaked. Mazzy announced that we were all to go out before school and clear the Harstans. It was the kind of public-spirited activity she thought was good for us. Some of the grammar school boys passed us while we were scraping away. The younger ones jeered at us, so Becky Simon lobbed a snowball and knocked a boy's cap off. Unfortunately, our ancient and ferocious German teacher was passing at the time and she called Becky over to harangue her on her unladylike behaviour.

'You should keep those young ones in better order,' she said to me. I knew this would go back to Mazzy. I didn't seem to be having much success with my special task for the term.

From my position at the top of the Harstans I looked down on a grammar school prefect's tasselled cap. As its owner climbed into view I saw it belonged to Christopher.

'Oh Dilly hello! How are you?' he said. 'You look like one of the heroic peasants of the Soviet Union, shovelling the snow. Mr Davis would approve.' My heart did a double somersault.

'Poor old Trotsky. He's in trouble with the Head now over some Communist play he wants to put on – something by Brecht. How's your romance with him getting on? He seems in a better mood this term, or he was, before the row over the play.' This wasn't what I wanted to hear.

'How's your romance with Ursula getting on?' I said, in what I hoped was a suitably contemptuous tone. He pulled a face.

'It's off. Her father's never liked me. I'm not very good at Latin. He was always sarcastic in class and he was just as sarcastic when I called round to see Ursula. I say Dilly you wouldn't..?' But at this point Mazzy appeared to see how we were progressing and Christopher left rapidly.

The next day it thawed and, as usual, the Boarding House roof started to leak. We returned from school to find the hall and landing full of chamber pots catching the worst of the drips. These, dating from the days when there had been chamber pots beneath each bed, were kept stacked in a cupboard and brought out at times of heavy rain or thawing snow. Previously when this had happened we had all thought it funny. Now it suddenly struck me as unreasonable.

'Why,' I said loudly, 'can't the bloody governors get the roof mended?' Mazzy came out of her room and looked at me gravely and sorrowfully.

'Dilly,' she said, 'I can see you are still in a troubled state.' I thought she was right but perhaps not in the way she meant. I was actually beginning to feel rather ill.

CHAPTER TWENTY ONE

Half an hour later I was lying in the San on an iron-framed bed, huddled under inadequate blankets. It was a dark, chilly room and to add to the gloom the walls had been painted a depressing shade of blue. Who, I wondered, could have chosen such a colour? Probably the same person who had chosen the only picture, two cairn terriers gazing wistfully at a bowl of greyish milk. There was also a framed copy of a dreadful poem entitled *An "If" for Girls*, which began,

If you can dress to make yourself attractive,
Yet not make puffs and curls your chief delight.
If you can swim and row, be strong and active
But of the gentler graces not lose sight....

and continued in this vein for several more verses. When in normal health and spirits it made me laugh. Now, however, it just added to my misery and when I reached the inevitable climax, *If you should some day meet and love another,* I started to sob. Unfortunately Matron came in at that moment to give me an aspirin.

'Goodness me!' she said. 'There's no need to get in such a state, Dilly. I expect you've got the flu. I just hope you haven't started an epidemic because I'm run off my feet as it is.' But she must have reported back on my sad state because Mazzy came in and called me 'a poor old thing', in quite kindly tones, reassuring me that she was sure I would be well enough to do my mock exams the following week.

I had started an epidemic. The next day Caroline joined me. At teatime Brenda came in with some books and I knew I ought to start revising but all I felt able to do was to read *Persuasion*, which I read with more emotional involvement than ever before. Suppose I had to wait eight long years before seeing the object of my love again. How could Anne Elliot have been so stoical? Captain Wentworth, rather improbably, assumed Mike's features. As I read, the headache I'd had all day grew worse and worse. Eventually I realised I was going to be sick. I made the washbasin in time, just as Matron brought in another feverish girl, saying,

'Any more of this and we'll have run out of beds,' and that she'd have to turn the commonroom into a temporary hospital.

As soon as I'd been sick I started to feel slightly better and lay there thinking about *Persuasion*. I imagined myself, some time in the future, at the farm, kneeling by a sofa, tending some unspecified relative; young Frank, now a sturdy toddler, had climbed on my back and was refusing to let go but Mike came into the room and gently removed him. But what was Mike doing at the farm? I needed to invent a plausible narrative and while I was doing this I fell asleep.

The next day Jane came down with flu and then two more girls and we were all moved into the common room. This was more cheerful; there were windows at each end of the room, one overlooking the garden and the other the Close. The fire was lit every morning so the room got reasonably warm and, as we began to recover, it became quite fun. Any disruption from routine was always welcome and we were heartlessly impervious to Matron's moans about extra work.

'It's a bit like the outbreak of fever at Lowood School,' I said to Jane.

'Ooh, I say,' said Becky Simon. 'Do you think if someone dies they'll be made to start giving us better food?' Of course, I thought, that precocious brat would have read *Jane Eyre*.

'Well, unfortunately for us, if someone does die, it won't be you,' said Jane. 'You're no saintly Helen Burns, so squash!' she added.

Doing revision was more or less impossible in this atmosphere but Mazzy was determined I was well enough to do mocks. When I appeared in school, Fiona said,

'You look awful Dilly. I'm sure you shouldn't be here.'

'Are you all right, Dilly?' asked Alithea. These were the first kind words she had spoken to me that term and I saw she was looking concerned, perhaps even guilty, at least something other than stonily indifferent. This made my eyes fill with tears.

'Not really,' I said and then sat down and put my head between my knees because I thought I was going to faint. I was sent back to the common room to convalesce. I eventually did my exams in the attic. The weather was slightly warmer so, though I still needed my coat, at least I wasn't impeded by gloves. My marks were disappointing but this was put down to the flu, so not much was said.

Once the drama of the flu epidemic was over, the term dragged on its weary way. Ursula heard she hadn't got into St Anne's and I felt in some obscure way I was being blamed for this. I was left with the general impression that everyone thought, not only had Oxford shown poor judgement, but I'd been allowed to get above myself and needed to be brought down a peg or two. Miss Seymour, in particular, seemed to take pleasure in pointing out my inadequacies. She seemed very thick with Alithea and I often saw them walking home together. I remembered Mike's comment on the magic Saturday afternoon that now seemed to belong to the remote past. 'Rather you than Joan Seymour.' Had he changed his mind? Alithea herself seemed low and spiritless. One day I came back into the form room to find her still sitting at the staff desk. She was resting her head on her hands and looked as if she had been crying. She looked up when I came in and I got up the courage to say,

'Are you all right, Mrs Davis?'

'Please go away, Dilly,' she said. So I went.

Life at the Boarding House was no better. Every Tuesday and Thursday after school, I trailed along suburban roads to the little semi-detached house where Miss Rush lived with her retired maths teacher friend and their over-indulged cat. Her spell in hospital hadn't improved her temper.

'Why did you choose Oxford?' she had asked me at my first lesson. She was a Cambridge graduate and seemed to take my decision as a personal insult. She also seemed quite annoyed by the improvement in my Latin.

'Mr Marlow didn't think it was necessary for me to learn a prose by heart,' I said one day when I'd failed to do so. She pulled her glasses down to the end of her nose and glowered over them. This had always terrified me, but now, made reckless by misery, I stared back at her.

When I returned from my lesson I found Brenda sitting in my place at the head of the table.

'Prep please!' she called out just as I entered.

'It's not time yet,' protested Becky Simon. 'Anyway, Dilly's here now.'

'Oh sorry,' said Brenda. 'I didn't think you'd be back so soon. I keep forgetting you're not going to Mrs Davis's any more.'

Fresh from my glaring match with Miss Rush, I scowled and pushed her books aside. The juniors smirked and sniggered at this display of bad temper. I knew it was undignified but I was finding Brenda more and more intolerable.

SPRING TERM 1956

The next day I returned from school to see Miss Rush's Austin Seven parked outside the Boarding House and knew she'd come to complain about me. Mazzy wasn't really angry but she kept saying how deeply disappointed in me she was, which was worse.

'I hope you will choose your friends wisely when you get to Oxford,' she said towards the end of her lecture. 'Remember you have been brought up with good principles. When you are young, it is easy to be dazzled by spurious glamour.' It was the nearest she could get to saying the Davises had been a bad influence.

As I was leaving she asked me whether I had noticed any improvement in Becky's behaviour. 'There still seem to have been one or two detentions.'

In fact my special project with Becky was getting nowhere. I didn't really care except that it seemed yet another example of my inadequacy. One evening Brenda burst into in the attic in a glow of self-righteous indignation. She had caught Becky and her friend Mary creeping in through the back door with a greasy newspaper containing the remains of some fish and chips.

'You'll have to come with me to Mazzy, Dilly. It's imperative to deal with this crisis immediately.'

I sighed. 'Oh, come on! Is it that serious? We all used to sneak out and get fish and chips – Well, I did - with Heather.' (Referring to a girl who had left rather suddenly.)

'Dilly!' Caroline looked horrified.

'Oh well, *Heather...*' said Brenda.

Jane avoided my eye.

'It was rather fun.' I remembered the thrill of sneaking out through the dark garden, dropping down over the wall at the end onto the Harstans, running panting through the Close to the fish and chip shop

221

in the street beyond the arch, then rushing back, clutching the warm parcel and handing it up to my co-conspirator.

'At least we always had the sense to get rid of the newspaper.'

'It transpires,' said Brenda, 'that the intention was to donate the remainder to Rags. I'm afraid I fail to find it amusing, Dilly.'

Reluctantly, I went with her to report it to Mazzy. Becky and Mary were banned from visiting the local shops on Saturday mornings and I had to make sure that they didn't.

I'd never much liked Brenda but after this episode I began to find her unbearable. Her long sallow face with its sneering expression, her pale goggling eyes, her pompous manner and pretentious vocabulary grated on me more and more. What made it worse was that she was always there. She was in the same form room at school, in the attic in the evening, in the dormitory where she even slept in the next bed. Every night, it seemed, I lay there awake listening to her rather adenoidal breathing. I almost felt like murder.

Caroline irritated me too. Whenever I snapped at her, as I increasingly did, a most infuriating look of Christian forgiveness came into her soft dark eyes, which made me even more bad tempered. I'd always liked Jane but I'd begun to find her teasing about my supposed passion for Hugh intolerable. It was difficult to get away from them as well. There was no privacy in the Boarding House.

On the next Saturday afternoon however, I was actually alone in the attic. The other sixth formers had all gone into town. The house was quiet; the juniors were out for their usual walk with Matron. I thought I would try to catch up on some work but it was no good. I couldn't concentrate. I started to flip through *The Oxford Book of English Verse* looking for sad love poems but, as they were all written by men, nothing quite met my case, so I started to write one myself. I had written poems before; we had sometimes been set them for English homework and some of mine had been published in the school magazine but this was different; for the first time I was writing about a subject that really mattered to me. I'm sure it was a terrible poem; mercifully it's been long lost, but it was the start of something. It was hardly emotion recollected in tranquillity, but, as I struggled with the technicalities, I began to feel better. Then I heard footsteps on the stairs and hastily hid my poem under *Lyrical Ballads*.

'Have you been crying, Dilly?' said Jane, returning in time for tea.

'Of course not - seem to be getting a cold.'

'Not unrequited love then?'

'Shut up!' I lost my temper completely and told her how irritating and stupid I thought her jokes were.

'All right! There's no need to be so mardy.' But I could see she realised she'd gone too far. She offered to bring me up a cup of tea. While she did so I went to bathe my eyes in cold water but both bathrooms were occupied and I couldn't be bothered to go down to the washbasin in the San.

CHAPTER TWENTY TWO

Into all this misery came Amber. She turned up the next day just as we were setting out for early Evensong.

'Dilly dear,' said Mazzy, putting her head round the door of her study. 'I have a young woman here who says she is your cousin.' I followed her in.

'Amber!' I exclaimed.

'Hello, our Dilly, what have you been doing with yourself? You look like a wet dish clout. Too much studying I suppose. Anyway I've come to take you out to tea. You look as if you could do with feeding up.' Mazzy looked at me in a rather startled way as if she was only just aware that I was looking pale and thin. I could see why she'd sounded rather doubtful about Amber's claim to be my cousin. Amber was perching on the dingy armchair and from the tiny, bright green hat on the back of her vivid hair to her stiletto-heeled shoes she looked as out of place as a bird of paradise. She was wearing bright orange lipstick and a lot of green eye shadow. Uncle Frank would have sent her straight off to wash her face.

'Bring your friends,' she added, hearing the other three muttering outside the door. Forced to accept our relationship was genuine, Mazzy said I could go to tea with Amber and take Brenda. The other two would be needed to supervise the boarders' tea and, of course, we had to go to Evensong first.

'Perhaps you would like to join them?' she suggested. Amber was noncommittal but once outside she said,

'Look, I'll meet you afterwards. I've got a friend with me and I don't think church going's much in his line.' For a moment I wondered if she'd brought Barry Wilson but then I saw someone smaller, fatter and, I thought, older, slink out from behind a buttress to join Amber.

'Meet us at the Northgate,' she said, referring to the less classy of the two hotels near the Close and, taking her companion's arm, she disappeared round the corner.

After the service, Brenda and I made our way round to the hotel. Amber and her friend were in the Tudor Lounge sitting in fringed armchairs by a coal-effect electric fire.

'This is Les,' said Amber. Les leapt to his feet. He had a moustache, which suggested to me that he might have been in the RAF, and I was riveted by his two-tone brown and white brogues. Were these, I wondered, what were meant when people referred derisively to 'co-respondent shoes'? Whether this was so or not I knew what my mother would say if she ever met him, 'What a common little man!'

'Well, ladies,' began Les, 'did you say a little prayer for me?' He continued in this manner throughout tea and laid on the flattery by the spadeful. He called us glamour girls, said he was surrounded by a bevy of beauties and compared us to film stars, Amber was Rita Hayworth, I was Grace Kelly and he couldn't think who Brenda reminded him of, which was hardly surprising, but eventually said it must be Marilyn Monroe.

'Go blonde, dear,' he advised her shamelessly, 'and you'll have the men at your feet.' I was appalled and couldn't help thinking nostalgically of Mike's easy charm. Only a short distance away, at that very moment, Mike would be sprawled in an armchair, wearing his old tweed jacket, perhaps burning holes in his trousers with his cigarette. Maybe Joan Seymour was sitting opposite him eating buttered toast. I only hoped the grease was running down her chin, as it was down Brenda's, and that it was making her equally unattractive.

Brenda loved it all. She giggled at Les's every witticism; she spoke in her most affected manner and told him she was a scientist.

'Not too brainy, I hope. I don't like brainy girls,' he said. 'Mind you, Amber here, is a wizard with figures. I'm talking about numbers, you naughty girl!' as Brenda giggled again. 'Cigarette?' Brenda took one and leant forward as he offered her a light. She inhaled deeply and closed her eyes. I refused, and wondered how Brenda could have been so self-righteous over the fish and chips episode. Smoking was a far worse crime.

Les told us a great deal about himself over tea. He had indeed been in the Raf, as he referred to it, 'stationed not a million miles from here,' and had come out with 'contacts'. He had been able to buy a small shop and gone 'from strength to strength.' He was about to buy his third shop 'and...' he finished, looking enquiringly at Amber.

'OK' said Amber, grinding out her cigarette among the cake crumbs on her plate. 'You might as well know, Dilly. I got chucked out of nursing months ago - not that I cared - I hated it. I've been working in a department store, Ladies Fashions. Les came in to spy out the land. We got talking and...'

'Luckiest day of my life,' said Les.

'But don't say anything to anybody yet,' she said. 'It'll all come out sooner or later. Les and I are going to get engaged.' Barry Wilson might almost have been more acceptable, I thought. At least he was local.

Les however was very generous. He kept ordering more teacakes and made sure we finished every scrap of jam and butter.

'Don't leave anything,' he said. 'It's all paid for.' He even made us stuff our pockets with sugar lumps although the waitress was looking on in disapproval. I couldn't imagine Grace Kelly doing such a thing; I was less certain about Marilyn Monroe.

'What a charming man,' said Brenda as we walked back to the Boarding House. 'Do you think I should go blonde when I leave?' I looked at her rather lank mousy hair and failed to imagine the transformation.

Over Sunday supper, as always leftovers from the rest of the week eaten in the kitchen, she told Jane and Caroline about Les. Caroline looked horrified. I could see Jane was trying not to laugh.

'And which Hollywood star are you like, Dilly?'

'Grace Kelly, I believe was mentioned,' said Brenda as I was chewing on a cold roast potato and so unable to answer immediately.

'Dilly! All immaculate with white gloves! She can't even keep her hair tidy! I can't see her marrying a prince.'

Strangely enough this bizarre tea party made me begin to feel better. I didn't wish Amber any harm but I realised her flashy life wasn't for me. Mazzy had just been drawing the green chenille curtains in her study as we returned to the Boarding House. When we'd knocked on her door to report back I'd felt an odd sense of relief, even homecoming, on seeing her book-lined walls, the piles of marking and the shabby armchairs. There had been something wholesome in the very drabness.

At least the episode had given me something else to think about. I tried to imagine Les at my uncle's farm. I wondered if he would advise Frances to go blonde and even smiled as I imagined her parents' horror.

From then on things started to improve slightly. When the post arrived at breakfast time on Valentine's Day, a pale blue envelope was passed down the table for me. For one heart-stopping moment I thought it might be from Mike and then I recognised Christopher's handwriting. However it was nice of him; it raised my spirits and impressed the rest of the boarders. Jane insisted it must be from Hugh and even the local postmark didn't stop her teasing me on the subject.

The days began to get longer and down at school the atmosphere was lightening too. Ursula went for an interview at Durham and was immediately offered a place. Her aunt might not be thrilled but everyone else seemed pleased and relieved.

'Well done, Ursula,' said Alithea. 'The English School at Durham has a very good reputation.' Mazzy went even further; she told Jane that English at Durham was of a higher standard than English at Oxford. Jane, as presumably Mazzy knew she would, passed this on to me and I realised I was still being punished for the sin of pride.

Rosa had been sitting the London University exams and soon after heard she had not only been accepted but had been awarded a scholarship. No one was sure whether this meant she had eclipsed my achievement or not, but I felt very happy for her and had a sense that some justice had been done.

'I suppose nobody's offered you a scholarship yet?' said my mother when I told her at half term, and I realised I would never be good enough to satisfy all her ambitions for me.

Soon after this Fiona had an offer from St Andrews. Miss Cutler told her not to accept it. She reiterated that Fiona wasn't university material, she wouldn't get the grades they required and should continue to apply to training colleges. A fearful row broke out and Fiona, most uncharacteristically, was several times in tears. During this crisis I was her main confidante. Our relationship was back to normal and I realised I'd missed our closeness during that strange heady time of my involvement with the Davises.

One lunchtime, when we were conferring in the form room, Alithea came in.

'I hear you've been offered a place at St Andrews, Fiona,' she said.

'Only conditionally and Miss Cutler says I shouldn't take it,' said Fiona.

'What rubbish!' said Alithea. 'Write and accept immediately, but don't say I said so. Mind you, I don't know why you want to go there. It's full of rich English girls from boarding schools, who failed Oxbridge. Bloody training college', she added, almost to herself. 'Old fool!' She obviously didn't mean Fiona. We looked at each other, shocked. She went out immediately, ignoring me and slamming the door behind her.

'Did she actually say 'Bloody'?' said Fiona. "Bloody training college.' I'd like to say that to Cutler, the old fool.' We started to laugh. 'Rich girls?' added Fiona thoughtfully, after we'd managed to control ourselves. 'Rich men as well, probably.' That evening she wrote to St Andrews and accepted their offer. Miss Cutler was annoyed but there was nothing she could do. Unless, I supposed, she hoped that Fiona would fail to get the required grades. Which, I thought, would be very unchristian of her.

'Nineteen!' Aunty Joyce had written in my birthday card, 'To think I was wed at nineteen!!' I presumed she was boasting. Her life, I thought, was nothing to boast about but everything made me aware I was too old to be at school. At teatime on my birthday I had to perform the traditional Boarding House ritual of running round the table, a circuit for each year, while the candles were still alight. No one had ever had to do nineteen laps before and I nearly didn't make it.

'In two years time I shall have a vote.' I said. My parents had come over that weekend to take me out to tea. We were at the Northgate and I had a feeling the waitress recognised me and was keeping an eye on the sugar lumps. My father said he was appalled at the thought.

'I think I shall vote Labour,' I continued, hoping to upset him further.

'You see what I mean?' he said to my mother. 'No sense at all. Lord help the country!'

At last the end of term was in sight but Alithea and Miss Carr had decided that before we broke up they would organise a theatre outing for the A level English group. We were to go to London by coach to see the Royal Shakespeare Company in *A Winter's Tale*. This was the first time I'd seen this on the stage and it's since become one of the plays I love best, so it's strange I can remember almost nothing of that particular performance. Instead it was the off-stage drama of the day that left the most powerful impression.

We had to set off very early in order to get to the matinee on time and at first we were all quiet and sleepy. Gradually however we livened up. A lot of people had never been to London before. I'd only been once, to visit the Festival of Britain. As the excitement grew, someone started singing and we all joined in, quietly at first but then we grew more raucous. Led by Audrey Dawson's gang, we started to sing,

Our sergeant major jumped from seventy thousand feet, to the tune of John Brown's Body.

And he ain't going to jump no more.
When we got to the second verse,

They scraped him off the pavement like a lump of strawberry jam, Alithea muttered something to Miss Carr and Miss Carr got up and spoke to the coach driver who almost immediately pulled into the side of the road. Miss Carr helped Alithea down the steps and Alithea disappeared behind some bushes.

'I think she's being sick,' said Audrey, standing up so that she could see better. Fiona looked at me,

'Preggers,' she whispered. I felt as if I had been stabbed through the heart.

'You're not going to be sick too Dilly, are you?' asked Audrey. 'You've gone really pale.'

'Well, certainly not for the same reason,' said Fiona.

'What do you mean?' said Audrey and then almost immediately, 'Really. Do you think so?'

Miss Carr got back on the coach.

'Sit down at once, Audrey. Mrs Davis isn't feeling at all well. I don't want to hear any more singing. Can you please remember that at this very moment the school is taking part in an act of worship. This is not the time to be singing vulgar songs.' Alithea returned to the coach looking white and rather fragile. We speculated quietly amongst ourselves about how far advanced her pregnancy might be.

'That means we'll have a new English teacher again next year,' said one of the Lower Sixth. 'Staff seem to be changing all the time nowadays.'

For some reason Rosa hadn't come on the trip; (perhaps she couldn't afford it) so, during the interval, it was just Fiona, Ursula and I who started to wander down a corridor in search of some fresh air. We passed an almost empty bar.

'Oh look,' said Ursula. 'There's Mrs Davis and isn't that the man who used to teach you Latin, Dilly?' Hugh and Alithea seemed to be in an intense conversation but at that moment Hugh looked up and seemed surprisingly pleased to see me.

'Dilly!' he said, 'How's the Latin going?'

'Not so well since you left.'

'Really? Come and tell me about it. Can I get you girls a drink?'

'I don't think we ought,' said Ursula but Fiona said,

'It's all right. We're all over eighteen,' and started to advance on Hugh, smiling confidently. Alithea signalled to me,

'Dilly,' she said quietly. 'Please get them to go. I need to talk to Hugh urgently and he needn't think he can get out of it.'

'Ursula's right,' I said to Fiona. 'We may be over eighteen but it's a school trip and we're in uniform. We can't go hanging around bars.' Fiona looked at me in amazement. I usually fell in with her plans quite meekly. All the same we left.

'Mrs Davis didn't want us to stay,' I explained to Fiona on the way back to our seats.

Alithea didn't turn up after the interval.

'Has anybody seen Mrs Davis?' said Miss Carr.

'I saw her outside,' I said. 'I think she wasn't feeling very well again.' Why was I doing this for her, I wondered, when she had been so horrible to me all term?

'Was that why she didn't want us to stay?' asked Fiona.

'Yes,' I lied.

'All the same I think something's been going on between her and that Latin teacher of yours. She was probably saying it had to stop now she was pregnant and they were saying an emotional farewell.'

I thought this was possible, but still it was strange. I remembered the Vicar's wife's friend describing Hugh as being 'terribly in love' with

Alithea. Surely in that case he should have been the one to want them to be alone together instead of seeming relieved to see us. Then, much as I'd wanted to believe that Alithea was in love with Hugh, I'd had to admit to myself that her attitude towards him had often seemed rather ambivalent. So why was she now determined to be alone with him and what exactly was he trying to 'get out of'? It was all beyond me. Shakespeare was simple by comparison. All I could say to Fiona was,

'I don't think she was very well. He was giving her a medicinal brandy.'

'My brother says the latest medical opinion believes you shouldn't drink when you're pregnant.' I couldn't think why Fiona's brother would be telling her this except that he'd started to be very know-all since becoming a medical student.

'Thank you, Dilly,' Alithea murmured as we got on the coach to go home. I hoped this might be a breakthrough in our relationship. I desperately wanted to talk to her. If she was pregnant all hope for me was at an end but it was better to know. However the next day she was off school and after that she was as cold and distant as ever.

PART 5

Easter 1956

CHAPTER TWENTY THREE

Finally the miserable term came to an end. As soon as I was in the car on the way home my mother said,

'You'll never believe this but Amber's engaged!'

'To Les?'

'You've met him?'

My mother was most annoyed that I hadn't told her about Amber's visit and not too pleased about Amber turning up at the Boarding House.

'Whatever did Miss Manzonni make of her? I hope she didn't look too..too...'

'Tarty?' I suggested.

My father exploded. He wanted to know where I picked up such words.

'I suppose that's one of Fiona's expressions,' said my mother. 'It isn't a word I would have used myself.' However she was unable to think of a better one and I knew that was what she meant.

I was questioned closely about Les.

'Apparently he was an officer in the RAF,' said my mother.

'He certainly mentioned he had been in the RAF,' I agreed. I tried to think of some uncontroversial things to say about Les.

'He has a moustache and he's quite a bit older than Amber.' All this fitted in with the story of his career in the RAF.

'How does he speak?' said my mother.

'Well he hasn't a *local* accent,' was the best I could manage. His style of conversation was, I felt, something it would be best for them to find out for themselves.

Uncle Frank and Aunty Joyce had taken the whole thing better than I expected. Amber's failure to qualify as a nurse was hardly mentioned. Now that she was going to get married they simply weren't interested. Amber had brought Les to the farm for Sunday dinner and he'd obviously modified his manner for the occasion. I wondered if she'd also made him change his shoes. What lay behind all this, I gradually realised, was her parents intense relief that Amber had not 'Had To Get Married,' something that probably had always terrified them. They didn't seem to realise it was usually the more careless or vulnerable girls that got caught out. Amber had far more sense.

The wedding was to be in early September when harvest was over and Aunty Joyce was trying to get ahead with the preparations. She claimed that Amber wanted Frances and me to be bridesmaids. A few years ago I would have found this thrilling and romantic; now I thought it was all regrettably bourgeois, especially when I heard we were to be decked out in pink organdie.

'I've told her it'll give her another evening dress to take to Oxford,' said my mother to her friend, Mrs Stewart, who had come round for tea.

'I'm not going to wear pink organdie in Oxford. I don't want to turn up at a college ball looking like…like Little Bo Peep.' Mrs Stewart went into peals of merry laughter.

'Well now there's a young lady who knows her own mind! And what colour would you prefer, madam?'

'I suppose green suits me best.'

'Oh no, you can't wear green for a wedding. It's unlucky. Didn't you know?' I didn't know and I didn't care but some remnants of my bourgeois upbringing restrained me from saying so.

'How about black then?' Of course Mrs Stewart realised I wasn't serious and this called forth more merry peals. My mother wasn't really listening.

'I don't know what we're going to do about your hair though. Have another scone Kirsty. Dilly pass Aunty the scones.'

'Would you like another scone, Mrs Stewart?' I asked, disassociating myself from all this childish 'Aunty' nonsense. My mother looked at me reproachfully but Mrs Stewart just said I was getting very grown up.

'The Minister's little girl has such lovely curls,' continued my mother. I was already getting heartily sick of this child's curls; they had been mentioned every day so far and we were only in the first week of the holidays. It was in the hope of silencing my mother on this subject that made me accept Mrs Stewart's offer to give me a home perm. She promised to bring the necessary kit round the following week and transform my straight locks into a mass of soft waves. As soon as Mrs Stewart had left I regretted having been so weak and although, for the time being, this stopped my mother complaining about my hair, it merely meant that she returned to her other favourite topic; Amber's wedding in general but, in particular, any information I could give her about the bridegroom. She obviously realised I was holding something back.

'I think it's very strange that Joyce hasn't asked us over to meet him.'

'I think he's very busy with his new shop.'

'All that money spent on her education and now she's marrying a shopkeeper!'

'What does that matter if she loves him?' I said this with some passion; but it was myself I was really thinking of, not Amber and Les. Theirs had struck me as a strangely commercial relationship. There had seemed to be no erotic charge between them; I thought this odd. Occasionally the image of Amber in the stack yard with Barry Wilson rose up before me. What did Amber think she was doing?

Variants of this conversation were played out daily until, when I was nearly at screaming point, my mother was distracted by another visit from Mrs Stewart who arrived at half-past ten one morning full of import.

Over the last few months I'd gathered from my parents that the congregation weren't too happy with their new Minister. Right from the start he'd been considered odd and public opinion was now hardening against him. He was was accused of preaching socialism. I'd baby-sat for him and his wife, unpaid, once or twice during the Christmas holidays and had been interested to see a copy of the *Manchester Guardian* lying around mixed up with the children's toys and other debris of family life. My mother didn't always approve of his sermons but the Minister was a Cambridge graduate, which impressed her. Also she had rather taken to his wife who, it turned out, was also a Cambridge graduate. But, while this discovery impressed my mother even further, it made most of the congregation suspect she was as unfitted to be a minister's wife as her husband was to be their minister.

In a way they were right. I never discovered why this unlikely pair had been sent to our small town. In a university town they would have been welcomed; in an inner city they would have done much good; but in an agricultural area like ours, Conservative in every sense of the word, people couldn't understand them and, before long, incomprehension turned to hostility.

The congregation's suspicions about the Minister's wife had soon been proved right. She took little interest in sales of work and other chapel activities. Sales of work were supposedly held to raise money but they were also important social occasions. The Minister's wife neither knitted nor sewed herself but; what was even worse, she showed no enthusiasm for buying crocheted dressing table mats or embroidered tray cloths. At first people had made some excuses for her; those two children must keep her busy and of course the couple were hard up; but she was rapidly becoming as unpopular as her husband and now Mrs Stewart had gone round that morning and found her sitting at the kitchen table reading.

'She hadn't even made a start on the breakfast things and when I pointed out that little boy of theirs was feeding his sister with spoonfuls of marmalade from the jar she said "Oh Justin, you'll make her sick," and laughed!'

'I said to her, "I was just asked to pop round and remind you it's the Young Wives' Club meeting this afternoon. I heard you forgot all about it last week," and she said, (you're not going to believe this) she said, "Oh I don't think I'll have time." That's what she said, "I don't think I'll have time." Can you credit it! And there she was at the kitchen table, reading. But it's as true as I stand here. There was a lot I could have said but you know me. I never like to cause trouble, so I just said, "Yes, well I can see you've still got the washing up to do." And then I left.'

During this monologue I'd been sitting at the dining room table supposedly revising European History but, as my mother and Mrs Stewart were in the kitchen, I could hear most of it through the serving hatch. My first reaction was to laugh. The image of the little boy feeding marmalade to his sister was funny enough. The thought of Mrs Stewart's face on encountering this scene was more amusing still. But then I felt a sudden rush of rage. Mrs Stewart had dropped her voice but I could still hear her sanctimonious murmur burbling on. The smug cow! I thought. She's really enjoying this. Sounds of departure were heard. No, Mrs Stewart hadn't time to stop for coffee. She must get on and let the chairwoman of the Young Wives' Club know the Minister's wife wouldn't be coming. Otherwise they might delay the start of the meeting waiting for her arrival and that would never do, would it? No doubt, I thought, she would meet a number of other people while on her mission of goodwill and be able to pass on the shocking story to any one who had the time or inclination to hear it.

My mother was rather thoughtful over lunch. She passed on some of Mrs Stewart's story but she wasn't totally unsympathetic to the Minister's wife. She was a keen reader herself and although her choice of literature was rather restricted, as she refused to read anything 'unpleasant', she had been known to neglect the housework in order to finish the latest Angela Thirkell. As we washed up she said,

'I think I might just walk down to the Manse and see if that young woman would like some help. It never seems to occur to people that perhaps she can't get to the Young Wives' Club if she has no one to look after the children.' I was astounded. Usually my mother said she was too exhausted to walk anywhere and the idea that she would then offer to look after two children who might euphemistically be described as 'lively' seemed unbelievable but I only said,

'Perhaps she's glad of an excuse to get out of the Young Wives' Club.'

'Well dear, the meetings may not be very intellectual but if you marry a minister you know what you're taking on and there are

EASTER 1956

certain duties.'

I blessed my new-found religious scepticism for saving me from such a possible fate.

All afternoon, while pretending to myself that I was reorganising my Wordsworth notes, I thought about Mrs Stewart's story. The neglected washing-up reminded me of Alithea. Up till this point I'd only thought about how her pregnancy affected me and my relationship with Mike. Now, for the first time, it was brought home to me this pregnancy would result in an actual child. What kind of a mother would Alithea make? Indeed what kind of a father would Mike be? Most fathers I knew didn't have much to do with their children. They went to work, came home and hid behind newspapers. The Minister had been regarded as rather soft after being seen wheeling his little girl along the High Street in a pushchair. Mike hadn't been brought up to be helpful about the house but somehow it was easier to imagine him as a father than Alithea as a mother... Alithea pushing a pram? Alithea taking her baby to the clinic to be weighed while she collected cod-liver oil and orange juice and chatted to other mothers? Alithea singing nursery rhymes? All these things were equally unimaginable. On the other hand I could certainly imagine her sitting reading while her child got into all sorts of mischief, possibly even danger. And if, some time in the future, she had two children and the elder one fed marmalade to its sibling to keep it quiet I didn't even think she would be amused although Mike might be. I began to feel rather sorry for this unborn child. Fond as I was of reading I felt I would be a better mother than either Alithea or the Minister's wife. It was a pity Mike hadn't realised that, but it was too late now.

My mother returned from the Manse in remarkably good spirits. She hadn't managed to persuade the Minister's wife, whom she now referred to as Janet, to go to the Young Wives' meeting, but she'd given her some good advice that had apparently been well received and she was very taken with the children. She thought they were both remarkably bright and made only a passing reference to the younger child's curls My mother was fond of small children. She'd doted on me until I became a sullen teenager; now, although she was proud of my recent academic achievements, she mainly saw me as a straight-haired, green-eyed, argumentative disappointment.

The first of these failings however was about to be rectified. On the following Monday, Mrs Stewart arrived with all her paraphernalia. I'd washed my hair as instructed and came down to the kitchen. I'd been promised soft waves and had begun to imagine being able to put my hair up with one big hair clip in a casual and artistic manner just like Alithea.

Mrs Stewart produced a box. On it was a picture of two identical, simpering, young women. One had had an expensive perm, the other a home perm, the kind she was going to give me. They looked equally awful. At this point I panicked.

'I only want the ends permed,' I said.

'Are you sure, dear?' and 'Oh, Dilly!' said Mrs Stewart and my mother simultaneously. But then Mrs Stewart said it would be quite difficult to do more as my hair was so long and my mother regretted she hadn't sent me off for a hair cut but she hadn't and so I was spared the worst. It was bad enough. As soon as Mrs Stewart started to mix up her potions, the kitchen was filled by a rotten egg smell with the suggestion of something more dangerous underlying it. My hair was tugged about and wound tightly into rollers. The process seemed to take for ever and, when all the rinsing, drying and combing out had been finished, I realised she'd managed to curl a bit more than the ends. Mrs Stewart proclaimed I looked 'sweetly pretty' and begged me to look in the mirror. I could see my mother was rather more doubtful and when I dared to look in the mirror I was appalled. It could have been worse I supposed if I'd let her loose on all my hair but the word that sprang to mind was 'soppy'. I looked soppy. What the mirror showed me was the kind of girl who would have been happy to go to a dance in pink organdie. I'd been taken over. I managed to be polite – just, but then I rushed upstairs and sobbed in my own room.

The next day things got worse. A parcel arrived from one of my Edinburgh aunts. It turned out to be a bright green Harris tweed suit.

'Oh look what Aunty Nettie's sent for you!' said my mother. 'Real Harris tweed and you were saying only the other day that green suited you.'

'Not that green.' I was staring at the hairy object with horror. My mother didn't hear. She was busy reading Aunt Nettie's letter.

'She says she's got a wee bit stout for it but she's sure we can find a little woman locally who will alter it to fit you and it's very warm. You can wear it when you're working in your room at college and want to save on the heating.' The dismal picture of university life this evoked, sitting on my own in a cold room wearing a bright green bristly skirt and jacket, almost made me feel, if it was the only alternative, I'd rather be the girl in pink organdie. I told her not to waste money on alterations by the local 'little woman' who was, in fact, a large lady with an electric Singer sewing machine in her front room.

'I'm not wearing it. I'd rather wear my school skirt.'

'Well then dear, you'll have to do that. We can't afford to buy you any more clothes and after all navy blue goes with anything. We might manage a new jersey, something bright.'

I was beginning to feel nearly as depressed as I'd been in January. Perhaps my mother sensed some of this. She thought I'd been working too hard which made me feel guilty, and suggested a trip to the department store where we'd bought my interview suit, to look for the bright new sweater.

As we approached the store we both stopped to admire a striking window display. Beneath a bold caption 'Scandinavian Style' was a teak dining table and six chairs. The table was laid with a plain blue glass water jug and six matching tall glasses. The stainless steel cutlery was arranged round woven tablemats in blue and yellow check. I admired the glasses; my mother seemed most taken by the tablemats.

'Those are just like Janet's. She says they save so much work, no tablecloths to iron. Of course she can't afford to send things to the laundry but I told her that anyway they just rip your things to shreds. Our tablecloths really are getting past praying for. They were all wedding presents you know.' I could see she was rehearsing the argument she was anticipating with my father. She bought the mats but they always looked out of place on our old-fashioned polished table. My father hated them and eventually they disappeared.

*

Years later, while I'm clearing out the house after my mother's death, these mats re-emerge, a poignant reminder of how she too had wanted a different kind of life . She'd been as charmed by the style of living at the Manse, their teak dining table with the woven mats and their lime green wall, as I had been by the orange paint and plank bookcases in Alithea's kitchen or the scarlet chairs in the castle. Fortunately, unlike my father, Steve has no views on tablecloths and as long as no one touches his books or papers he doesn't mind what colour the walls, or even the chairs, are painted.

CHAPTER TWENTY FOUR

I'd hoped that the first time I washed my hair it might start to look softer and more natural; instead it just turned into a mass of frizz.

'Oh dear!' said my mother when I came downstairs with a tragic face. 'That can't be right. I'll just give Kirsty a ring. It's a bit late now but perhaps she'll come over tomorrow and show you how to manage it.'

'Please don't! I've decided I'm going to get it cut.'

'Are you sure dear? Short straight hair can be very trying. It might make you look very plain.'

'You think I'm plain anyway.'

My mother's reply to this was so evasive that I completely lost my temper. In the midst of all my tearful recriminations I said something about some people had said I was pretty. My mother looked alarmed.

'You know Dilly there are men who will flatter you just to get what they want.' This remark was devastatingly hurtful but, because I knew she was thinking of Hugh, it had its comic side. The thought of pompous Hugh using flattery to seduce me over the poetry of Catullus turned my sobs into hysterical laughter. But at the same time I so wanted to convince her I'd had an admirer that I might easily have said something foolish about Mike. Fortunately at that moment the phone rang.

'It's Fiona.' My mother handed me the phone and hovered round suspiciously. I glared at her and made gestures. It was a measure of how shaken she was by my outburst that she actually went off into the kitchen and started clattering the supper things ostentatiously.

'What's the matter, Dilly? You sound upset.' I poured out the whole story of the perm.

'I don't want anyone to see me' I said, thinking of the Davises.

'Well, there's a really good new hairdresser here,' Fiona said. 'He does razor cuts. Why don't you try him? As it happens, the reason I was ringing was to see if you could come over. I've got something to tell you. It's not something we can discuss at school.'

'What sort of thing?' I was so intrigued that I was momentarily distracted from my troubles.

'Not the sort of thing you can talk about over the phone.' I was even more fascinated. I said I'd tell my mother I had to go over to meet Fiona because I wanted to have my hair cut by this new hairdresser. She was always complaining about the local one so she might be persuaded.

Just at this point however she came in to say I'd been on the phone long enough and remind me about the phone bill.

'Fiona's ringing me,' She returned to the kitchen but this reminded me of a possible problem.

'Is he very expensive?'

'Actually I think he charges seven and six.'

'Seven shillings and sixpence!' I was shocked but in my present mood I felt defiant and agreed to everything Fiona suggested. When I came off the phone my mother said,

'The MacDonalds must have more money than us if they can let Fiona chatter on the telephone like that.' It didn't seem a good moment to ask for seven and six to destroy Mrs Stewart's handiwork but I suddenly remembered my post office savings book. I decided after all I wouldn't mention the hairdresser. I said Fiona needed to see me about some history revision.

'Surely it can wait until you're back at school.' I said it couldn't, but perhaps Fiona could come to us. This was merely a tactical move.

Silence.

I knew my mother was remembering Fiona's appearance the Easter before last. She'd turned up at our house wearing bright red stiletto-heeled shoes with matching nail varnish and a straw boater with a red ribbon. A long red umbrella had completed the vibrant colour scheme and all this combined with a striped blouse and a pencil-slim skirt had confirmed my mother's worse suspicions about Fiona's morals. Interestingly, my father, who would have been appalled if I had appeared dressed like this, seemed amused. He described Fiona as 'a card' and when she was leaving offered her a lift down to the bus, thereby proving, as my mother said, that all men were the same really. Eventually it was agreed that I could spend a day with Fiona as long as I got a bus back by six because my parents didn't want to have to spend another terrible evening wondering what had happened to me.

Fiona had no time to tell me her dramatic news before my hairdresser's appointment. All the same I was so full of anticipation that at first, I hardly noticed that my hair was being cut with a razor while still wet, although I was very happy to see the detested frizz falling on the floor. Instead of sticking me under a helmet-like dryer, the hairdresser dried my hair with a hand dryer and then we all contemplated the results.

'There,' he said. 'I knew you could take the gamine look. Lovely high cheek bones, like Audrey Hepburn.' This seemed a more achievable role model than Grace Kelly and I felt happier than I had done for months.

'You don't think I look too boyish?' The hairdresser and Fiona both reassured me although Fiona thought I ought to buy some earrings and even persuaded me I should try mascara and eye-shadow which I'd previously resisted, probably because of Amber's rather unsubtle use of these cosmetics.

'But first,' said Fiona, 'I really must tell you about the awful thing I've heard. We'll have coffee at Mather and Coles. There might be people we know at Boots.'

Once we were seated in a suitably secluded corner of the department store's restaurant and Fiona had bullied a rather haughty waitress into bringing us coffee, I waited excitedly to hear the 'awful thing' Fiona had to tell me. However, having waited so long, she now didn't seem to know how to begin. She fiddled around with her spoon, asked if I had enough milk and commented that the coffee was even weaker than at Boots.

'Well, come on!' I urged her. 'What is it? Spill the beans!' It couldn't be anything to do with her family, I thought, or she would have been more upset. I got the impression that although she was shocked by something she had been rather looking forward to telling me about it. For one hopeful moment I thought maybe Ursula was involved in something scandalous; unfortunately this seemed unlikely.

'You know registry office weddings?' she eventually began. Surely, I thought, Ursula hadn't got married? It was a wonderful idea but even my imagination couldn't stretch that far.

'Yes?' I said, trying to get a glimpse of my new haircut in the gold-framed mirror across the room. She paused again,

'Well you know sometimes people, if they've got something to hide, might get married at the registrar's with just two witnesses.'

'Or if they thought their families might not get on,' I suggested. 'That's how the Davises got married,' I added casually. Fiona dumped her cup down, spilling the tepid beige liquid into her saucer.

'You already knew!'

'Yes, what's so terrible about that? Mr Davis told me that Saturday afternoon, you remember, when I went round and Mrs Davis and Mr Marlow had gone to Nottingham to see a French film.' Really! I thought. Was that all? I nearly said 'Don't be so bourgeois.' Surely there must be more to it than this.

'But Dilly, you must have got it wrong. That was ages ago.'

'Yes, last October.'

'But Dilly, he can't have told you then, not last October. That's what I was going to tell you. They only got married a fortnight ago. Early in the morning, with two witnesses who seemed to be complete strangers!'

I felt for a few moments as if I were living in a weird time warp. I tried to think what Mike had actually said,

'All you need to get married, Dilly, is quarter of an hour at the registrar's and two witnesses,' but he hadn't actually said that was what they had done, had he?

Implying rather than actually lying I'd come to call it. It was a technique I'd become rather skilled at lately.

'Now I come to think of it...' and I told Fiona what Mike had said. 'And so that means...'

'It means that for the two terms Mrs Davis has been teaching us she's been living in sin,' said Fiona, sounding alarmingly Presbyterian.

'But how do you know?'

'I know a woman who works in the registry office. She goes to our church. I bumped into her in town last Saturday and we had coffee together. She's a terrible gossip and she went on about how shocked she'd been recently when this couple had turned up and the woman looked as if she might be pregnant. I said surely that must often happen at registry office weddings? but she said these two were teachers and you'd think you could expect something better from people like that, even nowadays.'

'But how do you know it was the Davises?'

'She started to describe them. Apparently they were a very striking looking couple. She had a lot of dark hair and was wearing a red sweater, and slacks. Fancy getting married in slacks! - even at a registry office. This woman I know didn't take to her at all. She said she was in a foul temper. He was very charming apparently, very blue eyes. Has Mr Davis got very blue eyes, Dilly?' I nodded, unable to trust myself to speak about Mike's eyes. 'They all felt quite sorry for him but personally, I think he must be nearly as much to blame as she is.'

It seemed unlikely that there was another couple fitting this description anywhere in the neighbourhood but I still asked,

'Are you absolutely sure it was them?'

'Absolutely sure! I asked her if by any chance she remembered their name. She didn't want to tell me at first. She said she'd said too much already. So I said, "I suppose it wasn't Davis by any chance?" and she said "Oh no! You don't know them do you?" which was a bit of a giveaway, wasn't it?'

It struck me that the woman wasn't likely to survive in her job for much longer if she could so easily be trapped into giving away confidential information but I just said,

'Well there's nothing we can do about it.'

'Don't you think we should tell someone? I haven't even mentioned it to Mummy yet but I know she would go straight to Miss Cutler.'

'But what good would it do?

'It's a matter of principle. After all the High School is a Church of

England foundation.'

It occurred to me that maybe Miss Cutler might rather not know about this; it would be most inconvenient. We might not be very popular if we brought it to her attention.

'It would be difficult to find a new English teacher for the summer term,' I pointed out.

All this time, I thought, Mike had been free and I hadn't known. But anyway what could I have done about it? I was just sweet little Dilly to him. 'Legally, you are,' I remembered him saying when I told him I wasn't a child. Old enough to get married, of course, although not without my parents' consent and, after all, I still wanted to go to university. I remembered the college regulations I'd received. 'Members of the college *in statu pupillari* will be required to go down if they marry'. And what would it be like to go up to university wearing an engagement ring? It might cramp one's style a bit. For a moment it seemed possible to imagine a world beyond Mike. After all I had lovely cheekbones. Others might appreciate them. But, Alithea had seemed in a foul temper - poor Mike!

'Why did your friend think Mrs Davis was in a bad temper?'

'Apparently he tried to kiss her and she pushed him away.'

I was overwhelmed for a moment with grief and fury. She didn't deserve him. I would never ever have pushed Mike away. But I had to try to appear unconcerned.

'I've heard you can go off that sort of thing a bit when you're pregnant.'

'Dilly! Who told you that?'

'I can't remember - probably Jane - she always makes out she's the expert. Perhaps you'd better ask your brother if there's a medical reason for it.' Fiona started to giggle and we both went on laughing for no reason except that was what we sometimes did.

'We could always blackmail her into giving us a good report,' I said and we went off into fresh fits.

'This coffee is terrible,' I spluttered.

'It says on the menu it's made with real beans.'

'But it doesn't say what kind of beans.'

'Baked beans,' Fiona suggested.

We were both helpless with laughter. It looked as if Alithea's secret was safe.

'Have you two finished?' asked the waitress, snatching our cups. 'I have ladies here waiting for tables.'

'Come on!' said Fiona. 'Let's go and look for earrings.'

'What have you done!' was my mother's immediate reaction, but once she'd scolded me for ingratitude and said she didn't know what she was going to say to Mrs Stewart she started to admit that my new hairstyle suited me.

'I suppose you can take a rather different style from me,' she said thoughtfully.

'You look like a lad,' said my father.

'With earrings!'

'Well you won't be able to wear those at school.'

'Who cares about school. I'll be out of it soon. And then', I added, vaguely but threateningly, 'there'll be no stopping me.'

PART 6

Summer Term 1956

CHAPTER TWENTY FIVE

'Smashing haircut Dilly,' said Jane the first evening back at the Boarding House. The others agreed although Caroline said she always felt long hair was more feminine. Down at school, Hazel, the future beauty consultant, was more than just complimentary. She wanted the name of the hairdressers and to know who had cut my hair. I looked at her. She was as pink and white and delectable as ever but her face was rather round - not very distinguished cheek bones - I thought.

This term was always a bit easier at the Boarding House. As it was officially summer, the common room fire remained unlit, making it rather chill and dank on sunless days, but the juniors could play out in the garden, so life was less stressful.

Now the evenings were light again we could watch the comings and goings in the Close. Algy, the young actor, caused a minor sensation by appearing with his hair dyed red, obviously for some part he was playing. Jane screamed with laughter when she saw him. He turned round; we realised he must have heard her and this set us all off, even Caroline, although she said, between giggles, that we were all being very bad-mannered. Andrew Strong appeared once in white shorts, on his way to play tennis somewhere, causing much swooning among the juniors. The divine Mr Weaver strode to and fro in his cassock looking romantically contemplative; but there was no sign of Mike.

Alithea, however, seemed better tempered. Fiona said you weren't usually sick after the first few months. We noticed her waistline was thickening.

We had only been back at school a week when we heard that Rosa's father had died.

'We should send a card,' said Ursula, who always knew the right thing to do, but then, after Rosa had been off school for a few days, Miss Carr said she had asked for some work and perhaps one of us would be kind enough to take it down for her.

We thought it might be easier if we all went together. I was very nervous. I felt I wouldn't know what to say. I also wondered whether the coffin would be in the house and hoped not.

Rosa's street was halfway down the hill towards the town. Further down the slope there were more rows of redbrick terraced houses and you could see over their roofs to the engineering works at the bottom of the valley. The Cathedral Close on the top of the hill could have been in another city, another world.

When we knocked at the door there was a pause; we could hear a muttered conversation inside. We looked at each other. Were we doing the right thing? Then Rosa's mother opened the door and stared at us blankly. Fiona rose to the occasion.

'Mrs Green, I do hope we're not intruding on your grief but we were told Rosa had asked us to bring some work for her.'

'You'd better come in,' she said. The stairs rose up almost directly from the front door but there was just room for us to squeeze down the passage into the narrow kitchen where Rosa was working at a small deal table.

'Take your friends into the front room,' said her mother but Rosa ignored her. On our way to the kitchen we'd passed another room with a half open door, and I'd glanced in uneasily, wondering if the coffin might be in there but all I could see were some posters with writing in what I presumed was Russian. On the mantelpiece was a bronze bust of a man with flowing hair and a beard. I had an idea it might be Karl Marx. The three of us took up too much space in the kitchen and I felt we seemed too large, too loud and too highly coloured compared with small, pale Rosa and her thin, pale mother There would hardly, I thought, have been room in the house for the coffin.

Ursula had, of course, been entrusted with the work and the instructions but, that dealt with, we all stood there looking awkward, not knowing what to say and wondering how soon we could leave.

'Well,' said Mrs Green, 'can I get you all a cup of tea or something?'

'Mother!' said Rosa.

'That's terribly sweet of you,' said Ursula, 'but we have to get back to school before the bell goes.' I thought she sounded patronising and I wanted to be friendly so I burst in,

'Ursula's really missing your help, Rosa. She's having to make do with me and Fiona and we forgot all about moving the milk crates at break the other day. It was chaos!'

As usual in Rosa's presence I felt as if I was babbling and the other two looked at me as if I was being inappropriately flippant but Rosa gave a faint smile and said,

'I'm sure it's not that bad.'

As we left, I said,

'At least your father knew about your scholarship.'

'Oh that,' said her mother. 'Well I don't know what use that'll be now. Scholarships don't pay the rent. She may have to look for a job.'

'But she can't,' I said. 'She must go to university. She's so clever!'

'Like I said,' said her mother. 'Clever doesn't pay the rent.' But she followed us to the door and, as we left, said,

'Thank you for coming. It's nice for Rosa to see her friends. I hope we shall see you at the funeral on Thursday afternoon. Half past two, just at the cemetery. He wouldn't have wanted anything religious.'

We were all rather quiet on the way back. Eventually Fiona said,

'It must be awful to live in a little house like that.'

'Oh, I don't know,' said Ursula. 'It all depends what you're used to. I expect people like Rosa's family would feel quite lost in somewhere like the Deanery.' She gave a superior little snigger. 'By the way, Dilly. You really shouldn't have burst out with all that stuff about how Rosa must go to university. It wasn't your place to advise them. She may be happier, you know, doing some sort of office job. It would still be a step up for her.'

I waited for Fiona to support me, but she stayed silent. Why didn't the others see how wrong this all was? Because, I supposed, they hadn't had their eyes opened by the Davises. I suddenly felt lonely.

Then, after a few more moments silence, Ursula unexpectedly said,

'Of course I suppose one shouldn't really think like that. Mrs Davis was telling me the other day about the importance of the 1944 Education Act and how it meant people like her husband could go to university. If working-class people are really clever perhaps they should go to university but probably they're better off not going to Oxford or Cambridge. She says her husband has a bit of a chip on his shoulder about the way he felt he was sometimes treated at Oxford.'

Mrs Davis had been talking to Ursula! What was going on? And complaining about Mike…'a chip on his shoulder.' For some minutes I couldn't speak. Then, just as we were going in the school gates, I managed to say,

'Do you think we should go to the funeral?'

'Of course not,' said Ursula. 'It's a school afternoon.'

'It's only Games.'

'I don't think my father would like me to go to an atheist's funeral,' she added. I felt, rather oddly, that this was an unchristian attitude.

Later that afternoon I met Miss Carr in the corridor and she enquired about our visit. I said I thought Rosa's mother had been pleased we had all gone and she'd asked us to go to the funeral on Thursday afternoon.

Miss Carr looked taken aback and, rather stupidly, I said we'd only be missing Games. My reluctance to take part in organised sport was notorious; Miss Carr said I needed my exercise and I didn't argue any more. Perhaps if I had she might have asked Miss Cutler to let us, or at least me, go to the funeral but, as with the Davises' party, I didn't ask properly for fear of an outright refusal. However this time I was more defiant. I decided to skip Games and go anyway.

I told Fiona of my plan. After her first objections she volunteered to come too but I said I wanted her to cover for me.

'Say you think I suddenly felt ill.'

'But Dilly, that would be lying.' I realised she wasn't as advanced in deception as I had learnt to be.

'No it won't. I shall be feeling sick with terror.'

'Then why go?' but she agreed to do her best.

On Thursday I removed my Games kit from its bag and replaced it with the soberest clothes I could lay my hands on. My school skirt was dark enough. Fiona lent me a black sweater and a pair of prohibited nylons. In a moment of vanity, I included my new silver earrings that I kept at the back of my top drawer, tied up in Mike's grimy handkerchief. This latter unromantic object was my only relic of him; my only reminder of that Saturday afternoon we had spent together during the previous autumn. Now, all possibility of returning it having passed, I couldn't bear to discard the thing, or even wash it.

I had no real idea about appropriate clothes or behaviour at funerals. I hadn't gone to my grandparents' funerals as my family considered such occasions unsuitable for children. I remembered seeing female members of the Royal Family in black veils at the King's funeral but rightly guessed that such excesses would be thought inappropriate by normal people.

The games field was on the outskirts of the town; conveniently the cemetery was just beyond it. When the others turned in at the gate I waited for a moment and cycled on. I was early and had time to discard my school blouse and cardigan behind a hedge, wriggle into Fiona's sweater and put on my earrings. People began to arrive. Suddenly I saw Mike. He looked unfamiliar in a dark suit but when he saw me he gave his lopsided smile; my heart did its usual double-somersault. I realised that I wasn't over him yet, that I had secretly hoped he would be there and that was why I was wearing my earrings, although, I told myself, I really did care about Rosa and her mother as well.

The hearse arrived, followed by a black car. Rosa and her mother got out. Another car drew up and more people got out. They looked very respectable and, I thought, rather disapproving but perhaps they were just looking solemn as befitted the occasion. I guessed they were Rosa's mother's relations. Mike was talking to another, very different, group of people who I supposed were from the local Labour Party. They looked slightly less respectable but rather more amiable. The undertakers watched grim-faced as the coffin was taken out of the hearse by six men who looked uncomfortable in their black suits. I noticed their hands were knotted, scarred and blue-veined and realised they were probably miners, old friends of Rosa's father from South

Yorkshire. Everybody moved towards the graveside. Rosa suddenly saw me, and her smile removed all my doubts about my right to be there. The men lowered the coffin into the grave and I thought, - is that all? - But it wasn't.

Mike moved forward. He said that his friend Harry Green wouldn't have wanted a priest at his graveside. Along with his hero Karl Marx, he had believed religion to be the opium of the people. (At this point I noticed some of the relatives definitely looked set-faced.) However, Mike continued, Rosa and her mother had asked him to say a few words and he was deeply honoured. Although he had only known Harry for a few months he had come to respect his courage and integrity and admire his intellect. (The expressions of the relations became ever more rigid.) He went on to say how proud her father had been of Rosa. How he had fought to stay alive for her sake and had at least managed to see her future secured by her scholarship to London University, (but it isn't, I thought). For this reason he wanted to read this poem by a compatriot of his, Dylan Thomas. (The relations' faces now appeared to be set in stone.)

Mike opened a book but clearly he didn't really need any prompting,

'Do go not gentle into that goodnight,'

I could feel my eyes filling with tears. His voice resounded through the graveyard; Richard Burton was as nothing compared to this. By the time he had reached the final,

'Rage, rage against the dying of the light,' the tears were rolling down my face. As usual I had lost my handkerchief; I surreptitiously wiped my face on the sleeve of Fiona's sweater. I looked across the grave and saw Rosa was crying too. I'd hardly ever seen her show any emotion apart from scorn.

The six miners now stepped forward and stood round the grave. One of them nodded and they started to sing,

'The people's flag is deepest red,

Their voices were a bit uncertain but then Mike joined in. I suddenly remembered Uncle Frank,

'Nice singing voices though, the Welsh' and in spite of the emotion of the occasion, for a moment I wanted to laugh. By the time they came to the chorus,

'Then raise the scarlet standard high!
Beneath its folds we'll live and die.'

the local Labour party group were singing as well. Their voices were ringing out loudly making me wish I knew the words and could sing with them. Some of the relatives had started to move away, tight lipped, obviously wanting to disassociate themselves from such goings on. As the anthem came to its conclusion,

'Though cowards flinch and traitors sneer
We'll keep the red flag flying here.'

Rosa stepped forward and threw a handful of earth on the coffin.

'Thank you for coming,' said Rosa's mother.

'Yes thanks, Dilly,' said Rosa.

'Are the other girls here?' said Rosa's mother looking round.

'No, they couldn't manage to get away.' As they moved towards the car Mike came over,

'Dilly! I hardly recognised you. You look...grown up. Haven't you done something to your hair? You look lovely. You should wear black more often. It suits you.' These were almost lines from my fantasies but too late, too late. 'He charms everybody' I reminded myself, but it was no good.

'Have you heard by the way?' he looked a bit shamefaced, - self-conscious and, at the same time, smug - I told myself. 'Allie's expecting a baby, in the autumn.'

'We haven't exactly heard but we guessed.'

'Oh you girls! Are you the only one here, by the way? Where are Rosa's other friends?' It didn't seem the moment to explain that Rosa didn't really have any friends.

'School thought rounders was more important,' I said. 'I'm not supposed to be here myself. If it comes out I'll probably be expelled.' Mike looked concerned.

'Oh I'm sure they'll understand,' he said. 'We've missed you Dilly, you know,' he continued. We? I thought. I looked at him and felt tears welling up again.

'Oh Dilly!' he said. 'Oh Dilly!' He took my hand in his and then put his other hand on top imprisoning mine. 'I hope… You're such a lovely girl.' (At least he didn't call me a sweet kid, I thought) 'You're such a lovely girl – some man is going to be so lucky one day. I hope…' I realised it was the nearest I was going to get to an apology. I squeezed my eyes shut for a moment to get rid of the tears; then looked him in the eye and said as firmly as I could,

'Perhaps you need to be more careful in future.' He gave me his lopsided smile.

'Perhaps I should.' (But, I thought, I don't think you will be. You can't help it.)

'I hope you'll both be very happy,' I said.

'Well, yes.' He looked a bit worried for a moment, and I wondered if he thought I was referring to their surreptitious wedding. 'Allie's rather… she's finding it difficult to get used to the idea,' and then he brightened up, 'but I'm sure when the baby's here, it will be wonderful.' He leant towards me as if he was going to kiss me but then looked round at the dispersing group.

'No,' I said. 'Better not.' I released my hand. 'Goodbye.' I felt pleased with myself for gaining some control of the situation and I walked away with dignity only marred by the fact that I was wearing my best shoes and I wasn't very used to walking in high heels especially when the landscape kept blurring before me.

I picked up my bike from the hedge and changed back into my school things, putting my earrings carefully in the top pocket of my blazer. I hoped to get back unnoticed, but I was no sooner through the door of the Boarding House than Jane grabbed me,

'Dilly, what have you been up to? Mazzy wants to see you at once. She's absolutely furious about something.'

CHAPTER TWENTY SIX

I wasn't scared - I told myself - I bloody well wasn't scared of any of them. They could do as they liked. What could they do anyway? I'd soon be out of it all.

I banged boldly on Mazzy's door.

'Come in!' I walked in, shoulders back, with what I hoped was a defiant stare on my face.

'Perhaps you can explain to me why you were not at Games this afternoon, Phyllida.'

Mazzy knew perfectly well why I hadn't been at Games that afternoon; lying would be pointless.

'I went to Rosa's father's funeral.' I'd like to think I stated this fact with dignity or even defiance but I suspect I just sounded sullen and guilty.

'And why did you think you could do this without asking anyone's permission?'

'Well, I sort of mentioned it to Miss Carr, and she didn't seem very keen on the idea, but I don't think she actually said "No".'

'But you didn't have permission.' And so the interview went coldly on.

At one point I attempted to justify myself by explaining Rosa's mother had asked us to come.

'I'm sure Mrs Green meant no harm but people from her..her background don't always quite understand.'

'People from her background!' My voice rose - I was almost shouting. 'People from her background! I thought you voted Labour.' I terrified myself. I felt possessed and the look on Mazzy's face was terrifying too.

'I vote by ballot, Dilly. That is what we do in this country.' I think she must have realised I was beside myself because she suddenly changed; she became sad, reproachful, disappointed. In a way that was worse. She was full of concern for my spiritual welfare. Once again, she said I had been 'subject to influences.' She had hoped, with my upbringing, I would have been able to withstand these but she supposed I was still very young. It was not too late for me to learn from this experience. Once again, she warned me to be careful about my choice of friends when I got to university where there would be many temptations. I hoped she was not going to offer to pray for me; to forestall this possibility I said,

'But the funeral was an inspiring experience. His comrades stood round the grave and sang *The Red Flag*.' I decided not to mention Dylan Thomas. She'd probably guessed Mike would have been there but there was no point in drawing her attention to this. As it was, I thought I saw a faint flicker of amusement on her face. 'What's so funny?' I wondered. Finally she said,

'Well Dilly, the matter is out of my hands now. Miss Cutler wants to see you first thing in the morning. Prep should have started by now and I expect Brenda is having to undertake your duties once again.'

In spite of my bravado I couldn't help worrying about my interview with Miss Cutler. I thought it very likely she would take my prefect's badge away. I knew I lacked leadership qualities. From the moment I had been made a prefect I'd half expected this to happen. Only once before had a prefect been demoted. I remembered Miss Cutler announcing at prayers that this particular girl had shown she was no longer fit to be a prefect. None of us knew exactly why - we were fairly junior at the time - but someone hinted it was because she had been seen on a float, at the Festival of Britain parade, with her arms round an American airman. At least, I thought, I would be demoted for a nobler reason.

Miss Cutler quite reasonably wanted to know why I hadn't asked properly if I could go to the funeral. She said Miss Carr had been surprised by the suggestion and I could have made my case sensibly. I was too impetuous but of course I had also been deceitful and involved Fiona in my deceit. She needed some time to consider whether I was fit to continue to be a prefect. How could I hope to have any moral authority over the juniors if I behaved like this? However she admitted there were some mitigating aspects. She did realise I had wanted to help Rosa at this sad time. In the meantime, I was suspended from prefect duties and I should stay out of the prefects' room.

As soon as I went into the form room Fiona came up and signalled to me to come out into the cloakroom.

'What did she say?' I explained I was suspended. 'Never mind. I thought that might happen. I've brought a flask of coffee for break. We're not going to go back to milk bottles and straws at this stage in our career.'

'Are you suspended too?'

'No, but you don't think I'd leave you by yourself in the form room with Audrey's gang and that half-witted Hazel, do you? Anyway I'd rather stay out of Ursula's way for the moment, thank you!' Then she told me how I'd been found out.

Fiona had told the Games teacher I was feeling sick. She had been suitably vague about whether I'd gone back to school or to the Boarding House and it seemed entirely probable that nobody would have bothered to investigate further. I was no loss to the rounders team. The Games staff had given up on me years ago. But, at that moment, Fiona told me, Ursula had spoken up.

'She said,' - Fiona mimicked Ursula's priggish tones - 'Are you sure Fiona? I'm pretty certain I've just seen Dilly cycling off past the field down the road towards the cemetery. Perhaps she's had permission to go to Rosa's father's funeral after all.' When challenged later, Ursula claimed that she had made this remark in all innocence. Neither Fiona nor I believed her.

*

Steve has never been able to understand my continuing distrust of Ursula. He's always thought it's most commendable, considering her background, that she's become so left wing.

'You mean,' I say,' like there's more joy in heaven over a sinner that repenteth?' Steve does not care for the analogy.

This particular conversation is taking place some time in the seventies when Steve and Ursula's husband, Clive, are, for a time, colleagues in the same university department. We're walking back from a dreary evening in their house. I continue,

'Her politics may have changed; she hasn't. They just give her still more justification to be self-righteous. She still wears the proper uniform, only now it's dungarees. And that meal! I remember, when we were all about thirteen, she once asked Fiona and me to tea. We ate bread and margarine and teeth-shattering rock cakes in an icy room with portraits of her depressing ancestors glowering at us from the walls and Fiona and I got a helpless fit of the giggles. Now it's boiled chops and Chairman Mao. I think I'll give her that poster of Che Guevara. He's better looking than Mao. It might sex up her cooking a bit.'

Reluctantly, Steve laughs and I'm silent, remembering how my

SUMMER TERM 1956

introduction to radical politics had involved poetry, art, jazz and Mozart, red sweaters, pale cream nail varnish, Algerian red wine, spaghetti bolognese and scarlet painted chairs.

*

For two days I remained in limbo. The Boarders, who had some vague idea that I was in trouble, kept asking what was going on but I'd been forbidden to say anything to anybody. Then Miss Cutler sent for me and told me I could remain a prefect.

'I think,' she said, 'you should know that what has finally decided me is a letter I have had from Rosa's mother. I didn't realise you and Rosa were such particular friends. You should have made this plain at the time and then of course you might have been allowed to go to the funeral. Perhaps you might like to read this? I knew Rosa's father was an intelligent man but I didn't realise her mother... one wouldn't have thought...' She trailed off as she handed me the letter.

Nor would I have thought Rosa's mother capable of writing such a letter; nor did I think she had. The handwriting might be that of Rosa's mother's but as I read I could hear another voice coming through as clearly as if Mike was actually in the room and I felt tears coming. Fortunately it didn't seem inappropriate to be touched by such eloquence.

'Yes,' said Miss Cutler, and she actually smiled, 'a very moving letter. Very kind of her to take the trouble.' Then, just as I was leaving, she said, 'I wonder how Mrs Green knew that you were suspended?'

'I didn't tell Rosa,' I said defensively. She looked at me enquiringly. I hoped she didn't know that Mike Davis had been a regular visitor at Rosa's. She usually tried to pretend teachers' husbands, in any case a rare species in our school, didn't exist. Although, as Alithea's pregnancy became more and more obvious, this must have been becoming increasingly difficult. I left her looking thoughtful.

That was almost the end of the matter. Miss Carr told me I'd been 'intellectually dishonest' which was her most crushing rebuke but Mazzy said no more on the subject. I returned to the tedium of prefect duties and the prefects' room coffee, which was inferior to Fiona's flask; however I was spared the indignity of being demoted. Strangely enough I now felt more secure about staying a prefect. After all, if I hadn't lost my badge over this incident I was unlikely to lose it by merely being inadequate.

Back on corridor duty, I saw Alithea approaching.

'All right, Dilly?'

'Yes, thanks. Thanks a lot.' And we exchanged a quick, secret smile. 'Oh, Mrs Davis...' but she'd walked away.

Rosa returned to school a few days later. She was obviously still going to try for a State Scholarship and there was no mention of taking a job. As soon as I could get her on her own I asked her what was happening.

'Oh, I'm going to college,' she said. 'Mum and I are moving in with my aunty, Mum's sister. She's a widow too. When Dad got ill we moved down from Yorkshire to be near Mum's family, but her sister's the only one that's ever helped. She's the worst off too but that's always the way: isn't it?'

'I'm so glad,'

'Well, what you said helped. Mum was quite surprised. It started her thinking and, of course, Mr Davis was wonderful. Mum thinks the world of him. What he says goes.'

Yet another member of the Mike Davis fan club - I thought. It helped, I realised, to have a slightly cynical disposition. I decided to cultivate it.

'Of course,' Rosa added, 'there's not much room at my aunty's. Mum and I will have to share a room but I'll soon be away a lot so we'll manage.'

I imagined having to share a bedroom with my mother. It was an appalling thought.

'This is he of whom I said. After me cometh a man which is preferred before me: for he was before me.'

Miss Cutler was reading from St John's Gospel. We were in the middle of one of our weekly Scripture lessons. We'd been studying St John's Gospel since the beginning of term; sometimes it felt like since the beginning of time; so far we'd reached chapter one, verse thirty. 'Let us consider,' Miss Cutler continued, 'what is implied by the two "befores" in this context.' But, just as we were beginning to consider the implications of the 'befores', there was a piercing scream. – Someone's finally cracked - was my first thought, but it was Audrey who was screaming and she was obviously in pain. She writhed at her desk doubled up and sobbing. Ursula was told to run to the office and get them to telephone for an ambulance. The class broke up in confusion and before the bell had gone for the end of lesson Audrey had been borne out on a stretcher, still shrieking intermittently.

The official line was acute appendicitis but the rumours spread fast. We soon knew Audrey had had a miscarriage of a particularly agonising sort.

'It was an ectopic pregnancy,' said Fiona learnedly. Her brother as usual was the source of this gynaecological information. Audrey wasn't coming back to school, and her friends said her parents were insisting she must marry Bobby as soon as she had recovered, although neither Audrey, nor, apparently, Bobby, were by now very enthusiastic about this. Nor could I believe her parents really wanted their only child to go and live in America. Bobby came from a small town in Iowa. Her friends got an atlas from the geography room and discovered Iowa was right in the middle of the United States and very flat.

'It's not as if she's going somewhere glamorous like Hollywood or New York,' said Hazel.

'I don't see why she's got to marry him,' I said. 'Now there's no baby.'

'Surely Dilly, it's a matter of moral principles.' said Ursula.

'Why if they involve making everybody miserable?' I surprised myself by saying. I felt my ideas about a lot of things were beginning to change and I wished I could talk to someone about them. Well of course I wished I could talk to the Davises but presumably this particular subject would have been a sensitive one at the time even if I had still been seeing them.

Then, once again, Fiona's indiscreet friend at the registry office had an interesting story to tell. Audrey and her parents had turned up for the ceremony but Bobby had gone missing. He was presumably more willing to face a court martial than marriage to Audrey.

'He's probably got a wife back in Iowa,' said Fiona. 'Poor Audrey, no one will marry her now. She's damaged goods.' I wondered if Audrey would have to live as a social outcast like Maggie Tulliver, in *Mill on the Floss*, a tragic death her only hope of redemption.

CHAPTER TWENTY SEVEN

Exams had begun. One of the first papers was European History. That morning Hazel drifted in. While peering in the cloakroom mirror, apparently examining her flawless complexion for blackheads, she asked vaguely,

'Is it European or English history today?' Fiona and I looked at each other but in a way I was quite impressed by her insouciance. As I had predicted, we had the question about the decline of the Spanish Empire in the 17th Century. I knew all the facts. Unfortunately I was, by this time, completely bored by them. I expect the examiner was equally bored by my answer.

'Told you we'd have that question on 17th Century Spain,' I said to Hazel afterwards. She looked at me blankly. 'Don't you remember? The day we got into trouble for being in the Physics lab.' But the row about the Physics lab had left as little impression on Hazel as the fate of the Spanish Empire.

In a way I envied Hazel. I still cared about the exams but I just couldn't concentrate on revision. The evening before the Romantics paper I did make some attempt to revise Wordsworth but could work up little enthusiasm about the *Small Celandine* nor feel much concern for the ramblings of the tedious old leech gatherer. Instead I started, surreptitiously, to read through the *Songs and Lyrics* in Alithea's Donne - she'd never asked for it back and I didn't feel like reminding her about it. Ever since she had introduced me to the Metaphysicals I'd become more and more obsessed by Donne's love poems. Seeing Mike again at the funeral had made me realise I was more in love with him than ever and only Donne seemed to fit my mood.

'*My ragges of heart,*' I repeated to myself '*can like, wish and adore, But after one such love, can love no more.*'

Hearing me murmur these lines Jane looked up.

'A bit late to be learning quotations now, Dilly.'

'M.Y.O.B. bossy boots!'

'OK. OK. Keep your hair on!'

This childish exchange rather ruined the image of myself as a tragic heroine. Reluctantly I returned to Wordsworth.

Once the exams were over we were supposed to fill our days by doing a local history project. At least it gave us an excuse to get out of school. Fiona had the bright idea that, for the purposes of our research, we needed to visit some village churches. Even Ursula saw no objection to this plan and so for several days Rosa, Fiona, Ursula and I cycled off together into the countryside. Fiona and I were, by this time, managing to be reasonably civil to Ursula. Any observer who happened to see the four of us sitting around among the tombstones in the long grass of some ancient churchyard sharing chocolate, or in Fiona's case radishes, as she was slimming again, would have thought we were an amicable enough bunch.

On one of these days we saw a group of archaeologists working lower down on the escarpment. We cycled down to investigate and found they were excavating the site of a Roman villa. It was an interesting diversion but the main thing I remember about the episode was an argument Rosa had with Ursula and Fiona about the benefits or otherwise of Roman civilisation. Fiona had just expressed her amazement at the high level of sophistication in Roman living standards revealed by the excavation.

'The Ancient Britons really ought to have been terribly grateful,' said Ursula. I thought this was the kind of thing her aunt, the Dean's wife, might have said in the past when the Dean was just a vicar. I imagined her marching round the parish, trying to impose middle class standards on resentful council estate tenants, convinced that they ought to be 'terribly grateful' for her advice. Alithea, I felt, still had some way to go in turning Ursula into a Socialist. I could see Rosa was annoyed. Her pale face became flushed, always a dangerous sign. She spoke with quiet passion,

'Why should they have been grateful? Don't you realise they had their own culture? Like all Empire builders, the Romans rode roughshod over local customs and local boundaries, just as we've done in Africa.' This was too much for Fiona, always a loyal imperialist. Even if it meant being on Ursula's side she had to speak out in defence of the British Empire.

'Yes,' said Ursula, when Fiona had finished 'As Fiona says we did bring some benefits to Africa, although, of course,' she added, sounding surprisingly apologetic, 'we did some terrible things too.' These last few words, almost muttered, seemed rather more like Davis-speak than Ursula-speak but, before Fiona could protest, she reverted to her normal style, saying she thought the Celts must have benefited overall from Roman rule.

'The women didn't,' said Rosa. 'Celtic women had much more respect and status. They could rule in their own right.' As the rest of us had only the haziest notions about life in pre-Roman Britain there was nothing more we could say.

'At least the Romans had central heating,' I said, to break the awkward silence that followed. 'That's more than can be said for the Boarding House.'

I was, in fact, more interested in what this conversation had revealed about the current state of Ursula's thinking than in the argument itself.

*

Once, being in Oxford for the day, I decide to visit my old tutor. She's reading when I arrive but puts her book aside. As she does so I catch a glimpse of the title, 'Women in Celtic Britain' and I'm suddenly reminded of our argument beside the dig on that far off summer day. The memory makes me wonder if the book is, perhaps, by Rosa. By this time I've lost track of her. Steve never comes across her at the annual Labour Party Conference but I can't imagine she's abandoned left wing politics altogether, so I've begun to wonder if she really is a Communist just as Fiona had once suspected. However I'd kept up with her long enough to know she'd got a First and had become an academic.

I'm just going to ask about the book when my tutor kindly enquires 'And how are all your tribe?' Her attitude towards my large family and their eccentric behaviour is one of tolerant amusement that I find rather comforting, especially compared with my mother's growing disapproval, so I'm easily distracted and, in recounting the latest of our dramas, I forget all about 'Women in Celtic Britain'.

*

We cycled back from the excavations towards the city along lanes bordered with fading cow parsley and hedges entangled with wild roses. The larks sang high above the fields of green wheat and I was beginning to feel happier again.

This return to happiness was mixed with nostalgia. After all these years we were doing things for the last time. The Commemoration Service was nearly upon us. A small rotund monk from the local

SUMMER TERM 1956

Anglican monastery came as usual to help us rehearse plainsong.

'*My soul doth magnify the Lord,*' we chanted.

'Each word separate, like beads on a string,' he pleaded, as he did every year.

And, as we did every year, we filed into the nave of the cathedral, smart in blazers, berets, school ties and dazzling white blouses, to sing the familiar hymns and yawn through the Bishop's address. But for me and for Fiona and Ursula and Rosa and Brenda and Hazel and all Audrey's friends, although, of course, not Audrey, this was for the last time.

When we returned to the Boarding House after Commemoration, it was clear something unusual was in the air.

'Miss Manzonni has an announcement to make after tea,' said Matron. We crammed into the study, and as soon as we'd all found a patch of floor or somewhere to perch, Mazzy spoke,

'I feel I must let you know, before rumours start to spread. I shall be leaving my post as housemistress at the end of this term.' We were silent. It was inconceivable. No one could remember the Boarding House without Mazzy. I knew I had to say something.

'Everyone will be very sorry...' I began.

'Where are you going, Miss Manzonni?' Jane interrupted. Mazzy's solemn expression lightened.

'I shall be taking up a teaching post in Miss Robson's school. Of course, I shall miss being a housemistress, but I think it is time for a change.' We shuffled out, trying to come to terms with this momentous news.

I realised that I really was sorry. During the evening, while the others speculated about what a new housemistress might be like, I analysed my feelings. It wouldn't affect me, but somehow I'd thought

Mazzy would always be there. I'd imagined even in my new life I would come back occasionally and find everyone there as usual. The Dean, the Fish Bish and, of course, the divine Mr Weaver, would still be crossing the Close on their various errands. Each morning the boarders would still be going down the Harstans to school where the same staff would still be teaching the same things they had been teaching for years. Matron would still be complaining and the Boarding House roof still leaking and there would still be shepherd's pie for supper on Tuesdays. Absurdly I'd even imagined Hugh and the Davises would still be living in their basement kitchen. For years school life had seemed predictable, sometimes monotonous. Now I began to be aware nothing was permanent.

Another end of school year tradition was The Doctor's Talk but this was for leavers only. One afternoon near the very end of term, we filed into the school library where a woman doctor was to tell us about sex. It was too late for Audrey but it wouldn't have been much use to her anyway. We were given no information about birth control, just warned about the uncontrollable passions of men. It was up to us to keep these passions at bay. Even innocent kissing could lead on to all sorts of things including heavy petting. Hazel put her hand up.

'Please could you explain what's meant by heavy petting?' There was a slight giggle from one of Audrey's friends. I had a feeling they knew all about heavy petting and had put Hazel up to asking the question because she looked clean and innocent and they thought it might embarrass the doctor. The poor woman flushed slowly from the neck upwards before saying that it involved 'touching the most intimate parts of the body.'

'Honestly,' said Fiona afterwards. 'I was nearly sick.'

I considered my reactions. I remembered Jane telling us that a boarder a year or two above us had had an illicit date with a grammar school boy one Saturday afternoon. She'd returned looking very flushed. Later the rumour had got out that he had put his hand down her dress and inside her bra. Everyone was very shocked. But, I thought, with the right person this might not be so disagreeable. I attempted not to think who the right person might be.

As usual on the final Sunday of term, we went across to the cathedral for Evensong. Across the choir, almost where Hugh used to sit, was someone I thought I recognised, a tall white-faced, bespectacled boy, well, man really, Paul Longley. He'd been at the Grammar School a year or two above me and I remembered he was now at Oxford. At the end of the service he came over to speak to me. I was overawed. I had always thought of him as a different generation. Now he was graciously friendly. Ignoring the others he stared at me myopically through his horn-rimmed glasses.

'I hear you will be joining us next term,' he said, sounding rather as if he were the Vice-Chancellor himself.

'No more than four - if that,' said Jane, afterwards. 'He's just so hideous and he sounds so pompous.' I thought she was particularly annoyed about being ignored.

'Well, he's asked me to a party he's giving next term.'

'Dilly!' Jane shrieked. Then she added, 'I hope it won't be full of drips like him.' But I knew she was quite impressed that I'd had an invitation to a party before I'd even arrived in Oxford. I felt rather pleased about it myself. Paul might not be very attractive but surely there would be other more appealing men at his party.

On the last morning of term Ursula arrived in the formroom holding three neat packages.

'Just a small farewell gift for each of my team,' she announced, smiling graciously. Rosa as usual, looked impassive. She thanked Ursula politely if not effusively, and if she felt patronised she gave no sign, but Fiona and I felt rather awkward and also annoyed. We had never seen ourselves as part of Ursula's 'team'. Perhaps, I thought, we should also have bought her something but, feeling as I did about her, it would have seemed hypocritical. As it was we felt obliged to help her organise the end of term clearing up with more enthusiasm than we'd normally have shown.

That afternoon, at the end of term assembly, Miss Cutler officially announced which staff were leaving and praised their contributions to the school. Mazzy, of course got a long peroration. Finally she came to Alithea.

'Mrs Davis has only been with us a short while and we are sorry she is leaving us so soon but it's her husband's fault.' There was an audible gasp. Alithea's pregnancy was now quite visible and Alithea herself looked furious. But Miss Cutler carried on, apparently quite unaware that she'd said anything stupid. She blithely continued, saying it was because Mr Davis had, 'very bravely' as she put it, taken a post at a large comprehensive school in London and that he and Alithea would be moving down there shortly. She was sure we would want to wish them every success in their new life. We would now sing the end of term hymn, *'Who would true valour see'*. During the hymn a lot of leavers were crying, even those who had been saying all year that they 'couldn't wait to get out of this dump.' I was struggling with tears as well. The Davises were going to London. I would never see them again.

CHAPTER TWENTY EIGHT

Halfway up the Harstans for what, I thought, was the last time, I remembered I'd left Ursula's present on the windowsill.

'I need to dash back,' I said to Brenda. 'Tell Matron I won't bother about tea.' I flung myself into the formroom. There was someone by the window and I thought the cleaners had got there before me.

'Sorry' I gasped. 'Don't throw it away. It's mine.' Then I realised the someone was Alithea. She was standing by the window and the bulge of her pregnancy was clearly outlined against the light. 'Oh sorry,' I said again but in a different tone. We looked at each other. 'I've just come back for...' I waved a hand in the direction of the windowsill.

'Is this yours?'

'Yes,' I said. 'Ursula gave us, me Rosa and Fiona, leaving presents. We never thought...now we feel...perhaps when I go with my cousin. We're going to the Lake District but that's not till September...will be a bit late but I'm going to look at Dove Cottage ... maybe I can get something there.' Alithea still stared at me silently as well she might. I knew I was being totally incoherent. 'Of course,' I went on irrelevantly, 'I know you don't like Wordsworth...You prefer Donne...' The mention of Donne made me feel like crying and I stopped.

'Dilly,' she said, 'I'm sorry you got mixed up in our mess.' I didn't know what to say. It was my turn to stare at her in silence. Eventually I said,

'That's all right.'

'Oh good.'

Then I thought, no, no I'm a bit better, but I'm not all right. She's not getting off that lightly.

'No,' I said. 'It's not all right but I expect I shall get over it eventually.'

'Dilly, you're not trying to tell me you're still infatuated by my absurd husband?' Her tone of amused tolerance enraged me.

'He's not ..he's not..'. I couldn't get the words out; my eyes were stinging with tears and my throat felt tight. 'I'm not infatuated. I love him,' I said, and couldn't hold the tears back any longer.

She sat down on a formroom chair, pulled another one over and put her feet up. At last, I thought, she's going to talk to me.

'I can't stand for long,' she said. 'My ankles swell up.' I wriggled on to a desk, which looked more casual than pulling up another chair, and propped my feet on the cold heating pipe. I continued to snivel and couldn't find my handkerchief.

'Have a paper one,' she said, reaching for her briefcase. I remembered Mike passing me his grimy handkerchief, which I still kept at the back of my drawer, and this made me sob even more violently.

'Listen Dilly. He's not worth it. I know he's good-looking and charming and all that but you should just try living with him.'

'I wish I could.' I sobbed. She started laughing.

'You wouldn't for long – clearing up his mess - putting up with his laziness and the way he thinks he can get out of everything with that smile and those blue eyes. His bloody mother has a lot to answer for. If this is a boy,' she stroked her stomach briefly, 'I'll see he's brought up differently.'

'No cocoa and biscuits,' I managed, half laughing, through my sobs.

'Oh, you had that story too, did you? No, no cocoa and biscuits.' In a moment of female solidarity we smiled at each other and I felt a bit better. Part of me still thought I would willingly slave all day, every day, for Mike but I remembered the mess in the kitchen that afternoon the previous autumn. It was all right to clear that up once - but all the time? 'We men expect a lot I'm afraid,' he'd said. Well, why should they? I was too bright to spend my life washing up. I stopped crying.

'Why did you go to live with him, then?' She looked at me and raised her eyebrows.

'Oh, I know you weren't married until...', I hesitated.

'How?'

'Fiona. She knows someone who works in the registrar's office who gossips a lot and Fiona recognised you both from her description.'

'Well I'm grateful you didn't say anything. I should have thought Fiona would have been all moral outrage.'

'She was at first but I said that as you were leaving soon anyway, there was no point in causing trouble. Anyway I didn't want you to hate me even more.' Thinking about Alithea's treatment of me made the gripping pain round my heart come back. Tears started to roll down my face again. The paper handkerchief was getting unuseably soggy. She handed me another and said,

'What made you think I hated you, Dilly?'

'Because...because...'

'Because I started to ignore you?' I nodded. When I managed to speak again I said,

'Were you angry with me because your husband..because Mr... because Mike...' (I'd managed to say his name at last).

'Because Mike what?'

'Because of him having his arm round me in the car? Sorry I mean his having his arm around me in the car?'

'What?'

'Having is a gerund - verbal noun – takes the possessive. Miss Carr's very fussy about it'

'For God's sake, Dilly!'

'Sorry. I thought you might mind too.'

'About Mike or the gerunds?'

'Both I suppose.'

'Just at the moment, I couldn't care less about gerunds. As far as Mike is concerned, if I refused to speak to every female he made a pass at, I'd be excluding myself from contact with fifty percent of the human race.'

'But he liked me - he really did like me. I really believed I meant something to him - I did – I did!' I was sobbing again, almost howling.

'If you're going to get hysterical Dilly I'll have to stop this conversation now. Mike did – does - like you. He knows he made you unhappy and feels guilty about it. I think he's really fond of you. He was upset when I told him you were in so much trouble about going to Rosa's father's funeral and got Mrs Green to send that letter.'

'But he wrote it. Didn't he?'

'Oh, you read it did you? I told him frankly I didn't think the Head would be taken in.'

'She was a bit surprised.' I'd calmed down. I didn't like the idea of Mike pitying me and I felt being 'fond' of me sounded patronising but I reminded myself it was because he still saw me as very young. There was a pause during which I thought about how I could acquire more sophistication. I'd recently started writing in black ink and drinking my tea without milk, an affectation that enraged my father. Now I thought I might practise using more eye make-up before I went to university. I'd ask Fiona's advice about this. And I would read more Sartre.

Above us I could hear the cleaners at work in the assembly hall. They were shouting to each other; buckets were clanking and someone was whistling. They'd be down here before we knew where we were and there was a lot more I wanted to know.

'Anyway, Dilly,' said Alithea. 'I wasn't being quite fair to my dear husband - he only makes passes at pretty women - so let that be some consolation to you. Of course he has to be charming to everyone. Poor Joan adores him and he can't stand her because she's plain and then there's Rosa and I suspect Mrs Herbert, ancient as she is, is in love with him too. Look even I fell for it, although I had the sense to refuse to marry him until I got trapped into it.' She looked down at her stomach gloomily. If they can invent the atom bomb and talk about space exploration you'd think they could come up with a better contraceptive.' She looked so angry that I said,

'You'll probably really like the baby when it's born. My cousin's baby is lovely now he's sitting up and making noises and everything.'

'Oh Dilly! Don't whatever you do, start getting sentimental about babies. Don't be one of those boring girls who goes round flashing an engagement ring in her third year, thinking if they come out of university with a degree and a husband they've achieved all their ambitions. Try to do something with your life. Whatever Mike says, you're not just a sweet little thing. You're very immature – the result of a sheltered upbringing I suppose - but I believe you have potential. You could develop into a rather interesting person. I've heard you were a bit of a rebel when you were younger. The story in the staffroom is that Miss Manzonni reformed you - praying over you I imagine. But don't be brainwashed Dilly. Think for yourself. And don't think of getting married until you've worked out who you are.'

There was another pause. I could hear steps coming down the stairs and the clatter of buckets and mops. A stout, grey-haired woman in a flowered pinafore peered in the door.

'Oh excuse me, I'm sure.' she said.

'Would you be kind enough just to give us a few more minutes?' said Alithea. She smiled at the woman and I thought Mike wasn't the only one who could turn on the charm.

'Of course, ducks! I'll start on next door.'

We could hear her banging about in the Lower Sixth formroom. She started singing a hymn,

'The day thou ga...avest Lo...o rd has ended.'

'For God's sake shut the door!' said Alithea. I shut the door and went back to my perch. Alithea obviously had more advice to give me.

'The thing is Dilly, physical attraction is all very well but you have to remember you might be stuck with this person for the rest of your life. Of course Mike is...well obviously I don't have to tell you.' She gave a sly smile that I rather resented and then continued, 'But the only other thing we have in common is politics and actually not even politics really. Yes, we're both left wing but in a very a different way. In my family we have a wide outlook, international, cosmopolitan, liberal in our social attitudes – 'privileged' Mike says and I suppose he's right. With him it's all Trade Unions and the rights of the workers - male workers. They don't really include women. They're just there to make the tea.' ('That's a lovely cup of tea Dilly,' I remembered) and then he's so provincial and narrow-minded. He disapproves of homosexuals - well you saw what he was like with Ben and Danny - and he thinks all modern art is rubbish and he doesn't like foreign films.'

'But you both like literature.'

'Yes, but not the same literature. He likes reciting poetry in that beautiful voice - sounding like Richard Burton, but most of what he has by heart is Victorian sentimental verse. He loves Tennyson. If he really wants to annoy me he starts on *The May Queen*.'

We'd done Tennyson for O level so I knew the poem she meant and when I thought of Mike declaiming,

For I'm to be Queen o' the May, Mother,
I'm to be Queen o' the May.

I couldn't help giving a reluctant snort of laughter even if it turned into half a sob when I remembered *Phyllida my Phyllida*

'Just imagine, Dilly,' she said. 'Living with a man who prefers Tennyson to Donne!'

I tried to think seriously about this and then saw she was smiling, so I managed to smile back.

'But you wouldn't really have preferred Mr Marlow?' I must have sounded incredulous and she laughed.

'Well, no.' I was amazed to see her hesitate. 'His religion is absurd and his politics appalling but - I don't know quite how to put it - Hugh and I belong to the same tribe.'

'What! Is he half-Jewish too?'

'Hugh! Of course not. What I mean is we share certain things. We read the same books as children; we were brought up doing the same rituals, Oh I don't know - *Peter Pan* at Christmas, going to Daniel Neals for our school shoes - that sort of thing. Mike comes from a foreign country and I'm not talking about Wales. He took me home once. His family just didn't know what to make of me. I'd have been quite happy to discuss Marxism with his father but he and Mike went off to the pub. I had to sit there with his mother while she knitted, (so I was right about the sweater, I thought) and disapproved of me and then guess what?' I shook my head. 'When they came back from the pub his father had bought me a bottle of *Babycham*!'

All I knew about Babycham was from the advertisements. A little Bambi-like creature pictured leaping above a shallow glass of something sparkling but I could imagine, as alcoholic drinks went, it wouldn't pack the same punch as Algerian red so I managed to indicate sympathy and horror.

'I asked Mike how he could have let his father think I would touch the stuff and he just got annoyed and said he had meant to be kind. He couldn't see how patronising it was.'

'Did he bring some for Mike's mother?' I was trying to visualise the scene.

'For her? Certainly not. She doesn't drink. She's strictly chapel, no good talking to her about Marxism. It was a bit hard to be regarded as the scarlet woman for drinking bloody Babycham.'

I thought that at least Mike's mother would have approved of my teetotal upbringing but before I had time to consider this further Alithea continued,

'Also, you know, men who think they're God's gift to women don't always know how best to please them. Bear that in mind, Dilly. Looks aren't everything. Sometimes it's better to be the one that's adored.' I looked at her blankly. Yes, I could see that weedy Hugh adored her, but surely Mike spent his life trying to please women. That was his charm and his failing.

'Sorry,' she said, 'you don't understand, do you? You will one day.' I felt this was insultingly patronising and it also reminded me that Alithea hadn't answered my first question. Why had she suddenly refused to have anything to do with me? Was it because I was so naïve?

'Did Ben and Danny think I was very boring?' Alithea looked taken aback at this sudden change of subject.

'What?'

'Well if you didn't really mind Mike... if you didn't really mind Mike...' I started to cry again.

'If I didn't mind Mike making passes at you why did I stop asking you round? Is that what you're trying to say?'

'Yes,' I sobbed.

'Because I was told not to, you silly girl. Isn't that obvious. I think Miss Manzonni was already beginning to think I was a bad influence; so when your mother rang...'

'What!' For a moment I felt stunned.

'Oh, she didn't tell you? Yes, she rang Miss Manzonni and complained about us leading you into a den of iniquity – artists, homosexuals - although she probably didn't spell that out to your dear housemistress - alcohol and, as she thought Mike and I were married, I don't think she could begin to imagine him cuddling you – or is it his cuddling you, Dilly? –perhaps we should ask Miss Carr. Anyway from your star-struck state your mother guessed sex was involved somehow, and suspected you of falling for Hugh. She thought he'd been using the poetry of Catullus to seduce you. And then there was Hugh's play. Oh dear! She didn't want her daughter involved with anyone who had written such filth. So that was it. Of course, Hugh had left anyway. He fled back to London before Mike could punch his front teeth in - it actually came to blows you know. Well on Mike's part. But in any case your old Latin teacher was back. There was no real reason for you to come round any more but we wouldn't have cut you off entirely if it hadn't been for your mother. Miss Cutler had me in for a big lecture about professional conduct and how could she give me a reference if I did this sort of thing and it was important for teachers to keep their distance from their pupils – bad for discipline and so on and so forth. So no more tea and toast and lending you subversive literature'.

I said nothing. The news of my mother's interference had made me too angry to speak.

'*The voi....ce of prayer is never silent*' came from the next classroom, '*Nor dies the strain of praise away.*'

'I wish she'd just die away,' said Alithea.

'It's the end of the hymn,' I said.

'That was a joke, Dilly. I'm afraid,' she added, 'I did make use of you. I realised quite soon that Mike found you attractive. Women always fall for him but he prefers the pretty ones so that happened to be quite convenient at the time. I'm sorry if you got hurt but you'll soon get over it. You may look back on it as a useful experience.' She smiled. 'I gather when you saw him at the funeral you gave him a bit of a ticking off about his careless flirtations. He was quite impressed. That's what he needs, more women who'll make him think for a moment about the consequences of his behaviour. Anyway the thing was your adoration stopped him minding too much about Hugh and me. It distracted him when things were... well when they went a bit further than I intended... I don't think he ever entirely suspected... He's a bit of an innocent in some ways...'

I wasn't really listening. I felt she was being far too casual about my broken heart. But the mention of Hugh made me ask.

'Has he really gone to California?'

'Oh, Hugh, yes - he applied for a research fellowship. At Berkeley.' This meant nothing to me and, in my ignorance, I thought it odd that anyone would go to America to do research in the classical languages.

'It seems a long way,' I said, 'but I suppose if he's trying to forget you...' I wondered if going half way round the world would help me forget Mike.

'I think he's more worried the baby might look like him,' she said. 'Even New England wasn't far enough.'

It's extraordinary to realise that I didn't really take in the implication of this immediately. Perhaps because she made it sound like a joke - But anyway I was still brooding on her admission that she'd made use of me.

'You shouldn't have used me. You might have realised I'd get hurt. But I suppose I'm glad I met you. You've changed my ideas about a lot of things – made me think - so this year hasn't been a total waste of time. I know I haven't done well in these exams. I might as well have gone to France and I partly didn't go because...' My voice started to wobble again.

'Because of Mike.' she said. I nodded. 'Never hang around for a man, Dilly. If they really want you they'll follow and if not..well they're not worth it.' - that was all very well for her, I thought, She had all the confidence in the world. Poor, sad Hugh had trailed after her.

'I'm glad you think you've learnt something from us,' she continued. 'Miss Cutler accused me of favouritism. Ursula's father complained we'd given you an unfair advantage in the Oxbridge exams so I thought I'd better pay Ursula more attention. It's been not entirely unrewarding. I think I've managed to make her question some of her family's attitudes.' She laughed. 'Perhaps that's not what Miss Cutler intended.'

It was as I'd suspected. Alithea's influence was the cause of some of Ursula's recent uncharacteristic outbursts. But I didn't believe her influence would last long.

There were more footsteps and more clatterings of buckets. Another cleaner had arrived.

'There's someone still in there, Reenie. I was going to do the toilets first.'

'I can't help that Ethel. I've got a bus to catch. They'll have to move.'

'One of them's a teacher.'

'Teacher or no teacher, I've still got to catch my bus.'

'We'd better go,' said Alithea. A tougher-looking woman – dyed red hair escaping from a turbaned headscarf, peered round the door.

'Yes, we know,' said Alithea. 'You've got to catch your bus.'

We walked up the Harstans together, just as we had before Christmas. Half way up, I realised I'd left Ursula's present behind again but I decided it didn't matter. At the top of the steps we paused.

'You really will get over him, Dilly, you know. Men outnumber women six to one at Oxford - lots of choice. You'll have forgotten Mike ever existed by the middle of your first term.'

'Perhaps,' I said. 'At the moment I feel like Donne says in the poem, you know, *The Broken Heart*.' My voice wobbled but I managed to get out the quotation.

'My ragges of heart can like, wish and adore,
But after one such love, can love no more'

Then I suddenly remembered. 'Oh no, I've still got your Donne!'

'Oh, let me have it back some other time.' This filled me with hope. There would be another time?

'Well goodbye.' She hesitated and I hoped she might be about to suggest I came back to say goodbye to Mike, but at that moment Jane came rushing towards us.

'Dilly! Where have you been? Your parents are here. They're saying goodbye to Mazzy but I've been sent to look for you!' She paused and noticed my red eyes. 'You're not crying because you're leaving are you? Soppy date!'

'I thought you couldn't wait to leave school!' my father exclaimed, 'and now look at you. Crying your eyes out!' Actually, although most of my tears were for Mike, suddenly I felt quite sad about leaving. After all the Boarding House had been part of my life for a long time. It was difficult to imagine a world that didn't include Jane and Caroline and even irritating Brenda. I could come back to visit of course, but there would be a stranger in Mazzy's room and I knew from experience that old girls were a five minute wonder, a few exclamations and questions and then everyone would want to return to the concerns of real life.

I sobbed quietly all the way home. All my mother's attempts at bright conversation were rejected. I was in no state yet to have it out with her about that phone call. Meanwhile, the desert of a long summer holiday stretched before me.

PART 7

Summer 1956

CHAPTER TWENTY NINE

That night in bed I ran through my conversation with Alithea. I'd made a fool of myself undoubtedly – all that sobbing and declaring my undying passion for her husband. Still, on the whole she'd been nice to me. I could become 'quite an interesting person' she'd told me, which was flattering – well quite flattering. Once again I resolved to be more interesting. That evening, in an effort to cheer me up, my mother had talked about giving me a clothes allowance. Remembering that, at the funeral, Mike had said black suited me, I thought I might get a black polo-neck sweater for the autumn and perhaps a duffle coat. Thinking about this, I was on the edge of falling asleep, when suddenly it seemed as if I could hear Alithea's voice saying, 'Perhaps he was afraid the baby would look like him'. Immediately I was wide-awake.

That night, and during the next few days, I struggled to sort out my feelings. My first instinct had been to find some excuse to rush back and confront Mike with the possibility that the baby might be Hugh's. Then I thought of writing to him. Eventually I had the sense to realise I might be doing unnecessary damage to their relationship without doing myself any good. If the baby did turn out to be Hugh's – and unless it looked very like him who would know? It was up to Alithea to confess all, which seemed unlikely. And what did I think of Alithea now? Was this sort of behaviour all part of being an interesting person?

I found myself beginning to reassess Alithea. I can't remember in what order or exactly when these thoughts occurred to me. Perhaps some of them didn't become really clear to me until a later period but already I'd begun to see inconsistencies in what she'd said that last afternoon.

'Never hang around for a man, Dilly.' But she'd stayed in a place she despised to be with Mike and during their first year there she hadn't even had a job. Still perhaps she'd regretted this and was warning me not to do the same. Then I still couldn't see why, in spite of my mother and Mazzy and Miss Cutler, she'd needed to cut me off so completely. She could at least have given some explanation, been pleasanter to me in lessons, even spoken to me in the corridor. She didn't have to make such a point of ignoring me. It would, of course, have been almost impossible to invite me round and, I thought bitterly, with Hugh gone I was of no more use to her. I began to suspect that, without Hugh's attentions to herself she might have begun to find it rather annoying that Mike found me attractive. I was fairly certain she'd never invited Ursula round to their digs. We'd have all heard about it if she had. Would Mike have thought Ursula pretty? I found her smug pink face irritating but I had to admit she was by no means hideous. Fiona always said Ursula didn't know how to make the best of herself. She came from the kind of background where dowdiness was seen as a virtue. Certainly Alithea hadn't had any influence on Ursula's appearance. Also, I thought, if Alithea really cared so little for Miss Cutler's opinions why had she bothered with Ursula at all? Why had she tried to change her ideas? That surely wasn't what either Miss Cutler or Ursula's father would have wanted. Had she seen Ursula as a more interesting challenge than me? If she'd wanted a real challenge, I thought, she ought to have started on Fiona. The very idea made me smile.

As the summer wore on I had more than enough time to think

about all that had happened during the past year. I was supposed to be doing some reading for Oxford but as I sat at the dining-room table, surrounded by the prescribed books, I kept hoping the telephone would ring and it would be Alithea asking me to return her Donne. This wasn't just because such a call might lead to another meeting with Mike. Although I was beginning to feel more critical of Alithea, she still fascinated me and I longed for further conversation with her, if only to understand more clearly what part I'd played in her schemes.

The telephone didn't ring very often and, when it did, it was usually Aunty Joyce about the latest arrangements for Amber's wedding. Every time the post arrived I hoped there might be a letter from Alithea, at least giving me their London address so that I could send the book there; but there was nothing.

Eventually, unable to bear Alithea's silence any longer, I told my mother I needed a haircut. I'd only let the local hairdresser cut my hair once and fortunately my mother agreed it had been a disaster. She made my father give me the necessary seven and six, which he did, telling me I must never again take money out of my post office savings account for such a trivial thing as a haircut. I told them I'd also be meeting Fiona. Actually she had a part-time job and was working until lunchtime. However I had a plan for the morning, if I had the courage to carry it out.

All the way on the seemingly interminable journey my determination kept wavering but by the time the bus finally drew up at the stop near the cathedral, I'd made up my mind.

With a thumping heart, trying to stop my legs shaking, I walked up the once familiar lane. Pink roses were flopping over the railings, and the flowerbeds in Mrs Herbert's front garden were a tangle of nasturtiums, marigolds and sweet peas. I tried the door but it was locked. I lifted the heavy iron knocker and let it drop. The bang echoed through the hallway but if Mrs Herbert were out how would they ever hear down in the basement? Then, as I absent-mindedly picked at the blistered paint on the dark green front door, I heard a slow shuffling. There was a lot of clanking of chains and scraping of keys then Mrs Herbert peered out. As soon as she saw me she smiled.

'It's ..it's Dilly isn't it? Such a long time since I've seen you - that lovely carol singing. So sweet of you to call! I'm sorry I took so long to open the door. I never used to lock it but since the young people have gone I've found myself getting rather nervous.'

'Oh,' I said as casually as possible. 'The Davises have left then?'

'Yes, almost immediately after the end of term. I miss them so much. Mr Davis...' her eyes filled with tears. 'Mr Davis was so sweet. Do you know? He actually kissed me when they left.'

Well, no surprises there! I thought.

'Do you have their address by any chance. I have this book...'

'I'm afraid not, dear. They said something about writing when they were settled but I haven't heard anything so far.'

I had a cup of tea with Mrs Herbert in her dim, chilly parlour that smelt of damp biscuits, and promised to call again, although I found the place almost unbearably nostalgic. I was amazed when she told me she was getting another lodger in September, none other than Joan Seymour. How could Miss Seymour bear to be there, I wondered, feeling Mike's absence every day? Perhaps she'd have their address but I thought it unlikely she'd be willing to give it to me. Once outside again, in the sunshine, still clutching Alithea's Donne, I realised I must hurry or I'd be late meeting Fiona.

SUMMER 1956

Fiona, unlike the rest of the sixth form, had been determined not take a job at the local pea-canning factory. Instead she'd talked her way into working on the reception desk, not at the Northgate but at the other hotel near the Cathedral Close, the more up-market Swan. When I met her she was looking slightly stressed.

'I think they've begun to realise I can't type as well as I said I could.'

'You can't type at all,'

'Well, I'm learning quite fast. But now there's this letter. They want me to translate it.' She handed it to me.

'But Fiona, it's in Italian. You didn't tell them you could speak Italian, did you!'

'Not *speak* it exactly but I said I understood a little. After all it must be quite like Latin. The trouble is the vocab you learn in Latin is so useless. All that stuff about Caesar chucking bridges across rivers. And then Dido weeping and wailing and carrying on over pious Aeneas.'

The mention of poor, abandoned, Dido was painful. However my friend was in difficulties. This was no time to think of Dido's sorrows and so I suggested seeing if the public library had an Italian dictionary.

'Dilly you are clever! If only the Romans had booked into hotels.'

'They probably did,' I said. 'They just didn't write about it. The novel hadn't been invented.'

'Anyway,' Fiona added, as we headed downhill, 'the guests all seem to like me. I met a most charming Canadian yesterday. He gave me his address and said I must be sure to get in touch if I'm ever in Saskatchewan.'

Christopher's semi-permanent girl friend was on duty in the library. She greeted us both in a friendly way and guided us towards the reference section where we managed to find an Italian dictionary. I no longer resented her. After all, Mike had dismissed her as 'not having a word to say for herself,' at his party. I realised with a slight shock that this party had taken place only just over a year ago. So much had happened in between it seemed ancient history. In a studiedly casual manner I enquired after Christopher and was told he'd already been called up for National Service. He was doing basic training at Aldershot and wasn't enjoying it.

The Italian dictionary, at first, seemed of limited use.

'Why does this man keep calling the manager "she" when he knows he's a man?' whispered Fiona.

I consulted the dictionary further.

'Lei can also means you; it's the polite form.'

'How ridiculous! And what's all this at the end? *Le porgo i miei più distinti saluti.*'

'I think it's just a flowery way of saying, "yours faithfully".'

'What a language! No wonder they lost the war. After all that, all he seems to want is a double room in September.'

'With a matrimonial bed' I said, which made us start laughing so that we got glared at and shushed by the other readers.

Coming out of the library, on the way to my hair appointment, we bumped into Audrey who, far from immersing herself in works of charity in repentant seclusion, was hand in hand with another young man in uniform. She'd probably had enough of Americans however. This one was in the RAF.

'Only a pilot officer,' said Fiona, 'but at least he's got a commission, and I suppose he'll get promoted.'

*

When we saw Audrey again at Christmas she was flashing a large diamond engagement ring and the following summer they had a spectacular white wedding. Fiona sent me the picture from the local paper. 'Such hypocrisy!' she had scrawled across it.

*

Alithea still didn't write and I felt more and more depressed. The preparations for Amber's wedding did nothing to alleviate this. Frances and I had a final fitting for our pink organdie bridesmaids' dresses.

'How could Amber have chosen these?' I complained to Frances. 'Surely we'll clash with her hair?' But it seemed it was Aunty Joyce's decision. Amber was taking very little interest. She was too busy helping Les organise his latest shop.

One day it occurred to me that Ben and Danny might know what had happened to the Davises. I was still rather scared of Ben but I knew Danny would be kind. I looked for a map. When I actually found Bellingthorpe Castle I felt almost surprised. It had never seemed quite like a real place. Now I discovered one of the prosaic green local buses passed by the gates every few hours. It seemed almost sacrilegious. All the same, the idea of casually calling on Ben and Danny, while frighteningly daring, gave me something to hope for.

Knowing my mother's views on the pair I said nothing, but one hot morning in late August she got a phone call from the Minister's wife who seemed upset about something and clearly thought my mother was her only friend. My mother agreed to go to see her that afternoon and left me at the dining-room table ostensibly working.

As soon as she had gone, I escaped. I managed to catch the right bus, that put me off near the castle, but when I arrived at the iron gates they were closed and tied up with rope. I spent some time trying to undo them before giving up and clambering over the wall. But I'd already begun to suspect I was too late. I banged on the front door for some time but there was no response. I peered through the windows and saw the unidentifiable objects were still standing around under their dustsheets. I stood in the warm sunshine and listened, but the only sound was of the grasshoppers chirping away in the long grass of the neglected lawn. I tried to find a way round the side and failed, so I trailed back down the drive that was already disappearing under the encroaching grass and weeds.

I was just climbing back over the wall when an evil-faced old man appeared.

'Hey!' he shouted. I thought I was about to be told off for trespassing. 'What were you doing in there?'

'I was...' I began.

'I hope you weren't looking for them nancy boys.' He peered closely at me; his breath smelt of beer. 'I wouldn't like to think that a pretty young girl like you would have anything to do with the likes of them.' He laughed nastily, 'Ran 'em out of town we did. This is a decent English village. Pub wouldn't serve 'em. Shop wouldn't serve 'em. We ran them out of town.'

He leered at me and I began to feel terrified. He put his hand out as if to grab me but I suddenly saw the bus, presumably on its way back, and waved frantically. I scrambled on board. A stout woman looked at me sympathetically.

'Was he bothering you, ducks? He ought to be locked up, that one ought.' There was a generally murmur of agreement.

My mother was already back when I arrived home but fortunately she was so full of the drama unfolding at the Manse that she was only vaguely interested when I said I'd just had to get out for a bit. Apparently people at the chapel were beginning to complain about the Minister's sermons. There was to be an investigation by the stewards.

'Of course,' said my mother, 'he has a lot of silly Socialist ideas but then he's still very young.' That evening she and my father were arguing about this - my father being inclined to support the stewards - when the phone went. It was Aunty Joyce to tell us they'd just received a telegram from Amber. She and Les had got married in Nottingham, by special licence. Aunty Joyce was hysterical.

'Well,' said my mother. 'You know what that means!' But she was wrong. Amber was far too knowledgeable to have 'Got Herself into Trouble' as the saying went - a curious construction that made it sound as if girls got pregnant through parthenogenesis. I should have guessed Amber wouldn't go through with the wedding. She'd never have let Aunty Joyce dress us in pink organdie if she'd been serious.

'At least you'll still have another evening dress,' said my mother. This time I didn't bother to argue but I'd no intention of taking a pink organdie dress with me to Oxford. That wasn't at all the impression I intended to make.

All these dramas meant less attention was paid to my disappointing A level results, although my mother kept talking about 'distractions' and 'bad influences' to anyone who would listen. She obviously blamed the Davises for my failure to win a State Scholarship. Fiona rang to say she'd got the required grades for St Andrews.

'So much for not being university material. I hope old Cutler will write and grovel but I bet she won't.'

I said how pleased I was and then asked,

'How did the others do?'

'You'll be happy to hear Ursula didn't get a State Scholarship either.' I was rather ashamed of my relief so, in an effort not to sound too happy and remembering how unpleasant her aunt had been at the carol-singing, I asked how her family were taking this.

'I don't know but I do remember her saying her father didn't believe girls could ever do as well as boys because we were too emotional and had smaller brains, so I suppose this will just confirm his views. Rosa's done well though - distinctions all round.'

This was another piece of good news. A State Scholarship added to her London University scholarship would make Rosa comparatively well off.

Just before I left for Oxford, the Minister called round. He urged me to join the University Methodist Society.

'I believe there's a very nice Presbyterian Church,' said my mother. She'd already told me I'd meet a better class of person there. Having no intention of going near either I stayed non-committal while they politely battled for my soul.

I quite liked the Minister. Who knows, if I hadn't met the Davises and learnt about Socialist-atheism, I might have given the Methodists a try and then perhaps my life might have taken an entirely different direction.

PART 8

Interim

CHAPTER THIRTY

In October I left home for freedom; freedom to stay out until 11.15pm, freedom to entertain a man in my room between two in the afternoon and seven in the evening; freedom to sit in the gallery at the Union and watch male undergraduates posturing and debating and freedom to study anything in English literature as long as it was written before 1830. It was all mildly exciting.

There were also parties. As I'd promised my mother I wouldn't drink alcohol until I was twenty-one I drank a great deal of weak orange squash. To make up for this I tried to smoke convincingly while answering questions about what year I was in, what college I was from and what I was reading. Often someone in the background was strumming a guitar and crooning *Frankie and Johnny were sweethearts*. Sometimes I was asked to jive, which was slightly more exciting.

At first sight Paul Longley's party didn't look even mildly exciting.

Although Jane had classified Paul as a four, I'd been certain there would be other more attractive men among his guests. However when I pushed open the door of his room in Balliol I thought perhaps I'd been over-optimistic. The room was full of intellectual-looking men in dark suits talking intensely to each other. There were only a few women and they were talking amongst themselves with a kind of desperate animation while the men ignored them. Not, I thought, that the women should care. There was hardly a man in the room to whom Jane would have awarded more than a six. I was just about to disappear as quietly as possible and search for better entertainment in the Union Cellars when I caught the eye of a tall, dark young man. Something about his height and his ill-fitting suit reminded me of Mike the last time I'd seen him, at Rosa's father's funeral. The expression on my face must have shown this stranger what I felt about the party, as he moved towards me and said in a reassuring northern accent.

'Let's get out of here. There's a pub down the road.'

Most people, I've observed, are attracted to a particular physical type. Friends who remarry always seem to pick someone who resembles their previous spouse even if their first marriage has ended in bitter feelings and broken crockery. Is this attraction something innate or are we all trying to recapture a lost first love? For whatever reason I was immediately attracted to Steve. And yet I soon realised Steve was a very different personality from Mike. In some ways I thought this was a good thing. Steve, I told myself, had stern integrity not facile charm. All the same, when I introduced him to my parents a little more charm and a little less integrity might have eased the situation.

Steve, like Mike, was a miner's son. Perhaps that too was part of his attraction for me but he wasn't the kind of boyfriend my mother had hoped I would acquire at Oxford. Soon after she first met him she asked, in an unconvincingly casual manner, whether I ever heard anything of that young man who had taught me Latin? That bad! I thought. Was she now sorry that she'd put a stop to my supposed romance with Hugh? I replied with some satisfaction that I believed he was now in California.

I made a great point of telling my parents I'd joined the Labour

Club, which, of course, was another bad mark against Steve. But I was very quickly disillusioned by politics. Being an inadequate school prefect had taught me early that I'd neither the desire nor the aptitude for power but student politicians seemed obsessed by it. All their energy seemed to be directed towards internal power struggles rather than looking outwards and trying to change society for the better. It was all very tedious.

Today the expending of powers
On the flat ephemeral pamphlet and the boring meeting.

I quoted to Steve as he was walking me back to my college one evening.

'Who said that?'

'Auden.'

'Well he's sold out, hasn't he?'

Steve judged all poets by their politics and very few passed the test. Wordsworth had sold out and Shelley probably would have, so Steve claimed, if he'd lived long enough. I remembered Mike reciting Dylan Thomas over Rosa's father's grave. Had Dylan Thomas sold out? Had he ever indeed opted in?

Steve's attitude discouraged me from saying much about my own poetry and in any case the spirit of the time seemed against me. Auden, the renegade, was at that time Professor of Poetry. I'd seen him in the Tackley Café on The High surrounded by young men. That, along with the content of the English syllabus, clearly indicated that women couldn't be taken seriously as poets. My writing became a clandestine activity of which I was slightly ashamed.

I drifted away from politics and became involved in university drama. The acting set could be vain and bitchy but I didn't expect such high ideals from them and they were more amusing. Most of the time I lurked in the wings handing out swords or cigarettes or whatever else was appropriate for that particular production and once I got a small part in a college play.

At the end of my second year I went on a trip to Europe with a Shakespearean production. Steve didn't come. He always had to take a factory job in the Long Vacation to pay for his keep at home. It was the first time I'd been abroad and I think my parents only agreed to it because they thought it might get me away from Steve. This stratagem nearly succeeded. The trip was a shambles; we ran out of money and got dirty and hungry but there were endless jokes and new places to see. I'd never been so happy. On the way back I decided I must chuck Steve. But at Dover there he was standing in the rain, patiently waiting for our coach to drive off the ferry. He'd hitched all the way to meet me and I couldn't do it.

By the end of our third year we were engaged. Sometimes Alithea's words came back to me. Was I now one of those 'boring girls going round flashing an engagement ring', thinking that if I 'came out of university with a degree and a husband' I'd achieved my ambitions? What had happened to the Dilly who'd had the potential to become, 'quite an interesting person'? But, unlike Alithea, I knew I couldn't just go and live with Steve as she had with Mike. And, I thought, even she had given way to convention and married Mike when she found she was pregnant.

Still at least I couldn't be accused of 'flashing' my ring. Knowing Steve had so little money I'd persuaded him to get me a second-hand one. I loved it and thought it much more interesting than the row of three diamonds most other engaged girls were wearing but it was yet another thing for my mother to complain about. Fortunately when I was told to show it to Mrs Stewart she said the setting was rather similar to Princess Margaret's, which immediately made it more acceptable.

There was another pressure to marry early. We were living under the shadow of the Cold War. Ever since Russian tanks had rolled into Hungary, during our first term, the international situation had seemed more and more precarious. I remembered Mike that day at the castle and wondered if he still believed the USSR was a peace-loving nation. However one thing was certain; I wanted to experience as much as possible of life, by which I really meant sex, before the bomb fell.

My mother in particular did all she could to discourage our marriage. Even when Steve got his First she wasn't impressed.

'After all it's only in PPE.'

I didn't know where she'd got this idea from, perhaps the Minister. He and his family had moved on to some more suitable environment but my mother was still in touch with his wife.

Eventually, having accepted we would get married anyway, she decided to make the best of it and concentrated on inviting as few as possible of Steve's relations. Unfortunately he came from a large extended family.

'Just invite them,' I said. 'They won't all come. Most of them haven't got cars.'

'People like that,' said my mother, 'are quite capable of hiring a charabanc.'

At this I exploded.

'If there's any more fuss we'll just go to a registry office and get two witnesses off the street. That's all you need to get married.'

'Do you want to break my heart?'

Had Alithea's mother been heartbroken by her daughter's casual marriage? I wondered. It seemed unlikely. She would have been too busy attending important meetings with other internationally minded Socialists to bother about such trivialities.

Once again I was saved by Fiona, this time unintentionally. While searching for a suitable bride's mother's outfit in a local department store my mother bumped into Fiona's mother. She appeared distraught. Through some rich friends at St Andrews, Fiona had met a man from a wealthy, upper class family in the Borders and he wanted to marry her. All this would have sent my mother into a paroxysm of envy if it hadn't been for one thing. He was a Roman Catholic. I'd already heard some of this but had been told not to say anything so I tried to appear surprised.

'It really is too bad of Fiona,' said my mother. 'Her mother is quite frantic and, you know, she really is a very decent little body.' After this news, she became almost grateful that I was marrying someone who was, at least nominally, a Protestant even if he was from the working class.

As the Catholic family were against the marriage as well. Fiona was dispatched to stay with relations in Canada, so that she could 'think things over'. I wondered whether she would get in touch with the charming Canadian from Saskatchewan. However she returned from Canada still determined to marry Alcuin and in the end both families capitulated. Fiona refused to become a Catholic.

'But,' said my mother, 'they'll get her in the end and of course the children will be bought up RC – very sad.'

*

In later years, however, my mother became quite impressed by Fiona's wealth and social status. Once, when Fiona was visiting her parents, my mother met her out shopping. When she next came to stay with us she told me pointedly how smart Fiona had looked.

'Did you tie-dye that tee shirt yourself?' she asked almost immediately afterwards.

She was also impressed by Fiona's children.

'Very nice manners.'

'Camilla's at a convent school,' I said maliciously, 'and her brother is at the prep school for Ampleforth.'

'Well, they speak very nicely.' She sighed and looked out of the window at her own grandchildren who were having a water fight on our battered lawn. I could hear Jonathan swearing, but fortunately she was getting a bit deaf.

*

The older generation seemed to be convinced that we were all setting out to cause them maximum distress. The phrase 'after all we've done for you' was repeated frequently. Amber's divorce had caused considerable horror. Nothing like this had ever been heard of in her family. Amber broke the news of her intentions just before my wedding and Uncle Frank and Aunty Joyce were so mortified they said at first that they didn't think they could show their faces in public. They were even inclined to stop Frances being my bridesmaid such was the shame and disgrace Amber had brought upon the family.

'Now Dilly,' said my mother, 'you see what happens when you have a registry office wedding.' Absurd as this remark was it made me wonder for a moment whether Mike and Alithea's marriage had lasted, but that line of thought was too dangerous to pursue for long.

Eventually Uncle Frank was persuaded they should all come, apart of course from Amber, but they didn't exactly add to the merriment of what was already a rather stressful occasion.

A few years after Amber's divorce, another storm broke over the family, caused, of all people, by Frances.

For some time I'd worried about Frances. After Amber's defection from nursing, her unsuitable marriage and finally her divorce, Uncle Frank wasn't likely to risk Frances going wild at training college and, as no eligible young farmer appeared, it looked as if she was destined to stay on the farm for ever. Then one evening my mother rang.

'I'm afraid I've got some upsetting news about Frances.' Before I could panic, she continued, 'Apparently she's gone and got engaged.'

'What's so upsetting about that? At last she'll be able escape from home.'

'You haven't heard the whole, Dilly. The young man is coloured.'

'What sort of colour? Green? Is he a Martian?'

'It's not funny, Dilly. Joyce is very upset.'

'But where on earth did she manage to meet him?'

'At a Sunday School teachers' conference.'

Then I really did laugh and I wrote to Frances immediately, promising our full support. It looked as if Steve and I would be the only relations at her wedding. But, at the last minute, Amber turned up.

'I don't say I approve,' she said, 'but she is my sister.'

The rest of the family came round eventually. Remembering Uncle Frank's views on the peculiarities of Jews, the Welsh and Lancastrians, it amazed me to see how indulgent he became with Frances's two children when they visited the farm. But as my mother never failed to point out, they were very well behaved.

INTERIM

It was strange that Fiona, Frances and I all defied our parents in our choice of husbands. Unfortunately this hasn't made me closer to either of them. Instead the lives we have chosen have driven us apart. I still see Frances but prefer to do so without Steve. Steve has no problems with her husband's race, quite the reverse in fact, but can't accept his religion. He's still determined to argue him out of the darkness of faith into the pure light of reason and however many times I've told him to let it go he just can't resist another attempt. As for Fiona, leaving Steve's disapproval aside, our lives have drifted so far apart that we now, as Alithea might have put it, no longer belong to the same tribe.

It's all rather sad; I've no siblings so, in their different ways, Frances and Fiona were once my closest companions. Although I've made many other good friends since, these are the only two who share my past and all the memories of our youth.

CHAPTER THIRTY ONE

Although, as time passed, I regretted not seeing more of Fiona, I never made much effort to keep up with anyone else from those years. The intervening decades were such a time of social upheaval and my life became so different from the one I'd once imagined that my schooldays seemed to belong to another world.

For a time I attempted to keep in touch with Rosa. We wrote to each other intermittently but her letters were frustratingly laconic. When I wrote back I felt I was babbling unnecessarily and as I became more absorbed in my children while she seemed dedicated to a life of scholarship we seemed to have less and less in common. What I really wanted to ask was whether she still heard from Mike, but there had always been uneasiness between us on that subject. I was fairly certain that she too had been in love with him and, while he'd been very kind to her and her mother, I knew he didn't 'fancy' her, as my children would have said. I also knew that, although it may only have been a passing attraction, he'd definitely fancied me and that she was aware of it. I realised this must have caused her some pain. Anyway our correspondence petered out and although I wondered about her occasionally I made no serious effort to find her.

There were other people, Jane, for example that I wouldn't have minded seeing again. I'd have liked to know if she'd managed to meet any man who'd scored ten on her scale or if she'd had to make do with a nine. But I did nothing about it.

There was just one person I definitely never wanted to see again. In gloomier moments during the early years of my marriage I sometimes imagined that Alithea might have kept in touch with Ursula. At our last meeting Alithea had claimed she'd made Ursula question some of her family's attitudes and I wondered if she might have felt she needed to stay in touch with her to complete her mission. However even if Ursula had been able to give me news of Alithea I'd no desire to go looking for her. It was a nasty shock therefore when, one Easter, she turned up on the Aldermaston Easter March.

Almost from the beginning of our relationship Steve and I had gone on protest marches: one of our early dates had been the Anti-Suez demonstration in London. When we were first married we'd lived in a basement flat in Islington and every Easter we ended up at Aldermaston. Whenever we were on the march I half hoped we might bump into Mike and Alithea. Every time I saw a couple with a baby in a backpack or a child in a pushchair I imagined for a moment it might be them. Instead, one Easter, I was amazed to see Ursula.

'Goodness Dilly,' she said patronisingly, entirely ignoring the presence of Sophie in the pushchair. 'What are you doing here?'

'Same as you I suppose.' Afterwards, I thought I should have said, 'It's what we've done every year since '58.'

'This is my husband, Clive'. She indicated a stern-looking young man in a bobble hat who was carrying a placard proclaiming, 'Ban the Bomb!' He nodded curtly. Steve, who had been impeded by the weight of Anna on his back, staggered up to join us.

'Oh no!' said Ursula. 'You haven't got one of those trendy baby-carriers, have you? How bourgeois!' I was further astonished. Bourgeois was a favourite left wing insult at the time: used indiscriminately whether you were refusing to sleep with some undesirable character or had been detected using tablecloths. But I'd never expected to hear it from Ursula.

'This is Ursula,' I said to Steve.

'Oh, Su please. I call myself Su now. Spelt S U.'

'Not so bourgeois, I suppose,' I said. I'd forgotten Ursula had never understood sarcasm. Clive continued to scowl. Smiling and general civility were clearly bourgeois conventions. However, when he did eventually condescend to speak, it was obvious that he was the product of a public school education however much he would have liked to disguise it.

Clive and Ursula seemed to know everyone. I saw Ursula speaking confidently to Canon Collins. Even though we'd been coming on the marches longer than they had, she contrived to make me feel an outsider.

This turned out to be our last Aldermaston March. Soon after that Steve got a junior lectureship at a northern university and the arrival of our third child made travel more difficult. Unfortunately, thanks to Steve's political connections, we still came across Clive and Ursula more frequently than I would have liked. My only consolation was that, when I asked about Alithea, she dismissed her as 'Rather a champagne Socialist I seem to remember.' And Alithea had obviously never introduced her to Mike.

When we were still in Islington I half-expected I would meet the Davises again. Islington was still relatively cheap in those days, although the process of gentrification was beginning, and it seemed like the kind of place where they might choose to live. The furniture and decoration of our flat owed much to Alithea's influence, although it was somewhat cleaner, perhaps through the influence of Aunty Joyce.

Steve didn't share my enthusiasm for planks propped on bricks and made some proper bookshelves, but being indifferent to colour schemes he didn't object to orange walls. He even helped me paint them.

Until Sophie was born I used to go to local Labour party meetings with Steve, though I half admitted to myself this was less to do with political commitment and more to do with the hope that one or both of the Davises might turn up. I imagined inviting them round for a supper of spaghetti bolognese and rough red wine. I would show Mike that I'd recovered from my broken heart and discuss Donne or Italian cooking with Alithea. But it never happened and, when we moved back north, I gave up all hope of meeting them by chance.

Life was busy enough in the following years to distract me from these thoughts, although sometimes, on a winter Saturday afternoon, the sound of *Cwm Rhondda* drifting from the living room would draw me irresistibly towards the television. I would glower at the sprawling male bodies apparently transfixed by the screen. But while I was saying 'Can't anyone give me a hand,' or 'Your bedroom's a mess,' or 'Have you done your homework?' - at the same time, I would be watching intently in case, for one moment, the cameras might pick out Mike's face from among the crowd.

As the years went by, I wondered if I would even recognise him. He must be grey-haired, perhaps even bald and maybe that hard, desirable body had run to fat. I was getting older too. Would I really want to meet Mike again now?

Yet odd incidents could still set me wondering what had happened to him and to Alithea and Hugh and even Ben and Danny but especially to him.

If I happened to be in Oxford, I sometimes used to call on Paul Longley who'd become a don in his old college. I once asked him if he heard anything of Christopher. Was he now a vicar? But Paul told me that he'd never been ordained. Apparently Christopher had lost his faith while doing National Service.

'I think he was very influenced by a history teacher who came in my last year. The fellow was a rabid atheist. A chap called Davis. I don't suppose you would remember him.'

I admitted I'd known the rabid atheist quite well and, while I was explaining how I'd first met him, I found myself blushing just as I'd done as a schoolgirl. Paul looked at me rather quizzically and so I didn't feel able to ask him more about his memories of Mike, as I should like to have done. But the conversation left me feeling disturbed for several days.

Then, not long before Miss Cutler's funeral, another meeting with someone else from my past affected me even more profoundly.

Not many people make a living through poetry and so, even after I began to be published, I used to take odd teaching jobs from time to time. This time I'd been asked to fill in at a rather traditional girls' school, during someone's maternity leave. Steve strongly disapproved of the institution but it was quite peaceful compared with some of the places where I'd taught so I ignored him. This school, like the grammar school I'd been to, was an Anglican foundation and like my school had an annual commemoration service. A few weeks before, the headmistress announced with some pride that this year the Bishop would be preaching.

Bishop Dave, as he liked to be called, had, for a long time, been just a disembodied voice on *Thought for Today*. Now I wondered whether I would recognise him either after so long. But, as the procession came down the aisle, Dave in the full splendour of his robes, I immediately saw the chubby face beneath the mitre was a replica of his father's - that cheerful proprietor of the corner shop where I had bought a tin of peas so many years ago. At the reception after the service we managed to have a few words together about old times.

'It's become very bijou round the Cathedral now,' he said. 'That pork butchers where my mum used to buy haslet has become a deli.' I rather admired the way he spanned two worlds with the reference to his mum and the word bijou, which certainly wouldn't have been in his mum's vocabulary. 'So I hear your friend Fiona never went over to Rome?'

'No. She actually told a cardinal it would be intellectually dishonest.' He raised his eyebrows.

'It was a favourite expression of our English teacher's.'

'What? Not the delectable Mrs Davis?'

'No, Miss Carr.'

'Alithea Davis,' he said, lingering almost voluptuously over her name. 'I'll never forget that red sweater.'

'Yes, I remember you and Christopher dragging us round there at the SCM carol service. Do you still hear from Christopher?'

'Christopher?' he said as if dredging something up from the depths of his memory. 'No, no, not for ages. I think he married that girl who worked in the library.'

I would have liked to talk to him longer but a bishop has social obligations. He moved on and the crowd washed over him.

However, brief as it was, this conversation had an extraordinary effect on me. It brought the past back so vividly I could think of nothing else for days. I remembered the carol-singing, the old house at the back of the Close, the smell of the paraffin stove in the damp hall and the Algerian red on Mike's breath, the feel of his tweed jacket. It was useless to tell myself I was the mother of five grown-up children, soon to become a grandmother. Part of a line from a poem by D H Lawrence kept running through my head, *..I weep like a child for the past.*

After I'd recovered a little I decided that I would make an effort to find Rosa. I felt sure she would have kept in touch with Mike and this time I'd be brave enough to ask her about him. It was difficult to know where to start my search and I was still thinking about it when I opened the *Guardian* one morning and was shocked to find myself staring at Rosa's obituary. As I'd suspected, she had been the author of the book on Celtic women as well as a number of other scholarly works. I first thought how ironic it was that my tutor had been reading a book by a distinguished scholar who, years before, had been refused a place at the college all through the absurd snobbery of their history don. Then I felt sad; but mixed with my sadness for her comparatively early death and my regret that we'd lost touch was also the thought that I now had no idea where to start looking for Mike and Alithea. Over the next few days there were quite a few letters in the paper about Rosa and my heart skipped a beat when among them I saw the name Davis. But it was from an Angharad Davis in Cardiff, not Mike after all.

Although the name Davis was common enough even in England I could never see it without wondering if the owner had some connection with Mike. So when, not long after my meeting with Dave, I took a group of sixth form girls to the Barbican to see an RSC production of *Much Ado* the first thing I noticed on the programme was that the actor playing Benedict was called Gareth Davis. He was extremely good-looking in a way I felt I remembered all too well and I started to fantasise that he might be Mike and Alithea's baby. But I soon realised that he was too young. Of course he could have been a younger sibling but, checking the programme notes, I saw he'd been born in Cardiff. Somehow I failed to imagine Alithea settling down to family life in Cardiff.

After his success as Benedict, Gareth Davis began to attract quite a lot of attention. He was interviewed in the colour supplements and I kept coming across his name. In some of these articles he mentioned the influence of his mother who sounded very different from Alithea. He said she'd failed the eleven-plus and had been trying to make up for it ever since through evening classes, the Open University and, finally, a doctorate at Cardiff University. She was a passionate Nationalist and all the children — he had a brother and two sisters — had been brought up to be Welsh speakers. He said less about his father, who was a headmaster, except that he'd encouraged his son's acting because he would like to have been an actor himself if his own mother, who had been strict Chapel, hadn't been so against it. I remembered Alithea had described Mike's mother as strict Chapel and wondered if Mike, with his wonderful voice, would also have liked to be an actor. After all, he'd told me that he and Alithea had met during a production of *Mother Courage*.

Soon after this Gareth Davis left the RSC and started appearing in the kind of films that are known as 'rom-coms'. I knew Steve would never go to such a film but, once when he was out canvassing for the local elections, I watched one on television - and, I thought, the resemblance I'd first noticed had not been entirely imaginary.

PART 9

The Past Unearthed 1997 - 2000

CHAPTER THIRTY TWO

December 1997

The morning after Miss Cutler's funeral, I oversleep after a restless night. Memories of my last year at school had kept me long awake and when I finally fell asleep my dreams were full of confused images of that time. In the morning it feels odd to see a mature Fiona sitting calmly at the breakfast table when in my dreams she'd been a schoolgirl again.

'Pour me some coffee,' I say, yawning.

'Didn't you sleep well?' I admit to dreaming about the past. 'Especially the Davises,' I add.

Fiona needs reminding again about the Davises. Even the shock and horror we felt when we discovered Alithea had, as Fiona once so memorably put it, 'been living in sin' is, to her, only a dim recollection.

'It seems extraordinary now that we were so scandalised,' I say, thinking of the complicated love lives of my children. 'Nowadays, most people would think you were mad not to try living together before you got married. You know Francesca's moved in with Marco.' Fiona is silent and I say defensively,

'I think she's sensible finding out if she likes living in Milan before she commits herself. It's not easy marrying someone from another country, even if you do speak the language fluently.'

'It's not easy marrying someone from another religion,' says Fiona. 'At least you don't have that problem.'

'Oh, I don't know. Atheism can be quite challenging.'

'Atheism isn't a religion Dilly.'

'It is with Steve. Fundamentalist Atheism, just as trying as any other kind of fundamentalism.' Fiona looks blank, so I return to something nearer her concerns.

'I suppose Marco must be nominally a Catholic, but he never seems to go anywhere near a church. It doesn't really seem to matter any more. Like class. When I think of the fuss my parents made about Steve!'

There is a silence while I attack my bacon and eggs. Fiona sips her orange juice and frowns. Many years ago she tried to dissuade me from marrying Steve. Since then she always does her best to ignore his origins. She looks out of the window and observes that it's very misty but perhaps it will clear later.

'Of course the Davises were a big influence,' I add, refusing to change the conversation. 'I'd been madly in love with Mike Davis, so when I found Steve was also a miner's son, it gave him a certain romantic glamour.'

Fiona shakes her head in a bewildered way. She says it all sounds like something out of D H Lawrence and I say I certainly wouldn't have fancied him; 'so opinionated and ugh! - that little red beard.' Fiona, reverting to her old self, laughs and so makes me laugh, as she always did.

A shadow falls over the table.

'You seem very merry,' Ursula rebukes us. All merriment immediately dies away. 'Idling over breakfast I see.'

Ursula, who never idles, says she's waiting for Clive, who will be calling in to pick her up before they go on to London and in the meantime she has some papers to read before an important meeting of some committee or other and to my relief she marches off.

'You didn't tell me she was staying here.'

'I didn't know,' said Fiona. 'Very smart, that red jacket.'

'Yes, it's practically uniform for New Labour women.'

'So you're obviously not one?'

I'm not sure whether this is a question about my politics or a comment on my jeans and sweater. However I decide to treat it as the former. I usually avoid politics with Fiona but feel I must admit I'd been pleased by the election result the previous May.

'Mind you,' I add, 'I don't expect the New Jerusalem, I just hope life will get a bit better for ordinary people and that this lot will have more integrity, perhaps ... I see they've already compromised on cigarette-advertising. *All power tends to corrupt...*'

'*And absolute power corrupts absolutely,*' concluded Fiona. 'Goodness me! It's a long time since I've heard anybody quote Acton. I live in such an intellectual backwater these days. Anyway,' she finished rather surprisingly, 'I was so disgusted by all the recent immoral behaviour in our party, 'sleaze' as the papers called it, that I voted Green this time. Such a nice woman came round canvassing. She was most impressed by the composting system in our gardens. Of course I didn't tell Alcuin. It would have been difficult for him as chairman of the local Conservative Association.'

'Well you don't have to vote the same way as your husband' I said, trying to hide my amusement.

'But most women do,' said Fiona. 'Look at Ursula.'

'Oh, I'm sure Ursula had begun to change her mind before she met Clive. Alithea Davis had a lot of influence on her in her last two terms at school. Being rejected by Oxbridge probably had some effect as well. Her family were very unkind about it. Her horrible aunt said she wouldn't even hear decent English spoken in Durham.

'It seems,' says Fiona, 'these Davises had an enormous effect on everyone but me. It's strange I can hardly remember her. I don't think I ever met the husband.'

'If you had, you'd certainly have remembered.'

'Really Dilly, you sound as if you're still infatuated. What became of them?'

'I don't know. I wish I did.'

'Perhaps it's just as well you don't.'

'You're right though,' I say, ignoring her comment. 'They did have quite an effect – on Christopher for example.'

'Christopher?'

'You must remember. My boyfriend, the one with the ears.'

'Oh, the Grecian urn!'

'That's the one.' I relate the story of Christopher's loss of faith. 'He argued with Mike Davis all the time he was being taught by him but then look what happened…Oh that reminds me. I met his friend Dave last year - taking the school commemoration service - now a bishop - would you believe it! His dad kept a corner shop just down the road from the Roman arch.'

'Well there you are Dilly. That's what a grammar school education could do for you. How many boys from corner shops could hope to become bishops nowadays?'

'Absolutely none from round where we live,' I say laughing. Their families would disown them. They want their sons to become doctors, or failing that, accountants.'

Fiona looks blank but after a moment says,

'Oh, I see what you mean. Now that's another thing, what do you think this government is going to do about immigration?'

I don't want to discuss immigration with Fiona and so attempt to distract her by reminiscing about other characters from our schooldays. This isn't an entire success. Fiona now likes to think of our old school as being rather more socially exclusive than it was. But I persist.

'Do you know, I once ran into Audrey - years ago now. She'd become quite grand. She said her husband was a group captain. I think this was supposed to impress me but I haven't a clue about ranks in the air force. They'd just come back from a tour in Singapore and she was full of their wonderful social life out there. I nearly said, "It sounds better than Iowa," but I thought that would be too unkind.'

'Iowa?'

'Surely you remember?' But it seems Fiona doesn't. Audrey's romance with the American who 'wasn't even an officer' and all the scandal of her pregnancy has been deleted from her memory. Nor is she interested to hear that according to Audrey the exquisite Hazel was running a beauty salon in her husband's five star hotel. When I mention Rosa however she is a little more receptive.

I recount the shock of seeing her name on the *Guardian* obituary page and realising she had indeed been the author of the book, *Women in Celtic Britain*, that I remembered seeing my tutor reading,

'I wonder if she ever realised the college had turned down someone who was to become such a distinguished scholar?' All this interests Fiona but when I start to reminisce about our visit to Rosa's house after her father died, the tiny room, the bust of Marx on the mantelpiece, her eyes glaze over, so perhaps it's almost fortunate that at this point Ursula reappears with Clive.

'Clive just had to come to say hello.'

'Indeed, indeed,' says Clive, graciously. 'And how is that husband of yours? Still toiling away in the constituency? I'm afraid I didn't really have time to have a chat with him at the Conference - so many committees. A shame! We can't do without useful people like him - the backbone of the Party.'

I look above me at the ornate and weighty-looking chandelier and imagine the pleasure I would feel if it suddenly broke loose and crashed down on Clive. Disappointingly it remains firmly attached to the ceiling. A shrill trilling noise comes from somewhere about his person; he fumbles in his pockets and produces a mobile phone.

'Hello..hello! Can't hear you. Reception's terrible. We're out somewhere in the fucking sticks. Su dragged me up here. Funeral of some old bat - headmistress or something - no one important – waste of valuable time.' All this is clearly directed at Ursula. She stares resentfully into the distance.

'Have to take this outside. That was Alistair,' he says furiously to his wife.

Ursula, obviously mortified, said a hasty goodbye. Soon after I look through the window and see them obviously in the middle of a huge row.

'Well that got rid of them.'

Fiona says nothing but looks a great deal.

'At least Steve has integrity,' I say with feeling.

After Fiona has driven off in her 4x4 I go for a walk. The big iron bell pull has disappeared and there is a neat panel of half a dozen buttons beside the Boarding House door indicating the place has been converted into flats Mist wreathes around the cathedral towers. I tread softly under the dripping branches of the sycamores, over the gravestones, up to the basement railings and try to look into the dining room. Prepared to peer into shadowy depths, my gaze is brought up short by a magnolia painted wall. The long dining room has obviously been divided in two. I wonder whether, if could go inside, I would recognise anything of the original layout. In my memory I can still revisit the place, room by room, the reality might be destructive. I walk down the Harstans, noticing on my way that the tithe barn has been turned into garages, and prowl around the red-brick, gabled, Victorian building that used to be my school. The grounds look unkempt; a rather tatty sign reads *College of Art* but later I hear that the building is about to be incorporated into the new university. Everything is locked and I can't see much, as the laurels at the front are so overgrown. I wonder what happened to the honours' board where, presumably, my name along with Fiona's, Ursula's and Rosa's would have been inscribed in gold after we were awarded our degrees.

I make my way back up the Harstans remembering the years I toiled up to the Boarding House with a satchel full of homework and notice that the gargoyle has gone. Perhaps, I thought, it had dropped off, starved to death once Becky had stopped feeding it with leaves. I return to the Close noting that the actors' lodgings are now the offices of the Dean and Chapter: walk past the re-named Northgate Hotel, now part of a chain, and round the back of the cathedral towards the little lane where Mrs Herbert and her strange trio of lodgers once lived. Little here has changed outwardly although the garden is tidier, with a bay tree in a tub and neat pots of spring bulbs, already showing green tips, arranged under the window. I linger by the gate until a brisk woman arrives hauling along a small dog and carrying a wicker basket containing a few expensive-looking groceries, including, I notice, extra virgin olive oil.

'Can I help you?' she enquires coldly and I say,

'No, no, that's fine,' and wonder what her reaction would be if I said, 'Yes, I'd like to look in your basement.' Instead I carry on, pass out of the Close and walk down the little shopping street where I notice the butchers that sold the bright pink mince and the mouse head stewing steak has become a 'Purveyor of Game'. The other shops have become even more unrecognisable but include an expensive-looking hairdressers, an antique shop and the delicatessen mentioned by Dave, presumably once the pork butcher's where his mum used to buy haslet.

Later I decide to go to Evensong. The choirboys are all on post-Christmas holiday so there's rather a small choir and I'm offered a laminated sheet explaining the order of service. It all seems to be set up for the tourists, the Cathedral Experience rather than an act of worship. The old form of the prayer book is used but a laywoman reads badly from a modern translation of the Bible and I'm left feeling things aren't what they were. I remember Hugh's dramatic genuflections. Nobody in the sparse congregation seems inclined to go to such lengths today and I almost regret this. I feel a bit depressed but remind myself it's not for me to criticise what the Church of England does to keep itself in business.

I return to London in what Steve calls 'a funny mood'.

CHAPTER THIRTY THREE

My funny mood lasts for a long time. The encounter with Dave had left me feeling disturbed for several days, but returning to the actual scene of those past events has had an even more distressing effect. I can't settle to anything. Returning to dust, dead holly leaves and the bare-branched Christmas tree standing on a thick mat of pine needles isn't a good start.

'I tried to tidy up a bit,' says Steve, seeing my expression, 'but I didn't really know what to do with the Christmas things and I've been busy.'

'You always are.'

I clean the house and fill vases with early daffodils.

'Who am I doing this for?' Steve is never in. The children still look on this as their family home but they can only visit occasionally. This is all mainly for me and I don't need all this space. Nor all this work, I think, as I vacuum, dust and polish rooms full of things but empty of people. When I take the Christmas decorations up to the loft, I look at all the boxes of the children's possessions.

'Don't throw those away just yet,' they plead, so there they all are: Action Men, dolls, Lego, piles of old NMEs, A level notes, letters from ex-boyfriends or girlfriends... I feel oppressed by the sheer weight of stuff above our heads.

'I feel as if I'm keeping a museum,' I say one day at breakfast. 'I want to clear stuff out. Move somewhere smaller; live somewhere more interesting.'

Steve looks horrified at the idea of his life being disturbed and this is only the beginning of a number of arguments on the subject. Feeling I'm getting nowhere, I decide travel might be a cure for my restlessness. Anna has asked us both, several times, to come and visit her in Sydney but Steve always says he can't spare the time. Now I decide to go by myself. I fly into summer and while I sit drinking strong Italian coffee in beachside cafés I'm reminded of a particular incident, years ago, that made me return to writing poetry.

When the first three children were old enough we'd gone on a camping holiday in southern Italy. One day I'd seen an interesting-looking woman sitting in a café by the edge of the sea battering away at an old typewriter. We'd smiled at each other and, inspired by this glimpse of another kind of life, I decided that one day, when the children were grown up, I'd take off to some warm place by the sea and begin to write poetry again. But then, I'd thought, why should I wait? I could write poetry anywhere. This was just as well. On our way home we stopped off in Rome. Something about the decadence of the place affected even Steve. We sat around in cafés and, in a final burst of extravagance booked into a hotel. One hot afternoon we left the children asleep in the bedroom and made passionate love on the bathroom floor. But I'd run out of contraceptive pills and, after the twins were born, foreign holidays were beyond our reach for several years.

Returning from Sydney the plane plunges through thick cloud towards Heathrow. It's already March but everything is still gripped by winter. I feel I've returned too soon. Steve says he's missed me but the rooms in our Victorian house seem dark and narrow after Anna's big sunlit spaces. Then Francesca rings from Milan and says she's pregnant. Despite Steve's protests I decide to go to Milan. Once there I remember the woman with her typewriter at the beach café and have a

THE PAST UNEARTHED

half-formed idea of travelling further south, finding some place by the sea where I can concentrate on writing. But, before I can talk to Francesca about this plan, Steve rings to say he's coming out to join me. I'm not sure that I'm totally delighted by the news. Steve has never been very good at holidays and, since the children have grown up, has been increasingly unwilling to take any time off work. It's understandable; from the moment he passed the eleven-plus, he'd been constantly told how privileged he was. All his life he's been trying to justify not going down the pit.

But, when he comes through the gate at Malpensa airport, I notice how grey his hair has become and surprise myself by a rush of tender affection. It seems that my absences have worried him and he's been thinking things over. He starts to talk tentatively about the possibility of moving and perhaps taking more time off; so I agree to return to England with him. Perhaps, I think the woman in the beach café might have envied me surrounded by my children; such is the human propensity to want what one hasn't got.

Then, once back in England, strange coincidences start to occur. It's as if by revisiting my past I've unconsciously started an archaeological excavation and now fragments of that past start to re-emerge.

When the summer finally arrives, Steve, who is struggling to learn to enjoy life, actually suggests we go down to Cornwall. Francesca's twin, Sebastian, is there. Since he left art college he's been travelling with a puppet theatre. (A career choice that Steve has, so far, found hard to come to terms with). And so it happens that in St Ives, while wandering around its steep streets with their sandy corners, I pass a small studio. Seeing the poster outside, I think it's advertising a

Jackson Pollock exhibition. I slither grittily to a halt and look more closely. *Ben Walker: A Retrospective.* Of course!

'Good God! I met that artist once, years ago. That day at the castle.'

'Which you've told me about so often,' says Steve, pre-empting any possible repetition.

Inside, a middle-aged man is sitting in the corner guarding the catalogues. These have a photograph of Ben on the front, older, thinner, much thinner - gaunt in fact, and underneath, *Ben Walker 1932-1985.* The dates and the photograph tell it all. I wonder if the man in the corner was his younger partner, perhaps now kept going on retro-virals and what happened to sweet Danny. Was he too destroyed by AIDS?

There is a brief biography. I discover that shortly after I met Ben he went to New York - I remember 'Paris is finished' - and then on to California. Following Hugh I wonder?

I soon realise - although I daren't say so while the man in the corner, who has the air of a keeper of the flame, could possibly overhear me - that Ben never had a single original idea although he got much more skilled at pastiche. Then I stop before three little watercolours quite unlike anything else in the exhibition.

'Bellingthorpe Castle!' The man in the corner looks at me suspiciously but I'm entranced. There is a view of the castle from the front, a view of the park through one of the Gothic windows and an interior with a lightly sketched figure, shadowy in a corner, who, I am almost certain, is Danny.

As we leave I tell the man that I once met Ben, at Bellingthorpe, and he becomes quite friendly although he stiffens up when I mention Hugh, and says some people let Ben down very badly. I think it better not to enquire about Danny, whom anyway I suspect got left in

England when Ben sailed for New York.

Later that afternoon, while we are looking at the Barbara Hepworth sculptures, Steve disappears and I assume he's bored. It isn't until Christmas that I find he has bought me all three paintings as a present. I tell him it's the nicest thing he's ever done for me and he says,

'Well there's not a lot of competition in that direction, is there?'

The next fragment to be uncovered is a small volume in a second-hand bookshop.

'To loveliest Alithea from her still ever devoted Hugh' - *'Vivamus mea Lesbia atque amemus'.* I stand staring at the flyleaf in disbelief. I recognise the small neat handwriting from the corrections in the margins of my Latin proses. *The Poems of Catullus, a new translation by Professor Hugh Marlow, University of Melbourne.* Perhaps California wasn't far enough. Had the baby looked like Hugh? Had Mike pursued him to the very shores of the Pacific? *'Let us live my Lesbia and let us love.'* This seems somewhat optimistic unless Alithea eventually went to Melbourne to join Hugh. Unlikely, although it could explain why I had never been able to find out what became of her. However *'Still ever devoted'* seems to have a plaintive, unfulfilled ring to it, which suggests she didn't. Poor Hugh.

I ask the owner if he has any idea where the book may have come from and fortunately he's able to be quite informative. It turns out he bought it, among other books, from the library of a recently deceased, moderately famous novelist.

'They were sold by his latest ex-wife,' he says, obviously enjoying the chance to gossip. 'I think she was number three but there was a slight reconciliation in his final illness – he was an alcoholic I believe.'

He admits that he noticed this book because it was an oddity; the others from that source were mainly review copies.

A new idea strikes me. Could Alithea have been one of these ex-wives, and if so what happened to Mike? I buy the book and look at it from time to time hoping it will yield other clues but the only thing I notice is that it's in good condition – hardly read in fact. Poor Hugh.

The last piece of the past to turn up is, however, more than a fragment.

In the early March of 1999, I find myself in the café of an Arts Centre somewhere in East London. It's the kind of place that goes in for a lot of brown, chunky food. I chew my way through some lentil soup and a lump of bread full of various seeds, wishing there were something more stimulating to drink than organic apple juice. I've come to see a play written by a girl I once taught at an inner city comprehensive.

Her letter had arrived a few weeks before.

'Sometimes I think I wasn't such a bad teacher after all'. Steve, at the other side of the breakfast table, looks at me over his glasses.

'I wish you wouldn't do that, Steve. You remind me of my terrifying Latin teacher – Miss Rush. Do you try to intimidate your students like that?'

Steve removes his glasses and waits for me to explain myself further.

'Do you remember the only bright spot when I was at the Keir Hardie Community School was the sixth form and, in particular, one girl, Joanne. She had a lot of talent - I tried to encourage her writing.'

THE PAST UNEARTHED

'Vaguely.'

'Well she's written a play which is being put on at an Arts Centre in Deptford but may go further if things work out. Anyway she wants me to go and see it.

'How will you get to Deptford?' This is hardly the response I'd hoped for, but I let it pass.

Now, sipping my apple juice, I'm beginning to worry that Joanne's play will be very bad and I won't know what to say.

It's apparently International Women's Day - something that has passed me by until this moment – and we're being urged to inscribe the names of women who have influenced us on large sheets of paper. I've no intention of doing any such thing but it makes me think. There were quite a number, one way and another: my mother, who first read poetry to me; Aunty Joyce, domestic standards, though not to the extent of ironing tea towels; my Edinburgh Aunts with their passion for education and careers for women; Amber, for first making me understand the meaning of sensual; Fiona, for whatever sophistication I may possess; Rosa, for making me question my right to a comfortable middle-class upbringing; Mazzy, self-discipline; Miss Carr, English grammar but also for saying – 'Well my dear. It's your life' - and of course Alithea... My thoughts are interrupted by the arrival of a nervous Joanne who has to be reassured.

Sitting in the tiny theatre I peer at the programme and a name jumps out at me. Phyllida Morgan! Good God! Is anybody else called Phyllida? Most people make the same mistake the Vicar's wife made so many years ago and think I'm called Philippa; I don't usually bother to enlighten them. More recent friends call me Pippa, which sounds a bit livelier than Dilly.

Much to my relief, the play is quite good, certainly promising. I watch Phyllida Morgan with interest. She is one of the strongest of the cast and also very pretty. I think she'll do well – that is if she has any luck in her precarious profession. But what on earth made her choose, or at least choose not to change, such a name as Phyllida?

After the play, Joanne wants to hear my opinion and she asks me to join them all at the pub.

The small, dark pub near the river hasn't been too excessively heritaged although there are a number of coy references to past smuggling connections in Gothic script on the walls. It's cramped and in the general scramble for seats I find myself next to Phyllida Morgan.

'A pint of bitter for you Meg, wasn't it?' says one of the men slopping down a glass in front of her.

'So Phyllida is your stage name?' I ask.

'Yeah that's right. I'm like technically, Megan Davis but I didn't want anyone thinking Oh, Gareth Davis! and going, "Are you related" and I'm like, "Well, yeah he's my brother but..." Well you know... I mean basically I'm me, so I took my Mum's surname and then Megan Morgan... too alliterative and too bloody Welsh come to that. I mean Gareth Davis! I'm surprised people don't mistake him for a rugby player.' She looks at me for the usual reaction. But I'm not really interested in her famous brother.

'But why Phyllida?'

'It's my second name. It's from a poem.'

'Yes, I know.'

'Really? I've never known anyone apart from my dad who has even heard of it.' I feel a slight prickling sensation – a slight shortness of breath.

'Does your dad ever quote it?'

'Well,' she laughed, pulling a face. 'Basically, only too often. He likes reciting poetry, old fashioned, sentimental stuff - embarrassed us rotten as kids. *The May Queen* - that was another one. Do you know that too?'

I nod.

All the time she'd been speaking I'd been studying Megan. I could see the similarity to her brother but now I'm searching for another similarity and can't see it. Megan is dark-eyed. Can I even remember what he looked like?

I need to be sure.

'So you were called after that poem?'

'Well sort of. Basically they were running out of ideas and apparently Dad suggested it like a bit of a joke. He's a bit sentimental about that poem – probably some girl in his past – "Just one of a long line," Mum says. I've tried teasing it out of him but he won't let on. The most I've ever got out of him, but he was laughing at the time, was that he owed her something. Mum just rolled her eyes and said "An apology I expect."'

I pick up my beer but my hand is shaking so much I have to put it down again. Still I've got the opening I need. Doing my best to keep my voice steady, I say,

'Is your mum...' I wondered how to phrase this. 'Sorry, but can I ask? Had your father been married before?' She looks at me, surprised.

'Yeah.' She pauses, puzzled. 'So you don't want to ask me about my famous brother - that's a nice change.'

'I'm more interested in your father.' I immediately realise this perhaps isn't the best thing to say to Mike's daughter. Especially as I remember, from the articles about Gareth, that his second wife sounded rather formidable. I notice Megan looks amused, so I hastily say,

'Sorry! What I mean is, I think your father's first wife may have taught me English and I've often wondered what became of her. She was called Alithea, Alithea Davis in those days. I suppose she's changed her name.'

'Several times,' she said grinning. 'That's the one. Well how amazing. So did you ever meet Dad?'

'Yes, actually I did.'

'And fancied him, I suppose.'

'Well...' I attempt to dismiss this with a light laugh. Megan is not deceived.

'And I expect he encouraged you. I gather he was a bit of a lad until Mum took him in hand. Even now, when his hair's white and he's put on weight, he can still turn on the charm - like Gareth. Wasn't his last film gross?'

It would be safer to discuss Gareth's last film but there are things I really want to know even if it's tactless to continue.

'Do you mind my asking - have you got a half-brother or sister?'

'You don't know Simon as well do you?'

I shake my head.

'It's just Alithea was pregnant when she left our school and I wondered...' I can't think how to continue. I try again. 'It's just Alithea made a great impression on me and I'd be very interested to hear what happened to her.' This seems the safest line to take.

'Basically the story's like complicated...' she begins.

The pub is filling up. I can see the young man who bought her the beer is trying to attract her attention so I say,

'Look, I really want to hear it but somewhere quieter would be better. Perhaps I could buy you lunch sometime soon, next week, say, and you can tell me the story then? If you could give me your mobile number I'll give you a ring.'

'On what I get paid, I'll never turn down the chance of a free meal,' she says scribbling down her number. As she hands it to me she smiles. Her smile is slightly lop-sided and suddenly I see Mike – of course I can remember what he looked like! I've hardly touched my beer but I feel rather drunk. However I pull myself together and go to talk to Joanne.

CHAPTER THIRTY FOUR

It's more than a week before I manage to meet Megan Davis. During that time I'm reminded of how the children used to be before big events, Christmas, birthdays, holidays. 'I can't wait' they used to say, 'I can't wait'. It used to drive me mad. Now I know how they felt and I'm ashamed of myself. I try to analyse my state as calmly as possible. I tell myself it's because I'm at last going to find out what happened to Mike and Alithea. But that, although interesting, is hardly something to get so excited about. Then Megan had hinted at some secret about Alithea's son, Simon. But I already have a good idea of what that secret might be. Finally I tell myself firmly that my impatience has nothing, absolutely *nothing*, to do with any chance of meeting Mike again and, even if such a chance should arise, how could that be of any possible significance at our age?

I distract myself by trying to think where I can meet Megan. I don't want to intimidate her by taking her somewhere too grand but all the cafés and little bistros I can think of are noisy places where I'm likely to run into someone I know. I feel Megan's may be a long story requiring a calm ambience with no interruptions, so finally decide on a small Italian restaurant where Marco took us when he and Francesca last came to London.

While we're still settling in and unfolding our stiff white napkins, we avoid the subject we've come to talk about. Instead we talk about our families. Megan is the youngest; her siblings are all quite a bit older than her and she describes herself as having been, 'basically a surprise'.

I order some red wine, a good Barolo. The waiter recognises me and lets me try out my Italian, which I'm trying to improve, now that I have a half-Italian granddaughter. As we study the menu we talk intermittently about the pros and cons of bringing up children to be bilingual. Megan says they were all brought up to speak Welsh because their mother is a passionate Welsh Nationalist.

'But your father isn't a Welsh speaker, is he?' I realise there may be a side to Mike I never knew about. She laughs,

'He'd forgotten any that he knew until Mum took him in hand. In his day being educated meant speaking English.'

'And when I knew him he was very left-wing.'

She looks at me, raising her eyebrows, and I realise I've already revealed I know more about Mike than I care to admit. Fortunately the arrival of the antipasto provides a distraction and gives me time to think. I explain I had a boyfriend who always talked about his Socialist-atheist history teacher. I add that Alithea was almost the first middle-class person I'd met who'd openly claimed to be a Socialist.

'The two of them made rather an impact in a quiet cathedral city in the fifties.' I hope this isn't a tactless thing to say. I don't know what she feels about her father's first wife.

'Oh, Dad still votes Labour, much to Mum's annoyance, but he's not very politically active - one politician in the family is enough.'

I remember from the article about Gareth that Mike was described as a headmaster 'And so,' I say, trying to keep it casual. 'Is your father still working?' (I keep trying to imagine Mike as a headmaster.)

'No. He took early retirement – got pissed off with all that paperwork. He's happy to be out of it. He's always said he wanted to act when he was young. Gran was against it – insecure and, I think she thought, irreligious. She was some scary woman, that one! But he's always been involved in everything to do with theatre when he could: now he's mainly into producing.'

Up from the depths of my unconscious floats a picture of Christopher standing in the snow, saying 'Poor old Trotsky! He's in trouble with the Head about some Communist play he wants to put on....'. Words that had barely registered at the time, so concerned as I'd been with my own misery.

'But anyway as Mum's out so much with all her committees he's more or less taken over the housekeeping.'

I nearly choke on my wine.

'The *housekeeping!*' She looks surprised.

'Yeah, he's pretty competent. Of course Mum gives him a list. She's dead organised.'

So, I think, this woman succeeded where Alithea failed but then things are very different now. I feel once again that I've given away too much; so, by the time we've decided on a main course I think it's time to change the subject.

'You were going to tell me about Simon. I think that's what you said he was called?'

'Oh yeah. Well. Simon. Where can I start? Oh course a lot of this happened before I was born but I've picked up the story in bits and pieces - basically through Mum and she got most of it from Dad - so hardly impartial.'

As Megan starts to relate how much she knows I've already anticipated the end of the story but I'm still interested to know how it all unravelled. Alithea, as I'd already suspected when I was only nineteen, had made an indifferent mother. Mike had often returned from a day's teaching to find the flat empty. The baby had been left with her parents or rather with their housekeeper. (That ever useful refugee, I remember), and he'd soon found that Alithea was having an affair with a television producer. This was the final blow to what had been from the start a rather dodgy marriage. I imagine that the differences in their respective backgrounds would have made things even more difficult when they got to London. Anyway he'd soon headed back to Wales where he'd met, or rather re-met, Megan's mother.

'They were at primary school together and Mum had fancied him from when they were both six. But when he went to grammar school and then Oxford she thought she'd lost him.'

(So, I think, he started early – already charming the girls at six). But, aloud, I just say,

'What happened to Simon?'

'Well basically he was just a baby so he stayed with his Mum,'

'Or the housekeeper.'

'Yeah, probably. When Mum and Dad married,' she continued, 'there was some talk about Dad trying to get custody but I'm not sure Mum was that keen and although Dad used to go down and visit, he didn't really press it. Mum felt he found it hard to bond with Simon. Odd! I mean, Dad's basically such a warm affectionate father and he totally like adores his grandchildren. Still when Simon got old enough we had him to stay in the holidays. I think that like suited Alithea. She couldn't really be bothered with him when he was young.'

'No cocoa and biscuits for Simon then.'

'What?'

'Sorry, just remembering something.'

'I don't think he got on too well with the others – being so much younger I can't remember him very well but Gareth thought he was a stuck-up prat - very English - oh sorry!'

'It's all right,' I say. 'I know what you mean.'

'Anyway eventually,' Megan continued, 'he got sent off to boarding school, Winchester. She said it was a family tradition. Mum says they had quite a row about it and apparently while they were arguing something came out - and this will really amaze you!'

I doubt it, I thought.

'In the midst of this row about Winchester, Alithea said something mega-weird. Dad was protesting he should have some say because Simon was like his son as well and apparently she said, "Well, I suppose." Now, at the time Dad basically just thought she meant he had a right to his own opinion, but then, about ten years later it must have been, the shit really hit the fan.'

By now I've guessed what's coming but I try to maintain an expression of detached interest.

'Anyway, basically Simon had just like graduated from Oxford. He came up to visit us and at supper that evening – and I do remember this even though I was quite little - he was sitting there looking, well you know, looking as if he thought we were a bit of an uncouth rabble –Mum always tried to say he was just shy but I dunno... Anyway, Dad, trying to be friendly and interested like asked him what his plans were and he talked about some opening in the City. Dad tried to persuade him against it. There was a bit of an argument; Dad lost his cool and said, "I wouldn't like to think any son of mine." And then Simon, in that cold English voice of his, said, "Well perhaps I'm not." Oh my God! All hell broke loose. Of course I'd no idea what it was all about then but apparently about the time Alithea was teaching at your school there was this guy...'

'Hugh Marlow!' I say before I stop to think.

'You knew him as well!'

'He used to teach me Latin. I'm sorry. I've spoilt your story.'

She gives me a puzzled look and I wonder whether Mike ever said that the sympathetic Phyllida was having extra Latin lessons.

'Do go on,' I say hastily. 'What happened next?'

'Well Mum started to say it was time for me to go to bed but I kept asking why Dad was so upset. Nobody would explain to me what was going on and I was really worried. Dad looked as if he was crying – perhaps he was. I heard a car drive off – it was Simon leaving. The next day Alithea turned up. It's the only time I've ever seen her. She's very striking isn't she - and amazing clothes. I think she was wearing some kind of velvet cloak. Well, it was the late 70s. And Simon came back. Mum had arranged for me to spend the day with a friend but as she was hustling me out I heard Alithea say, "But Mike, I couldn't be sure." Then Dad said, "Well, just look at him." None of it made any sense to me at the time but it's true Simon wasn't at all like the rest of us. People used to comment and Mum would say he looked like his mother. But there was his Mum at our kitchen table, dark-haired and nearly as tall as Dad and there was Simon fair-haired and slightly built. Even I noticed it. While Mum was driving me to my friend's I said, "But he's not like his Mum, is he?" Mum told me to leave it alone. Well that's basically it. When I got back they'd both gone and Simon never came to stay again.

It was only when I got older I started to ask about it. I remember Mum said Dad had had his suspicions but basically the dates didn't like work out. He'd sent this Hugh guy packing before Alithea got pregnant.

'Yes,' I say, 'but I think they must have been meeting in London.' And I relate the story of the theatre outing.

A thoughtful silence follows and I can see Megan wondering just how far I was involved in this ancient drama.

'What did your Mother feel about it all?' I ask to distract her.

'Well she was rather sorry for Simon. Still she was glad we didn't have any more contact with Alithea. She's basically resigned to women falling for Dad's charm and usually just has a laugh but she does get a bit tight-lipped about Alithea. Dad still gets a bit emotional when her name comes up; I think Mum suspects he's never really got over her.'

For a moment I feel a pang of sympathy for this formidable second wife. Maybe I'd been luckier than I realised. But, now Megan has brought up the subject of her father's conquests I'm worried that it may lead her to enquire about her namesake. To distract her from this line of thought I ask if she remembers Mike ever mentioning someone called Rosa.

'Rosa! Of course I do. She used to come and stay, supposedly to talk to Mum – they were both interested in Pre-Roman Celtic tribal structures - but she used to follow Dad round with her eyes. I think she was a bit in love with him. How did you know her?'

'She was in the sixth form with me - very clever.'

'Yeah, but very quiet and mousy looking. There was someone else from your school came once as well, Joan somebody - a history teacher.'

'Oh God! Yes, Joan Seymour, I remember her!'

'Luckily, considering poor old Dad's weakness for a pretty face, neither of them was exactly a threat. Mum was quite kind to them but, of course, even though Dad obviously didn't fancy either of them he still had to turn on the bloody charm. I love my Dad to bits but honestly ..!. Phyllida never turned up though.' She looks at me. I change the subject.

'But your mum still minded about Alithea?'

'Yeah, fortunately she's far too grand for the likes of us now.'

'Is she?'

'Yeah, though basically, even though she's so posh, I think she's a bit of a slapper.' She sees the shock on my face and laughs, and I wonder how I could ever have doubted she was Mike's daughter? I can see him in every expression, every gesture.

I notice the waiter hovering,

'Dolce, signora?'

Megan says she would like pannacotta, which gives me the chance to ask further about Alithea. I'm interested to know what happened to her and anyway it will lead us away from any possible speculations about what happened to Phyllida.

After her affair with the BBC producer had broken up her marriage to Mike, Alithea had appeared in some satirical television programmes. I seem to have missed her brief moment of media fame.

A short marriage to the recently deceased novelist had followed which explained why Hugh's translation of Catullus had turned up in the bookshop. She hadn't even bothered to take it with her when she left. Poor Hugh! She'd had two novels published under her latest married name. The second came out about the time her marriage with the novelist was breaking up. He'd made sure it was badly reviewed.

'Although, Dad said, they were rubbish anyway,' says Megan. 'But of course he would, wouldn't he? I think there was a rather unflattering portrait of him in one of them. She made him Irish but he wasn't deceived.'

'So what did she do next?'

'Did you ever hear of a little feminist publisher called *The Crowing Hen?*'

'Yes! I sent some poems to them when I first started writing again. They didn't want them, though they said they'd like to see more of my work. But I never got round to it. It was about the time the twins were born.'

'Well, Alithea started that. Perhaps she thought as, thanks to her ex-husband, she was being turned down by all the like big names, she'd publish her own stuff. I dunno. Anyway it went really well for a few years - a very right-on seventies vibe. She sold out to Virago and made shit loads of money just about the time Dad found out about Simon. She actually offered Dad a share - in compensation for all those holidays when we paid for Simon's keep I suppose – although, of course, she didn't put it as bluntly as that. Dad was furious - even more furious! Then, basically, she just buggered off – nothing from her for years but when Gareth was at the RSC we suddenly got a Christmas card asking if this brilliant young actor was our Gareth. Mum said "Don't answer" but of course Dad couldn't resist, so now they regularly send each other boastful Christmas cards - you know the sort of thing...

*Simon has just flown in from New York. He's now hedge fund manager for Morgan...*or whatever they're called.

So pleased to hear Simon is doing well. (You liar Dad!) *I expect you've seen Gareth's latest film.* (She probably hasn't – not highbrow enough for her.)'

'And what's she doing now?'

'Oh that's really funny. A few years ago we got a card saying she'd decided it was time to settle down – settle down! She was over sixty - I suppose the affairs were drying up. Well that's what Mum said. She was marrying a very rich man – about ten years older than herself - nobody knew much about him. Someone described it as 'quiet money' but since then he's been in the media quite a lot. He amazed everyone by giving a huge donation to New Labour and he's started to collect contemporary art.'

'Not that one!' I said. She nodded. 'And I suppose it's all down to Alithea's influence – definitely too grand for the likes of us!' We both laugh.

'Dad was a bit upset about her marriage – "still carrying a candle" Mum said and he still hates that Hugh. Threatens to strangle him if they meet. Fortunately he's...'

'In Melbourne.'

'You seem to know an awful lot!'

I told her about the translation of Catullus in the bookshop. 'Just another coincidence, though meeting you was the strangest.'

'I'm very glad you did,' she said, spooning up the last of her pannacotta, as I sip my espresso. 'That was a fabulous meal. Italian food for me usually means takeaway pizza. Mind you, Dad's spaghetti bolognese is pretty excellent.'

'Your father makes spaghetti bolognese!'

'Yeah. You sound surprised. He's quite a good cook. Though I mean basically spaghetti bolognese isn't exactly the height of sophistication, is it?'

'It was once.' I decide it wouldn't be a good idea to mention I'd first seen it made by Alithea and, instead, say,

'Your mother must be a remarkable woman.'

'Oh, she is.'

Somewhere out in the April afternoon the sun is still shining but this discreet little restaurant is down a small alleyway and the pink shaded lights have been switched on. We're the only customers left and they're clearing tables around us.

Time to go.

As Megan prepares to leave she says,

'Thanks a lot, Pippa. I'll tell Dad I met you. I'm sure he'll be interested. What was your surname before you were married?'

'It was…' I start, and hesitate, and then think – what the hell! So I smile and say, 'Just tell him that Phyllida sends her love.'

CHAPTER THIRTY FIVE

A few days later, I'm sitting over my breakfast coffee trying to get up the energy to do some more clearing out. I've a longing for more space and greenery. But space and greenery in London are expensive. It's a beautiful spring morning - a good day for house-hunting. Steve, of course, is already at work on his book and I know there's no chance of persuading him to leave his desk. Then the phone rings.

It stops ringing before I can reach it. Steve will be irritated by the interruption. He comes through holding out the handset.

'Some bloody Welshman for you - a poetry reading I expect - wouldn't give his name.' I grab the phone and then drop it because my hand has started to shake. I manage to pick it up.

'Hello.'

'Dilly?'

The voice caresses me. Liquefying like a jelly left in the sun, I ooze onto the nearest chair.

'Can you guess who this is?' Play it cool, I tell myself.

'Um, it's either the ghost of Richard Burton or a disreputable Socialist-atheist I once knew in my youth called Mike Davis.' He laughs,

'Still the same witty girl.'

Witty? Was I? I don't remember.

'And still as beautiful as ever, my daughter tells me.' This is plainly such an outrageous lie that I can't think of anything to say. Possibly, under pressure of persistent questioning, Megan may have said that I didn't look too haggard considering.

'But listen Dilly, was that your husband who answered the phone? He sounded a bit grim.'

'You interrupted his work and he doesn't have much small talk. He's a Yorkshireman not a mendacious Celt.' Mike seems delighted by this insult but, when he has stopped laughing, his voice goes into caressing mode again.

'But is he good to you, little Dilly?'

'We try to be good to each other - it's called being married - and less of the "little Dilly". I've had five children. I'm not a skinny little schoolgirl any more.'

'Five children! I've got four. I used to think I had five but I gather Megan told you that story. That first wife of mine...however did I get involved with her and as for that little shit Hugh Marlow..if ever I get my hands on him!'

'Poor man,' I say. 'Exiled in Melbourne – too terrified to come back. I wonder what the Australians make of him?'

'I'd hoped they'd make him into a barbecue but I gather he became Professor of Classics in the university. Anyway let's not talk about them any more. What did you think of my little Megan?'

I'm able to praise Megan's looks and talent and general niceness enough even to satisfy her doting father.

'She ought to do well,' I say. 'But why did you give her that dreadful name that's plagued me all my life?'

'But it's a lovely name,' he says. 'And one with such fond associations for me. I'll never forget the sweet way you used to look at me, with those big green eyes, when those two were making my life hell.'

Were they making his life hell? I wonder. I remember how angry he'd been with Hugh. I suppose my obvious adoration must have soothed his hurt feelings and so he'd thoughtlessly encouraged it. At least at the funeral I'd tried to tell him how irresponsible he'd been. For once I feel quite proud of my younger self but then I wonder how much lasting effect it had had when he starts,

'But Phyllida, my Phyllida ...'

'Mike please,' I say quickly. 'Not that poem!' and he laughs, which I think is an admission that he's hamming it up.

'Talking of poetry,' he says, 'is your husband a poet by any chance?'

'Steve!' I say. 'No way. He's writing what he hopes will be a standard university textbook on the aftermath of British colonialism.'

'Oh, it's just that recently I've come across some good poems by someone with the same surname.'

'That'll be me.'

Mike's surprise and pleasure take the conversation onto a different level. He stops flirting and talks seriously and sensibly about my poetry. I do try to remind myself that this is a man who used to recite *The May Queen* to his children, but he has some intelligent things to say.

While we're still talking, a door slams somewhere in Cardiff, and Mike says,

'Oh God, that must be Angharad back and I haven't finished clearing the kitchen.'

Angharad! That was the name on one of the letters about Rosa. There surely can't be two Angharad Davises in Cardiff? Even in Wales, can there? I start to speculate that Mike may have a particular fondness for women with unusual names, although that would suggest he was rather more selective than I'd give him credit for. Aloud I say 'Yes, I heard you were a reformed character, domestically that is.'

'Completely,' he says. 'Better go. I'll ring again and we must all meet sometime.'

I go to put the phone back on its base and to my surprise Steve isn't working. He has the newspaper open and is scowling.

'That fool Patel thinks if the *Guardian* doesn't arrive it's all right to send the *Telegraph* instead,' he says, but I have a feeling that it isn't really the newsagent's lack of political awareness that is making him so annoyed.

'So that,' he says, a moment later. 'That was the legendary Mike Davis was it?'

'How did you guess?'

'Well look at you.' I see myself reflected in the mirror opposite and realise that my face looks lit from within.

'Guess what! He's read some of my poetry and he really likes it.'

'He certainly knows how to get round you, doesn't he!' And then Steve sees the light die out from my face and says,

'I'm sorry. I've done it again, haven't I?' He slings the despised newspaper on one side and says,

'Look, it's sunny and it seems quite warm out. Forget work. Let's take a train to Richmond, go for a walk by the river and have lunch in a pub.' When we get to the river, he takes my hand and we're walking along amicably together when we see the houseboat.

Of course it's crazy. Perhaps fortunately, there's no one of the older generation left to tell us how foolish we're being, although our friends do their best. The children seem rather proud of our eccentricity although Sophie worries a bit about her children falling in the river. We promise life jackets and say how wonderful it will be for them when they're older. Jonathan offers us a converted pigsty on his smallholding if it sinks. So far the boat has shown no sign of sinking.

It's an old Thames barge, amazingly spacious, full of light and reflections from the river - my world elsewhere.

Mike rings again, several times. In fact he rings me probably at least once a month. I suppose it's when Angharad is out and housekeeping gets too tedious. I sometimes wonder if he has several women he rings to chat up when he's bored. Steve likes doing jobs on the boat and if Mike's on the phone he usually finds it necessary to use the electric drill.

'Look, I know what he's like,' I say, 'but he makes me laugh.'

'And I don't, I suppose?'

'Not intentionally.' And then, seeing he looks hurt, add, 'Joke!'

But apart from making me laugh, Mike can talk interestingly about poetry. He's even started emailing me with some helpful suggestions about my work. In return, I agree to re-read some of his favourite poems and admit to liking Tennyson, although I draw the line at *The May Queen* and I absolutely refuse to listen if he starts on *Phyllida*. Once, foolishly, I joke about how Alithea said, 'Imagine living with someone who prefers Tennyson to Donne.' It's never a good idea to mention Alithea.

'A member of the Oxbridge elite that run the country.'

'You're Oxbridge yourself,' I remind him.

'Yes, but part of a brief post-war experiment when the Welfare State was strong, before Thatcher dismantled it. Now New Labour are dancing on the ruins. That ex-wife of mine and her public school gang still have the power.'

I watch a heron flying across the river. It comes to land on the island opposite. The boat settles slightly. The tide is going out; sunshine turns the mud banks iridescent, and glows on a red double-decker bus moving slowly across the bridge. I feel a poem stirring somewhere in the back of my mind. I'd like to get back to my desk.

'Well, don't they?' he demands.

'Sorry there was a heron.'

This distracts Mike for a moment. He likes to hear about our life aboard although he says from time to time it's not for him. I sometimes try to imagine where he's ringing from – somewhere like my parents' bungalow that he so admired? But then I reflect their house would probably have been Angharad's choice so I've no idea. Anyway I don't try to imagine too hard because that would mean replacing my picture of Mike then with Mike now. When Mike is flattering me and making me laugh, I imagine him as I last saw him, a tall, dark young man reciting Dylan Thomas over Rosa's father's grave, rather than as the rather portly, white-haired ex-headmaster that he must have become. No doubt he has similar delusions about me.

The past can't be recaptured. I shall never go back again to that cathedral city where I was at school. It's changed too much. Already my memories of it have been corrupted by my last visit. So when Mike returns to the subject of Alithea, while it occurs to me that he must know her address, I decide I won't ask him for it.

For a moment, while he rants on, I imagine ringing her,

'Perhaps you don't remember me but I've got two books of yours, your Donne and, coincidentally, the poems of Catullus …' In a way it's tempting. I'd like to show her that though she used me and then abandoned me, I survived – not only survived, but even flourished. But realistically, I know she wouldn't be interested – probably wouldn't even remember. Almost certainly I'm just one of a long line of people she's used and abandoned during her life. What puts me off even more, however, is Megan's comment, 'too grand for the likes of us.' It's not that this intimidates me; it's just that I couldn't bear to arrive at some mansion and find an elegant woman in designer clothes living among proper furniture. I'd rather remember her in jeans and that notorious red sweater, cooking spaghetti bolognese in the basement kitchen with its improvised bookshelves.

Mike pauses in his tirade. Some comment from me is required.

'Come on,' I say to Mike. 'She hasn't that much power.'

'She has influence, Dilly, a lot of influence. Look at her now! Getting that poor deluded old man she married to part with his cash for pretentious piles of rubbish.'

'You never did appreciate Art much, Mike!' Ignoring this he carries on,

'Now she's got him messing with politics. The Labour Party, even New Labour, shouldn't be taking money from someone like him. Perhaps Angharad is right – we should rebuild Offa's Dyke.'

I realise that what Megan said is true. There is still something between him and Alithea. He can't quite let her go and perhaps the way she's gone through husbands and lovers suggests she's never quite got over him.

I remember Danny that day at Bellingthorpe Castle,

'I adore Ben, Ben loves Hugh and Hugh loves that Alithea – Love's Roundabout, ducky'. He'd also noticed that I loved Mike and that Mike loved Alithea. I wonder how Danny survived being abandoned and whether perhaps Hugh fled to Melbourne not to hide from Mike but to escape from Ben. Most of us, it seems, have managed to find consolation elsewhere except perhaps Hugh. I've never heard of his being married, but maybe Simon's existence is some comfort to him. It must mean he still has a link with Alithea.

That reminds me of a question that I've been meaning to ask ever since I had lunch with Megan but first I tell Mike that he should be satisfied with his life. He's had a rewarding career in a place where he has roots, four successful children and now grandchildren he seems besotted by.

'So let Alithea chase celebrities. She hasn't really achieved that much. Teachers have a more lasting influence and you seem to have an amazing wife.'

'You may be right,' he says. 'And of course Angharad is amazing but...'

This sounds dangerous. Perhaps it's time to interrupt with that question. Why had he kept in touch with Rosa and Joan Seymour but disappeared out of my life?

'Because you'd sent that message.'

'What message?'

'That it would be better if we didn't meet again.'

Silence, I can't speak.

'Hello, hello. Are you still there.'

Finally I manage to explain that I'd wanted to come and say goodbye on the last day of term, that Alithea had implied we would keep in touch, that when I didn't hear from her I'd gone to their lodgings and to the castle searching for them, or at least for news of their whereabouts. As I'm telling him this, the misery of that time comes back to me so vividly that I feel on the verge of tears. When I've finished there's a pause and then Mike starts laughing.

'You should be flattered, Dilly. You know why she invented that message don't you? My dear ex-wife obviously felt I was beginning to find you a bit too attractive.'

I'd like to say, 'And were you?' but it seems to be one of those questions better left unasked. In any case, once again a door bangs in

Cardiff, and he says,

'Oh God! I haven't finished making the soup,' which is the way most of our conversations end.

I put the phone down still feeling shaken by what I've just heard. A line from a poem I once read is teasing me somewhere in the back of my mind. I identify it as Auden and go to look it up.

If equal affection cannot be,
Let the more loving one be me.

In that case, I think, Angharad, whose name I have discovered means 'more love' in Welsh, is lucky and Danny was lucky and perhaps Hugh is lucky though I doubt he sees it that way, and so, perhaps, is Steve. He's stopped me escaping at least twice. In spite of his rather graceless ways I know he loves me, maybe more than I love him.

And me? Well I do love Steve but I suppose a bit of me is still in love with someone who doesn't exist any more - a tall, dark young man reciting Dylan Thomas over a grave, which is why, so far, I've resisted any suggestions that we might meet. In fact Steve and I have no reason to go to Cardiff and I'm sure Angharad will have the sense to veto any plan of Mike's to meet in London either with her or on his own. Of course we might run into each other in Edinburgh this August. Joanne's play, with my suggested amendments, is on at the Fringe. She's expecting us to be there and Megan will be in it. If we do finally meet, I'm sure it will be very disillusioning. And, if it isn't?

Well, that might be worse.